A RAKE'S INTENTIONS

"You are the fairest maiden at the ball," Lord Lucan told Diana.

"Except that I'm no maiden," she murmured, then blushed at her own boldness.

Surprised, the earl's eyes narrowed a little. "No," he agreed. "A poor choice of words, perhaps," he added, grasping her chin in one hand so that she was forced to gaze into his eyes.

"You are so beautiful," he said huskily. "Diana the goddess, the eternal virgin. Maiden or not, that is how I view you."

She pushed his hands away, but his eyes still held her captive. "You must not say such things, Lord Lucan. There is no purpose in this."

He turned her words around. "On the contrary, there is a purpose. I am a man who always has a purpose in mind, Diana."

Suddenly, he knew he could not wait, that he meant to ask her here and now to be his wife. When she knew he wooed her in earnest, she would not be so reluctant.

"You know what I want, don't you?" he began gently, pulling her closer. "I want you, Diana, in every sense of the word . . ."

REGENCIES BY JANICE BENNETT

TANGLED WEB   (2281, $3.95)

Miss Celia Marcombe's dark eyes flashed with righteous indignation. She was not a commodity to be traded or bartered to a man
as insufferably arrogant as Trevor Ryde, despite what her high-
handed grandfather decreed! If Lord Ryde thought she would let
herself be married for any reason other than true love, he was
sadly mistaken. He'd never get his hands on her fortune—let
alone her person—no matter how disturbingly handsome he
was . . .

MIDNIGHT MASQUE   (2512, $3.95)

It was nothing unusual for Lady Ashton to transport government
documents to her father from the Home Office. But on this particular afternoon a gust of wind scattered the papers, and suddenly an important page was lost. A document desperately
wanted by more than one determined gentleman—one of whom
would murder to get his way . . .

AN INTRIGUING DESIRE   (2579, $3.95)

The British secret agent, Charles Marcombe, had done his bit
against that blasted Bonaparte. Now it was time to nurse his
wounds and come to terms with the fact that that part of his life
was over. He certainly did not need the likes of Mademoiselle
Therese de Bourgerre darkening his door, warning of dire emer-
gencies and dread consequences, forcing him to remember things
best forgotten. She was a delightful minx, to be sure, but it would
take more than a pair of pleading emerald eyes and a woebegone
smile to drag him back into the fray!

*Available wherever paperbacks are sold, or order direct from the
Publisher. Send cover price plus 50¢ per copy for mailing and
handling to Zebra Books, Dept. 3278, 475 Park Avenue South,
New York, N.Y. 10016. Residents of New York, New Jersey and
Pennsylvania must include sales tax. DO NOT SEND CASH.*

Change of Heart

Julie Caille

ZEBRA BOOKS
KENSINGTON PUBLISHING CORP.

ZEBRA BOOKS

are published by

Kensington Publishing Corp.
475 Park Avenue South
New York, NY 10016

First printing: January, 1991

Printed in the United States of America

To my parents
Priscilla and Robert Burns
with all my love

Chapter One

Of the seven Farington offspring, only the two eldest daughters bore their mama company the cold March afternoon the letter from Great-aunt Serena arrived. Warmed by the dancing fire not five feet away, the three women were comfortably grouped about a low table in the Small Saloon, a room whose once-plush seat coverings and faded carpet hinted at the impoverished state of the rest of the house. Yet it was hardly a gloomy place, for the Farington family kept the house scrupulously clean and well-lit, and their many domestic doings filled its chambers with, if not continual noise and mayhem, at least a close approximation thereof.

Diana, the elder daughter, watched her mother slit open the letter with outward dispassion, but beneath her cool exterior she was far from calm. Her sister's future hinged upon their great-aunt's reply, and after her own appalling experience, Diana could feel nothing but dismay at the thought of her darling sister being paraded before the overcritical eyes of the London *ton*. Of course, Great-aunt Serena might well refuse to sponsor Aimee, for not even the most doting relative could claim that their great-aunt was anything but capricious. A refusal was something that Aimee would deem a calamity of the first magnitude, but Diana, having already experienced the deepest of pitfalls during her own London Season, could not agree.

She said nothing, however, but shot a veiled look at her seventeen-year-old sister, Miss Aimee Farington. From the expression on Aimee's face, one might think the letter merited the same degree of veneration that might surround, for example, the creation of new mountain ranges or the shifting of continents. Her heart-shaped little face was flushed with anticipation, and her lovely blue eyes sparkled as if some long-awaited treat were about to be bestowed upon her. Her small hands gripped each other convulsively as she leaned forward, her dark hair tumbling from its fastenings as if it, no more than her emotions, could be contained.

"Oh, Mama, do hurry!" breathed the younger girl, bouncing with impatience. "I simply cannot *bear* the suspense! I cannot *think* what I shall do if Aunt Serena does not agree to present me—die of despair, I suppose! But she must do it, mustn't she? After all, she took Diana, didn't she? Oh, I know she'll do it! I know it!"

Mrs. Farington had thrust the newly arrived missive out at arm's length in an effort to bring the spindly handwriting into focus. "It's of no use," she said at last, heaving a disgusted sigh. "My eyes just are not what they used to be. Diana, you must read it, for I cannot make heads or tails out of this blur."

Perfectly willing to perform this office, Diana rose from her chair and moved gracefully across the short space to her mother's side. Ignoring Aimee's moaning appeals to read it aloud, she returned to her seat and scanned the letter, reviewing one section in particular with a startled frown.

At four-and-twenty, Mrs. Farington's eldest daughter was a striking young woman. She was of medium height and very slender, with an elegant carriage, a straight little

8

nose, and sweet, finely molded lips. Where her sister's hair was black as jet, Diana's hair shone like molten honey, and her eyes were some curious mixture of brown and gold. However, it was not these attractions which made one stare, though they should have been reason enough. It was the look in, or rather *behind* those unusual eyes that piqued the interest, for there was such a shuttered look, such a vulnerable quality in their depths, that one could not help but wonder what could have been its author. As it happened, she was a widow, having married one Edmund Verney at the age of eighteen. His death, however, was not the cause of that look.

"Aimee is quite right," stated the young widow when she finished reading. "Great-aunt Serena is quite willing to finance Aimee's Season in London. She does not agree that she should wait another year. She says my notions are poppycock." Concealing her distress, Diana glanced at her mother. "The whole letter sounds just like her," she added dryly.

Aimee looked ecstatic. "Then it is settled!" she cried, clasping her hands to her bosom. "I shall go to London! I shall see Cousin Charles!"

A troubled frown touched Diana's brow as she took in the flush of color in her sister's pretty cheeks.

"Apparently so," she said, allowing a tiny ripple of disquiet to creep into her voice. "I don't agree with Aunt Serena, however. Are you absolutely set upon going this year?"

Aimee widened her blue eyes. "Well, naturally, Diana! I think it beyond everything that I shall have a Season when I will not even be eighteen until next Christmas. I cannot wait to tell Eliza—she will be mad with envy! But, of course, that's not why I wish to go," she amended, noting her sister's frown. "I shall have the whole Season with Charles, you see. It may be the only chance I will ever have to make him notice me. *Really* notice me,

9

I mean."

Diana was unimpressed. "Yes, well, likely he will still be there next year," she coaxed. "Listen to me, Aimee, dear, if only just this once. London is huge and strange— not at all comfortable like our little village. There will be scads of people, none of whom will care a rap for you or your feelings. You will have to conform to a rigid pattern of behavior. And that is something you will find difficult, I assure you, for I found it nigh to impossible myself."

She might as well have been addressing the small potted plant on the table beside her for all the heed her words were given. "No lectures, *please,*" begged her sister, adding brightly, "Yes, I do want to go, and no, I don't want to wait until I've grown a little older. It is boring in the country, Diana!"

Diana sighed. She honestly did understand her sister's feelings, for she remembered experiencing almost identical sentiments—once. It was really, she thought, her own emotions which were the source of the problem. It seemed so long since her own lips had curved into the light-hearted smiles that came so easily to Aimee. She knew most people assumed this was because she was still mourning the death of her husband. Her lip did curl a little at that absurd thought

"When does she wish Aimee to come?" inquired Mrs. Farington, fussing with the folds of her skirt. As Diana raised the letter and opened her mouth, her mother added quickly, "Only the bare facts, if you please, for I've no desire to listen to Aunt Serena's sarcastic form of wit, if I can avoid it. Will she pay the travel expenses? For I'm sure your Papa's carriage will never make the journey in one piece, and we cannot afford for her to travel post, and—"

"And I absolutely refuse to ride the Mail!" declared Aimee, secure in the knowledge that she would never be asked to do so.

Diana's gaze went to her sister. "She says she will pay for us both to travel post, and to bring either a maid, or Miss Tilden."

"Both!" echoed Aimee and Mrs. Farington at once.

The first to recover from surprise, Aimee clapped her hands in delight. "You are coming, too, Diana? Oh, how famous! We shall have such fun!"

Diana's leaden silence caused her mother to eye her uneasily. "Why, how . . . how kind of Aunt Serena," she ventured. "I think it might be good for you, Diana. Will you consider it?"

Having steeled herself to resist an entreaty, the tentative question put Diana at a loss. "I . . . I don't know, Mama," she answered, staring past her mother at some memory from the past. "You know how I feel about London."

Mrs. Farington's rosebud mouth turned down sadly. "Yes, Diana, dear. But all that was long ago. Edmund has been gone now for three years. People will have forgotten all about what happened."

"I have not forgotten," her daughter reminded her softly. "I shall never forget."

Her mother sighed. "Of course not, love, but you must learn to live again. You are too young to want to bury yourself in the country like this. With Edmund's money, you could have been living in town somewhere, enjoying yourself, making friends, perhaps meeting another gentleman who could—"

"Who could make me as miserable as Edmund managed to do!" interrupted the young widow with her first flash of impatience. "Look, Mama, if I did go to London with Aimee, it would be simply to bear her company and keep her from falling into scrapes! I have absolutely no intention of marrying again."

"Or of ever having any fun," inserted Aimee daringly. "Oh, Diana, I *am* sorry, but it is difficult to remain

11

cheerful when you talk so. And I do not intend to get into any scrapes."

Diana forced a smile. "One never does. Oh, I know how I must sound to you, dear. And, believe it or not, I am not trying to cast a damper on what must seem to you the ultimate good fortune. But as for my coming with you, well, I would have to give that a great deal of thought."

Recognizing the obstinate set of her eldest daughter's jaw, Mrs. Farington tactfully abandoned the subject, and turned her attention instead to the younger girl.

"It would be foolish for us to depend upon it, of course, but if you *were* able to attach the interest of your cousin Charles, your papa and I would be excessively pleased. He is such a fine, steady sort of man, so exactly what one would wish! And so very well set up in the world! Of course, I am the last person on earth to push you to marry for such a vulgar reason as money, for only look at your poor papa and me! And we, as you know, are as happy as two ducks on a pond—despite the fact that the roof is sadly in need of repair." Struck by this melancholy thought, she heaved a long, regretful sigh. "Well, there is no denying it would be a great comfort to know you were married to a man who could provide for you. Aunt Serena will not be here forever, after all. And there are Elizabeth and Dorothy and Louisa still to consider, and Jeremy's school fees, and little Nick's, when he is older."

"Do you think Cousin Charles will remember me?" inquired Aimee, rather anxiously. "It has been nearly three years since we visited the Perths. He may not even recognize me."

"Well, you have changed a great deal," agreed her mother. "It is quite possible he may not, so you ought to be prepared if that turns out to be the case. But that may be all for the best, for you were sadly plump in those days,

12

were you not? And correct me if I am wrong, my dear, but did you not have spots?"

Aimee scowled. "Only a few," she retorted. "Both Elizabeth and Dorothy are far worse! It is only people like Diana who can escape them altogether. You have such glorious skin, Diana."

But Diana was staring at the carpet, her thoughts far away. They were neither new nor pleasant, these thoughts, but over the years she had learned to distance herself from them. Objectively, she knew that, yes, she ought to get away from home. She was feeling only half-alive these days, as if a portion of her soul had died along with Edmund. But that was ridiculous. Escape from her role as Edmund's wife had been one of the most providential releases of her life. Not, of course, that she would have wished him to die, but since he had gone and gotten himself killed in a vulgar tavern brawl, there was really no more to be said. If he had not died, she would certainly have left him by now. Of that she was certain, even though she was sure of little else.

"She doesn't hear me," said Aimee. "She's wool-gathering, again."

Diana glanced up. "I'm sorry?" she murmured, her attention returning to the present. "I'm afraid I didn't hear what you said."

"Never mind," said Aimee. "I was just saying that you never had spots."

"Oh?" replied Diana vaguely, missing the worried look her mother and sister exchanged. "Goodness, look at the time. I'd best get back, for Tildy will be missing me. Let me know when you're going to write to Aunt Serena. I must think this over very carefully."

When she had gone, Mrs. Farington shook her head. "You know, when she came back to live near us after

13

Edmund died," she confided, "I thought it was a wise decision. I thought that for her to be near us would be good for her, that it would help her grow away from her misfortunes. I never thought she would just stay on here, growing older and more unhappy. I really think she ought to go to London with you, Aimee. She has no future here."

Aimee chewed her bottom lip, hesitantly forming the question preying on her mind. "Just what was it about Edmund she hated so, Mama? What was it about him that was so beastly?"

Mrs. Farington patted her lace mobcap nervously, and glanced down at the letter on the table. "Oh, Edmund was all wrong for our Diana. She should never have married him. She *would* never have married him, were it not for his . . . ungentlemanly conduct. When a lady is forced into a compromising position and the gabble-mongers get hold of it, well, there's really no alternative. She marries the man in question, or retires from society forever to live in disgrace." She cleared her throat, and continued firmly, "It is unfair, but true. The sad part of it is, your sister married Edmund to avoid scandal, then hid herself away in the country as if she were still in disgrace. But our Diana has never had a reason not to hold her head up. What happened was not her fault."

This was the first Aimee had heard of the true circumstances of her sister's marriage. Her blue eyes very big, she protested, "But, Mama! I cannot imagine Diana allowing a . . . a man to impose on her in such a manner. She is the most poised, controlled person I have ever met!"

Her mother smiled slightly. "Yes, well, you have not met a great many people, my love. The Diana of today is not the Diana of yesterday. You've forgotten, haven't you? She used to be so carefree, so spontaneous, so full of life—oh, how can I explain it? She was young, Aimee and

14

he was such a horrid young man. He cared nothing for her feelings. She has never said, so I draw my own conclusions, but I fancy he did not treat her well in private. *That* part of marriage is not easy for some women, my dear, and if the man is not gentle . . . but I should not speak of it to you! You are so young, so innocent!"

She dabbed at her eyes with her handkerchief, struck anew by the enormity of what her first daughter had suffered.

For a few moments, Aimee studied her mother, then said, rather suddenly, "She *shall* go to London, Mama, for if she does not, *I* will refuse to go, and then she must change her mind. And once we have her there, why, I shall look about and find her a proper husband. And don't think I cannot, for I know what suits Diana better than anyone in the world."

"So selfless! Such an angel!" sobbed her mother, still dabbing.

"Oh, pooh!" said Aimee. "That's farradiddle, Mama. I'm shockingly selfish and you know it. But I do love my sister and I hate to see her unhappy. So I shall find her another husband, only one who loves her this time. I daresay that will solve everything."

If Diana had heard these remarks, she would have been quite touched. She was closer to Aimee than any of her sisters, and had long been determined to prevent her from being hurt. And remembering how easily it could happen sent a shiver of foreboding running down her spine.

There was no dismissing the feeling. It gripped her, and what before had been a mere ripple of disquiet became a positive tidal wave of worry. What if a man tried to do to sweet little Aimee what Edmund had tried to do to her? The thought made her ill, and her expression grew bleak as she wended her way along the dirt road leading to the small house she had been leasing for the past three years.

It had not been quite as easy to come back as everyone imagined. Just the notion that others might know what Edmund had tried to do to her, the reason for her strange marriage, was enough to bring a flush of humiliation to her cheeks. When one was very private and very sensitive, such a sordid chapter in one's life was almost beyond endurance. Just knowing her name had been bandied about the drawing rooms of London was enough to make Diana want to curl up and die. Even here in this sleepy little corner of Wiltshire, she had never been completely comfortable.

When people asked, as they occasionally did, why she had never returned to London after her period of mourning was over, she could hardly think of a civil reply. Does one venture to return to the place where one has suffered the ultimate mortification? Does one seek out the very people who whispered about the scandal behind their hands? No, one does not. But, of course, she could not say this. And so she let them assume that town life had not suited her, and that she preferred the country. It was the simplest solution.

In fact, nothing could be further from the truth. Diana had loved London. She had reveled in the crowds, the color and excitement, the very busyness of it all. She had loved seeing the street vendors and the merchants, hearing their boisterous cries rising above the rumble of rolling carriage wheels and the clopping of horses' hooves on the rough cobbles. Every part of it had made her feel so alive, so a part of the rest of humanity. The balls, the plays, and the parks had been but an added bonus. But Edmund and the hypocrisy of the life had spoiled it for her.

So-called friends had turned her misfortune into the latest *on-dit*. Congratulations on her marriage had been extended by those who were aware of how much she detested her betrothed. The fact that he was a lecherous beast who tried to paw every girl he met made no difference. His uncle was an earl, and so, of course, he was rated a fine catch. She must be pleased with her achievement.

Her wedding night had been a nightmare. Even now, she closed her mind to the memories of Edmund's roughness, his utter indifference to her terror. The number of times they had been intimate had actually been very few, for she had quickly grown adept at avoiding his embraces. Fortunately, he had not appeared to care, for among various other outlets for his lust was a mistress in Chelsea. Like a good wife, Diana had stayed in the country and turned a blind eye to his infidelities, an action that had, ironically, earned her praise from Edmund. She had laughed scornfully when he had told her that the marriage was not turning out so very badly after all. And then she had thrown a Sèvres vase at his head. Not so badly, indeed!

By the time Diana arrived back at her house, she was thoroughly chilled by the stiff March wind. Hurrying upstairs, she threw off her dress and unpinned her hair, quickly drawing a comb through its long mass of tangles. Since she did not reside in town, she did not conform to the modern practice of cropping one's hair into short curls. As she retwisted it into its neat coil, she wondered whether going to London would mean having to cut it all off. She shuddered at the thought that any eccentricity on her part would give rise to gossip. She still recalled the awful, naked, helplessness of being a victim, and having others look at you as though you had brought all your troubles on yourself.

Although she was quite alone, Diana still cringed when she thought about it all. She had never dared tell anyone how it had all come about, that she had purposely crept upstairs at the Edgerton's ball to peer out the upstairs window at Sir Henry Neyle walking with one of her rivals on the balcony below; that she had cherished some very warm feelings for Sir Henry and that jealousy had prompted her to eavesdrop upon the pair of them; that she had dared to believe the handsome blond baronet had looked at her differently, that his smile meant so much more than his actual words. And through her own foolish actions, she had managed to bring about her own downfall.

Edmund Verney, loathsome creature that he was, had followed her up the stairs and caught her spying on Sir Henry. He had laughed at her, then forced his horrid mouth onto hers, digging at her lips with his revolting tongue. She had kicked and bitten like a wildcat, but Edmund had proved surprisingly strong for such a thin young man. When their hostess walked into the room half a minute later, he was already half atop her, one hand clamped over her mouth, the other fumbling beneath her skirt. Though Lady Edgerton pretended sympathy, the scene was utterly damning in the eyes of such a malicious gossip. It mattered not that Diana was still chaste. To their hostess, it was simply too good a story not to tell.

By the end of the following day, their betrothal had been announced. Oh, Edmund had not been honorable enough to make the offer himself. He had sulked like a little boy when, like an avenging fury, an outraged Great-aunt Serena had descended upon his uncle, Lord Bathurst, and flung animadversions at him while brandishing her cane like a dueling sword. It was she who demanded that Edmund make amends for his despicable action, she who had the wit to fight rumor with counterrumor. When Diana wanted only to hide, Great-aunt Serena took her to the opera, flaunting her great-niece as if nothing in the least untoward had transpired. Within hours, the story was diluted into some nonsense about a secret betrothal and stolen kisses, which most people accepted simply because they disliked Lady Edgerton. The fact that the woman was well known for her tendency to exaggerate was largely what saved Diana from complete social disgrace.

Yet even in private, Edmund was so far lost to all sense of decency that he had the effrontery to deny the whole of it. Then, when he finally admitted his misdeeds, he declared that he had no wish to marry Diana. However, in the end, he had succumbed to Aunt Serena's verbal thumbscrews, for it was the easiest way out of the hornet's nest he had created. One thing Edmund had always lacked was backbone. He had no shame either, for he never displayed, either in private or in public, any contrition or embarrassment over the entire episode. Indeed, Diana had been mortified to hear that he had bragged of his easy conquest in one of the men's clubs.

Was it any wonder that she was reluctant to return?

Wearing a fresh gown, Diana entered her small dining room to find that Miss Tilden, the nurse of her childhood years, and, more currently, her companion, was already seated at table, calmly engrossed with her knitting.

For as long as Diana could remember, Miss Tilden had been a knitter. In her sixty-six years of life, she had made an incalculable number of garments, both for charity and for people she knew. Her current project was stockings, vast piles of woolen stockings, which she eventually intended to donate to the Foundling Hospital in London. To Diana, the clicking of knitting needles was the most comforting sound in the world, associated as it was with blurry childhood memories of warm milk, buttered toast, and the drowsy crackling of hearth fires.

As soon as she crossed the threshold, Miss Tilden's amiable face wrinkled into a welcoming smile. "Ah, there you are, Diana. I was just wondering where you might be. Did you have a pleasant visit with your Mama?"

Diana hesitated. "Oh, well enough," she said evasively. "I am sorry to be so late. You must be famished."

Her elderly companion put aside her knitting and Diana rang for her maid to bring in the soup. While Bess ladled the steaming liquid into their bowls, Miss Tilden cast a shrewd look at the girl she had known all her life. "Something's troubling you, I think. Did they hear anything from your aunt? I do hope it's not bad news."

Diana smiled what Miss Tilden called her bright, false smile. "On the contrary, everything is splendid. Great-aunt Serena has offered to frank Aimee's entire season, as well as the cost of traveling post. For both of us."

Miss Tilden, who had just picked up her spoon, put it down abruptly. "Both? My dear, what can you mean?"

Diana's own spoon dipped determinedly into her soup. "I mean," she said, after discovering it was too hot, "that I am invited as well. And you, for that matter. I suppose that Aunt Serena imagines enough time has passed now. She wants to try to auction me off again."

Miss Tilden looked pained. "Dear Diana, pray do not speak in that cynical way. It is most distressing! You cannot truly believe that is her only motive? Surely she is just being kind?"

"Oh, no, I doubt it," Diana responded coolly. "If the invitation had come from you, Tildy, then I would have said the same. But dear Aunt Serena is far too didactic a personality for that. She's probably bored and has forgotten how much trouble I caused her the first time."

"I see." Miss Tilden gave a delicate cough. "So, ah, are

20

we going?"

Diana shrugged. "I have no wish to see the place ever again."

"Diana," said the older woman quietly, "when you were a little girl, I could always tell when you were lying by the way you would shrug your shoulders in just that way. This time, perhaps you are lying to yourself."

Diana shut her eyes, one hand flying up to touch her head as if it hurt. "Oh, Tildy. I'm such a coward. Just the thought of seeing some of those people again throws me into a quake. Just talking of it makes my heart begin to pound."

"Stage fright," pronounced Miss Tilden, with less sympathy than Diana expected. "Good heavens, love, of course you're nervous. But surely it will pass."

Diana's hand fell limply to her lap. "It must pass," she said tonelessly. "Because I'm going, Tildy. I made up my mind while I was walking home. I have to go for Aimee's sake."

Miss Tilden looked blank. "Aimee's sake?" she repeated uncertainly.

"Yes. I have to protect her from men like Edmund. I must guard her, as must you, Tildy." Diana's mouth was set in a firm, stubborn line as she spoke.

Without hesitation, her companion assumed her meekest expression. "You are perfectly right, of course," she murmured. "We must go to protect Aimee. Now, why did that not occur to me, I wonder? To be sure, it is perfectly obvious. So sensible! I must be getting old."

"I'll go on one condition," Diana told her mother the following afternoon. "I will not stay with Aunt Serena. I want to hire a house for the Season."

"Hire a house?" repeated Mrs. Farington faintly. "Mercy, Diana, think of the expense! Particularly when

21

you can stay with Aunt Serena in Arlington Street. Such a distinguished address!"

"Distinguished or not, I won't stay there," said Diana flatly. "I've enough money to do it. And since you persist in refusing to take any of it for your own needs, I may as well spend it on this. Oh, Mama, I don't want anything grand! Just a small respectable place where I can have some privacy. I'm *used* to being my own mistress, Mama. I cannot imagine spending several months under Aunt Serena's roof. You know what she is."

"Yes, but will Aimee like it?" wondered Mrs. Farington.

"Aimee will love it. And you need not worry about respectability because, after all, I *am* a widow, which, thank the Lord, gives me some level of freedom. And dear Tildy has consented to bear me company. We shall go on very well. I trust Aunt Serena will still sponsor Aimee, even if she resides with me?"

Her mother sighed, unable to argue with her strong-willed daughter for any length of time. "I trust so, my love. I shall write to her on your behalf, if you like. Will you write to Edmund's man of business as well? I'm sure he will look into the matter of the house for you, if you request it."

Diana's brow furrowed thoughtfully. "Yes, that's an excellent idea. I can describe specifically the sort of house I am looking for. Perhaps he can find something near Aunt Serena so as to pacify her. But not too near," she added, with a grimace.

"As you wish," said her mother. "I know your papa will not object." She paused, her caring gaze resting upon her daughter's face. "Are you sure this is right for you, Diana? I want you to go, but believe it or not, I do have some understanding of how you must feel."

The concern in her voice threatened Diana's control. Catching up her mother's hand, she gave it a loving squeeze. "Oh, Mama, I am a little scared to go back," she confessed, swallowing the lump in her throat. "I'm afraid all the gossip will be revived, and I'll have to face them all down again. And I don't want Aimee exposed to their maliciousness. It's difficult to know what to do."

Mrs. Farington pulled her daughter close, one hand stroking her hair tenderly. "You've decided to go, why don't you let it go at that? Aimee will be fine. You want to go, Diana. There's no shame in admitting it, and nothing to be frightened of, either. Just don't lump all the people you meet into one category. And remember, some of the best people are the ones who don't try too hard to impress. Try not to judge too quickly or too harshly. That's my little piece of motherly advice."

Eyes bright with unshed tears, Diana pulled back her head and managed a small laugh. "I'll try, Mama, but you know what a suspicious nature I've developed."

"You've changed," agreed her mother gently. "Life does that, I'm afraid, but it seems to me that too much of the old Diana went away. And despite her very quick temper, I miss my other Diana very much."

Diana sighed. "Oh, she's still right here, believe me— only a little more in control. I fear her shocking temper is never very far from the surface, though. No doubt it's only waiting for just the right person to set it aflame."

Chapter Two

In entrusting the selection of a house to Mr. Perkins, Diana was making a wise decision. A capable man, Perkins had served not only her husband, but her husband's uncle, Lord Bathurst, and was quite unfazed by her request. With his typical dedication to duty, he spent several days viewing a large number of the various dwellings available for hire, and after much peering about into bedrooms, kitchens, and attics, he narrowed the list of candidates down to three. His letter detailing the location, rent, and floor plan of each establishment arrived the following week.

To Diana's dismay, the cost of hiring a house was a trifle more than she had anticipated, but after carefully checking her records, she found the expense to be within her means. Each of the houses was located in the fashionable part of town. The first, in Clarges Street, had a great many advantages, but on the whole it sounded too large, and since it was the most costly of the three, Diana quickly eliminated it as an option. Of the remaining two, one was situated in Jermyn Street and the other in Clifford Street. The latter's proximity to Bond Street weighed heavily in its favor, but after more debate, she selected the Jermyn Street address. It was within walking distance to both Aunt Serena and the mews where she kept her carriages, an advantage when one considered the expense of purchasing and maintaining any sort of equipage. It seemed a reasonable assumption that since Aunt Serena owned both a barouche and a landaulet, as well as an elegant town coach and a large traveling chariot, she would allow them the use of one of these conveyances. As for riding, Diana shrugged that aside. Aunt Serena kept nothing but carriage horses.

Mr. Perkins's letter assured her that all three houses were adequately furnished, so that all she need be concerned with was the hiring of domestic staff. If she was desirous that he should look into that matter as well, he would be more than happy to oblige. He recommended, as a minimum, the employment of a cook, a butler, and either a footman or a pageboy, as well as at least one abigail. Since he had already demonstrated to her satisfaction the excellence of his judgment, it was with some relief that Diana decided to leave the business of interviewing and hiring servants completely in his hands.

Another week passed before she heard from him again. This letter informed her that the four menials she had requested had been engaged and were prepared to commence their employment on any date she chose. Since the Season was fast approaching, Diana wrote back to tell him they would be leaving at the end of week, and she would be pleased if the house was open and ready when she arrived. She then put on her bonnet and gloves, and left the house to inform Aimee and the rest of her family of the date of departure.

Diana's steps were light as she trod the short distance to Farington Place. It was a glorious feeling to be so in charge of one's life, she reflected in a sudden burst of optimism. There really was something to be said for being a widow. To be able to make one's own choices without male interference, to have the freedom to set up one's own establishment, this was what she found most tolerable about widowhood. And since she had not loved Edmund, she had not been forced to suffer the agonizing sense of loss that normally accompanied such a bereavement.

True, she had had to settle some of Edmund's gaming debts, but on the whole, she had come out of it very well. Edmund had not been complete master of his own purse strings, and so had not been able to squander his money in the manner he would have liked. His uncle had been delegated trustee of the small fortune her husband had inherited, a responsibility Lord Bathurst had made sure to take seriously. He had insisted that Edmund make a will in Diana's favor, which later proved a fortuitous precaution. Thanks to that will, Diana had inherited all her husband's money rather than the half-share the law would have allowed her if he had died without a will. As long as she was not extravagant, it was enough to make her financially independent for the rest of her life.

Naturally, Diana's first impulse had been to try to assist her own family with their pecuniary problems, but her parents stubbornly refused to accept anything other than the odd gift or two for the children. Perhaps they felt their eldest daughter's sufferings entitled her to whatever profits she eventually reaped. Whatever the case, they insisted that Diana's money remain her own, that it made them breathe easier knowing she had it. And then, of course, there was the hope that Great-aunt Serena would remember them in her will.

The Dowager Lady Torrington was the matriarch of the family. She was shockingly rich, having been an heiress in her own right before her marriage to a wealthy viscount. Neither she nor the viscount had approved of gaming or improvident spending, and so their combined fortunes had increased over the years, endowing the viscount's widow with the power to rule over the family with an iron rod. Her despotic temperament made her a positive terror to those members of the family within swinging distance of her cane. Diana could recall times in her childhood when she had been quite frightened of Great-aunt Serena, but as an adult she saw her differently. In her own way, Diana had just as much steel in her as the dowager, and did not shrink from the prospect of facing her displeasure. If only she could face the London *ton* with as much fortitude, she thought wistfully.

The journey to London via post-chaise was accomplished with a minimum of discomfort, although Aimee chattered so much she eventually gave poor Miss Tilden a headache. And then, rather to Diana's amusement, she took such great care to keep silent that she did not, in fact, speak again until they rolled past Hyde Park Corner more than two hours later.

"Look, Diana! There is Hyde Park!" she exclaimed, pressing her face against the glass in wonder. "We are here! Oh, you must look, Miss Tilden! I am sure it will make you feel better."

In spite of the way her palms had begun to perspire, Diana found herself smiling. "Yes, Aimee," she said softly. "We are here."

Everywhere there were people. Aristocrats and beggars, ladies and ladies' maids, footmen and pageboys, thieves and pickpockets, errandboys, street hawkers, flowergirls, jarveys, sedan chairmen—these and a host of others were what made up this seething pocket of life that Diana remembered so well. She had not been in London since the day she had married; just knowing she was back made her realize how greatly she had missed it.

From then on, it seemed only a short time before they

27

reached their destination, 30 Jermyn Street. As Diana paid off the postboys, excitement went charging through her, supplanting the calm she had been trying to sustain. The tall narrow brick house was very like every other house on the street, each attached to its neighbor like so many links in a chain. Without speaking, she studied it eagerly, heartened by her own unexpected surge of elation. Here was where she was going to live, she told herself wonderingly. It was *hers*, at least for these next few months.

Drawing a deep breath, she glanced at Aimee, who stood watching her out of alert blue eyes. "Well," she said, making her tone brisk, "let us hope Mr. Perkins was right, and there is someone inside to let us in!"

As it happened, that good gentleman's assurances had not been in vain. The door was opened by Lawrence, her new butler, and their trunks and valises were fetched in by a tall, well-muscled footman named Felix. Within the hour, the ladies were well on their way to being settled into their new home.

Diana explored the house with a great sense of satisfaction. It was not at all commodious, yet it had the requisite number of reception rooms. The ground floor had a small, neatly decorated morning room, a slightly larger dining room, and a tiny back room which was meant for a study. Most of the first floor was devoted to the drawing room, although another tiny room at the back had been allocated for a boudoir. There were three bedrooms on the second floor, and the attics above that, while the kitchen, servants' quarters, pantry, and scullery were relegated, in the usual manner, to the basement. It was just the sort of house she had envisioned, Diana thought contentedly.

The first thing she did after supervising the unpacking of her trunk by Meg, her new abigail, was to sit down and compose a carefully worded note to the dowager viscountess informing her of their arrival. This was borne off to Arlington Street by a cheerful Felix, who returned half an hour later with a rather curt response from that imperious lady. This dispatch contained the peremptory statement that she wished to see them the following morning, and she trusted they could find the means to get themselves there. She would expect them at eleven o'clock.

Diana rubbed her suddenly burning eyes, relieved that at least Great-aunt Serena had not demanded to see them at once. It was too late in the day to be making calls, and they were all tired and in need of a good night's rest. Though her optimistic mood lasted for most of the evening, later, as she slipped into her nightdress and crawled into bed, Diana was struck with another rush of anxiety. Had she made the right decision? How would she feel when she began to meet people she had known six years before, people who had known the disgraceful reason for her marriage to Edmund? Her eyes squeezed tightly shut, Diana prayed that her self-control and ability to hide her true feelings would be enough to get her through whatever was to come.

Diana awoke the next morning feeling extraordinarily refreshed. Whatever dreams she had dreamed must have been pleasant, she mused, as she stretched her slim arms above her head and yawned. Swinging her legs over the side of the bed, she glanced toward the clothespress, wondering what she could wear that would be both elegant and subdued. Having no desire to call attention to herself, she would leave Aimee to cut her swath in the paths of fashion alone.

However, the celestial blue walking dress she finally selected was hardly subdued, for in truth, Diana adored bright colors. Her spencer, too, was rather dashing, composed as it was of white striped lutestring ornamented with braiding. The brim of her bonnet was not large enough to be truly fashionable, she reflected, but her matching blue kid shoes and straw-colored gloves were very smart. But when she surveyed this costume in the mirror, her brow furrowed. Instead of making her appear dignified and sure of herself, it made her look young and a little frightened. Well, perhaps this was because her hair was not yet dressed, but hung loosely down her back in a thick wavy mass. Laying aside the spencer, bonnet, and gloves, Diana rang for her abigail, who had assured her the previous evening that she knew just the way the mistress's hair ought to be arranged.

Meg soon proved her contention to be no idle boast. She seemed to possess just the knack for getting Diana's thick hair to do what she wanted, combing and twisting her honey gold tresses into an attractive, intricate style, while leaving some wispy curls to soften the perimeter of her face.

" 'Twould be a shame to cut all this off," remarked her pretty young abigail. "Still, the modern styles would suit you just as well. Miss Aimee says she wants to have hers cut. You'll be wantin' to bring in one of them fancy coiffeurs, I reckon. I couldn't undertake to do that for you."

"I suppose so," said Diana, thinking it was just as well Aimee wanted to follow the conventional road. She did also, but somehow that did not extend to a willingness to change the way she wore her hair. She had always kept her hair long; it was a part of her.

After partaking of a light breakfast in the dining room with Aimee and Miss Tilden, Diana went to the study to make a short list of things she needed to do. Shopping for Aimee headed the list, as well as sending a polite note to Lord Bathurst, Edmund's uncle. She knew a visit from him would not be too traumatic, for although his lordship was a pompous sort of man, he had always been kind, and had written her a most conciliatory letter when Edmund had died. Mulling for a while over which shops they should visit, and in what order their purchases should be made, Diana made notes in her neat, concise handwriting. She was nearly finished when Aimee came to remind her it was time for them to visit Aunt Serena.

Diana had decided that they would walk. It was perfectly respectable for them to do so, and the distance was not so very great, even for Miss Tilden. Moreover, although it was a trifle windy, the sun was shining, and the sky was clear and bright. It would have been a shame for them to have taken a carriage when the weather was so fine, she told Aimee cheerfully, while pulling on her gloves.

As they strolled along the street, Aimee began to twirl her parasol in what she told them was meant to be a coquettish manner. "For I quite intend to make a stir among the gentlemen," she confided. "Oh, of course, I mean to have Charles in the end, but first I intend to enjoy myself. In my bones, I feel sure that I will be very good at flirting, Diana. And I want to practice as much as possible, so I can make Cousin Charles jealous. It will be so romantic!"

Miss Tilden looked quite shocked, and Diana said quickly, "I hope you will do no such thing, Aimee. It is not at all the thing for a young innocent girl to flirt, no matter what that hoydenish Eliza Fingleshaw may tell you. Honestly! If you'd told me that before we left, I should have done everything I could to keep you at home."

Aimee gave her a sidelong glance. "Well, that is why I did not tell you, Diana," she pointed out, rather blithely. "Oh, now, do not be working yourself into a fidget! I won't do anything to embarrass you or bring shame upon myself. I simply want to have a little fun. Surely you can understand that?"

Diana was about to answer when two figures rounded the corner some distance ahead of them, advancing in their direction. Her heart skipped a beat. *Surely* that could not be . . . oh, dear Lord, could it actually be Sir Henry Neyle? It was beginning, she thought, in a sudden panic. Her hard-won poise was deserting her. Would he recognize her? If he bowed, should she speak? Nearly dizzy at the prospect of seeing him again, Diana barely glanced at his companion, a tall, strong-featured gentleman whose cool gray eyes had already locked upon the three women.

Carefully averting her eyes so as not to be caught staring, Diana turned to make some idle comment to Aimee. Aimee answered, but Diana did not hear, for the two gentlemen were getting very close and all her attention was focused on the laughing blond baronet. At the last possible moment, she turned her head, as if to give them a bare, uninterested glance. To her gratification, she saw Sir Henry's eyes widen in recognition, and instead of passing by, he stopped short and swept off his hat.

It seemed the most natural thing in the world to greet him. "Good day to you, Sir Henry," she said, hoping her voice did not quiver with the self-consciousness she was feeling. "How good to see you again."

Sir Henry bowed, his smile so angelically sweet Diana felt her heart turn over. "Why, it's . . . Mrs. Verney, isn't it?" he inquired. "It seems like years since you've been to town, ma'am. I'd quite given up hope you would ever again grace a London drawing room with your fair presence."

His gallantry brought a sweep of becoming color to Diana's pale cheeks. "Six years, to be exact," she told Sir Henry shyly. "May I introduce you to my sister Miss Farington? And, of course, my dear friend and companion, Miss Tilden."

As the ladies acknowledged the introduction, Sir Henry clapped a hand on his companion's shoulder. "Do you know Lord Lucan, Mrs. Verney? If not, pray allow me to bring him to your notice. Make your bow, Geoffrey, old boy."

Unoffended by this remark, the gray-eyed gentleman looked straight into Diana's eyes. "Actually, Mrs. Verney and I have met," he said, his voice low and pleasantly masculine. His gaze extended to Aimee and Miss Tilden. "Ladies," he added, with a bow.

With some effort, Diana pulled her senses together and looked more fully at the man she now remembered was an earl. "Ah yes," she replied, a trifle flustered by the frankness of his regard. "How do you do, my lord."

"Well," said Sir Henry, "how absolutely delightful that you have returned! Dare I hope that you are here for the entire Season?" At Diana's affirmative, he went on, with flattering alacrity, "Then, may I call upon you sometime soon? I should very much like to renew our acquaintance. Where are you staying?"

As Diana answered, she was suddenly conscious of Lord Lucan's wandering gaze. What on earth was he— Good heavens! The man actually had the audacity to stand there and study her figure! How *dared* he, she thought furiously. The fact that the wind was whipping her thin muslin gown rather revealingly against her frame was absolutely no excuse!

Speechless with indignation, Diana shot the earl her frostiest dagger look, which the outrageous man feigned not to notice until his perusal was complete. Then, up went his brows as he flashed her an oh-so-innocent smile. Unhappily aware that she was beginning to blush, Diana raised her chin disdainfully and answered Sir Henry's next pleasantry—a polite inquiry about the health of her family—with enhanced cordiality.

Though she favored Sir Henry with her most dazzling smile, Diana's parting nod to Lord Lucan was distinctly cool. As the three women moved off down the street, Diana's emotions were chaotic. How dreadfully unfortunate that Sir Henry had been with that particular man! The earl was one gentleman whose acquaintance she had no wish to renew. Now that she saw him again, she recalled very well the few occasions they had been together. He had the annoying tendency to stand too close, that was it, so that when they talked she was forever wanting to take a step or two backward. He always made her feel as if she were threatened in some way, though by what she was unable to explain.

Although Diana would later puzzle over a reason for her next action, she would never produce one that made any sense. Surreptitiously, she glanced over her shoulder at the two men. To her horror, the insufferable earl looked around at precisely the same insant. His eyes met hers, and with a grin that to Diana seemed brimming with wickedness, he raised his fingers to his lips and blew her a kiss.

Aghast, Diana's head snapped back to the front so fast it almost hurt. Dear God, why had she done it? Overwhelmed with embarrassment, she fixed her eyes rigidly on a point somewhere in the distance and increased the length of her stride. And of course, she thought savagely, he would think she had been looking at *him!* The man obviously had an inflated opinion of himself.

"Diana," gasped Miss Tilden suddenly, "must we walk quite so fast? I find I am quite out of breath. Are we late, my dear, that we must hurry so?"

With a murmured apology, Diana relaxed her pace, but unfortunately the damage was done. The brief surge of confidence she had experienced while talking to Sir

Henry was already beginning to ebb. Had she learned nothing in these past few years? she wondered miserably. Surely marriage and widowhood should have had given her some veneer of sophistication, some ability to recognize and prevent potentially unnerving situations. Yet perhaps not, for it seemed that she was as impressionable as she had been at the age of eighteen.

The memories were sweeping in now, like the gathering wind before a storm. That man had always tried to stare her out of countenance, hadn't he? And wasn't he married? Yes, he was, to a very beautiful woman by the name of—was it Laurette? And here he was, up to his old tricks again. Heaven help that poor woman who was forced to bear his name! He was probably another such as Edmund, out chasing women while expecting his wife to sit chastely at his hearth, waiting for him to crook an arbitrary finger in her direction.

Well, she might still blush as easily as a schoolgirl, but Diana knew a great deal more about men now than she had at eighteen. In particular, she knew how deceptive were their smiles, and how selfish their lusts. This time around, she promised herself grimly, Diana Verney would no longer play the easy target. With all the contempt she could muster, she would snap her fingers in Lord Lucan's smirking face next time they met!

"What a perfectly exquisite creature," remarked Sir Henry languidly, as the two men continued along Jermyn Street. "I always admired her, you know. I even thought of making her an offer once."

"Oh?" Lord Lucan's deep voice was noncommittal. "What prevented you?"

"Oh, well, I was madly in love with Denise at the time. You know, that ravishing little French actress playing in some of the Drury Lane farces? And I thought to myself,

35

really, Henry old boy, two such beautiful women, and how is one supposed to divide oneself, you know? I'd wear myself out between them. And I remember asking myself, why should I get married when *la petite* Denise is so charmingly accommodating? And then, of course, there was that nasty business with Edmund Verney. I was a bit surprised at that, I must say."

His companion's expression grew a little hard. "Yes. Edmund Verney was the last person I'd have expected her to marry."

"Well, she's free of him now," sighed Sir Henry, negligently swinging his cane. "And since I have no Denise to amuse me at the moment, I really think I may try my luck with the fair widow. I'd say she's ripe for the plucking, wouldn't you? Who knows? I may be lucky. She seemed to look favorably upon me just now."

"She did, didn't she?" mused the earl. "Still, I think she liked me a little, too."

Sir Henry let out a chortle. "You? No, no, Geoff, old boy, you've got it all wrong. You haven't quite learned the knack of pleasing the ladies, have you? I mean, ladies of quality, of course," he added with a small guffaw. "If you must study the more interesting parts of their anatomy, my dear fellow, you simply *must* learn to do it when they're not looking. That's what they want, don't you see? If they catch you at it, then they must needs look insulted and *that* spoils all the fun. You bungled it this time, old boy." He laughed again. "I'll wager she won't even give you the time of day next time you meet."

Lord Lucan gave him a quizzical look. "You think not? How much would you care to wager on that? She'll give me far more than the time of day before I am through."

Sir Henry's eyes lit. "Oh, I say! You mean it? Oh, this *ought* to be amusing! No, *really*, you choose. What shall it be? A contest between us? Winner gets the widow *and* the gold."

The earl hesitated. "I think not," he said finally, a curious glint in his gray eyes. "I never wager on anything serious. You see, Harry, I'm after the lady's hand."

"Her *hand?* Egad, do you really want to go and get yourself leg-shackled again? She's a widow, old boy. You don't have to *marry* her!" Sir Henry looked askance at the thought.

"You think not?" retorted the other, rather musingly. "I wouldn't be so sure. She doesn't strike me as the sort of woman who'd accept a carte blanche, and at any rate, I've a fancy to marry again."

The baronet laughed and gave him a sidelong look. "A fancy so strong you've never so much as mentioned it before, eh? It sounds as if the hard-hearted Geoffrey Trevelyan has been struck by one of Cupid's darts. Or should I say the fair Diana's arrows? Oh, this is *marvelous!* I wish you luck, old boy, but to be frank, I wish *me* even better luck. You don't object to a little rivalry, do you?"

The earl raised his brows. "Rivalry? You're not suggesting you want to marry her, are you?"

A derisive snort hissed from between Sir Henry's teeth. "Not unless she's an heiress, and as far as I know, she's not. Anyway, what's the point? She knows what's what by now." He gave a small laugh. "Married to Edmund Verney, she'd have to."

"She won't accept you."

It was a statement, flat and sure, and it goaded the other man.

"Oh? Well, we'll have to see about that, Geoff, old boy. I've a certain way with the ladies, don't y'know? Boyish charm, and all that. *Ma chère mère* tells me I'm perfectly irresistible."

The earl's lip curled. "Odd. My mother says the same

about me, Harry. But I don't make the mistake of believing her."

The three women were ushered into Great-aunt Serena's drawing room fifteen minutes later by a tottering and extremely stiff-lipped butler. As regal as a queen upon her throne, the dowager sat in the center of that huge salon, her voluminous blue skirt spilling about her like water around a peninsula. The gnarled fingers of her left hand were tightly wrapped about the silver head of her long ebony cane.

"You're late!" barked the old woman, before they had taken more than a step into the room.

"Nonsense," said Diana, moving forward to kiss her scowling relative on the cheek. "It is precisely eleven o'clock. It cannot be that which has you miffed."

Her aunt glowered at her. "You're still as saucy as ever, I see. Well, go ahead, sit down, sit down! Barclay!"—this was addressed to the lingering butler— "Pull over those chairs for my nieces and Miss, ah, Tilden, is it? They're too far away from me. Now, Diana. I suppose it's too much to expect that I might be given an explanation?"

Sinking into the chair nearest her aunt, Diana raised her delicate brows questioningly. "An explanation, ma'am? What can you mean?"

The dowager had obviously been nourishing her complaints. "To start with, I want to know why you must waste good money setting up a household of your own when you could be staying here under my roof! What's wrong with my house?"

"Nothing," answered Diana calmly. "But I felt I would prefer to be on my own, having been accustomed to it for so long now. I thought Mama explained all that."

"And *my* feelings do not enter into the matter, I suppose?"

Diana smoothed her skirt, irritated by the dowager's accusing tone. "I did not think you would object. Indeed, I can think of no reason why you should."

Her aunt reached for her sherry. "You can't, eh?" she said, taking a hefty sip.

"No, and what's more, my dear ma'am," retorted Diana baldly, "I've purposely chosen to live nearby, thinking it would please you. But it seems I set myself an impossible task."

The response fared well with the dowager, who had always preferred spunk to spinelessness. "Hrumph! And so you could use my carriages, I'll hazard a guess!" she threw out, in a slightly less peevish tone.

Diana studied her fingertips. "Only if it suits you, madam," she said evenly. "Otherwise, I will gladly purchase my own."

The dowager peered at her for a moment, then let out a cackle. "Oh, hoity toity! Aren't we the proud lady now! *Madam*, indeed! You used to call me 'Aunt Serena,' for land's sake!"

"And I still shall, if you like," said Diana, with a reluctant laugh. "But when I am in your black books, Aunt Serena, I don't dare take such liberties."

"Liberties, be damned! I'm your aunt, Diana. Oh, now I've shocked your Miss Tilden. Haven't you told her I'm a plain-spoken woman?"

This time Diana's voice quivered in amusement. "I rather fancy she knows it. But as for my setting up house on my own, are you truly that put out by it?"

The dowager finished her sherry, and reached for the hand bell to ring for tea. "If you were to ask me, Diana, you're no more fit to be on your own than little Aimee, here," she pronounced. "Just look what a hash you've made of your life already."

"Oh, no, Auntie Serena," protested Aimee, quick to intervene. "That is unfair. Diana has done very well, and we have the snuggest little house in Jermyn Street. Diana knows just how everything ought to be done, I know she does."

Pleased by this mark of sibling loyalty, the dowager merely sniffed, and said, in a conceding tone, "Well, it ain't a bad address, but why the devil you must bury yourself alive since that rascally husband of yours died, I cannot begin to understand. If I'd had my way, I'd have had you up to London years ago to find you a decent mate."

Diana opened her mouth to reply, but as Barclay chose that moment to bring in the tea tray, she closed it again, and cast a speaking glance at her sister. When he was gone, she continued, in a more moderate tone than she had meant to employ, "But I don't wish to remarry, Aunt Serena. I'm perfectly happy as I am. I am here to assist you with Aimee's Season."

"I didn't pay for you to come all this way to help me play chaperon," retorted the dowager, a trifle sharply. "Now, what I want to know is this: did Edmund leave you well enough set up to meet this ridiculous expenditure? I won't have any niece of mine getting herself behindhand in the world."

A little surprised, Diana said mildly, "Oh, I can afford it, Aunt Serena, but, as you guessed, I would prefer not to have the additional expense of buying and stabling a carriage and horses."

The dowager waved her hand dismissively. "No, no, there's no need for that. It would be a shameful waste of money when you can use mine. But we'll have to purchase a couple of nice ladies' hacks for you to ride, eh?" As if reading Diana's thoughts, she continued,

"For God's sake, don't look so amazed! What an old lickpenny you must think me!"

Blinking, Diana remarked, "No, I never thought you that, Aunt Serena. It is simply that I find you so unpredictable!"

Taking this as a compliment, the dowager snorted. "It's a damned good thing to be! Take my advice, Diana, and always keep 'em guessing! That way, you won't ever be called a dead bore. Now then," she said with evident relish, "let's get down to business. I've picked a date for the ball and made up the guest list. No sense in wasting time, I felt. Let us hope, Aimee, that we can fire you off without starting any scandals."

Again, Aimee deflected the barb. "That is kind of you, Auntie," she responded, with her sweetest smile. "Perhaps I should warn you, though. I have already quite made up my mind to marry my cousin Charles."

The dowager cocked her head. "My grandson? Oh, aye, that would be a fair enough match—*if* you can bring him up to scratch! The young fellow's been devilish slick at avoiding the altar." She grinned ferociously. "I've been trying to put some spirit into the boy for years, but it's no use. He's terrified of me, did you know?"

"I can't imagine why," said Diana dryly.

The dowager gave her a suspicious look, then allowed her mouth to relax. "Never mind him. What's this nonsense about not wanting to remarry?"

"Just that, Aunt Serena," replied Diana shortly, her mind on something else she wanted to say. "About the ball. Did you by any chance include Sir Henry Neyle on your guest list?"

"Why?" Her aunt's tone was equally abrupt. "Don't tell me you're still hankering after *him!*"

Diana stiffened. "I'm not *hankering* after anyone, Aunt Serena. But we met him in Jermyn Street a short

41

while ago, and he was most courteous. I think it only civil that he receive a card."

Aimee, exchanging a swift glance with Miss Tilden, said ingenuously, "Oh, and do not forget Lord Lucan, Diana. I think he has an admiration for you, also."

The dowager's small brown eyes snapped with interest. "Eh? What's this? You've already caught *his* eye, have you? Well, I'm not altogether surprised. "Now, *he* would make you a fine husband!"

"But I don't want a husband," wailed Diana. "And I don't care a straw for the odious man. Anyway, Aunt, you know perfectly well he is already married."

"No, he ain't. That wife of his ran off with some American two summers ago and drowned herself. Oh, no, not on purpose. There was an accident at sea—she fell overboard, or some such thing. They rescued her, but it was too late. Anyway, he's well rid of her! She was a wicked, faithless woman, and a poor excuse for a wife!"

"Well, I'm very sorry, I'm sure, but that does not mean I'm interested in taking her place. I don't even *like* the man!"

The dowager's tones were tart. "At least he's a man and not a mincing Jack-a-dandy like Sir Henry Neyle. Why, the man's as pretty as a girl, Diana. You cannot seriously expect *him* to make you happy!"

Diana eyed her aunt in growing exasperation. "No, I don't. Because I—am—not—looking—for—a—husband!" she ground out, through clenched teeth.

"All right, all right," said her aunt, changing her tactics. "No need to fly up into the boughs about it. You like being a widow. Why, so do I, for that matter! Just as long as you understand that widows as young and attractive as yourself are considered by some to be *fair game*. I trust I make myself clear?"

Diana's expression turned bleak as the meaning

behind these words sank in. "Fair game," she repeated with effort. "I see."

The old woman watched her for a moment, and was pleased to see the resolute tilt return to her chin.

"Well," replied Diana, the light of battle entering her eye, "I shall be very much on my guard. But I still must request that you invite Sir Henry Neyle to the ball."

"Very well," agreed the dowager blandly. "And the Earl of Lucan, as well."

Chapter Three

If he were asked, Lord Lucan would have said he was not a romantic man. He had never been in love, and, if he thought about it at all, would likely have said that falling in love was not a very practical thing to do. Remarriage, however, was eminently practical, and choosing a woman who suited his exacting taste was high on his list of priorities. Once he had decided that Diana Verney was that woman, it was typical that he wasted no time, and set out to commence his wooing the following day.

He had never been given to mulling over decisions for vast lengths of time, but this was not because he was impetuous. His thought processes might be lightning quick and his decisions seldom subject to reconsideration, but this did not mean the earl had not given serious thought to the matter of choosing a new wife. The truth was that having met Diana six years before, she had registered—and remained—in his mind as the most intriguing woman he had ever met.

In appearance, she was his ideal woman—soft and feminine, neither too short nor too tall, with a lovely face and wonderful figure. Astonishingly, her demeanor and disposition also attracted him. In fact, he could recall quite clearly the searing effect she had had on him at the time of her come-out.

He had noticed her immediately, for she had stood out from the other girls like a candle in a throng of rushlights. He remembered experiencing quite a pang of regret that he was already married, there being something about the way she held her head, something in the proud tilt of her chin that had caught his fancy. Curiosity had driven him to converse with her and his interest, he recalled, had quickly heightened. Though she had been a little shy, her responses had been intelligent, and as for her spirit . . . *that* he had found amusingly evident in the flash of her eyes and the slightly disapproving tone in her voice. Of what she had disapproved he was still unsure, but he had longed to further the acquaintance and find out. Such a fascinating young woman had been utterly wasted on a man like Edmund Verney, he thought with a frown.

But now she was back, and he lacked a wife. When fate offered a second chance, only a fool would fail to take advantage of it. He would begin his courtship without delay.

Having been granted the use of the dowager's town coach, the two sisters had spent the entire morning shopping, and had managed to make a fair dent in the monumental task of supplying Aimee with the items of fashion she would be needing for the London Season. Miss Tilden had accompanied them, and as she had become quite exhausted, was soundly asleep upon her bed when his lordship arrived.

Downstairs in the study, Diana was halfway through a letter to her parents when the clang of a bell brought her head up with a jerk. Her expression alert, she found herself paying unusual heed to the firm tread of Lawrence's footsteps as he went to the door. Though she tried to remain calm, her pulse began to flutter in an odd anticipation. Could it be Sir Henry? Surely it must be he, for the odious Earl of Lucan would not dare have the impertinence to come here . . . would he? Rising from her chair, Diana was nearly to the door when a deep male voice brought her to a halt.

He *had* come! Her worst fears confirmed, Diana froze, her hand just inches from the knob. The door was ajar, and through the crack she caught a glimpse of the earl as he stepped into the hall and followed Lawrence up the creaking wooden stairs to the floor above.

As if transfixed, she stared at the spot where he had been. Though she could not think him a handsome man, she was forced to admit his presence was imposingly masculine. He was very tall and very solid, at any rate, with a wide pair of shoulders and a broad chest. It was impossible not to be aware that most women rated such features high on their list of ideal male attributes; as for Diana, she could not recall ever having given the matter a great deal of thought. Why was it, then, that she abruptly (and rather perversely) decided she preferred fair men? This, of course, could have nothing to do with the fact that her uninvited caller was very dark, both of hair and skin. His features, too, were too harsh to please, and there was a certain arrogance in his stride that she disliked.

Stalling for time, Diana raised an unsteady hand to smooth her hair, while casting her rose-colored gown a critical glance. It would not do, she reasoned, to appear to disadvantage, since there was little doubt she would need all her confidence to survive an encounter with this man. She hesitated another few seconds, catering to her reluctance to face what was sure to be a difficult interview. She would be very cool—no *cold,* she corrected, so that he would be quite put off and— But where was Aimee?

The question effectively shattered what little poise she still possessed. Terrified that her innocent young sister was upstairs alone with a man of libertine propensities, Diana rushed up the steps to the next floor with an energy seldom displayed outside a cavalry charge. Her fears, however, were quite unwarranted; when she burst breathlessly into the drawing room she found the earl to be alone. Indeed, he looked distinctly taken aback by her unconventional entry.

Knowing how foolish she must look, Diana made a hasty attempt to salvage her dignity. Arching her brows daintily, she said, "My lord" in a tone just icy enough to suggest that there could not possibly be a rational reason for his visit.

The earl bowed. "My dear Mrs. Verney, there was no need to run," he assured her, with an irritating smile. "I had no intention of leaving before you arrived."

"I was *not* running!" she responded hotly, entirely forgetting that a dignified person would not respond with such vehemence.

How dared he laugh at her!

"Weren't you?" he inquired, his amusement annoyingly evident. "Then I can only say you are the most energetic woman of my acquaintance!"

It took all her resolution to ignore this. "Just why are you here, Lord Lucan?" she demanded.

"What, weren't you expecting me?" He surveyed her, his black brows rising in apparent surprise. "I thought I made it quite clear I wished to know you better."

So Aunt Serena was right . . . !

"No, of course I wasn't expecting you," she lied. "I hoped you would have the decency to leave me alone."

"Decency?" His head cocked to the side. "No, really. That's doing it too brown, my dear. What's indecent about paying you a visit?"

Diana eyed him suspiciously, then gave a slight sigh.

"Nothing," she conceded, yielding to his logic against her better judgment. "Pray, be seated, my lord. I will ring for refreshment."

"Now, that's better." He stepped forward, then waited for her to take a seat before he did likewise. "I was beginning to think you didn't like me," he added with what she felt was far too satisfied a smile.

"Your remarks," said Diana, nervously smoothing her skirt, "are most improper. I must ask you to refrain."

"Refrain from being improper?" He looked amused. "Very well, I'm willing to give it a try, at least for a bit. What shall we talk about? The weather?"

Since at this juncture Lawrence arrived with a tray laden with wine and cakes, Diana was forced to bite back her response. She dismissed her butler at once, however, so as to allow herself the pleasure of saying, as waspishly as possibly, "The weather, my lord, is very probably the only subject upon which you and I could agree!"

"Now, why on earth would you say a thing like that?" he responded, helping himself to a biscuit. "You certainly seem to be in the sullens. Did I do something to offend you?"

Diana glared. "Lord Lucan, my extremely brief acquaintance with you is enough to assure me that you are being deliberately provoking. You must know that your behavior yesterday was excessively impertinent. I am amazed you had the effrontery to show your face here today."

She said it with such stiff dignity that he ought to have been firmly put in his place. However, Geoffrey Trevelyan, sixth Earl of Lucan, only stretched out his long legs and regarded her with what could almost have been called a twinkle. "You're supposed to offer me some sherry," he pointed out in a kindly manner.

Biting her lip, Diana reached for the decanter and poured him a drink. "Aren't you going to answer me?"

she inquired, resisting the powerful urge to hurl it in his face.

As if reading her thoughts, he hurriedly accepted the glass. "Thank you. So you think I was impertinent. How so?" He gave her a quick side look as he sipped his sherry.

Diana clenched her hands into fists, convinced she was on the verge of a strong spasm. "I wonder if it will rain this afternoon," she remarked, in a pointed manner.

Although a gleam of humor entered his gray eyes, her aristocratic caller showed no sign of taking the hint. "Surely you did not take exception to the fact that I saw fit to admire you?" he persisted.

Diana's bosom heaved indignantly. "In far too blatant a manner!" she snapped.

"I see. Then I assume you did not care for the kiss, either?"

Eyes flashing, Diana lifted her chin in just the manner he remembered. "I care nothing for your kisses," she informed him, in the most withering accents she was capable of summoning. "I may as well tell you, my lord, that I found such a vulgar display the veriest epitome of insult. And I shall take leave to inform you that I am *not* the sort of female you seem to imagine!"

"Ah. I see we have a little misunderstanding," said his lordship, setting down his glass. He leaned forward, and dropped his bantering tone. "Now, why do you instantly assume I rank you low? I meant only to flirt with you, but if you deem it an insult, I must certainly apologize. I assure you, Mrs. Verney, I don't view you as anything but a lady of unimpeachable virtue. We seem to have gotten off to a bad start, I am sorry to say." He paused and gave her one of his direct looks. "When you came in just now, I thought you looked a bit worried. I only sought to make you smile. Perhaps it was presumptuous of me."

"Oh." Somewhat appeased, Diana eyed him un-

49

certainly. But then . . . why are you here?"

His lordship sighed ruefully. "I see we have come full circle. My dear Mrs. Verney, although you hardly know me, you may believe me sincere when I say that I have long admired you. My purpose in coming here today was merely to beg the pleasure of your company tomorrow. I should like to invite you to drive with me in the Park."

"Oh," repeated Diana, her emotions in a jumble. "I'm sorry, my lord, but I cannot."

"Why not?" he said. "I'm a competent whip; I won't overturn you."

A rebellious sparkle crept back into Diana's eyes. "Lord Lucan, when a lady declines an invitation, she is not required to give an explanation for her refusal."

"Is this one of those interminable rules of etiquette? I never abide by 'em, my dear. They're far too confining." A sudden glint entered his eyes. "That one about not receiving gentlemen alone, for instance. *Most* confining."

Diana was suddenly assailed with a vexing urge to giggle. She controlled it, however, and managed to say, with only a trace of a gasp, "Miss Tilden is sleeping, my lord, and anyway, I am far too old to require a chaperon."

"Quite in your dotage, in fact," he agreed. "Come, I have no wish to be at outs with you. Shall we be friends?"

"Very well," said Diana, wondering how on earth he had managed to maneuver her into a tractable mood.

Her answer obviously pleased him, for he surged out of his chair with a twisted grin. "Capital! Then I'll come for you tomorrow a little before five."

"What?" she exclaimed, rising with him. "I did not mean . . . You know very well I did not mean . . . Oh! Where are you *going?*"

"I think I can find my way out," he explained, his long legs carrying him swiftly to the door.

"It is extremely rude," said Diana, her voice gathering strength as she spoke, "to walk out of a room when someone is speaking to you!"

She was but two steps behind him, and he startled her by turning suddenly and reaching for her hands. "If I stay any longer," he said, with an odd little curl to his rather hard mouth, "I really will kiss you. And since you barely know me, and care nothing for my kisses, I think it best that I go. Unless you've begun to feel differently?" His flaring nostrils belied his playful tone, leaving Diana no doubt that given the slightest encouragement he would do it.

"Go!" she gritted, trying to pull away. "Go, before I have a fit of the vapors! Impossible man!"

He grinned, and his grip tightened. "Until tomorrow, then. Be ready."

Then he released her and rather to her surprise, favored her with a formal bow. "And in the meanwhile, Mrs. Verney, rest assured that I remain your most obedient servant . . ."

"That man is simply too much!" she told Aimee a few minutes later. She watched Aimee adjust the tilt on the saucy little bonnet she had purchased that morning. "I am glad you had the excellent sense not to join us. There are some gentlemen, my dear, who do not know how to behave themselves in the company of innocent young girls."

Her back to Diana, Aimee was watching her sister's face in the mirror. "You like him, don't you?" she said suddenly.

"Like him!" Diana gave a careless laugh. "Don't be ridiculous! He has the manners of a country bumpkin. He is far too bold, and those gray eyes of his stare too hard for my comfort. He makes himself entirely too free in my

51

house, and purposely misinterprets my words to gain his own way! I detest him."

Aimee swung around and stared at her sister. "Gracious, Diana, you sound so unlike your usual self! Are you all right?"

Diana shrugged. "Just disappointed, I suppose. I had hoped it was Sir Henry come to call."

Aimee removed her bonnet and went to sit near her elder sister on the edge of the bed. "Tell me about Sir Henry," she prompted with interest.

"Oh, there is really nothing to tell," replied Diana uncomfortably. "Except that he is the most complete gentleman, the very opposite of Lord Lucan. If *he* calls, it will be perfectly safe for you to meet him."

"I see," said Aimee. Her speculative gaze rested on her sister's face. "He is very handsome, isn't he? Once, long ago, did you perhaps cherish a *tendre* for him?"

Diana looked at the floor. "Long ago," she answered, with a long sigh. "I was very foolish then. Things worked out so differently."

"Mama told me a little. I am so sorry, Diana."

"Then you understand why it is so important for me to be here with you. It would kill me, Aimee, if anything like that were to happen to you. We must be so careful."

Aimee covered her sister's hand with her own. "I shall be careful, dearest."

"What you said yesterday about wanting to flirt, well, it frightened me," Diana confessed, rather abruptly. "It's a dangerous game, Aimee. You can have no notion how the slightest encouragement can affect a man. All noblemen are not gentlemen, you see. Think of Edmund!"

"Wouldn't it be better if we did not think of Edmund?" Aimee suggested wisely. "He is best forgotten, Diana. You owe him nothing."

Diana's hands slid over her face, as if to erase some

unpleasant memory. "I know it. But marriage to him changed me, somehow. I just don't want that to happen to you."

"Oh, it won't," Aimee assured her confidently. "I promise."

The following afternoon, Diana decided to take an inventory of her own clothing to see what she would need to purchase to see her through the Season. Since she subscribed to several ladies' magazines, she had been able to keep up with the latest styles, but she suspected that her gowns were far fewer in number than what she would require. She had made most of them herself, in some cases meticulously copying the fashion plates, in others, improving upon them. Although she disliked embroidery, she had always enjoyed making her own dresses. There was a sense of accomplishment in completing something one could wear that she did not feel by merely covering a pillow with some frivolous pattern. She had made gowns for her sisters as well, which was a large part of what had kept her occupied for the past three years.

Staring into the clothespress, she wondered what to wear for her drive with the Earl of Lucan. While she had no intention of making any effort to impress the man, she could not forget that it would be her first public appearance, and her pride demanded that she look her best. There were members of the *ton* who would be only too eager to label her a dowd; things would be bad enough without that, she knew.

Fashions had changed since she had made her comeout. After Waterloo, skirt bottoms had widened and become much more decorated, and the waistlines seemed to have come up even higher than before—a difficult feat, one would have thought. Gone were the plain, columnar, figure-revealing frocks which had reigned so popular before the time of Napoleon's exile. Trimmings of every

53

sort were increasingly the mode: ribbons, bowknots, ruffles, flouncing, lace, artificial flowers—the possibilities were endless. Diana was just as well satisfied that this was so. Some of the thin muslin gowns she had worn at age eighteen had revealed a great deal more than they had concealed, making her feel decidedly uncomfortable when in the company of gentlemen. Besides, she thought the various trimmings quite attractive, as long as they were not carried to extreme.

After much debate, she pulled out a very pretty round dress of dove gray bombazine, a fabric which was still considered very elegant. It would do very nicely, she reflected, for its high collar and long sleeves would shield her from the wind, while its subdued shade and design would surely provide her with an aura of mature dignity, something the brighter colors did not seem to do. She had completed it only a month earlier, and was pardonably pleased with the results. Its severity was alleviated by a band of peach-colored satin under the bust, and a double rouleaux of the same at the hem and base of the sleeves.

Without bothering to ring for Meg, Diana slipped out of her morning dress and into the handsome carriage dress. She had added peach satin trimming to the jaunty cottage that she had purchased to go with it. Placing this upon her head, she assessed the effect in the mirror. She found the style of the bonnet's crown, which resembled a man's, to be quite dashing, and a new confidence flowed through her. No, she decided defiantly, Diana Verney was not going to be labeled a dowd. She was going to take the shine out of them all!

Nor would she allow Lord Lucan to bring down her defenses. Her topaz eyes held a militant gleam as she mulled over all the things she would say to him. She would tell him, quite calmly, that he was insolent, that he was overbearing and rude, that she disliked being manipulated and that she was not going to put up with it.

Someone scratched on her bedchamber door, interrupting these delicious plans to put Lord Lucan in his place. Sounding apologetic, her abigail's voice floated through the thin wood.

"Sorry to bother you, mistress, but there's a gentleman to see you."

Could it be Sir Henry at last? Or would this prove to be another disappointment? "Meg," she said in agitation, "come and help me with the fastenings to this gown. Oh, do hurry!"

Aimee peeped into the drawing room, and, recognizing the blond gentleman within, tripped happily in to join him. "Hello," she said, her guileless smile tilting the corners of her pink lips in just the bewitching way she had been practicing. "Aren't you Sir Henry Neyle?"

Sir Henry bowed, his golden-lashed blue eyes moving over her in an appreciative manner. "I am. And you are the little sister, if I remember correctly. I *do* beg your pardon, my dear, but I've quite forgotten your name."

Knowing full well the man must know her as Miss Farington, Diana's young sister favored the handsome baronet with a single provocative bat of her long black lashes. "It's Aimee," she revealed in her most flirtatious voice. "Aimee Farington."

Sir Henry's smile altered subtly. "Well . . . Aimee . . . what a very pretty creature you are, to be sure. You don't resemble your sister much, do you?"

This time Aimee's lashes fluttered several times. "I fear not," she admitted with a deeply regretful sigh. "I take after Mama's side of the family, you see. Is Diana not the most beautiful girl? If I weren't so prodigiously fond of her, I would be quite green with envy. And she is the strictest chaperon, is it not unfortunate?"

His fancy tickled, the baronet studied her from head to

toe. "I see. And you are a little minx, aren't you? Here to be presented into society, like your sister."

Aimee regarded him soulfully. "It is so. Will it be too dreadfully dull for me, do you think?"

"It can be as dull or as exciting as you wish it, little Aimee. Your fate lies in your own hands," Sir Henry told her with an intent look.

"Oh," Aimee responded, dramatically clasping her hands together at her bosom, "I must have excitement, Sir Henry. I simply *crave* excitement."

The baronet's hand lifted for an instant, then dropped to his side. "Remind me of that some other time, Aimee dear. I think I hear someone coming."

As Diana entered the room, Aimee abruptly ended her experiment. She watched Diana calmly greet Sir Henry, and struggled to evaluate the entire episode.

It had been her first taste of flirtation, and she could not deny that it had been an exhilarating experience. As she had expected, Sir Henry had seemed to flirt back, but not quite in the manner she had anticipated. While she had not completely understood the underlying meaning to his words, she was aware that he ought to have been more formal with her. Was he a rake? If so, he would definitely not make a good husband for Diana, for Aimee had come to the conclusion that if a gentleman were right for her sister, he ought not to flirt with other ladies, and most especially not with herself. This was the gauge of measurement she had decided to use, and in her youthful mind, it seemed a good one.

"Have I caught you at an inconvenient time, Mrs. Verney?" Sir Henry was inquiring. "You look as though you were about to go out."

"Actually, no," Diana explained. "I was just trying on the dress to see if it fit properly. I may wear it later."

"I can see no flaw in the fit," he said smoothly. "Whoever made it for you did an exquisite job of it."

She smiled. "Why, thank you. Since I made it myself, your words are music to my ears."

"Did you really?" Sir Henry put up his quizzing glass. "How extraordinary! Mrs. Verney, I find you an amazing woman."

Feeling a little embarrassed by his scrutiny, Diana gave a self-conscious laugh. "Hardly that, unfortunately. Sewing is merely an outlet for my energy." Seeking to change the subject, she said, at random, "Have you any interesting news to tell me? I fear I've been sadly out of touch with practically everyone since . . . since my marriage." This was not what she had meant to say, and the sentence ended rather flatly.

But Sir Henry took no notice. "Gossip, you mean?" His fair brows went up. "Oh, *loads*, my dear. But I cannot remember six years worth this instant. Why don't you drive out with me later? Then we can have a cozy little chat about it all."

Diana opened her mouth to accept, when, unbidden, a vivid and thoroughly disconcerting image of Lord Lucan entered her mind. "I—I cannot, I am sorry to say," she heard herself respond. "I have a prior engagement."

A master at the game he had chosen to play, Sir Henry did not press the issue. "Well, perhaps another time, then," he offered carelessly. "And when is Miss Farington's presentation, if I may ask?"

Aimee smiled sunnily. "It is to be in two weeks, Sir Henry. Aunt Serena is sending out the cards for my ball this very day."

Sir Henry shot her an enigmatic look. "And shall I be invited, do you think?"

"Our aunt intends to invite some of my own friends, as well as the younger set," Diana put in quickly, unsure what Aimee's response might be. "I believe your name was one of those included. Naturally, I—we—will be

57

pleased if you will join us."

The baronet's lazy eyes did not miss the quick, involuntary rise and fall of Diana's bosom. "Why, I would not miss it for the world," he said easily. "You are both such lovely ladies, one would have to be addled not to attend what promises to be a most diverting affair."

It lacked but one minute to five o'clock. Diana, garbed in the dove gray ensemble, stood tapping her foot, her serenity gone, her temper more on edge than it had been in months. Where was that exasperating man? The prospect of facing the *ton* had put her nerves on such a fray that the additional delay was pure torture. How could he be so inconsiderate?

It was another ten minutes before Lawrence's footsteps told her the earl had arrived. "Lord Lucan awaits you in the drawing room," her butler informed her with a wooden countenance.

Diana swept into that room with every intention of starting a battle. Putting on her most wrathful expression, she began, "I thought that perhaps you had found something better to do today, my lord!"

The earl's brows flew up. "Something better?" he repeated, sounding quizzical.

"I mean," she said tartly, "that you are late. But perhaps it was foolish of me to expect punctuality. I am sometimes afflicted with the strangest notions."

The earl consulted his timepiece. "You baffle me, my dear. Look, it is just five now."

"It is more than ten minutes past that hour," she corrected, gazing significantly at the clock upon the mantelshelf.

"Oh, no. My watch always keeps perfect time," he said, quite kindly. "Your clock must be fast. I recommend you have it checked."

Irked by the knowledge that he was laughing at her,

Diana retorted, "Well, you should have been here well before the hour. You must know how crowded the Park becomes."

He must have heard something odd in her voice, for his steel gray eyes studied her thoughtfully. "Something's bothering you, isn't it? Will you tell me?"

Diana gave her gloves an unnecessary tug. "Nonsense! I was simply—Oh, never mind! Shall we go?"

His eyes narrowed a little, but he did not pursue the matter. "Very well. My carriage awaits, my dear," he said, with a courtly gesture of his hand.

For some unaccountable reason the gallantry erased Diana's other concerns, replacing them with a raw, dangerous awareness of the six-foot man in front of her. "I am not your dear," she replied, stammering a little. Annoyed by her weakness, she whirled away so that he could not see her face. "And I beg you will remember it!" she snapped.

It had little effect on the earl. "Not yet," he murmured. "But that is easily remedied." He had moved forward so that his mouth was close to her ear, which startled her nearly as much as the brush of his finger as he pushed back a stray golden curl.

The touch of his hand, and the warm breath upon her cheek combined to send a startled shiver down Diana's spine. Obviously, she decided, the only thing to do was to pretend she had not heard. Head held high, Diana sailed out of the house, her mind completely unable to come up with a suitably scathing response for this new outrage.

Outside, Lord Lucan handed her into his curricle with amazing cheerfulness. "Well, at any rate, I'm pleased you did not forget our engagement," he said. "I half-feared it might slip your mind."

"It was a temptation," Diana told him coldly, watching him swing his long body into the open, two-wheeled carriage.

A glint of humor warmed his eyes. "Ah, now, if we are

to speak of temptation, Mrs. Verney, perhaps we should dispense with my groom."

Diana's hands clenched. "Don't you *dare!*"

He laughed softly. "Very well. James shall play duenna, if it makes you more comfortable. Although, of course, you are far too old to need one," he reminded.

The groom, responding to a motion from his master, released his hold on the horses' bridle and made a deft leap for his perch. The carriage rolled forward over the cobbles, but Diana soon realized that James's presence made little difference to the earl.

"You look quite charming in that gown," was his next remark, "but I liked the other one better. Blue becomes you a little more, I think."

"That seems to be less a compliment than a piece of advice," she pointed out. "Are you always so clumsy with words, my lord?"

His quick look was difficult to read. "On the contrary, I make it a practice to say exactly what I mean."

"I see. Then should you care to criticize anything else whilst you have the chance? My hat, perhaps? Or my gloves?"

His teeth flashed white against his bronzed skin, and Diana was conscious of a curious jolt of gratification that her response had amused him. "No, everything you wear is completely *sans reproche*, Mrs. Verney. Rather, I would like to compliment you on your failure to cut your hair— an admirable piece of restraint, in my view. However, as I suspect my doing so will cause you to immediately rush home and hack it all off, I believe I will refrain."

A sudden urge to giggle poked holes in her gravity. "Well, as long as you do not mention it, I promise I shall not," she assured him, with only the slightest quiver in her voice.

He grinned at that, and a short, surprisingly companionable silence prevailed between them for several

60

minutes. They reached the entrance to Hyde Park, and the earl guided his curricle through the gateway with the careless skill of one who was renowned as something of a nonpareil. Once inside, his curious gaze immediately shifted to probe Diana's expression. She was looking extremely pale, he observed, when but a moment before her creamy skin had been aglow with confidence, the healthy, rosy hue he so admired.

Indeed, Diana's mouth had gone completely dry. Sprinkled all along the winding road ahead of them, in droves of carriages, was the *ton*, come to parade its finery like so many cocks in a barnyard. The moment had finally come when she was to face them, but somehow none of the stern little self-lectures she had prepared for just this occasion came to mind. All at once the scene blurred, and the ladies were proud, chattering harpies darting sly glances in Diana's direction, their escorts sharing the joke with typical male crudity. During her repartee with Lord Lucan, Diana had been able to forget her fears, but now they resurged, dominating her so completely that her palms grew damp and her stomach churned with nervousness.

"Easy, now," soothed her companion. "They don't bite, you know."

Too upset to remark his perception, Diana swallowed hard and answered automatically. "I know that, but it— it doesn't help, somehow."

"Would it help if I held your hand?" he inquired, his lazy eyes watching her keenly.

Diana's head turned in confusion. "Hold your—*what* did you say?" A small sparkle entered her eye. "Did you say what I think you said?"

"I don't know. What do you think I said?"

"Did you just ask to hold my hand?" she demanded.

"Not at all," he assured her, a suspicious tremor in his deep voice. "You could not have been attending, my dear

61

Mrs. Verney. I merely asked if it would help if I did so."

"Oh, you are impossible!" she exclaimed, her complexion heightening. "And, if I might add to the list, arrogant and presumptuous and overbearing—"

"Oh, come now," he protested, rather mildly. His shrewd gaze swung away from her face to scan the carriages in the immediate vicinity. "Look, there is Lady Jersey and Mrs. Drummond-Burrell waving to us from that barouche. Now you must nod and smile, very graciously. There's a good girl. You're quite marvelous, did you know that?"

Startled by this praise, Diana gave him a puzzled look. "I don't understand you. You're doing this on purpose, aren't you?"

"Doing what? Flirting with you? But of course I am," he said smoothly. "The temptation to do so is quite irresistible."

Diana felt the betraying warmth seeping into her cheeks, and decided to give voice to what was to have been a highly satisfactory set-down. However, at the instant she opened her mouth, her horrified gaze fell upon a certain person not thirty yards ahead of them.

The set-down flew from her mind. "Lady Edgerton," she whispered, barely knowing she spoke aloud. "Oh, Lord."

Supreme among her apprehensions had been this—the moment of meeting with the malicious woman who had found her that night with Edmund. Suppressing the urge to clutch at his lordship's sleeve, Diana gave him one wide, frantic look before assuming what she prayed was an expression of total indifference.

Until now, the earl had not made use of his quizzing glass, a fashionable frivolity which the average cynical nobleman would have classed as a virtually indispensible weapon. Diana's entreaty for help, though mute, was neither to be misunderstood nor ignored. Without hesitation, his lordship leveled his weapon upon the rapidly approaching Lady Edgerton.

"An odiously fat woman," he pronounced, inspecting his victim pitilessly. His dark head gave a mournful shake. "She reminds me of an overfed orangutan. How in the world do you think she gets into her corset in the morning? Or out of it at night, for that matter?" His glass swiveled suddenly, and his large magnified eye hovered over Diana. "Speaking of which, my dear Mrs. Verney, you appear to have preserved your own figure very nicely, despite your extremely advanced age. I'll wager you don't even wear a corset. You certainly don't need one, and that's something very few females can claim!"

"My lord!" gasped Diana, very much shocked. "I'll thank you not to— Oh! You're trying to make me laugh, aren't you?" And she shocked herself even more by giving way to a nervous giggle.

Glancing down at her, Lord Lucan's mouth twisted into that same curious half-smile that she had noticed before. "Perhaps I am," he acknowledged. "Still, I happen to find the topic of some interest—for future reference, you understand. You don't wear them, do you? Come, you can tell me." Lady Edgerton's fleshy countenance, angled for the moment away from them, was but a horse's length away.

"I certainly will not!" Diana retorted with asperity. Almost absently, she found herself giving Lady Edgerton a cordial smile and nod as that astonished lady's eyes came to rest upon her face. "Such a question is completely improper, my lord," she admonished, hardly noticing Lady Edgerton's attempt to stare her out of countenance before Lord Lucan's gargantuan eye forced her to look elsewhere. "I have never been so shocked in my entire life!" she finished, with less heat than might normally have accompanied such impassioned words.

Then it was over. Lady Edgerton had passed on, and Diana realized that the first—and probably the most dreaded—of the ordeals was painlessly concluded. Gradually, her tension began to abate. Things were going to be all right after all, she reflected. And she owed the man beside her a great round of thanks.

Observing her relief, Lord Lucan knew he had accomplished his objective. But just to be on the safe side, he lowered his lips to whisper in her ear. "Sooner or later," he said in a devilish whisper, "I'll find out, you know. I'm determined on that score, Diana."

"Oh!" she sputtered indignantly, her complexion now completely restored to what his lordship considered its proper shade of rosiness. She clenched her gloved hands into small fists, and tried very hard to ignore her companion's wolfish grin. "You . . . you . . . *Oh!*"

But scowling was strangely difficult, for at this precise moment Diana was making a staggering discovery. How could it possibly be, she wondered? How was it that such harsh features as Lord Lucan's could suddenly seem so amazingly attractive?

Chapter Four

As Diana entered the room, Aimee snapped shut the book of poems she had been endeavoring to read. It had failed quite dismally to engage her interest, for something had occurred which overrode any desire she might have felt to escape into the idyllic world of odes and sonnets.

"Oh, I am so glad you are back, Diana!" she exclaimed, her words pouring forth as they invariably did when she had worked herself into a dither. "Did you enjoy yourself? Was Lord Lucan pleasant? Did you see anyone you knew? Come and tell me how it went!" She patted the chair next to her invitingly.

Diana sat down, unaware that Aimee's sharp eyes were taking in the flustered twisting of her fingers. "Well," she said slowly, "it went better than I expected, actually. He does tend to make the most unconventional remarks." She hesitated. "But all things considered, I suppose it went very well."

Aimee's curiosity was roused. "Why, what sort of things does he say, Diana?"

"Oh, well—" Diana gazed pensively at her fingertips. "He is a shocking flirt, of course, but in a kindly sort of way. That doesn't make much sense, does it?"

"Not much," agreed Aimee, diverted by this explanation. "Did he try to kiss you?"

"Of course not!" Diana gave her young sister a reproving look. "Whatever put that notion into your head?"

Aimee shrugged. "Eliza Fingleshaw says that is all the gentlemen really want." Belatedly recalling her sister's opinion of Eliza Fingleshaw, she added hurriedly, "Well then, what does he do?"

"Nothing really," insisted Diana uncomfortably. "He just talks about things he knows he should not. Like, er, corsets." At her sister's incredulous stare, she added quickly, "I think he only did it to make me laugh. That horrid Lady Edgerton was there and it was she, you see, who spread those awful rumors about Edmund and me . . ." Her voice drifted off in a faint shudder of remembrance, before surging vibrantly back. "Evidently, he realized I was very ill at ease and decided to come to my rescue. He stared at that woman through his quizzing glass in *such* a way, Aimee. It was really quite comical, now that I think about it."

The undercurrent of laughter in Diana's voice caused Aimee to give her a considering look. "Well, that was extremely obliging of him," she remarked. "You cannot now say you detest him!"

After a pause of a few seconds, Diana met her sister's inquiring gaze. "Yes, well, I suppose that word is a bit too strong," she admitted. "Rather, let us say that I am *wary* of him, my dear, for there is no disputing the fact that he is very much a man of the world. You see, I know what he . . . what he wants from me, and I am not about to agree to it. To my sorrow, I have already discovered how easily one's reputation can be damaged, and I have no intention of allowing anyone to sully mine ever again."

"No, of course not." Aimee's expression sobered for a respectful instant, before she plunged once more into ebullient speech. "Well, let me tell you who was here while you were gone! No, *not* Cousin Charles, I can see that is what you are guessing. It was only Aunt Serena. She arrived just twenty minutes after you left, and I rather fancy she was not at all pleased to find you gone— until I told her who you were with, that is," she added, with an arch smile. "Then she laughed in that odd way of hers, and said she might have known. I do not know what she could have meant by that."

Diana made a small grimace. "Aunt Serena is the most *managing* female alive! That, as you are probably aware, is the real reason I did not wish to live with her."

Almost too airily, Aimee replied, "Yes, well, I intend to turn her managing nature to very good account. In fact, I have already done so, and you will never guess how, Diana! I have convinced her to have us to dinner tomorrow evening, and to invite Cousin Charles!" She sat back triumphantly. "Now, wasn't that clever of me?"

Diana could not refrain from laughing. "Yes, very! Next you will be telling me Aunt Serena has agreed to frighten Cousin Charles into making you an offer!"

"Now, Diana, you know that is not what I want! Arranged marriages may be very much the thing, but that will *not* do for me! It is essential that Charles fall in love with me. He must offer for me because he wants to and not because he has been coerced into it." Aimee beamed. "I explained all this to Aunt Serena, and she agreed."

Diana stared in disbelief. "She did? Are you sure you understood her correctly?"

Aimee's dark curls bobbed as she nodded. "Absolutely. Auntie can be very reasonable, I have found."

"I do not think," said Diana carefully, "that we can be talking about the same woman. There must be something you're not telling me."

Aimee's eyes grew round with innocence. "Why, what can you mean? Goodness, Diana, you *have* grown suspicious all of a sudden."

"Now, Aimee, you know I can always tell when you're trying to cut a wheedle with me." Diana studied her sister suspiciously. "Out with it, now."

"But I promise you, there is nothing!"

Unconvinced, Diana eyed her sister for one long moment, then gave a tiny shrug. "Very well, Aimee. We shall let it go at that."

"I need you both to help me decide which gown to wear, for I simply *cannot* choose. Should it be the pink, the lavender, or the white?" appealed Aimee, the following afternoon. "Which is most likely to impress Charles? Which becomes me more?" She whirled away from the mirror and looked expectantly at her audience. "I cannot think how I will choose when all the other gowns arrive!"

Diana cast a deliberative eye over the three choices, then exchanged a glance with Miss Tilden. "Well, the white does make her look a positive angel doesn't it, Tildy? But I am not the one to ask since in the end I will always choose a color. You'd better leave it to Tildy."

Aimee turned eager eyes upon Miss Tilden, awaiting her verdict.

"What about the lavender?" suggested Miss Tilden musingly. "With that coal black hair and those eyes—! And the little white lace collar so demure! And yet," she debated, "there is a great deal of favor to be found in the pink. A perfectly delicious dress, my dear. It reminds me of some sort of confectionery!"

Aimee's nose wrinkled. "Well, I am sure I do not wish Charles to view me as a confectionery! Perhaps it should be the lavender, then. But won't it make a better impression if I wear white? Or does white make me look too young?"

Diana laughed. "Never that, dearest. All three are extremely lovely, which makes it difficult to advise you. But I do think Tildy is right. There is something about the lavender that appeals to me. Pink and white are so commonly worn. The lavender is distinctive, and we can thread a matching satin ribbon through those beautiful curls of yours. *Not* that you would not stand out in any color, for you always look a picture in anything! I'm persuaded you'll have no trouble at all catching Cousin Charles's eye. And I plan to wear mauve, so we shall harmonize."

"But, Diana," grumbled Aimee in mock distress, "you forget I may have to compete for Charles's attention. There will be someone else present whom he might find more interesting than my poor self."

"Oh, who?" said Diana, looking surprised.

Her sister dimpled. "You modest creature, don't you know?"

"Oh, for heaven's sake, Aimee!" Diana's brown-gold eyes warmed with affection. "You are far more vivacious than I, besides being of marriageable age, which I am not! I *do* hate to discourage you, but your difficulty is more likely to lie in the fact that our cousin appears to prefer being a bachelor. Aunt Serena will have it that he has been at considerable pains to remain so."

"Yes, she told me that, also," retorted Aimee, in a more subdued voice. She glanced a bit anxiously into the cheval mirror, as if to seek reassurance that she had some small chance of attracting such a determined bachelor. She was not beautiful, but she was certainly a far cry from being unattractive, she told herself stoutly.

Reaching for the lavender gown, she held it up and surveyed it critically. "Perhaps," she mused aloud, "what I need is a more sophisticated gown. Something with a lower neckline so as to show off as much of my bosom as possible. Eliza says the gentlemen just adore

69

seeing a little glimpse of—" She broke off, catching sight of her sister's horrified expression. "Well, it was only a thought," she added quickly.

"I should certainly hope it was only a thought!" said Diana feelingly. "If Eliza does not know any better, at least you should. Such an indecorous notion should never even cross your mind!"

Aimee looked dismayed. "Truly, Diana? Didn't you *ever* consider doing such a thing? Even to attract Sir Henry?"

"Aimee," interposed Miss Tilden sternly. "I think your sister should be spared such prying questions, don't you?"

Noting her sister's silence, Aimee realized that she had inadvertently stepped into forbidden territory. "Oh, I *am* sorry, Diana," she said unhappily. "Forgive me?"

Diana forced a small smile. "Of course, dearest." She rose to her feet. "I think I will have a bit of a rest now. I have the oddest feeling this evening with Aunt Serena is going to be very wearing upon my nerves."

Diana returned to her room feeling a trifle guilty. She should have answered Aimee's question, she thought, hating herself for being such a coward. It was just that anything to do with attracting men in a physical sense made her uneasy. Of course, there was little harm in what Aimee had said, but she found the mere idea of her sister pulling such dangerous tricks alarming. Was Aimee going to be more difficult than she had anticipated? She *did* tend to get herself into scrapes, but thus far each of them, in the final evaluation, had been fairly harmless. Here in London, however, it was far easier to attract real trouble.

Diana yawned suddenly, knowing her sleep had been restless the night before. What on earth could she have dreamt that had so interfered with her rest? Knowing Meg was nearby she nearly reached for her hand bell, then stopped herself with a chuckle. How easy it was to become spoiled, she thought drowsily. As if she could not undress herself now that she had an abigail!

Free of her gown, she crawled into bed and shut her eyes determinedly, hearing Meg's quiet movements in the next room as she fussed with Aimee's gowns. Before drifting off, a small, involuntary smile touched her mouth. She wondered what Lord Lucan would say if he knew he was perfectly correct. She didn't even own a corset.

It was nearly six o'clock when she awoke. Meg must have come into the room while she slept, for her mauve dinner dress was laid out neatly across the chair. As this thought went through her head, a soft scratch upon the door heralded her abigail's arrival.

"Ah, you're awake," said Meg, setting down the jug of hot water for the wash basin. "I stepped in before but thought 'twas a shame to wake you when you was sleepin' so peaceful like." She moved about the room, chattering happily as she did her duties. "Miss Aimee has been fillin' my ear for the past hour with tales about this Mr. Charles Perth. I was struck all of a heap when she told me he was a-going to be one of them viscounts someday! Oh my stars, I cried! And ain't she going to make a grand viscountess! Some of them ladyships keep their noses so high in the air, I say 'tis a refreshin' change to meet someone who ain't too high and mighty to gibble-gabble with someone below her station!"

Attending with only half an ear, Diana rubbed her eyes. "Yes, well, the gentleman in question knows next to nothing about my sister, so perhaps she shouldn't count her chickens this soon," she said absently. "Is there time for you to fetch me up a cup of tea?"

This Meg was more than happy to do, since it would afford her a chance to converse with Felix the footman, whom she privately considered more interesting than ten viscounts or even a royal duke.

Left alone, Diana pulled off her chemise, and made good and thorough use of the hot water. She had not taken a close look at her body in the mirror in a long time, but from the moment she'd returned to London, Diana had been struck with an inexplicable urge to do so. Now, as if a magnet pulled her to the looking glass, she felt compelled to take critical stock of her own proportions.

Dispassionately, she knew she ought to be thankful. Her high, pink-tipped breasts were shapely and full, yet not so full as to present a problem when it came to the high-waisted styles of the day. Her sparse eating habits had kept her stomach enviably flat, while her gently rounded hips and buttocks curved smoothly into slim, supple thighs. For a time, when she was married to Edmund, she had hated the sight of her own body, for that was the only thing about her that had interested her lascivious husband. He had told her in one of his more magnanimous moments that she was as luscious a morsel as he had ever set eyes on—as though she were a succulent round of beef to be consumed! *Luscious!* She had despised that particular word ever since.

Her lips twisting in bitterness, Diana suddenly wondered whether Lord Lucan also thought of her as a luscious morsel. Or, to use a more acceptable term, did he find her desirable? For one unsettling instant she pictured herself with him, before the hot color flooded her cheeks. Appalled at the unintentional direction her thoughts had taken, Diana spun away from the glass and snatched up the clean chemise Meg had laid out for her. Pulling it roughly over her head, she castigated herself. What in heaven's name possessed her to think such a thing, and about *him*, of all people? She had long ago decided that *that* sort of thing was not for her. It was disgusting and degrading, and any decent woman avoided it at all cost. Thank the dear Lord she was a widow, and would never have to go through it again! A woman would have to be insane to seek out such an experience voluntarily, she told herself angrily. Yet, part of her had always argued against this logic, for why was it that so many women did?

She dashed an impatient hand into the air, unwilling to explore this very reasonable objection. What was more to the point was that she must never lower her guard, never lose sight of her own, very personal reason for not encouraging any gentleman's attentions. And it would be all too easy to do this, she feared, for the truth was she had always liked the company of men, preferring their sensible conversation to the uneducated, insipid prattling of her own sex. It was just that she could not always fathom their way of thinking.

As for flirtation, she could never claim to be a match for a man like Lord Lucan. He was obviously very skilled at the art of dalliance, for had he not already vanquished her anger twice with his whimsical charm? And in two short days, no less! He was very dangerous, she decided. His admiring glances and clever compliments were designed to feed her vanity and lull her into submission. And as for his assertion that he regarded her as a virtuous woman—poppycock! She would stake the few jewels she owned on the expectation that the Earl of Lucan would, sooner or later, be making her a dishonorable proposal.

And then there was Sir Henry. Diana frowned, surprised that he had not entered her mind in over twenty-four hours. She was neither so vain nor so cynical that she believed every gentleman who smiled at her was similarly bent upon offering her insult. Surely there were some men whose intentions were honorable, and surely Sir Henry Neyle was one of these?

Even after all this time, she could not help but think of the baronet as an exceptional man. Though she had not consciously yearned for him over the years, it had not come as a complete surprise to her that her heart still beat a little faster when he was near. At eighteen, she had held him in girlish fascination, had, in fact, pictured herself in his arms all too often. Why, she could not recall one instance of his ever doing anything even remotely forward or disrespectful. His eyes were always laughing and gentle, never bold or penetrating, like Lord Lucan's.

These ponderings began to lead her up the old, half-forgotten path. *If* Sir Henry were to look her way once more, and *if* he were to make her a declaration—? Disgusted with herself, Diana made an exasperated sound. What foolishness! She could not, *would* not, consider remarriage, not even with Sir Henry.

However, there was a small voice inside her which taunted: *Oh, yes, you would, you weak, little hypocrite. With Sir Henry Neyle, you would indeed.*

Meg's bustling appearance effectively brought Diana's broodings to a halt. "Here's your tea, ma'am," she announced, her cheeks still flushed with the satisfaction of knowing Felix's eyes had followed her up the stairs. "Hot and black just the way you like it," she continued. "Miss Aimee's already dressed and ready to go." The abigail set the cup and saucer on the small table next to Diana. "You'd best let me help you into your gown so I can get started on your hair. Did you get rested?"

"Yes, thank you." Diana reached gratefully for the dainty china teacup. Perhaps a few swallows of strong tea would dispel the nonsensical notions from her head.

Half an hour later, Meg was putting the finishing touches on Diana's hair when Aimee put her head inside the door. "Aren't you ready yet?" she inquired anxiously. "The carriage Aunt Serena sent for us has arrived." Casting an admiring glance at her sister, she added, with mock remorse, "Oh, you look simply divine in that color! Now I *know* I haven't a prayer's chance with Charles. I may as well stay home and knit stockings with— Oh, all right, all right. Don't glare so, Diana. I'm only funning. I'll run and bid Tildy good night. Do hurry, now!"

Diana's abigail gave a giggle as Aimee ducked out of sight. "She sure is anxious to see her cousin, ain't she, ma'am? I just hope she remembers what I told her. Miss Aimee, I said, mind you don't let the gentleman see how taken you are with him. Cool and mysterious, that's what the gents like. Nothing catches a man's fancy like a bit of challenge, no matter what his age or rank!"

Diana's brows shot up. "You told her that?"

Meg nodded, her garrulous affirmative including several more worldly remarks of similar nature.

The young widow's eyes closed for a moment. "It may be true," she remarked, half to herself, "but how my dear sister will choose to interpret 'cool and mysterious' remains to be seen. Oh, I cannot *wait* for this evening to be over!"

Contrary to what the dowager believed, the Honorable Charles Perth was neither spineless, nor easily intimidated. Yes, as a child he had gone in terror of his grandmother, but that fear had long since ceased to exist. Since both his parents resided in the country, it fell to him to see to his grandmother, whose dragonlike personality did not match her frail constitution. He considered it his duty to try to keep her happy, and if it pleased her to think she could bully him, why, it was all one to him. He was loath to admit it, of course, but he did bear some affection for the old woman, though she had never done anything very much to deserve it. After all, she *had* locked him in a closet once, something he had never quite forgotten. So it was with a certain understandable caution that he approached his grandmother when she summoned him to her side.

He knew he had been invited to her house for a definite purpose. Like many unmarried men, Charles had developed a sort of sixth sense which alerted him to danger of the matchmaking kind, and tonight's dinner party had, for some obscure reason, aroused his suspicions. However, he considered it fruitless to think of turning down the querulous old woman's invitation, for, like many females, his grandmother could be relentless in her persistence, as well as extremely cunning. At the age of nine-and-twenty, he could only wonder that, thus far, he had been spared any attempts to settle his future. Perhaps, he reflected darkly, she had only been biding her time.

The problem was, he had no intention of allowing his grandmother to choose him a wife. An eloquent shudder ran over his tall, angular frame at the thought. It was his usual wont to avoid the dowager's wearying displays of temper by simply letting her have her way, but a fellow had to draw the line somewhere, dash it! Unfortunately, he knew that when he began to drag his feet, some particularly abrasive fireworks were going to go off.

Which cousin his grandmother might wish him to wed he was unsure, but he suspected it was his cousin Aimee. After all, when Cousin Diana had been to town six years before, the dowager had made no effort to throw the pair of them together. Almost, he wished she had, for perhaps he might have been there to save her from that blackguard, Edmund Verney. A chivalrous man, Charles had been aghast at his cousin's predicament, and had his grandmother requested it, might have married the poor girl himself, simply out of compassion. However, such a solution had never been suggested, for he'd been in Newmarket on the fatal night, and by the time he'd returned, Diana's betrothal was already a *fait accompli*.

Being also a reasonable man, Charles refused to form a prejudice against Cousin Aimee before he met her. After all, he told himself, it was hardly her fault if his grandmother had decided to play matchmaker. Come to think of it, he'd seen the chit at the family reunion three years before, hadn't he? Without much success, he attempted to summon up some recollection of her appearance, but all he could remember was that she had dark hair and was rather plump. Of course, there was a chance she had improved, for wasn't Diana well above average? Well, all he could do at the moment was hope for the best.

By many, Arlington Street was considered to be an extremely agreeable avenue in which to reside, for not only did its graceful thoroughfare run parallel with St. James's Street, it lay directly adjacent to Green Park. It was not, perhaps, as awe inspiring as a Grosvenor Square address, but it was more pleasant and more convenient. Its residents were blessed with their very own entrance to the pretty little meadow; those fortunate enough to dwell on its west side were afforded a delightful, pastoral aspect from their windows. Indeed, Arlington Street appeared to offer one all the advantages of the country within easy distance of the countless diversions that only the Mayfair area could provide.

The street was said to be well inhabited, for many persons of the first rank and consequence chose to live here. Historically, its list of illustrious residents had included such names as the great Lord Nelson and Mr. Charles Fox, as well as a vast number of dukes, marquises, earls, and other members of the aristocracy, particularly those in ministerial positions. Diana's great aunt, the dowager Lady Torrington, resided in number five, a large house which held the distinction of being once owned by Sir Robert Walpole, and subsequently, by his witty and well-known son, Horace.

The dowager's home was in its way a showplace, for it boasted, among other things, a particularly elegant mahogany staircase, a superb collection of paintings including two by Sir Joshua Reynolds, and a magnificent gold and blue Axminster carpet woven especially for the drawing room. It was an impressive house, and as always, Diana was touched with a sense of wonder as she followed the dignified footman up the sweeping stairway to the first floor, her gloved hand lightly grazing that exquisite rail with its finely carved, barley-sugar balusters. Intoning their names in suitably stentorian accents, the tall, peruked servant stepped aside, allowing the two sisters to move past him into the drawing room.

Seated in the center of a blue velvet Sheraton couch, Great-aunt Serena dominated the scene in a gown of flowing purple. With brief surprise, Diana realized that Cousin Charles was not the only other guest, for an elderly, rather rotund gentleman was in the process of rising to his feet. To that gentleman's left stood Charles, elegant in a coat of dark blue superfine, cream-colored pantaloons, and a neckcloth whose intricate folds proclaimed it the work of a master.

From the manner in which the dowager introduced the older gentleman, Diana deduced that Lord Hervey's friendship with Great-aunt Serena had strengthened since last she was in town. His stays creaking noticeably, the old peer executed a portly bow, and beamed benevolently at the two sisters.

"'Pon my word, Serena," he remarked, "of *course* I remember your niece! Couldn't forget a pretty face like that! Evening, my dear. And this is Miss Farington. How-de-do, young lady."

While Diana smiled and shook hands with his lordship, she was conscious that Aimee's greeting to Lord Hervey sounded, at least to her ears, a trifle distracted. One quick look was enough to supply the reason. Aimee's blue-eyed gaze had encountered Charles's, and to Diana, it was clear that something more than a mere courtesy glance had been exchanged.

Nudging her blushing young sister gently, Diana said, "It's lovely to see you again, Charles. I trust I find you well?"

Recovering from her daze, Aimee added her greeting. "Hello, Charles," she said softly.

Charles's smile, as he replied, held a slightly bemused quality, and Diana could not help noticing how his green eyes kept shifting back to Aimee. It seemed the lavender gown had done the trick, she thought in amusement.

"Now then," interrupted Great-aunt Serena with a thin cackle, "we can all be comfortable. Charles, go and pour out some sherry for your cousins, will you? And there's madeira there, as well as brandy if you want it. Thurstan will take the madeira."

Charles readily performed this task, for it offered him the chance to move to a position where he could inspect Aimee without her knowledge. While he was no callow youth to be riveted to the floor by a mere pretty face, to say that he was pleasantly surprised would be to understate the matter. Could he possibly be this lucky? he found himself thinking.

By *Jove*, she *had* blossomed, he marveled, as the red liquid splashed into delicate crystal goblets. Covertly, his eyes drank in every entrancing detail. Such a dainty figure! Such angelic features! Her heart-shaped face was just as sweet as anyone could wish, and as for those melting blue eyes—! They seemed to Charles to hold everything he had ever yearned for in their sparkling depths. However, Charles was unquestionably a gentleman, and had far too much delicacy of principle to embarrass a gently bred girl by making sheep's eyes at her. And so, after gratifying Aimee with those first few looks, he made sure not to glance at her again, at least not more than any other person in the room.

Disappointed, Aimee waited in vain for Charles's sea-green eyes to seek hers once more. Minutes passed. She darted yet another look at him, but he appeared wholly engrossed by Lord Hervey's lengthy dissertation on the trials and tribulations of persons afflicted with gout. How they had arrived at the topic she had no notion, for she had paid heed to no one but Charles since she stepped into the room. And Charles had not spoken since Lord Hervey began to talk, some five or six minutes before. Even Aunt Serena looked absorbed, for she kept nodding, the single ostrich feather adorning her turban bobbing up and down with fascinating regularity.

Frustrated, Aimee cudgeled her brain. What could she do to make him look at her again? What was it Meg had told her? Cool and mysterious, that was it! The advice had a sound, sensible ring to it, but how on earth did one go about looking mysterious? The best she could do, she finally decided, was to stay with what she already knew.

It seemed like ages before she was able to catch Charles's eye again, and then she quickly seized the opportunity to send him the sirenic smile she had practiced in her mirror. Once she was sure he had noticed, she added, for good measure, the single eyelash bat which had seemed so effective on Sir Henry.

Charles blinked. What the deuce was the girl up to? In his opinion, virtuous young ladies ought *not* to bat their eyelashes at gentlemen in that precise way, and certainly not in such an inviting manner. To be sure, he did not wish to marry a flirt, for in his experience such females harbored some vain urge to continually add to their list of conquests. That might be good enough for some men, but not for Charles Perth!

However, a second later he decided he must have imagined the whole thing, for Aimee's eyes had dropped demurely to her lap, where her hands lay modestly folded. No, he assured himself, such a fair creature as Miss Aimee Farington could not be anything but perfect. He would ask her to go driving tomorrow.

It was but a few, short minutes later that Diana began to realize the dowager was expecting another guest. Of course she ought to have known, for Aunt Serena had always been a stickler for social conventions, and was unlikely to sit down to dinner with an uneven number of covers. Moreover, the missing guest would need to be a gentleman, so that the same number of representatives from each sex might be maintained. Now, who else would her aunt invite? Diana wondered. She soon had her answer, for not five minutes later the door to the drawing room was flung grandly open and the latecomer's name announced.

As the gasp escaped Diana's lips, she shot an accusing look at her aunt. How dared Aunt Serena pull such a sly trick! No doubt this was what Aimee had been concealing from her!

The young widow's bosom rose and fell, heaving with the unbearable indignation of being forced into what she considered an untenable position by her meddling, matchmaking, unscrupulous relative. How could the Earl of Lucan have had the *audacity* to come here tonight? Oh, how could Aunt Serena *do* this to her!

Chapter Five

Undisturbed by Diana's outrage, Aunt Serena beckoned to the earl. "Well, come in, come in!" she told him imperiously. "Diana, Aimee, you both know his lordship. For pity's sake, Diana, don't just sit there gaping like a henwit. The man doesn't have two heads, does he?"

Diana's rigid stare could not have more clearly conveyed her belief that Lord Lucan was encroaching where he had no business. However, if her perturbation had been less, she might have taken the trouble to notice the almost imperceptible check in his stride at his moment of entry. As it happened, the earl had believed himself a last-minute addition to a sizable dinner party, an impression shamelessly given him by the wording in the Dowager's invitation. However, save for the presence of Lord Hervey, he instead found himself in the midst of a small family gathering—moreover a family he scarcely knew! Only his good breeding saved him from appearing as disconcerted as he actually was. And by the look on Diana's face, he was not the only one who had been duped.

Though he maintained his outward impassivity far better than Diana, he was nearly as angry as she. If the wager viscountess thought she had done him a favor, by God, she was wrong! Not only had she placed him in an awkward position, but there could be little doubt that whatever progress he had made with Diana was in danger of being negated. But he could hardly expect otherwise, could he? It would be illogical as well as unreasonable to think Diana would welcome the very interference he resented. He would simply have to repair the damage—somehow.

He soon began to realize the challenge he had in store, for the lady was making a studied effort to ignore him, and he could not catch her eye. Eventually, however, he saw her sneak a peep in his direction, an action which filled him with a relief so great it ousted his vexation. She was simply playing obstinate! Well, let her, he decided in amusement. It was far more stimulating this way, after all. He had never liked things to be too easy, and why should wooing the lady of his choice be any different?

The conversation of the evening did not begin to prosper until the weather, the fading state of the old queen's health, and Princess Charlotte's pregnancy had all been perfunctorily discussed. The Prince Regent's latest extravagances were discreetly passed over, as were the shocking antics of his despised wife, Caroline of Brunswick, who had taken up residence in Italy with an Italian adventurer named Pergami. The red-faced, hard-drinking Princess of Wales had become such a source of embarrassment to her country that to introduce her into polite conversation was not considered particularly nice, especially by the highest sticklers.

By this time, they were seated in Aunt Serena's dining room, a large salon brilliantly lit by candelabra, as well as the great crystal chandelier suspended just above the center of the rosewood dining table. Rich damask curtains hung at its windows, fine paintings adorned its satin-covered walls, while at one end, a fire crackled in a marble fireplace, providing the diners with an ample amount of warmth.

Although Diana would not for the world have admitted that anything about Lord Lucan interested her in the least, her ears automatically pricked up when Cousin Charles asked him about his country estate. Curiously, she listened to the earl's description of his holdings in Cornwall, its location but a bare mile inland from the great granite cliffs edging the turbulent, often savage, Cornish sea. With a few swift words, he sketched for them an image of that faraway part of England where, he assured them, superstition still ran rampant and the past could seem more real than the present.

Intrigued in spite of herself, Diana studied the earl's face. "It sounds as though you miss the place," she said, careful to keep her voice neutral. It was the first time she had addressed him directly.

He answered her gravely. "I do, Mrs. Verney. When I am not there, I miss it very much."

"Then I wonder you do not stay there," she countered, wondering if she merely imagined that gleam of mockery in his eye.

The earl's broad shoulders lifted in a slight shrug. "Like all good things, I appreciate Cornwall more when I have been away from it for a while," he said smoothly. "And I like to see for myself what is happening here in the hub of our country. Many Cornishmen think the pixies are of greater concern than any of England's more tangible problems."

"Pixies!" snorted the dowager, pushing her food around her plate. "What poppycock!" She obviously felt that the subject had been adequately discussed, for she steered it into another, quite unrelated channel.

"Speaking of poppycock, would you believe that Thurstan"—she gave Lord Hervey a fond look—"wants to see me decked out in jewels? A woman of my age! Preposterous, ain't it?"

"What jewels?" asked Aimee with interest.

Aunt Serena looked smug. "I mean the Charles II tiara, of course. The fool man thinks I ought to wear the ugly thing!"

"But why do you not, Auntie? I have never even seen the Torrington diamond."

"Because it's too damned ostentatious to wear," snapped the dowager. "And don't get any ideas into your head, missy, because you ain't going to wear it either."

"It'd look wonderful on you," said Lord Hervey loyally. "You wore it when you were young."

"That was different! I was beautiful then," she grumbled, casting her elderly crony a frowning look. "But I won't be bamboozled into making a spectacle of myself now. Aimee, how was your shopping expedition? I suppose you spent enough to ruin me."

"Oh, we had the grandest time shopping, Aunt Serena! But we could not decide about one thing. Shall I truly be needing a riding habit?"

"Of course you will, silly girl," responded the old woman severely. "Oh, you mean, am I really going to buy you a horse, is that it? Didn't do it last time Diana was here, did I? Can't recall why. Silly of me. Well!" Her voice altered. "Charles?"

Fork paused midair, Cousin Charles fixed her with a wary look. "Yes, Grandmama?"

The dowager's voice was piercing. "Your driving skills may be lamentable but I cannot deny you have an eye for a horse. I should like you to procure a suitable mount for your cousin Aimee."

Charles's fork went down. Horses were serious business, and the assessing look he shot his young cousin held none of its former bemusement. "I could, of course," he said bluntly, "but without knowing how well she can ride—"

"I ride very well!" put in Aimee with an indignant look.

He sent her a charming smile. "Yes, of course you do."

His fingers ruffled through his auburn hair. "But, ah, how well?" he added.

Aimee smiled back. "Extremely well. Perhaps you would like me to prove it to you?" she suggested with pert hopefulness.

Those blue eyes, like two bits of night sky, were too much for Charles to resist. "Ahem. Yes, perhaps that might be a good notion." He saw his grandmother's sudden grin. "Makes sense, after all," he explained lamely. "Can't buy a lady a horse without knowing what sort of cattle would suit her."

"But what about Diana?" queried Aimee, unwittingly providing the dowager with her opening.

To Diana's horror, Aunt Serena's small, glinting eyes fell on the earl. "Rumor has it, Lucan, that when it comes to horseflesh, you ain't one to be taken in by mere show. Got a sharp eye for quality, they say." She gave one of her thin cackles. "Perhaps you would be good enough to oblige an old woman and find a horse for Diana."

Diana's fork clattered to her plate. "Aunt Serena!" she objected, in a strangled voice.

"Ah . . . naturally, I would be delighted to be of assistance to your niece," said the earl, his annoyance with the dowager returning. "But perhaps Mrs. Verney would prefer her cousin to purchase her mount?" he suggested, searching for a route out of the quagmire.

The dowager cut short Diana's sputters. "Oh, stop your fussing, girl! Four eyes are better than two! They can go looking together! We ladies don't wish to be bothered with the rubbishy details of the business."

With a slight cough, Charles came to the earl's rescue. "Shall we take a look-in at Tatt's tomorrow?" he offered. "It ain't a sale day, of course, but it don't hurt to see what's available."

Angered by the way in which her needs were being attended to without her consent, Diana said tightly, "Is it too much to hope that I might have some say in the matter? It might save his lordship a great deal of trouble if he were acquainted with what would suit *me!*''

"By all means," put in the earl, beginning to appreciate the humor in the situation.

Diana's eyes flashed. "First of all, I will *not* ride a horse whose tail has been docked—"

"Very wise," he agreed.

"Because it is a cruel practice," she continued, ignoring him, "of which I heartily disapprove. And secondly, I refuse to be put upon a slug of any sort. I require a horse with spirit." She raised her chin at the earl. "I trust you can recognize spirit when you see it, my lord?" she added in a sweet tone.

The earl could no longer conceal his amusement. "Aye," he said softly, his gray eyes alight with laughter, "I recognize it, Mrs. Verney."

Once the ladies left the gentlemen to their port, conversation between the three men remained desultory until Lord Hervey excused himself and wandered vaguely out of the room. The dowager had most expressly desired him to do so, and so the obliging little man made his way down the corridor to the music room, where he settled himself in a comfortable wing chair and eased his gouty foot upon a stool.

Left alone with the earl, Charles Perth cleared his throat. "S'pose I ought to apologize for my grandmother," he remarked, gazing absently into his glass. "I'm afraid there's nothing anyone can do once the old girl gets the bit between her teeth. Hope you understand."

"Actually," remarked the earl, fingering the stem of his goblet, "I'm beginning to find her rather entertaining."

"Are you?" Charles leaned back in his chair and stared thoughtfully at the other man. "You might not think so if you had to deal with her all the time. Got you here tonight by some trick, I'll wager."

Although he did not mention the deceptive invitation, the earl's silence gave Charles his answer. "I confess I was surprised," he said finally. "I cannot claim more than a slight acquaintance with the Dowager Lady Torrington, so I suppose I assumed there would be quite a number of other guests." He did not add that he had hoped that Diana had requested that he be invited. That had clearly not been the case.

"Well," said Charles comfortably, "between the two of us, we ought to be able to see that the girls have decent mounts. I wonder if Miss Farington rides as well as she claims."

"It appears that you are destined to find out."

"It does, doesn't it?" A tiny smile twisted the corners of Charles's mouth, and a few seconds went by before he gathered his thoughts to focus on another matter. Leaning forward to direct a frank look at the older man, he said carefully, "Y'know, I'm devilish glad to see my cousin Diana back in town. She's a fine girl."

The earl scrutinized Charles. "Indeed," he agreed imperturbably.

"A dashed fine girl," repeated Charles with emphasis. "Don't know what my grandmother has in mind, but, dash it, I s'pose it's my responsibility to keep an eye on her. Female relative and all."

The earl's left eyebrow shot up, and Charles shifted a little in his chair. "Ahem. Yes, well, perhaps you're thinking I ought to have done a better job of it the last time she was here."

"You were not the girl's chaperon," Lord Lucan pointed out, very kindly exonerating him. "It would hardly be fair to hold you in account."

"Uh, yes, but a fellow still feels he should have done something more." His fingers ruffled through his hair, effectively completing its disarray.

Charles found himself being examined by a pair of keen gray eyes. "You would have been what? About four-and-twenty or thereabouts?" inquired the earl, his tone casual. "Just the age where it would have been natural for you to have fallen under the spell of a lovely young girl like your cousin. I imagine her marriage must have dealt you quite a blow."

Charles straightened, recognizing that, as far as probing was concerned, the tables had just been effectively turned. "What? No, no, beg your pardon, Lucan, but don't misunderstand. I mean, Diana's a capital girl, and all that, but I never—" His eyes filled with dawning comprehension. "I think what you want to know is if we'll be stepping on each other's toes in Jermyn Street. Is that it?"

Whatever the earl was thinking, his face did not betray him. He said only, "I prefer to know who my rivals are."

Pleased that he had not been forced to ask the earl point-blank about his intentions toward his cousin, Charles reached to refill both their glasses.

"Like that, is it? Thought so. Well, I wish you luck, Lucan, but bearing in mind those black looks Diana keeps throwing you, I'd lay odds against your chances of success."

The earl sipped pensively at his port. "Yes, well, tonight would certainly suggest that conclusion," he murmured.

Slowly, the amusement vanished from Charles's expression. "I may as well warn you, if you mean to court my cousin, you'll be seeing more and more of my grandmother's meddling. She's enough to provoke a saint—which I ain't!"

"Perhaps someone ought to have taken a crop to her

backside when she was young," offered the earl dryly. "I wonder what she was like at, for instance, Miss Aimee Farington's age. Very like, I should imagine."

Taking instant exception to this ludicrous comparison, Charles opened his mouth to say, "Oh, come now, Lucan," when he suddenly recalled Aimee's coquettish smile and fluttering eyelashes. His mouth closed abruptly and he stared at the earl. "Good God. I wonder if that look she gave me was really meant to be . . ." His voice faded.

Lord Lucan favored Mr. Perth with a commiserating look. "I saw it. She's going to lead you a devil of a dance, you know."

And so, when Lord Hervey reentered the room a short while later, it was to discover that the conversation between the two men had lapsed into meditative silence. Indeed, each man wore such a remote look upon his face that Lord Hervey could not help wondering if Serena had been mistaken. What could her grandson and the earl possibly have had to discuss privately, after all?

The portly little man shook his head in perplexity, and muttered the word, "Females!" under his breath. This short utterance, rather to his surprise, brought both men's heads swiveling in his direction.

"Just so," agreed the earl in an ironic tone.

Charles nodded gloomily.

In the drawing room, Diana was attempting to explain to the dowager just why she was so excessively agitated.

"But it was positively insupportable of you, Aunt Serena!" she was saying in acute frustration. "To encourage the man in this way is ridiculous, and I utterly refuse to allow it to continue! Aimee," she accused, "*you* knew he would be here tonight! Whatever possessed you to be a party to this?"

"Balderdash," grunted the dowager, rapping her cane sharply on the floor. "I merely wanted to test the man. Handles himself well, don't he? Far better than you do, missy! Lord, girl, I thought you was going to disgrace me by succumbing to a fit of the vapors!" she added in disgust.

Eyes flashing, Diana warned, "It would have served you right, and I may do so yet! And, I promise you, Aunt Serena, if you ever do this to me again, I shall do more than that! I shall . . . I shall go into strong convulsions and take to my bed for a week!"

"Don't be a fool, Diana," said the dowager repressively. "It don't at all become you. I quite fail to understand how you can kick up such a dust over the matter. I can think of a score of women who'd trade half the teeth in their heads to be in your position, you featherbrained girl! Don't you realize that Geoffrey Trevelyan is a marital prize of the first order? You ought to be thanking me for inviting him, instead of flying off into a pelter! No doubt you'd have fallen on my neck with joy if I'd invited that Neyle popinjay!"

"Sir Henry Neyle is not a popinjay!" corrected Diana with considerable heat. "And I should not have desired you to have invited him either! It would have been just as bad—no, worse!"

"Aye," snapped the dowager. "Worse, because the man hasn't any breeding to speak of!"

"You know, Diana," said Aimee suddenly, "poor Lord Lucan did offer to let Charles buy your horse. I think he felt very awkward about it, and I think you are being most unfair. None of this is his fault, you know."

The truth of this struck Diana with blinding force. And with this came the realization that she was behaving with such ingratitude that she had completely forgotten his chivalrous action in the Park. And even though he'd had an ulterior motive for acting as he had, still, she *was* being unfair.

Ashamed of herself, Diana bit her lip in chagrin. "Yes, Aimee, you are quite right. I should know better than to place the blame at the wrong door."

So it was that when the three gentlemen joined the ladies a few minutes later, Diana determinedly sought the earl's eyes and sent him a swift, embarrassed smile. His response, a slow, sensual curve of his mouth, told her she was forgiven but it also contained a message. His pursuit of her would continue, it said, as clearly as if he'd stated the words aloud.

The latter half of the evening passed more felicitously than the first, and when Diana tumbled into her bed much later that night, the only conclusion she was able to reach about the state of her emotions was that they were in hopeless disorder. In fact, never before in her life could she recall being so torn between the clearly logical and the obviously imprudent. For she was prepared to concede—in the darkness of her own room and only to herself—that there was something about Lord Lucan that made him impossible to dislike. Even while she had been angry with him, a tiny inner voice had whispered confidently that it would pass, and that he would forgive her display of temper. Goodness, she had not indulged in such irrational behavior in years! Where was this so-called composure for which she was known?

Rolling to her side, Diana punched at her pillow in frustration. Well, so what if she did like the Earl of Lucan? It would be senseless, even foolhardy, to encourage the abominable man. However, perhaps if she stood firm it might be possible simply to be his friend. Yes, that was a thought. She would rather like to be his friend. But was that at all likely? Would a man like Geoffrey Trevelyan be satisfied with mere friendship?

*   *   *

The earl did not go directly home after the dowager's dinner party. He went instead to the house of a fashionable, rather dashing widow who was neither so young as Diana, nor so weighted down by social or moral convention. Knowing this, Diana might have leaped to the conclusion that Mrs. Clement was his lordship's mistress, but she would have been wrong. If the earl had, once or twice, accepted the lady's invitation to spend the night, it would be rather unfair to fault him for this. After all, he had the same needs as any other man, and the truth was, he liked Mrs. Clement very well. And the lady could be very persuasive.

Cynthia Clement was renowned for her late night parties. Her rooms during these sparkling little affairs were often a trifle thin of the company of ladies, but the numbers of gentlemen who flocked to that small house in Cork Street invariably made up for it. For although Mrs. Clement was only moderately pretty, among the gentlemen, at least, she was very much admired. She had an informed mind, a lively and generous disposition, and above all, she possessed the infinite good sense to be very, very discreet.

Relinquishing his hat and cloak at the door, the earl mounted the stairs to the first floor salon, where the din of voices told him the majority of her guests were gathered. He paused at the threshold, surveying those within with a faint smile on his lips. Spying him immediately from the far side of the room, Mrs. Clement excused herself from the gentlemen who surrounded her and approached him with a wide smile and outstretched hands.

"Why, Geoffrey, I had quite given you up! You naughty boy, wherever have you been?"

Her light tone assured him she did not expect an answer. "Good evening, Cynthia. How lovely you look," he said courteously, raising her delicate hand to his lips.

93

Her pleased expression displayed uneven teeth. "What fustian! I look perfectly dreadful, as you well know, but never mind that. Do you care to play faro? There's a game begun almost an hour ago in my dining room. Lord Ivor is holding the bank, and Mr. Pennistone was just trying to persuade me to join them."

His lordship's idle glance swept the room. "Faro?" he said absently. "No, I don't think so. Not tonight."

Though he was unaware of it, the earl was a favorite with Mrs. Clement. His elusiveness attracted and intrigued her, while their few encounters had left her astonished at his ability to give as much pleasure as he took. She had frequently wished that some of the other gentlemen were as patient and as sensitive to her needs. However, she was too wise and too lazy to chase him, and too content with her lot to dwell upon what she knew was not to be.

She therefore sighed, and said, without petulance, "There now, I might have expected you to be difficult. You've come for some purpose, I'll wager, and I don't suppose it's to see me."

He glanced down at her, a quirk in his smile. "Of course I came to see you, Cynthia. You and one other, that is."

"So frank," she murmured, her dark eyes peeping up at him from under darker lashes.

"You prefer me that way, remember?" he reminded her.

"I do, indeed." She tapped his arm with her fan. "I'll leave you on your own, then. Will you be staying long?" This time, it was as close as she would come to a bolder invitation.

He did not misunderstand. "No," he said gently. "Not long."

* * *

94

"Your bet, sir?" prompted Lord Ivor in an impassive voice.

Sir Henry Neyle hesitated. Faro, he decided sourly, was rapidly becoming a dead bore. He glanced around the room as if in search of inspiration, and instead beheld the Earl of Lucan framed in Mrs. Clement's narrow doorway. Wasting no time, he quickly seized this as a face-saving excuse to leave the game.

"What, you here, Geoff?" he called out jovially. "Stay a minute and I'll join you, old boy. So sorry, Ivor, but I must be on the toddle." Coolly, he scratched out his vowels, then nodded farewell to the group of men huddled round the widow's dining table.

"So what brings you here?" he inquired, ambling over to join the earl.

Lord Lucan shrugged indifferently. "The same as you, I suppose." He turned and made his way back to one of the emptier rooms, where a pair of armchairs near the fire had been recently vacated.

"How were you doing?" he asked, settling himself into the closer of the two.

"Oh, well—" Sir Henry waved one pale hand languidly as he sank into the second chair. "Truth to tell, I was losing, and losing don't agree with me overmuch. It does tend to alleviate the tedium of the moment, however."

The earl yawned. "I could suffer a little tedium over the thrill of gaming away my blunt. You're going to be dodging the duns if you're not careful, Harry."

Sir Henry lost some of his languor. "I know, dammit. I expect it's time to start looking about me for an heiress I could stomach in my bed. A depressing thought, since heiresses tend to resemble their horses—at least in facial structure. Last year's crop was the sorriest lot I ever saw in my life."

Without emotion, Lord Lucan watched the other man

withdraw a small enamel snuffbox from his pocket. "Have you been to see Mrs. Verney?" he said abruptly, coming to the point of his visit.

A trace of mockery glinted in Sir Henry's pale blue eyes. "Certainly. I'm as interested in the enchanting Diana as you are, old boy. Any objection?" he added, his tone holding a challenge.

For a long moment, the earl made no answer. "Actually, yes," he said frankly. "I won't have her offered insult, Harry."

The baronet's fair brows rose haughtily. "Oh, really?" he drawled. "You don't credit me with much finesse, do you? I suppose you're still hoping to wed the wench. A pity she's not an heiress, or I'd give you a run for your money. I'd win, too, for it's you, old boy, who lacks finesse." A new gleam entered his eye. "How bloody provoking that no one knows where that aunt of hers is leaving her fortune. The old girl's so full of juice one might be tempted to give her a little . . . squeeze . . . just to see what dribbles out." He flipped open his snuffbox with one thumb and helped himself to a generous pinch.

The earl's gray eyes raked the other man's face. "I trust that was a joke, Harry. You would not hurt an old woman."

"Hurt her? You mean physically?" Sir Henry looked genuinely shocked. "Good Lord, man, do I look like a murderer?" He shuddered eloquently. "Come, come, Geoff, old boy. Can't you recognize a jest when you hear one? 'Twas but a flash of wit, nothing more."

"Very witty," remarked the earl dryly. As if unable to bear the other man's presence any longer, he rose to his feet. "I'll bid you good night, then."

"Of course, Geoff, old boy," the baronet murmured, as he watched his friend depart. "But then, there's more than one way to squeeze an orange, now isn't there?"

*   *   *

Lord Lucan's thick black brows were drawn sharply together as he made his way along the streets of Mayfair toward his town house in Bruton Street. Absorbed in thought, he paid no heed to the late-night chill or the tendrils of thick gray fog swirling about his heels.

Sir Henry Neyle, he was musing, was not exactly his bosom friend, but until now they had seemed to find each other's company tolerably amusing. Until now, thought the earl, his scowl deepening. Now he was no longer amused.

It was rapidly becoming plain to him that the bonds of friendship did not stretch as far as he had thought. Sir Henry quite clearly subscribed to the precept that all was fair in love, except that to the earl's way of thinking, there was very little of the loverlike in the intent to offer a virtuous lady like Diana Verney a slip on the shoulder. Even were it offered with the greatest finesse in the world, Lord Lucan was sure that Diana would consider such an offer an insult. And he could not help but agree.

Of course, there were women who, far from being offended by such an offer, would consider themselves flattered, and they were not necessarily women of low birth, either. But Lord Lucan was confident that his beautiful Diana was not one of these. Moreover, since he strongly suspected that her marriage to Edmund Verney had been unpleasant, he preferred that she be spared any further distress. Why he should feel so strongly about this all of a sudden, he did not pause to analyze. But just the thought of that scoundrel Verney being married to Diana brought the earl's fingers bunching into hard fists. He'd been barely acquainted with the man, but he'd known enough *of* him to be disgusted by the stories he'd heard. And he damned well did not want Harry causing her more pain!

As he had quite truthfully told Diana, he had admired her for a very long time. Could it really be six years since he had first seen her? He could recall as if it were yesterday exactly how she had looked when he'd first clapped eyes upon her, how her golden hair had been piled high atop her head, how her demure white gown had clung so tantalizingly to her figure. A small corsage of pink roses had been pinned at her breast, he remembered.

A mere minute of conversation with her had been enough to assure him that the proud tilt to her chin sprang, not from a sense of her own consequence, but from courage, a feisty, stubborn kind of courage that demanded she conceal her own nervousness. He had thought her beautiful, of course, and wildly desirable, and that, combined with the spirit she'd clearly possessed, had been enough to make him want her, a wanting that had never quite gone away.

With a tired sigh, the earl breathed in the cold night air, his hands thrust deep in the pockets of his coat. Even yesterday in the Park, he thought, hadn't she shown courage? Even when her pale, strained features had betrayed her inner apprehension, she had held her head high. And after his assistance with the Lady Edgerton business she had rallied gamely, not faltering once throughout the remainder of the drive.

The major mistake of his life, he reflected, was allowing his father to arrange his first marriage. He had not expected love, nor had he looked for it or even desired it, particularly. However, he had wanted companionship, hoped for children, and expected faithfulness . . . and his wife had given him none of these things. Despite all this, he did not feel bitter, since he doubted whether Laurette had been any happier than he. And since she had been dead now for nearly two years, he had had ample time to come to terms with his feelings. He knew he did not want to spend the rest of his life alone, and therefore it was logical that he remarry.

A pity he had gotten off on the wrong foot with Diana that first day. He realized now that he ought not to have studied her so openly, but he'd been unable to prevent himself from doing so. His nature had always been direct—too direct for some. Briefly, he wondered if his elevated station in life had encouraged him to be this way. No, he decided, that was gammon. He would have been the same had he been born in a haycock and raised in the meanest circumstances.

Dammit, if only he had been free to woo her the first time around! Since Laurette's death, he'd been making more of these periodic visits to London, hoping Diana would eventually come back. As she finally had.

Well, he would win her now, he told himself, his jaw set in a stubborn line. And it would have to be soon. If she accepted an offer from him, Sir Henry would never have the chance to make his dishonorable offer, and she would never need know of the intended insult. It was, he reasoned, a most satisfactory solution to the problem.

And so, though some inner voice was urging him to go very slowly in his courtship, another part of him was equally determined to move swiftly. After all, there was no doubt in his mind that he was the right man for Diana.

All he had to do was convince her of that.

Chapter Six

The next few days were unseasonably warm and bright with sunshine. For Diana, they were days of unalloyed pleasure, for no dark event occurred to mar their early spring glory or make her regret her decision to come to London.

On the first morning after Aunt Serena's dinner party, she, Aimee, and Miss Tilden set out for the nearest lending library. There, they encountered a number of people, mostly ladies who were known to Diana. Most of the women greeted her with a mixture of surprise and kindness, which in turn surprised Diana, for she had been prepared for much less in the way of welcome. She was even more gratified when three of these ladies proceeded to pay her a call the following day, and in return, Diana began making her own morning visits, dutifully introducing her young sister to various members of the *ton*. Best of all, she managed to avoid Lady Edgerton completely, which she could not deny was a factor in the success of these hours.

Cousin Charles called upon them twice, which cast Aimee into such raptures that Diana was forced, out of a sense of duty, to remind her young sister that there was really nothing remarkable in their own cousin paying them a visit. She did not, of course, wish to be deliberately unkind but she firmly believed that Aimee needed to be brought to a sense of reality about the situation. After all, there was no guarantee that Charles was looking to marry and she did not want Aimee to be hurt. Whether her warning was sown upon fertile ground, however, was uncertain.

The second time Cousin Charles came to call he brought Lord Lucan with him. They had been looking at horses together earlier in the day, and it seemed to Diana that the two men were getting along amazingly well. Upon this occasion, she welcomed Lord Lucan's company, it giving her sister a chance to converse with Charles without their cousin feeling obliged to give Diana equal time. And since the earl said nothing too provoking, she was able to enjoy the time she spent in talking with him without reservation. Indeed, they had more than once exchanged amused looks at some of Aimee and Charles's discourse, which they could not help but overhear.

Aimee had worn a pout after each of Charles's visits. "He is so very proper, Diana," she complained. "I thought he would pay me compliments and flirt with me. Eliza told me that is what the London gentlemen are wont to do."

Diana regarded her sister earnestly. "It is greatly to his credit that he does not," she protested. "And hardly surprising either, considering you are chaperoned. I can think of no reason why Eliza Fingleshaw should be held as an expert on these matters. Anyway, I don't believe Cousin Charles is the sort of gentlemen who, er, flirts."

"But, Diana," said Aimee, disappointed. "I can't quite believe that."

"And why not?" inquired Diana, threading her needle. She was mending a torn flounce on Aimee's gown.

"Well," said Aimee, mulling her answer over with

101

some care, "I know it will sound shockingly vain, but I . . . I cannot help but think he admires me, Diana. I can't explain it, but . . . it's in his eyes, you see. I daresay you don't know what I mean," she added naively.

"Actually," remarked Diana, recollecting a similar expression in the earl's gray eyes, "I believe I do. But Aimee, what you probably see is his . . . attraction to you physically. It does not mean he is in love with you. *That* is completely different. It is very important that you understand that. Nor is love necessarily accompanied by a desire to flirt."

Aimee looked crestfallen. "Well, then, how will I know if he is in love with me?"

"I expect he will show it in other ways," replied Diana, quite firmly.

By prior arrangement, Cousin Charles brought round a perky little brown mare two mornings later for Aimee to try. Diana had no reservations about allowing Aimee to go, for their cousin was not only a complete gentleman, but a bruising rider, as well. He ought, she reasoned, to be able to curb any desire on Aimee's part to display her riding prowess to an excessive degree. At least Diana placed her reliance on his being able to do so.

Aimee's eyes widened with pleasure at her first glimpse of the horse. "Oh, Charles, what a beautiful creature!" she cried, in the most natural fashion she had yet used with him. "Is she truly for me?" Her glowing gaze was riveted on the mare, so that she missed his amused expression.

"Well, the truth is she ain't exactly ours yet," he answered, shoving his hands in his pockets. "Belongs to a fellow named Montague. Friend of mine, y'see. He agreed to let me borrow Pansy so you could try out her paces. Dashed silly name, but we can always change it. If she's

102

right for you, then I'll make him an offer."

"Oh, I'm sure she'll be perfect," replied Aimee caressingly, more to the horse than to her handsome cousin. Her hands reached out to stroke the mare's satiny neck. "Won't you, Pansy? What a little beauty you are!" she whispered.

Thinking to himself that the term fit the girl better than the horse, Charles watched his cousin indulgently. After all, he had gone to a dashed lot of trouble to persuade Monty to consider parting with Pansy, so he was pleased to see that Aimee apparently appreciated his efforts on her behalf. Since at the moment, at least, Pansy had drawn the whole of her attention, he turned aside to deliver a message to Diana.

"Lord Lucan is fetching a horse around for you to try, Diana. Sent his apology for the short notice, and asked me to tell you . . . ah, I mean *ask* you to . . . ah . . . be ready." As Diana's face stiffened, her cousin's voice grew hesitant. "Ought to be here soon. Hope it ain't a problem . . ." Charles dwindled into uneasy silence.

Although Diana did not immediately reply, the glint of wrath in her brown-gold eyes would have been evident to anyone. Be ready! So now, *now*, she was supposed to make herself ready at the earl's least command! Dictatorial, arrogant man! Forcing herself to respond as evenly as possible, she retorted, "All right, Charles. I'll go and change into my habit, then. Thank you for telling me."

Diana walked briskly into the house, wondering crossly what sort of a horse he would attempt to foist upon her. Since this would be the first time she had ever ridden in London, the earl could know nothing of her abilities in the saddle. And since she had not deigned to defend those abilities, as Aimee had done, she found it difficult to believe he would take her at her word and bring her a worthy mount. If he did not, she thought

103

mutinously, she would soon show him how wrong he had been not to listen to her! It was irksome enough to feel she had to prove herself capable of handling the beast before it was purchased!

Still stewing, Diana paced back and forth the length of her bedchamber. He ought to have called and let her know. He ought to have asked if she were free. At the very least, he could have sent her a note! She had nearly made up her mind to deny him admittance when Miss Tilden peered hesitantly into her room.

"Diana, dear, do you have any idea where I put my— Why, whatever is the matter?"

"That man!" ground out Diana, halting her steps. "That horrid man has *dared* to send me messages through my own cousin. He dares to tell me to be ready for him when he arrives at some unspecified time which is probably soon! Can you credit such arrogance, Tildy? He deserves to be punished!"

Miss Tilden looked perplexed. "What horrid man are you speaking of, my dear? Do we know any horrid men? I cannot conceive who—"

"Lord Lucan!" interrupted Diana fiercely. "He is bringing me a horse and I am supposed to make myself ready for him."

Miss Tilden blinked. "Well, in that case, perhaps you ought to begin putting on your habit, my dear."

Diana stared at her companion. "Tildy! Do you seriously expect me to do this man's bidding? Simply drop everything and jump to obey?"

Miss Tilden cast a quick glance around the bedchamber. "But what is it that you must drop?" she inquired, in reasonable bewilderment. "I thought you said you had no plans for the morning."

Diana waved an impatient hand. "I do not! But what is that to the point? I *might* have had other plans! He could not have known!"

"But do you?" continued Miss Tilden, with what Diana considered exasperating persistance.

Frustrated, Diana resumed her pacing. "No! That is— no! But, do you not see? Here is a man who . . . a philanderer, Tildy, who—"

"A philanderer?" repeated Miss Tilden in bafflement. "Are you sure, Diana?"

"Positive," asserted Diana fervently. "He has *flirted* with me, Tildy. He had dared to—*ooh!* I cannot speak of it."

Miss Tilden looked askance. "Well," she declared, with an air of disapproval, "if he has flirted with you, Diana, you must have nothing more to do with him! We cannot allow him into the house again! You are not to go riding with him. You must tell her ladyship that—"

"No, Tildy, no!" protested Diana, oddly unwilling to go to such extremes. "You do not understand. He is not that bad! He is not like Edmund, for heaven's sake. It is just that he is so . . . so . . . irritating. So *infuriating!*"

Miss Tilden's bombazine-covered chest rose and fell in a slightly reproachful sigh. "I cannot make heads or tails out of what you are saying, Diana. Are you or are you not going riding with this man?"

Her eyes focused somewhere in the distance, Diana suddenly smiled. "Oh, I daresay I shall, Tildy. But not, I fear, today. I have suddenly recalled several letters that I must write. If his lordship wishes for company, I shall suggest that he ride with his groom!"

Miss Tilden looked dubious. "Goodness, Diana," she quavered. "I do hope you know what you're doing . . ."

In preparation for the impending confrontation, Diana changed into her most becoming morning gown, and was on the point of descending to the first floor when sounds from below told her the earl had arrived. Unable to resist stealing a look out the window of her bedchamber, Diana tiptoed back into her room and peered downward. Below her in the street stood his lordship's groom holding the reins of a large bay gelding and a smaller, rather unprepossessing gray mare. Obviously, the bay belonged to his lordship, so the mare must be for her. Well, the animal did not look like a *complete* slug, she mused, but of course one could tell very little without closer examination. As with people, a horse's appearance could be misleading.

As she entered the drawing room, Diana could not help noticing that Lord Lucan looked far more at home in his riding coat and breeches than he had in formal evening clothes. Somehow, the very casualness of the attire accentuated his masculinity, reminding her of the underlying reason for his presence. This man, she told herself warningly, was only here because he wanted her to become his mistress. It would not do to forget that fact.

Ignoring her greeting, the earl took a step forward, then seemed to check himself. "My dear Mrs. Verney, did you not receive my message?" he asked, rather abruptly.

"What message was that, my lord?" inquired Diana in an innocent tone.

His eyes passed over her gown. "Your cousin was to ask you to be ready for riding. You look quite enchanting, my dear, but I must ask you to put on your habit as quickly as possible. I've brought you a horse I think you will like."

Diana yawned delicately. "My dear Lord Lucan, I fear you can have no conception of how busy I am. I cannot possibly go riding this morning. I am sure I have at least a dozen things to do. Of course, had you made your request—dare I call it a request?—in a less peremptory style, perhaps I could have rearranged my schedule."

"Ah, I see," he murmured, a hint of lazy humor entering his voice. "This is a display of claws. Well, then, what are they?"

Diana stared at him. "What are what?"

"What must you do that is so important?"

Taken aback, Diana answered, "Why, for one thing, I have letters to write—"

"Write them later," he advised. "The horses are waiting and the weather is perfect."

Diana bristled. "Has anyone ever told you that you are insufferable?"

"Yes, you!" he replied with a chuckle. "Now, be a good girl and go put on your habit—" He paused, then added, in a disarmingly humble voice, "please."

She eyed him for a long moment, then saw the faint quiver at the corner of his mouth. "Oh, you are odious!" she exclaimed. "I would send you about your business, my lord, except for the fact that—" She stopped.

"Yes?" prompted the earl, an unholy glint in his eye.

"—that it would not be fair to the horse!" she finished, with something of a snap.

The earl was left kicking up his heels in the drawing room for a mere fifteen minutes, for Diana, once deciding to relent, was not about to waste time dallying when she could be enjoying her favorite form of exercise. Her crop tucked beneath one arm, she soon returned, and even went so far as to bestow a genuine smile upon the earl.

"Well, shall we go?" she inquired. "I should not like to keep this spirited animal you have brought me prancing in the street."

The provocative words slipped out automatically, for this verbal sparring with him was becoming a habit. And not only that, she realized suddenly, it was actually exhilarating to speak thus. But how foolish she was to allow the mere bantering of words to excite her, she thought in embarrassment.

As if trying to read her thoughts, the earl cast her a slightly quizzical look as he gestured toward the door.

"After you," he said.

Once outside, Diana approached the mare critically. It was certainly not the showiest horse in the world, but that did not matter in the least. What concerned the young widow was the mare's quality, and with this in mind, she began circling the horse, assessing every detail of the animal's physique.

She was interrupted by the earl's amused voice. "I assure you, my dear, she's quite healthy. No spavins, cataracts, corns, or dropsy. Her teeth are good, her hocks are not enlarged, and no respiratory disease has yet settled in her lungs. Nor does she bite, kick, or bolt, as far as I have been able to determine."

Ignoring his bantering tone, Diana replied fairly, "Indeed, in appearance, at least, she seems satisfactory. And her tail has not been docked, thank goodness. What is her name?"

He made a wry face. "Ophelia. Someone apparently had a liking for Shakespeare. I trust that neither of you will end your days floating down the Thames, however."

Diana smiled involuntarily as Ophelia tossed her head and shifted her feet, as if to suggest her disdain for such a notion. "There, now, we won't allow that to happen," she told the mare. Reaching into her pocket, Diana withdrew a small lump of sugar. "Here, Ophelia," she offered, her voice soft and coaxing. "I've brought you a treat."

As the mare's nose nuzzled gently into Diana's hand, the earl took the opportunity to study the woman he intended to marry. She appeared absurdly young to him at that moment, as if the six intervening years had never been, and she was no more than a young girl of eighteen or nineteen, an innocent in a world of sophisticates. Her face, he observed, was clear of the tiny lines which many women her age already wore about their eyes and brow. Not only that, but she still retained that indefinable air of purity he'd noticed long ago, well before she had entered into that travesty of a marriage. How this could be was a bit of an enigma to him. In fact, there was a good deal about Diana that he failed to understand, but he was becoming more and more determined to do so.

About to comment upon the mare's friendliness, Diana glanced up, catching her breath as she encountered the earl's speculative gaze. There was that expression in his eyes again. It burned her, that look, and filled her with . . . something. Confusion? Fear? No, not fear, but an uneasy, shaky sort of feeling that brought a weakness to her knees.

"My lord?" she inquired, summoning a reproving tone. "Is there, perhaps, a spot on my nose to make you stare so?" It would never do to let him know how strange he made her feel.

He answered immediately, breaking the spell with some easy reply as he offered her a hand up onto Ophelia's back. What he actually said Diana would have been hard put to repeat, for her thoughts were in such a whirl that she barely attended. That smile of his was dangerous, she reflected a little nervously. Good gracious, it was nearly enough to wipe away her suspicions, nay, her *knowledge* of his true intentions! Such a state of affairs must not be allowed to continue! But what on earth was she going to do about it?

It may or may not have been this episode that brought both riders to a state of somber reflection, but whatever the case, they reached the Park without much conversation passing between them. It was still early enough that the dew sparkled wet upon the grass, and as they urged their mounts to a brisker pace, a small flock of starlings rose up from some nearby sanctum, objecting shrilly to their presence. Of either Aimee or Charles, there was no sign.

109

"Come," said the earl, turning to Diana. "Let's give these horses some exercise. Brutus is longing for a chance to stretch his legs, and at a guess, I would say that Ophelia shares his sentiments."

Diana's eye brightened at the opportunity to display her horsemanship. As they eased the horses into a canter, she discovered that Ophelia, far from being a slug, was just about the sweetest-goer she had ever been privileged to ride. The mare responded instantly to her rider's directives, her silken mouth sensitive to the slightest movement of the reins. She was fast, too, and Diana, delighted by Ophelia's unexpected fleetness, narrowed her eyes against the wind and gave herself over to the enjoyment of the ride.

When at last they slowed, the earl turned to observe her reaction. "Well?" he inquired, one dark brow rising. "What do you think of her?"

"I think that I owe you an apology," Diana told him ruefully. "I honestly did not think much of your choice until now."

"Ah," said the earl in satisfaction.

"She is a perfect lady," she continued, reaching down to pat Ophelia's glossy back, "yet with enough spirit and passion in her to satisfy the most particular rider. I should very much like to own this graceful, splendid animal."

The earl maneuvered his gelding nearer to Diana. "A perfect lady for a perfect lady," he stated simply. "Each with more than her share of spirit . . . and passion."

Diana flushed a little. "My lord, please. You must not say such things."

Lord Lucan regarded her intently. "Why not? There's no one but you to hear me. Come, let's neaten you up a trifle." He startled her by reaching casually to tuck back a golden curl that had escaped from its confining coil. As he did so, his thumb brushed her cheek—on purpose,

Diana was convinced—causing her to involuntarily tighten her grip upon the reins. To her embarrassment, the mare's obedient sidling brought the two horses even closer, so that the side of her leg pressed against the earl's top boot.

"I think Ophelia has developed a liking for Brutus," remarked the earl in a lazy voice. "How very convenient."

Hastily urging her mount into a walk, Diana searched for an appropriate response. Finally she said, in a faint but dignified voice, "You have not yet indicated, my lord, whether I passed muster."

Following beside her, the earl's brows lifted, and a trace of laughter crept into his voice. "Passed muster, my sweet? Once again you are confusing me. As charmingly as ever, of course."

She threw him a resentful look. "I refer to my ability in the saddle, of course. Are you satisfied that I can stay on a horse without falling off? Will you purchase Ophelia for me?"

To her discomfiture, he laughed. "My dear Diana, I fear you are laboring under a misapprehension. Ophelia is yours. I've already paid for her."

Diana stared at him, torn between amazement and an unseemly urge to scratch the smile from his face. "I have not given you leave to make free with my name, my lord," she pointed out, seizing upon the inconsequential with icy determination.

"Not yet," he swiftly conceded. "An omission we shall have to rectify."

"And I was under the impression that my aunt was to pay for the horse!" she pursued, eyeing him with suspicion.

"Oh, I promise you I'll send her the bill. Good God, did you really think I would put you on trial? I shouldn't dare, you know." He had the temerity to grin at her.

"Oh?" she said, glaring back.

"I've already had a taste of your temper," he reminded her, by way of explanation. He chuckled again, a deep sound that was curiously infectious. "In any case, I never for a moment doubted your ability to ride well."

Diana was puzzled. "But my cousin merely borrowed the horse he brought for Aimee!"

"Ah, but that was different," said Lord Lucan enigmatically.

"And why is that?"

He decided to be blunt. "Because your sister is a regular minx, and will say anything to impress your cousin. If I were he, I wouldn't believe half of what comes out of her mouth."

"That's not true!" cried Diana, defending her sister hotly. "How can you say that? You don't even know my sister! And Aimee happens to be an extremely competent horsewoman!"

"Is she?" he said, with detached interest. "Well, good for her, then. But I still think she's bound for trouble. If you want my advice, you'll keep a tight hold on her bridle while she's in town."

Diana's lips tightened. "I really don't recall asking your advice," she countered. At his amused look, she added bitterly, "I suppose the next thing you'll say is that trouble runs in the family!"

The words slipped out before she could stop them. Horrified at the inadvertent reference to her own scandalous past, Diana averted her eyes, wondering what answer he could possibly make. Perhaps he was so shocked he would merely pretend he had not heard. *Dear Lord, that would be worse than anything else*, she thought, though she had not an inkling of a notion why that should be so.

His eyes compassionate, the earl said deliberately, "No, I wouldn't say that." When she did not respond, he sighed, and said, as gently as possible, "Diana, look at me. My poor girl, I would never say such a thing to you! What makes you think that I would?"

At length, Diana turned helpless eyes upon him. "I'm sorry," she said inadequately.

He reached out to clasp her hand. "Don't be sorry. Say anything you like to me, but don't apologize. It's the best way to deal with my sort. That's what I've been trying to show you. That we can bypass all the polite, conventional, empty"—he hesitated, searching for a suitable word—"*palaver* that most of humanity seems to indulge in. The poppycock, as your aunt would say. The inanities. I'm no great hand at that kind of thing, as you probably noticed."

"I noticed," said Diana, swallowing hard as she pulled her hand from his warm grasp.

"Besides," he added, "you didn't ask for what happened to you. That's the difference between you and your sister."

"Oh, but I did," she muttered, too softly for him to hear.

At the far end of the Park, Aimee was fast approaching the conclusion that Cousin Charles was not as easygoing as he seemed. The uncompromising set of his mouth told her that she had done something wrong, but why, she wondered, did he not say anything? Good gracious, his very bearing was condemnatory, she noted in distress. She must end this silence.

"Charles, are you . . . are you angry with me?" Aimee cleared her throat nervously and fixed him with an imploring gaze. "Please speak to me."

Thawing only slightly at the entreaty in her voice, Charles turned his head to send her a look of acute male exasperation. "Dash it, Aimee, you just don't *do* things

113

like that in Hyde Park! Neck-or-nothing riding is for the *country!* Don't you know that?"

"Oh," said Aimee, much abashed. "No, I didn't."

"What the devil made you take off like that, anyway?" asked Charles with a frown.

A lump began to form in Aimee's throat. "But I thought that . . . well, when you said there was nothing grander than allowing a horse its head I thought you meant . . . oh dear! I am so sorry, Charles. I see I made a mistake."

Once begun, Cousin Charles seemed intent on giving her a complete trimming. "You're dashed lucky no one saw you!" he grumbled, ignoring her apology. "No one but a pair of servants, that is, and a handful of nursery brats and governesses!"

Reaching out, he snapped his fingers under her pert little nose. "If they had, I'd have given *that* for your chances of getting into Almack's!" he told her brutally. "And what's more, word would soon have gotten around that Aimee Farington is a hoyden and a romp! What a pretty hobble that would have been, eh? Is that what you want? To set the London tongues wagging about your exploits?"

A single teardrop trembled in the corner of Aimee's eyes. "Please don't be angry with me, Charles. I won't do it again."

"And if that weren't bad enough," continued Charles irately, "you had to go and ride through the pond! Not around the pond, mind you, but *through* it!"

"I only did it to make the little boy laugh. He looked so sad, sitting there with his broken toy boat. I do hope his papa fixes it for him!"

Charles gave her a pained look. "Well, he laughed all right! So did all the other brats within a hundred yards of us! And who would not, to see such a spectacle?"

Unchecked, the teardrop slid down Aimee's pale

cheek. "Was I truly so very bad?" she whispered.

"Bad!" snorted Charles. He was about to add several more choice words upon her want of conduct, when he noticed the tear. "Oh, Lord," he relented with a groan. "For God's sake, now, don't cry, Aimee! I didn't mean to rip up at you." Realizing how heartless he must have sounded, Charles strove to make amends. "Hang it, if we'd been in the country, I wouldn't have objected in the least! You're a Trojan in the saddle, Aimee! Got a dashed fine seat, as a matter of fact. Who taught you to ride?"

Aimee brightened a little at the compliment. "My papa. He was once an excellent horseman, but he doesn't ride much any more. He had a fall a few years ago, and finds it uncomfortable."

"Well," said Charles matter-of-factly, "he knew what he was about, that much is obvious. I'll have to have a talk with Diana, though. We can't have you making these kinds of mistakes."

"No," agreed Aimee, her face once more downcast. This was not going at all the way she had planned, she reflected unhappily. She had meant to make a favorable impression upon Charles, not provoke him into lecturing her like a child!

As for Charles, his opinion of his cousin had, in the last half-hour, undergone a rapid and thorough transformation. His sanguine conviction that such an angel could not be less than perfect had fled faster than Pansy across the grassy fields of Hyde Park. Granted, she was a regular out-and-outer in the saddle, but a delicately nurtured, gently bred girl hardly out of the schoolroom ought not to behave in such a hoydenish fashion!

Lucan had been right, Charles sighed inwardly. Cousin Aimee would likely prove as difficult to handle as his grandmother. Did he really want to leg-shackle himself to a girl like this? Lord only knew what sort of a dance she would lead him on next! He was going to have to give this some serious reconsideration.

When Aimee's escapade came to Diana's ears, her first reaction was one of reproach. However, it very quickly dawned upon her that her sister was still smarting from Cousin Charles's strictures, and for her to add her own admonishments would be superfluous. Notwithstanding this, she did point out, as gently as possible, something she was sure their cousin's delicacy would forbid him to do.

"You see, dearest," she explained, compunction filling her brown-gold eyes, "because of what happened to me, you must take even greater care of your reputation. I cannot overstress this. There are those who would be only too glad to dredge up an old scandal. They would compare the two of us, you see. They would say that the Farington girls are all the same, that we are bold and ill-bred, and that no decent man would consider allying himself to one of us. And the damage could even extend to Elizabeth and Dorothy and Louisa."

Aimee stared incredulously. "But that is so unfair!" she cried out. "All I did was allow Pansy to gallop! And the pond was hardly a pond at all. Scarcely deep enough to wade in!"

Diana nodded. "Yes, well, it does seem unfair. I told you things were different in London. You must learn to conform, at least on the surface. Enough to fool people. I don't believe Cousin Charles would like you to become a complete pattern-card of propriety. How dull!" she added, with an encouraging smile.

Aimee scowled. "I am beginning to think Charles is a bit of a prig," she retorted. "He will not flirt with me, but he is only too ready to give me a rake-down when I make a mistake!"

"If you give it some thought," said Diana patiently, "I

think you will see that his actions can only commend him. He is trying to protect you from—"

"From myself!" flashed Aimee, springing to her feet. "Oh, I understand perfectly!" And with a tiny sob, she ran from the room, leaving Diana to stare after her in distress.

It was not the most propitious moment to receive a caller. Nevertheless, when Sir Henry Neyle was ushered into the drawing room less than a minute later, Diana was able to force away her frown and to greet him with a semblance of a smile.

It had been nearly a week since she had seen him, and she realized with some surprise that she had devoted very little thought to him in the interim. However, his presence served to reawaken her awareness of his existence. What a contrast he was to Lord Lucan, she found herself thinking. How incredibly handsome he was, so tall and slim, with so classic a profile and hair more golden than her own. She could only wonder why such an Adonis had never married, when he could surely have had his pick among the eligible young ladies.

"I am so very glad to find you at home," said Sir Henry, lifting her hand and pressing it to his lips. With a boyish smile, he went on, "I was moping around this afternoon, feeling quite ridiculously bored, and then I said to myself, Harry, old boy, why don't you just pay a visit on the charming Mrs. Verney? *She'll* cheer you up! And here I am!"

Diana's smile warmed in automatic response to his charm. "Well, I cannot promise to cheer you up but I shall certainly try. May I offer you some sherry?"

"Well . . ." His eyes sparkled with mischief. "What I'd truly like is a glass of brandy. Does that shock you?"

"Not at all," she answered, calmly ringing for Lawrence.

The brandy was soon delivered, and Sir Henry, glass in

hand, followed her across the room, and flustered her by easing his chair a little closer to her own. "Do I make you nervous?" he asked, watching her face.

"Nervous?" echoed Diana. "No. No, of course not."

"Good. I should dislike that to be so. I want us to be comfortable together." He crossed one elegantly clad leg over the other, and sent her another enchanting smile. "So, pray enlighten me, Mrs. Verney. I am dying to know the answer to the mystery."

"I beg your pardon?" said Diana in perplexity.

With a sip of his drink, Sir Henry appeared to be studying the tassel on his gleaming Hessians. "To put it simply, why the long rustication? Did you dislike London as much as that?" He sounded diverted by the possibility.

Diana gave a small laugh. "Of course not. I merely stayed in Wiltshire to be near my family. It is very pleasant there."

His raised eyebrow connoted disbelief. "Indeed? But *not* dreadfully exciting, I'll wager." He took another swallow of the brandy, savoring the fiery liquid as it ran down his throat.

"No," she admitted, feeling defensive. "But I was not looking for excitement, Sir Henry. I had just lost a husband, you may recall," she added, seeking refuge in this excuse.

He smiled. "Ah, yes. How could I have been so stupid as to forget? Allow me to extend my condolences, Mrs. Verney, though I realize, of course, that they're a trifle late."

"Thank you," she murmured, wishing she could come up with a more witty, more sociable reply.

Suddenly, the baronet leaned forward and regarded her intently. "I never forgot you, you know."

"Oh?" All at once, Diana felt breathless. "How . . . how kind of you, Sir Henry."

"Not kind," he informed her dryly. "The truth of the

118

matter is that it would be hard for me to forget a woman as beautiful as yourself."

Diana could only gaze at him in wonder. Had this divinely handsome man just told her she was beautiful?

"You won't run away again, will you?" he asked, setting down his glass abruptly. "Because I do want us to become more closely acquainted. That would make me so very happy."

Diana's heart began to beat faster. "It would make me happy, too," she answered shyly.

Slowly, the corners of the baronet's mouth lifted. "Good," he said, very softly. "You see? I knew you would cheer me up."

Chapter Seven

On the whole, the days preceding Aunt Serena's ball passed a trifle too quickly for Diana's peace of mind, and on the morning of that event, she was not yet mentally prepared for it. After all, the ball's purpose was to launch her beloved sister into the world of the London *ton*, the world that Diana had for so long chosen to eschew. Recognizing, however, that it was far too late for retreat, the young widow resolutely thrust aside her worries. It was perfectly natural, she chided herself, to feel a bit apprehensive, but it would not do to let her imagination run wild. Aimee would be fine, and as for herself, well, she was not about to cry craven now!

The ball, Diana knew, would trigger an onslaught of invitations to every sort of social function, making it necessary for them to plan each day with almost military precision. Indeed, she thought wryly, there were those who treated the London Season as seriously as one of Wellington's campaigns—the enemy, of course, being all unmarried gentlemen of rank and fortune.

To be honest, Diana supposed she was no better than the rest, for she was as anxious as any matchmaking mama for her sister to marry—though not just any gentleman would do, of course. It was still far too early to ascertain whether Cousin Charles would prove a contender for her sister's hand, but Diana could not deny that she would hail such an occurrence with relief. Aimee, she had decided, needed a husband whose steadying influence would counterbalance her volatility, and she rather thought that Cousin Charles might be that man. Without doubt, however, the sensible course was to encourage Aimee to keep an open mind, and this was what Diana had been attempting to do for the past few days. There would be many other young men as eligible as Cousin Charles, as she had dutifully pointed out to her pugnacious sister.

Beyond all this, there were other concerns preying on Diana's mind, not the least of which was her own future. Just lately, she had been unnerved to discover that what she had so wholeheartedly believed she wanted—to remain a widow—no longer seemed as enticing. Her doubts on the subject needed to be resolved, and when was she going to have a chance to reflect upon it? After tonight's ball, she would be lucky to have enough time to sleep, much less think!

Oh, if only her emotions would not keep flip-flopping! On some days, she would find herself believing that her only hope of happiness lay in remaining a widow, yet on others, she would discover that the notion of remarriage (if she did not dwell overmuch upon its implications) was almost appealing. This latter way of thinking occurred more when she was feeling lonely or tired or when Aimee's bright but ceaseless chatter reverberated in her ears. Widowhood seemed more attractive at night, when memories of Edmund's pawing sent shivers of revulsion up her spine.

Sir Henry Neyle, she decided, was largely responsible for this soul-searching, for his remarks of the other day had seemed to indicate that he was considering making her an offer. Diana did not know what answer she would make—that was one of the things she had yet to decide—but still, how very gratifying it was! There was so much to admire abut Sir Henry, she reflected. He was strikingly handsome, his conversation was light and witty, and it was reassuringly obvious that he cherished no dark, ulterior purpose in seeking her out. Furthermore, in his company she could feel more like the self-possessed, sophisticated woman she longed to be, a woman who was not thrown out of countenance by an overbold look or a mocking remark. And he did not stand so close to her that he affected her ability to breathe properly, as another certain gentleman was discourteous enough to do.

But she must not start thinking of *him*. Instead, Diana determinedly turned her attention to the ball gown she had chosen to wear for the evening. It was new and made of Italian crepe, its unusual color, according to the dressmaker, being the exact same shade of turquoise blue as the Aegean Sea. What would Sir Henry say when he saw her in it, she wondered? Picturing the scenario, her eagerness for the coming evening began to quicken. Sir Henry's divinely blue eyes would shine with admiration, and he would lift her hand to his lips, and murmur something perfectly delightful, something like—

"Diana!" A sharp rapping sound put an end to her reverie. "Are you there? Can I come in?" Aimee opened the door enough to poke her head inside the bedchamber.

"Of course," said Diana in resignation. "I was just about to come down." Observing Aimee's odd expression, she added, more curiously, "What is it?"

Instead of perching on the bed as she usually did, Aimee drifted across the room to gaze broodingly out the window. "I wanted to talk to you, that's all," she replied, her back to Diana. After a pause, she threw over her shoulder. "Do you think it is going to rain?"

"I hope not. But in case it does, I think we should do as Aunt Serena wants and take our evening clothes over to

122

Arlington Street. We can get ready over there just as easily, and Meg can come with us . . . Tildy, too, if she likes."

Aimee nodded absently. "You know," she said, "I've been thinking about what you said." She swung around suddenly. "About Charles, I mean."

"Oh?"

Wandering over to the dressing table, she began to finger the various articles on its surface. "I don't always listen to you, Diana, but this time I am wondering if perhaps you are right. Why should I marry Charles? Why should I wed someone who is going to do nothing but find fault with me?"

"Now, Aimee, I never said—"

"It would make far more sense to marry someone who adores me, someone who will worship the very ground I walk on. Someone rich, of course, and divinely handsome. Someone who will never tell me what to do, or, more importantly, what *not* to do!"

Diana eyed her sister. "I really don't think that—"

"Someone," continued Aimee relentlessly, "who will love me so much that if I even *look* at another man he will be jealous enough to blow his brains out!"

"Oh, dear." Diana sank helplessly into the nearest chair. "I fear you would not care for that, my dear, if you would but consider—"

Aimee's lip curled. "Naturally," she went on, "I should not desire him to go through with it. But would it not be wonderful to be so loved, so adored, so *venerated?*"

"It might sound pleasant, of course, but do you not think such devotion might become a bit wearying?"

Aimee put down the brush she had been holding and gave her sister a puzzled look. "Wearying?"

Diana searched for a better word. "Tedious, then. Or even oppressive. And only think how difficult it would be to feel deserving of such adoration!"

Ignoring the latter part of this speech, Aimee frowned. "Do you mean it might be boring? I hadn't thought of that."

"Perhaps you should," Diana advised, as gently as possible. "Marriage is not something to be treated lightly, my dear. It can be of very long duration."

Aimee's nose wrinkled. "But I can't always resolve these things just by thinking them out. For me, it works best if I can, well, try it first, to see for myself."

"Well, you cannot do that with marriage!" objected Diana, somewhat sharply.

Aimee gave her a surprised look. "I know that. I just meant that if I were to find a gentleman who *adored* me, I could better judge whether I liked it or not."

"Yes, but—" Diana began.

"I shall have to give this some more thought. Goodness, Diana, you have helped me excessively. Thank you so much!"

And before Diana could say anything more, Aimee flitted from the room.

Aunt Serena cockily prophesied a successful evening all around.

"People flock to my parties," she boasted to Diana, a short while before the preball dinner was due to commence, "because my house is large enough to accommodate 'em all in comfort, and because I put out more than an adequate number of chairs." Her beady eyes silently appraised Diana's gown as she rambled, "And I serve decent refreshments—no paltry skimping there, I'll have you know! Good wine and good food, that's the ticket! Parties ain't the place to pinch pennies, Diana. Remember it, and you'll never want for guests."

"I'll commit it to memory," promised Diana in a mechanical tone.

Why must Aunt Serena prate on about this now, she wondered? Surely her aunt must know there was no question of Diana giving any but the smallest, quietest parties—unless, of course, she remarried, thereby acquiring a home with sufficient space to . . . oh, drat Aunt Serena for harping upon the subject, anyway, thought Diana moodily. This was not the time to begin thinking about *that* subject.

Silence reigned for a short time while under the watchful eye of the dowager, Diana's abigail deftly arranged her mistress's golden tresses. When Meg had given a final pat to her work, she tactfully withdrew, leaving Diana alone with the dowager viscountess. Diana's features were set in a cool, pale mask as she turned to exchange stares with her aunt.

Scowling, Aunt Serena broke the silence, no longer circumventing the point she wished to make. "Your presence is a drawing card, too, Diana. Some members of the *ton* will be here just to have a look at you, to see if there's anything to gossip about. And they'll be wondering how little Aimee will conduct herself." *That* ought to bring the girl to life, thought the dowager grimly.

"It doesn't help me at all for you to say that, Aunt Serena," Diana replied, a trifle jerkily.

In response, the dowager's tone sharpened. "It's best if you know the truth! You may think you're up to snuff, but you ain't! You live with your head in some plaguey dream cloud half the time, girl." For emphasis, her cane thudded upon the wooden floor. "Watch yourself tonight! Get rid of that Friday-face and try to act natural. And for God's sake don't disappear anywhere. We don't want to start any talk."

Diana looked stubborn. "The point is taken," she retorted flatly. "Now, if you don't mind, Aunt Serena, I'd rather not discuss it any more."

Yielding to the steel in her niece's voice, Aunt Serena inclined her head. "Very well, Diana. As long as you bear it in mind. I've already warned Aimee, and I'm done warning you—my constitution won't bear any more scandals!"

There were to be thirty guests for dinner. Initially, Aunt Serena had dug in her heels at Diana's request that Sir Henry Neyle be included, but later, to her niece's surprise, she had suddenly capitulated. The truth was, the dowager had decided that more, rather than less, exposure to the baronet's scintillating charm might provide an effective cure for what she considered Diana's corkbrained infatuation with the man. With this new strategy in mind, she seated them together, while cunningly placing the Earl of Lucan within the young widow's view, next to a singularly ravishing (but married) young countess, who had been invited for this sole purpose. On Diana's other side, she put Lord Bathurst, Edmund's uncle.

Unfortunately for the dowager's plan, Sir Henry was on his best behavior this evening. As it happened, competition over a woman invariably heightened his desire to possess her, but in Diana's case, intuition also warned him he was treading on thin ice. Thus challenged, he remained confident but cautious, for even though Diana did not exactly fit his image of a dashing young widow on the lookout for a cicisbeo, Sir Henry could not conceive of a woman who would be unswayed by his powers to charm. He had, in short, made up his mind to play what he felt was a winning hand with a little additional caution.

As delighted as she was to find Sir Henry beside her at dinner, a quarter of the way through the meal Diana had still not been able to exchange more than a few polite words with him. This was due to Lord Bathurst, who was one of those not-so-rare human beings who loved the sound of his own voice, and, who, being very much aware of his own consequence, held the belief that Diana must be equally impressed.

Outwardly, Diana had been lending her late husband's uncle a polite ear, but inwardly she was chafing at his long-windedness. Would the man never stop talking? His lordship had never seemed quite so tiresome as he did at this moment.

". . . lament that I was absent when you arrived in London," he droned in Diana's ear. "My physician felt it advisable that I should drink the waters, y'know. Dreadful time of year to visit Bath. Dreadful! Waste of time, too, for it didn't do me a whit of good, and so I shall tell him, the old squeeze-crab! Every time I listen to that charlatan . . ."

Reaching for her wine, Diana sensed Sir Henry watching her, as he had been doing through much of the dinner. She shifted restively, not daring to look his way too often. Out of nowhere, she recalled her abigail's advice to Aimee. *Don't let the gent see how taken you are with him* . . . Well, that hardly made sense, did it? For how else would a gentleman know how a lady felt about him?

". . . have every right to expect your husband's nearest relation to be on hand to advise you," wheezed Lord Bathurst, patting her hand in a fatherly way. "Naturally you are confused and in need of counsel, for females, in general, are not equipped to make difficult decisions without the guidance of a male . . ."

Between mouthfuls, his lordship prosed on with boorish relentlessness, bringing Diana to the limit of her patience. Finally tossing caution to the four winds, Diana flashed Sir Henry a quick smile, and was elated to discover that she was still the object of his blue-eyed and rather pensive gaze. For Diana, it was a heady experience to have one of the most handsome men in London sitting next to her with his eyes pinned to her face.

". . . cannot entirely approve your decision to live on your own," rattled Lord Bathurst, growing, if possible, more pompous by the minute. "Had I been consulted, I should have advised against a step which might, for an older woman, be considered acceptable, but for a woman who is only just past the first blush of youth . . ."

As his lordship buzzed on, rather like a bee in a particularly fragrant flower, Diana nodded automatically and allowed her thoughts to roam. Although she was not at all sure she wished to remarry, still, how very agreeable it was to have a suitor—for such was she beginning to regard Sir Henry—who made her feel so safe. The emotions he kindled were temperate rather than fiery, and far easier to deal with than those disturbing, turbulent feelings Lord Lucan aroused in her breast.

It was really most unlike Aunt Serena to be so accommodating as to put Sir Henry next to her at dinner. Or had she known that Lord Bathurst would monopolize her so completely that she would have practically no chance to converse with Sir Henry? And whatever had possessed her aunt to place Lord Lucan next to the Countess of Uxbridge? She could not even understand why Aunt Serena would have invited her at all, for the woman looked out of place in this respectable lot of people.

As Lord Bathurst paused to drink, she took the opportunity to study Lady Uxbridge. Honestly, the woman was almost too beautiful, she noted in vague disapproval. With all that glossy, auburn hair and those heavy-lidded green eyes it was small wonder she managed to keep a bevy of gentlemen swarming around her everywhere she went.

Covertly, Diana watched Lord Lucan to see how he was reacting to all that allure. He was smiling at something Lady Uxbridge was saying, she observed with a flicker of annoyance. No doubt his reply would be as outrageous and flirtatious as those he fed to herself! For some indefinable reason this notion made her angry, and turning back to Lord Bathurst with a jerk of her head, Diana proceeded to bestow upon that gentleman such a brilliant smile that he decided that he must be even wittier than he had realized.

The truth of the matter was that Lord Lucan was not at all eager to converse with Lady Uxbridge, and would have been far better pleased with some other choice of dinner partner. Despite her seductive eyes and voluptuous figure, Lady Uxbridge did not attract him in the least. Be they ever so beautiful and high-born and discreet, he disliked women who foisted their more than half a dozen illegitimate offspring upon their long-suffering husbands. In particular, he decided he disliked this lady's perfume, a heavy musk, which seemed to have gotten into his food.

So far they had spoken only of trivialities, but as this was going through his mind, she leaned toward him, her scent wafting over his plate more potently than ever. "Such an insipid set of people," she drawled, her rich voice at so low a pitch that only he could hear. "I swear Lady Torrington has assembled in this one room some of the dullest folk in London—save you and I, of course, and perhaps the charming Sir Henry. It makes one wonder why one came, does it not?"

Out of courtesy, he smiled. "If respectability is insipid, madam, then perhaps you are right. Lady Torrington is a high stickler. I doubt you will find many scandals brewing here."

Any irony in his tone was lost on Lady Uxbridge, who generously offered him a fuller view of her bosom. "You and I could always brew one ourselves," she murmured with a suggestive side glance that might have floored a less experienced man. "I just *love* a nice little scandal," she added, licking her lips.

His sardonic reply was intended to squelch that little idea before it took further root in her mind. "We could," he said smoothly. "But then, I hesitate to tread where so many others have trod before. It seems a trifle . . . redundant. Don't you agree?"

This was the exchange that Diana witnessed, but by averting her gaze she missed Lady Uxbridge's furious expression. Diana knew only a sharp stab of unexpected misery as she beamed determinedly at Lord Bathurst. One need not be very much up to snuff, she reflected, a shade bitterly, to discern that Lord Lucan was very much a ladies' man.

Both Aunt Serena and Cousin Charles considered it entirely proper that he lead Aimee out for the first set of country dances. Aimee, certainly, considered it her due. However, she was piqued to discover that Charles felt it unsuitable for him to claim her hand more than once in the same evening. Completely forgetting her own assertion that her cousin was dull, she redoubled her efforts to attract his interest.

"Lady Jersey has given me permission to waltz, Charles," she told him very sweetly and very pointedly, as they waited for the musicians to begin.

Charles noticed her frown. "Oh? Well, that's good, ain't it?"

"Yes, of course it's good," she snapped.

He stared at her in puzzlement. "Then why the gloomy face?"

"Why, what can you possibly mean, Charles?" replied Aimee, her tone brittle. Racking her brain, she wondered how she could possibly make her meaning any clearer. Surely Charles could not be so stupid that he was unable to take a hint.

The dance began, and there was little opportunity to talk until it ended. As he escorted her back to the dowager's side, Aimee managed to hiss into his ear, "I have *one* unclaimed waltz, Charles."

He halted abruptly, and her hopes soared. "Let me see your dance card," he instructed.

Eagerly, Aimee handed it over, but Charles's next words left her nearly speechless. "You ain't got a dance with Lord Lucan, have you? Dash it, that must have been an oversight on his part. I'll just go drop a hint in his ear."

Aimee stared at him in outrage. "Charles," she said finally, "don't *you* want to waltz with me?"

He gave her a genuinely rueful look. "Can't do that, Aimee. Might cause talk. Once is enough."

"But you are my *cousin!*" she squeaked, her hand flying to her mouth as if to control her own voice. "No one would question your right to a second dance."

Charles cleared his throat uncomfortably. "Yes, well, we have to be careful. Reputation is everything, y'know. At least with this set of people it is." He did not add that people might assume that more than mere cousinly affection existed between them—and he was not ready to admit that there was.

Her heart filled with hurt and rage, Aimee spun away from him with a stifled sob. She would teach Charles a lesson, she thought. By the end of the evening, he would be very sorry he had not taken that dance.

Some hours later, however, all was not going according to plan. True, Aimee never lacked either partners or compliments, but none of this seemed to make her feel any better. She had just sent her current partner off to fetch her a glass of punch when she caught sight of

Diana, who was bearing down upon her for the very purpose of having a little talk with her high-spirited young sister.

"Diana," said Aimee in a strained voice, before her elder sister could speak, "who is that girl dancing with Charles?"

Diana turned to look. "I believe her name is Drusilla Low," she said tautly. "She is about your age, Aimee, and seems pleasant. Perhaps you might become friends."

Toying with her fan, Aimee wrinkled her nose in distaste. "I doubt it," she said, her tone as short as Diana's. "Have you noticed how our cousin dances with all the plainest girls? What do you think of that?"

"I think it is very kind of him," replied Diana. She drew closer to her sister and added in an undervoice, "And I also think your own behavior this evening has been most unwise."

"Unwise?" Aimee gave a tinkling little laugh. "What have I done? Certainly I have not danced *twice* with any man—as this Drusilla Low has done. Have you noticed that she is quite the plainest girl in the room?"

Diana rubbed her forehead, where a throbbing ache was starting to grow. "I had not given it much thought, Aimee. Why are you saying this? It is unlike you to be so unkind."

Aimee's cheeks pinkened with indignation. "Because it is *my* ball, and Charles is *my* cousin, and he has danced with that Low girl *twice*, Diana! And only once with me!"

With a sigh, Diana strove to keep her voice calm. "I strongly urge you to forget Drusilla Low and start thinking of Aimee Farington. Have you forgotten everything I told you? You promised to behave!"

"I *am* behaving! I am very popular, haven't you noticed? I told you I would be good at flirting! I have been putting your theory to the test, and so far I can assure you that being put upon a pedestal is far from dull!"

At that moment, Diana's hand itched to slap her sister's face. "You promised not to do that!" she accused.

Feigning innocence, Aimee arched her brows. "Did I? I don't recall. I do know that I am a grand success, Diana. Every one of my dance partners has begged to be allowed to call upon me tomorrow. All but one, that is, and it isn't very hard to guess who, is it?"

Hearing the pain in her sister's voice, Diana's anger fell away. She longed to comfort Aimee, but could only reach out to touch her arm in sympathy. "I am sorry, Aimee," she said quietly. "But you cannot expect Charles to follow you around like a lap dog! He is a grown man of nine-and-twenty, and has, I daresay, a great deal of experience with women. He will not fall for these tricks. Be patient and try not to behave like . . . like a—"

"Like a child!" Aimee's voice was rising and her breath was coming in short gasps. "You think it is childish of me to want him to like me, don't you?"

Diana sighed. "Aimee, please. I'm sure he does like you. But he is not going to make a fool of himself in front of—Oh, I didn't mean— Aimee, come back!"

But her sister had taken affront, and was already stalking back to Aunt Serena. A few minutes later, as she chatted with a young woman of her acquaintance, Diana observed that Aimee's next dance partner was Lord Lucan, and that the musicians were striking up a waltz. Her heart sank. If *he* let loose his charm on her impressionable young sister, there could be no telling what damage might be done. Prepared for the worst, Diana excused herself, and, locating a chair near her aunt, promptly collapsed into it. To her annoyance, Aunt Serena seemed to be paying scant heed to the girl she was supposed to be chaperoning. She could overhear most of what the dowager was saying, and it appeared that her aunt was exchanging a series of grievances with Lord Hervey, the follies of modern youth figuring chiefly among her complaints. Wondering uneasily whether either Aimee or herself had inspired this conversation, Diana tried not to listen, tried to watch her sister and Lord Lucan without appearing to, tried to forget the throbbing pain in her head, and tried not to be glad that the earl had not sought out Lady Uxbridge once during the entire evening. She also tried not to think about her own dance with Lord Lucan, which was soon to come, or to wonder why Sir Henry had not signed her dance card at all.

To Aimee's chagrin, Lord Lucan did not present the appearance of a man who was enthralled by the charms of his partner. Her fluttering eyelashes won no response from him, no more than did the archly vivacious remarks that the other gentlemen had seemed to find so amusing. Suddenly recalling her resolve to find a husband for Diana, Aimee was assailed with a flash of guilt. She had lately become so involved in her own problems, she had nearly forgotten poor Diana. She must be brave, she decided, and put aside her troubles. She must push forward with her original plan.

Brightening a little, Aimee studied the earl's lean, rather swarthy face. Well! The place to start was obviously here. She might be naive, but she knew that this man was interested in her sister in a way that he quite obviously was not in herself. And was that not a telling sign of a good prospective husband? After all, she reasoned, if he was truly in love with Diana, of course he should *not* be wanting to flirt with anyone else!

In a manner which lacked her previous coyness, she remarked, "I suppose you would not frown so if I were Diana." Rather to her surprise, it was actually a relief to speak in her own natural voice. Flirting was much harder work than she expected!

Surprised by the about-face in his partner's behavior, Lord Lucan assessed her with suspicion. "Your sister would give me no reason to frown," he said dryly.

Aimee flushed. "Meaning you do not care for my behavior, I suppose."

"I think," he said, studying her, "that if you continue as you are, you'll soon be out of your depth. To tempt providence, Miss Farington, can be foolhardy."

Aimee pouted. "Now you sound like Charles. You older men are all the same, I think. Lecture and scold, scold and lecture! It's all I hear, even from Diana."

The earl's hard mouth relaxed into a surprisingly sympathetic smile. "When one is seventeen, the whole world can seem an adversary. I remember quite clearly how it was."

Taken aback, Aimee regarded him silently, as if seeing him for the first time. Suddenly, without knowing why, she said, "Lord Lucan, do you think nine-and-twenty is too great an age to wed with seventeen?"

The waltz was about to end, and as the music drew to a close, the earl took this opportunity to form a careful reply. "Age is less important than circumstances," he said finally. "It is something to consider, but there are no magic formulas, Miss Farington. There are enough limits in life without that."

"Oh." Aimee looked thoughtful. "Yes, I suppose that is true."

"Is everything all right?" inquired Diana, seizing the first opportunity available to speak to Aimee after the earl had left. "I hope Lord Lucan did not say anything he should not. I watched you but I could not tell for sure."

Aimee gave a rippling laugh. "Everything is fine. His lordship did not flirt with me, if that is what you mean. In fact, he is very sober, like Charles, only even worse, I think. He behaves like an uncle. But he gave me some advice which I found most sensible, so the dance was

135

not a waste."

"Really? What advice did he give you?" Diana looked a little amazed.

Aimee shrugged. "Oh, something about not tempting providence, or some such thing. He thinks that age is not as important as love, Diana. He thinks Charles is not too old for me."

Diana's brows rose. "He said that?"

"Well, not exactly, but words to that effect." Aimee appeared more cheerful than she had in days. "I cannot talk anymore, Diana. The cotillion is next, Aunt Serena is waving at me, and that young man at her elbow is waiting for me. Do stop worrying, Diana. You'll give yourself the headache!" she added, and hurried away.

As she stared after her sister, an amused voice said, "My dear Mrs. Verney, are you worrying again?"

Diana jumped. As usual, he was standing too close, so that she could almost feel the warmth of his body across the small space which separated them. And how was it possible, she asked herself wildly, that one's heart could hammer so violently against one's ribs? For the love of heaven, why did he make her so nervous?

Lord Lucan's eyes slid over her with masculine approval. "What?" he teased. "Don't tell me you've nothing to say to me. No rake-downs? No scolds? I thought I'd be due for a tongue-lashing or two by this time."

Diana forced a light laugh. "You make me sound like such a harpy, my lord. Am I truly so difficult?"

The curl of his mouth signified his amusement, but he said only, "Don't be ridiculous, Diana. Come, let us walk upon the balcony. I'm devilish hot in this coat, and I'm tired of trotting around the room in time to music. There are several things I do well, but dancing really isn't one of them. That gown, by the way, is delightful. You are the fairest maiden at the ball, my dear."

"Except that I'm no maiden," she murmured, then

136

blushed at her own boldness. Even to herself she could not have explained why she felt compelled to point this out.

Surprised, the earl's eyes narrowed a little. "No," he agreed, a trifle shortly. "A poor choice of words, perhaps. Let us not refine upon it."

They made their way through the press of people to the double doors which led onto the long stone balcony stretching the length of the back of the house. To Diana, it was as if she were in a dream in which she was moving toward the inevitable. The doors stood open to let in the flow of evening coolness, and pools of light lit the center of the area, leaving the far recesses of the balcony shrouded in darkness. They were not the only couple who had stepped out that evening for a breath of air, but for the moment they were alone.

He turned her around with firm hands, but when she had braced herself to repel his embrace, his hand went instead to her chin, raising it so that she was forced to gaze directly into his eyes.

"You are so beautiful," he said huskily. "Diana the goddess, the eternal virgin. Maiden or not, that is how I view you."

In a sudden panic, she pushed his hand away, but his eyes still held her captive. "You must not say such things, my lord. I wish you would not."

"Why?" he asked in a caressing voice. "Tell me why, Diana."

He was too close; she could not think. "You must know why," she stammered.

"No, I don't." He was studying her intently. "You are not indifferent to me. In fact, I think you like me very well indeed."

"Yes, I do, but please," she implored, "you must say no more. There is no purpose in . . . in this. Oh, you will ruin everything!"

He turned her words around. "On the contrary, there is a purpose. I am a man who always has a purpose in mind, Diana." Gazing at her steadily, he tried to tease her out of her somber mood. "Don't you want to learn about the things I do well, my sweet?"

"I don't think so." She shook her head, a sharp jerk of absolute denial.

Suddenly, he knew he could not wait, that he had never meant to wait, that he had brought her to the balcony to ask her to be his wife. When she knew he wooed her in earnest, she would not be so reluctant.

"You know what I want, don't you?" he murmured, approaching the subject cautiously. "You know it's right, don't you, Diana? Sweet, sweet Diana." He reached for her hands, pulling her closer. "I want you, Diana, in every sense of the word. I want you to be my—"

"No!" Incredibly, she found the words to stop him, and she poured them out in a rush he could not interrupt. "Don't say anything more, I beg you! It's not right, at least not for me! You don't know me at all. Please, please believe me when I say that I have no wish for a . . . a warmer relationship with you or any other man."

Realizing how cold she sounded, she added pleadingly, "But I would very much like to be your friend. Just your friend." She moistened her lips. "I *am* fond of you— Geoffrey. Do you think that might be possible? Can we not just be friends?"

He was staring at her, his disappointment acute and unmistakable, even in the darkness. "You like me," he repeated slowly. "But not well enough to consider— Dammit, I don't believe it, Diana! I'll swear you feel what I feel!" His hands reached out to seize her, to kiss her against her will, but once more, miraculously, cruelly, she said the only thing that could have stopped him.

"Please, Geoffrey, don't treat me the way Edmund

did." There was a thread of naked misery in her voice. "Please be kind to me. Be my friend."

He had to force himself to remember she meant no insult. "Confound it, Diana, don't compare me to *him*."

"I'm sorry," she faltered. "I didn't mean to—" There was so much more she should have said, but then there were voices and laughter as two other couples, talking loudly, stepped out onto the balcony. "Let's go back in," she urged. "Aunt Serena will be furious if anyone has noticed I am out here with you."

Cursing himself for his own impatience, the earl scowled. "We are going to discuss this some more," he said flatly.

Diana laid her hand on his arm. "*No!* I've told you I want to be your friend. That's as much as I'm willing to give, my lord. And that is quite, quite final."

Chapter Eight

Lord Lucan sighed inwardly. He was leaning against the wall at yet another interminable ball, watching (with manifest indifference) yet another set of dancers—or was it the same confounded set?—wheel about the room. As always, he was at pains to disguise his true purpose, for the last thing he wanted was to give the gossip-tabbies something to sink their teeth into—which would happen if they realized he was only here to keep a proprietary eye on Diana.

She went past him at that moment in the arms of a retired captain of a Hussar regiment, a brash young man at least five years younger than himself. With a short sigh, the earl folded his arms across his chest, reflecting that it was foolish to be jealous of the man. To his knowledge, Diana never danced with any gentleman twice, and never gave the least indication that she favored one man over another. And from the looks on the faces of some of her partners, it was his conjecture that she could well have had her pick of the lot.

To be honest, if she had demonstrated partiality toward anyone, he would have to say it was himself. At least, in the two weeks that had passed since he had made the incredibly stupid blunder of speaking too soon, she had twice allowed him to drive her in the park, as well as accompanying him there on horseback a number of mornings. She had obviously been quite serious about wishing to be his friend, he thought wryly. One evening, too, he and Charles had escorted her to the theater, along with that madcap sister of hers and the dowager viscountess. Had it not been for the appearance of Sir Henry Neyle during one of the scene breaks, the evening would have been one of the most pleasant he had ever spent.

The earl's mouth hardened at the memory. Unless he was misreading the situation, Diana was far too impressed by Sir Henry. It had rankled him that the entire time Harry was in their box she had behaved unnaturally, as if she considered the baronet's visit some great, extraordinary honor. Of course, he mused, there was no real cause for alarm, since he could not imagine Diana consenting to become Sir Henry's mistress. What worried him was that the baronet might toy with her affections, for he was beginning to realize that Diana was a very vulnerable woman, and he did not want her to be hurt.

If only he had not been so bacon-brained as to offer her marriage before she was ready! Like the merest whipster, he had rushed his fences, attempting to build upon a relationship whose foundations were incomplete. He should have given her time to realize that she wanted him as much as he wanted her, instead of being so damned impatient! Now he could only cling to the hope that if he waited long enough, there might come a time when he would dare to broach the subject again. Certainly he did not intend to give up, for without doubt, platonic friendship with Diana would eventually become a torture in itself.

"My, my, what deep, dark thoughts must be taking shape in that head of yours!" murmured a teasing voice

141

at his side.

The earl glanced down, surprised that he had not observed Mrs. Clement's approach. "Hello, Cynthia." Suddenly glad of her company, he smiled affably, and pushed away from the wall. "Come. Let's find a more comfortable place in which to talk. How have you been?"

"Oh, horribly lonely," she complained, a spark of mischief lurking in her brown eyes. As his dark brows shot up, she added, "No, no, I am only funning, Geoffrey. You know me. I am never lacking for companionship—only money." The faint sigh which accompanied these last two words hinted at desperate struggles with creditors and tradesmen's bills.

He led Mrs. Clement to a nearby couch within an alcove, saying, in the forthright fashion which Diana found so disconcerting, "What, have you no protector at the moment to keep you in funds?"

Mrs. Clement's color heightened at his plain speaking. "I have several very dear friends," she said, hedging the question, "each of whom would help me if he could but—" She shrugged her white shoulders philosophically. "What can I say? I am not the only one with problems these days."

"I see." His gaze inscrutable, the earl fingered his quizzing glass. "How much do you need?"

She leaned forward eagerly. "Not a great deal. Five hundred or so would see me through to the end of the month." She saw his eyes drop to the expensive-looking jewels about her throat. "Glass," she confessed, with brief embarrassment. "I sold the original long ago."

"You know, Cynthia, if you would stop wasting the ready on all these parties—"

"I know, I know." She waved a hand at him. "But my parties are what make me fashionable, Geoffrey. And I have never been able to economize. I've never really needed to, although eventually I suppose—" She broke off with a smile. "What a bore I have become. Let us speak of something more cheerful."

He ignored this. "I will give you five hundred for friendship's sake. But only once."

The addendum brought a pinkness into Mrs. Clement's cheeks. "Naturally," she responded with dignity. "And I shall pay you back when . . . when I can."

He shook his head. "Consider it a gift," he ordered. "And in return, you can do something for me."

"Of course, Geoffrey. Anything at all."

"Really? Well, this is fairly simple." His keen eyes swept the room, then paused. "Do you see that woman directly across from us, the one in blue? Her name is Diana Verney."

"Edmund Verney's widow? Yes, I see her."

"I want you to keep an eye on her for me. You attend many of the same social events, I'm sure. In a sense, I want some assistance in guarding her."

Mrs. Clement's gaze grew speculative. "From any particular gentleman?" she inquired offhandedly. "Or all of them?"

There was a rough edge to his voice. "Only the ones who don't know how to behave themselves. I especially want to know whether she sees much of Henry Neyle. This is between you and me only, you understand."

"Of course," she murmured, giving him a reproachful yet curious look from under her lashes. "Is she the one you wanted to marry?"

"What?"

"You told me once, in one of your more, shall we say, loquacious moods, that the only woman you desired to be your wife was unavailable. And with Edmund Verney gone . . ."

Unable to recall making any such confidence, the earl regarded her quizzically. "Foxed, was I?" he inquired. "That must have been quite a while ago. And I suppose we were alone?"

She smiled slightly. "Yes, we were alone." Being a woman, she could not resist asking, rather wistfully, "Do you love her?"

"Love?" he repeated. His lips twisting wryly. "A word so often misapplied, so much abused. What does it mean, Cynthia? No, don't try to answer," he added. "The poets bend their minds to that task, and even they don't shed much light." He sat forward, prepared to rise. "Do not forget . . . this conversation was strictly between ourselves. And now, my dear lady, should you care to dance?"

"I should be delighted, my lord," replied Mrs. Clement, placing her hand in his.

Across the room, Diana had thanked her partner and rejoined Aunt Serena, who, perhaps because Lord Hervey was late in joining them, was behaving more querulously than usual.

"Diana," she grumbled, "I am uncomfortable. This idiotish chair is constructed all wrong for old bones like mine. Why Lucretia Corewood cannot put out something better than this for her guests is beyond me. She married above her station, which probably has a great deal to do with it. I told you we should have gone to the Rillingtons' soiree instead."

"Aimee wanted to come here, not I," Diana pointed out, a little dryly. Her own feet hurt but there was nowhere else to sit at the moment. With a sigh, she said, "Aunt Serena, would you like to go home? I am sure once Lord Hervey arrives he will be happy to take you—"

"No, no," interrupted her aunt curtly. "It's early yet. Where's that sister of yours?"

"I don't know." Diana glanced around. "She was with Charles a few minutes ago."

Aunt Serena lost interest. "Well, if the chit is with Charles she's safe enough. *He* knows where to draw the line, though some of 'em certainly don't! Have you spoken to her lately about her behavior? I thought I caught her doing the eyelash bit again with Captain Peterson. I swear the girl takes after me," she added cryptically.

Diana was startled. "You? Good God, don't tell me you used to—Aunt Serena, you never did!"

"Not after I was married," said the old lady coolly. "But when I was seventeen, by gad, they were lined up for miles outside my door. Went to my head a trifle, it did."

Somehow, Diana could not quite envision Great-aunt Serena fluttering her eyelashes and smiling coyly at some young man in . . . well, he would have been wearing a periwig, wouldn't he?

"Well, I must say," she remarked rather accusingly, "I think your behavior has been quite hypocritical. When I think of some of the things you have said to me concerning the need for propriety—"

"Poppycock!" said the dowager with a sniff. "I never got myself into a situation I couldn't handle, that's the difference between you and me! We were wiser in those days, I daresay. Knew enough not to trust a man. Never let 'em know it, either. Flattery! That's what they like. Men are as vain as peacocks about some things . . . like their virility. Worse than women, some of 'em. Like that Sir Henry of yours."

Such comments as this never failed to irritate Diana. "Sir Henry is not vain," she said defensively. "I cannot imagine what he could have done to make you dislike him so."

Aunt Serena made a disgusted sound. "I don't dislike him. I don't even know him! Don't want to know him either! My eyes tell me the man's a loose fish and that's enough for me." The dowager ignored her niece's expression. "Now, who's that dancing with Lucan?" she went on. "Oh, the Clement woman. Now, there's an example for you not to follow."

Her curiosity roused, Diana turned to look at the couple. In animated conversation, they might as well have been alone for all the notice they were giving those around them. "Who is she?" she asked.

A certain hollowness in her tone caused the dowager to give Diana a sharp look. "She's a widow like yourself," she said brutally. "A prime example of a woman who lives by her wits. Her wastrel of a husband died about ten years ago and, being a typical spendthrift, left her stranded with a mountain of debt. But she survived, paid 'em off, and can still put her foot into many respectable Mayfair homes. Many," she added with emphasis. "But not all."

"What do you mean?" faltered Diana, who had been noting how intimately the earl was smiling down at Mrs. Clement.

"I mean, Diana, that she sold herself for money. Oh, don't look so horrified—women do it all the time! It ain't their fault most often."

"But . . . but she is here—"

The dowager snorted a laugh. "Of course she's here. Egad, I never realized you was so naive, Diana. These so-called gentlemen with their polished manners and noble lineages . . . do you think they all sleep with their wives? Or live celibate lives if they've none?"

"I can't say I've given the matter much thought," replied Diana tartly.

"Maybe you should! Y'see, as far as society is concerned, it don't much matter what you do, as long as you don't get caught. The Clement woman's discreet, and that's why she's still accepted into all but the most select circles. Discretion is what counts, missy."

Such a life sounded very depressing to Diana. "Then how do *you* know about it?" she countered.

Aunt Serena sighed. "I ain't dead yet, Diana. I keep my

146

ear to the ground. But I can't tell you the particulars. If she and your Lord Lucan are more than friends, that's their business. I do know the Duke of Wellington was besotted by the Clement woman some years back, but that's ancient history. *Now* it's the Wilson sisters."

Caught between dismay and a certain fascination with the topic, Diana found herself asking, "Who are they?"

"Courtesans, Diana . . . demi-reps, if you like. Whatever you choose to call 'em, it amounts to the same. You've seen 'em driving in the Park, though 'tis possible not to know it, for they dress as finely as you and I. In any case, they need not concern you, as long as you understand and accept that they exist. I thought you knew all that seeing that Edmund—"

"Yes, yes," struck in Diana rapidly, "but I thought it was only he who . . . who went to such women."

The dowager rolled her eyes. "Lord have mercy! Well, never mind this now, the music is ending. Do you have a partner for the next set?"

Diana consulted her card. "Why, yes," she said, brightening. "Sir Henry."

"Lord have mercy!" repeated the dowager, more sourly.

Aimee's ratafia in his hand, Charles Perth stared at the empty chair before him, then rapidly scanned the faces in the nearby crowd. Dash the girl, where had she gone? Five minutes ago he had deposited her in this very chair and made it clear that she was to stay there while he procured her drink. He gazed around, starting forward as he spied a dark-haired girl about Aimee's height. But it was not she, he saw, as soon as she turned her head.

Racking his brain, he tried to remember what color she had been wearing. Pink, wasn't it? And a dashed fetching shade it had been, he thought inconsequently. It had made her little face look so enchanting, he had known he would be unable to concentrate on his dance steps, and had suggested that they sit out the set and partake of refreshment instead.

Could she have left the ball room? Perhaps she had only gone to the ladies' retiring room to freshen up? As this notion took root in his mind, Charles's frown began to fade. Yes, that was it very likely—though why she could not have mentioned it to him before, he could not conceive. He felt dashed silly standing around holding a glass of ratafia, vile beverage that it was. Why the ladies insisted upon drinking it he could never understand, for it was disgustingly sweet, and nearly as spirituous as a good glass of wine! Brandy, now, that's what women ought to drink!

Making a mental note to encourage Aimee to imbibe something more palatable, Charles dumped the ratafia into the base of a tall fern which had the misfortune to be placed nearby.

Quitting the ballroom, he glanced up and down the adjacent corridor. Several ladies and gentlemen stood about, exchanging conversation and gossip, but of Aimee there was no sign. He traversed the length of the passageway, passing by the room reserved exclusively for the ladies from which emanated a variety of female voices. He paused, but did not recognize Aimee's voice, though his sharp ears identified two or three others of his acquaintance. Where the devil *was* she? he wondered, his brow puckering. He had just begun to retrace his steps, thinking he ought to go and discover whether Diana knew anything, when he heard what sounded like an agitated giggle.

Pure instinct told him it came from Aimee, and he swung around, his green eyes alert. At first, he saw nothing. Then he noticed what looked to be a small alcove at the end of the hall, extending around the corner beyond the casement window overlooking the back of the house. A window seat followed the wall into the recess.

Gritting his teeth, Charles bore down upon this hideaway with savage exasperation. What game was the little minx up to this time?

It never occurred to him that she was not alone, and the sight which met his startled gaze so enraged him that his reaction was considerably more unrestrained than he would later care to remember. In fact, he so far forgot himself that he exclaimed, "What the deuce—!" a phrase he normally would not have used in front of a gently bred lady.

Aimee was sitting next to Captain Peterson, who, when Charles invaded the alcove, had just succeeded in capturing one of her dainty hands and was pressing it to his rather full lips—despite her attempts to prevent him.

"Just *what* is going on here?" demanded Charles, fixing the captain with a freezing stare. "Unhand my cousin, sir!" he added, his voice vibrant with indignation.

Looking chagrined, Captain Peterson jumped to his feet. "Er . . . hallo, Perth. We were just . . . ah . . . I mean the young lady and I were only . . ." His quick grin won no response from Charles. "I mean, there's no point in raising a dust about this, is there, eh? Miss Farington and I were only conversing. No harm done, eh?"

"Conversing," responded Charles in a curt tone, "can be done in the ballroom. We will detain you no longer, sir. Miss Farington accepts your apologies."

Favoring Aimee with a short bow, Captain Peterson cast Charles a sullen look and made his departure.

"Insolent fellow," muttered Charles under his breath. Then he scowled at Aimee, unaware that his next words quite spoiled the whole scene for his cousin, who until this point had been regarding him as something of a Galahad.

"Dash it, what were you at, to come in here with that fellow? You've no sense at all, have you? Bird-witted chit!" He ignored the stiffening in Aimee's expression. "Peterson ain't someone you should trust, dash it! Why, the fellow's a born rascal if I ever saw one!"

Aimee's blue eyes took on an angry sparkle. "Nonsense, Charles. How dare you speak so to me! I think it is very high-handed of you when I am sure this is none of your business! I don't have to listen to you, you know!" she added.

The two cousins glared at each other, each feeling shabbily treated by the other.

"What do you mean, you don't have to listen to me?" echoed Charles irately. "Ain't I your only male relative here in town?"

"That doesn't give you the right to tell me what to do!"

"Dashed if it don't! It gives me a share in the responsibility to see that you don't ruin yourself with your own headstrong behavior!"

Aimee stamped her foot. "Well, I do not intend to do that, Charles. You are making a great piece of work over nothing! Do you know what I think?" she threw out. "I think you are jealous!"

Charles snorted. "Of Peterson? Not likely! The fellow's got drooping shoulders. Has to pad his coats to get a decent fit!"

Aimee gaped at him. "Well, of all the things to say!"

Almost to himself, he remarked, "And to think that when I first saw you I thought . . ."

"You thought what?" demanded Aimee.

"Never mind," he told her in a voice of grim warning. "I sent Peterson off with a flea in his ear, and I'll deal the same way with any other fellow who tries to take liberties with you. Dash it, Aimee, what possessed you to let him hold your hand? What if someone other than me had come upon the pair of you?"

150

She would not tell him she had planned it so, that she had meant to stay in the corridor and had not known of the existence of the alcove until they were inside. She would not tell him that he was supposed to be jealous.

"Captain Peterson was merely complimenting me on the shape of my hands," she retorted, not without pride. "I have very nice hands, Charles, though I am sure you have never taken the trouble to notice."

"A likely story," scoffed Charles. "What a flighty chit you are, to fall for such a rubbishy excuse to manhandle you."

"Flighty, am I?" she gasped. "Well, you are starchy, that's what you are. Starchy and priggish! I pity the poor female who becomes your wife, Charles Perth, because she will be bored to death, do you hear me? Bored to death!"

"Well, it dashed well won't be you!" he told her crushingly. "I'd as lief marry a Billingsgate fishwife as a spoiled brat who won't listen to reason!"

"*Ooh!*" said Aimee furiously. "I hate you, Charles!" And gathering her skirts, she rushed past him back down the hallway into the ballroom, leaving her cousin staring after her in fury.

To Diana's relief, Lord Hervey soon arrived to take his usual place at Aunt Serena's side. Thus, by the time Sir Henry Neyle came up to claim Diana for the waltz, Aunt Serena and her elderly crony were deep in conversation, which was all that saved Sir Henry from the dowager's vitriolic tongue.

Unaware of his narrow escape, Sir Henry guided her suavely through the press of people. "How very charming you look this evening, my dear. I see you received my small offering."

Diana glanced down at the fragrant little corsage of

violets pinned to her gown. "Yes, and I thank you for them," she said with a smile. "It was very thoughtful of you to think of sending me flowers."

"I think about you a great deal," he murmured significantly. "Do you care to rest some more, or shall we dance?"

"Really, Sir Henry," she responded, relaxed enough in his company to be able to joke a little, "you cannot seriously believe that hovering over Great-aunt Serena is *restful?* By all means, let us waltz."

Diana by now had the opportunity to dance that most risqué of dances, the waltz, with a variety of gentlemen, and had formed the opinion that Sir Henry Neyle was the most graceful of them all. He was in every way perfect, she reflected. In looks, charm, grace, and address, he was surely every woman's dream. He was tall, his entire form was as exquisitely sculpted as a Greek statue—and he was unmarried. Each time she was with him she had become increasingly aware of the envious looks cast her by other women. How would it feel, she wondered, to be married to such a man as this? That would be turning the tables, wouldn't it? She would be an object of envy, instead of the butt of painful, wicked gossip. It was not the first time this notion had drifted through her thoughts, but it had never before seemed quite so alluring.

"You dance divinely," he complimented her as they turned about the floor. "I have been looking forward to this moment all evening."

"You, Sir Henry, are becoming a sad flatterer," she retorted, trying not to betray how much his words pleased her.

"Only since you came to town, I promise you," he replied, allowing his lips to twitch just enough to take the absurdity out of the statement.

She laughed, as he had planned she should. "I might

have come sooner had I known the reception I would get. You really must stop this, Sir Henry, else my head will be so swollen none of my bonnets will fit." Her eyes twinkled at him. "And since I cannot afford to buy any more for a while, that would place me in a predicament. I would have to stay at home."

Sharing the joke, his lips curved in amusement. "And what a great shame that would be," he agreed, giving her hand a light press. "You win, then, my fetching little widow. I'll pay you no more compliments tonight." Over the top of her head, his eyes moved restlessly. "Lord Hervey seems very devoted to your aunt," he said casually.

Diana nodded. "Oh, yes, I believe he is."

"Too devoted, perhaps," he suggested.

"Why, what can you mean?" Diana shot an involuntary glance at Lord Hervey. "I am sure he does her a great deal of good. She is lonely for those of her own generation."

Sir Henry cleared his throat. "Yes, well, lonely old women with more money than they know what to do with frequently attract . . . devoted admirers."

Diana looked shocked. "Oh, no, Sir Henry, Lord Hervey is not like that. I am persuaded his attachment to my aunt is most sincere."

"Oh? I must bow to your judgment then, for I do not know the man. I have heard, however, that he is none too plump in the pocket. If I were heir—or heiress—to a vast fortune, I would not care to see it usurped by someone else."

Diana hesitated before answering. "I am convinced Lord Hervey is innocent of such villainous motives," she replied, her answer even more direct than he had hoped. "I've no idea where Aunt Serena will leave her fortune, for she is impossible to predict. It will not be to me, at any rate, for I am too often in her black books." She smiled. "Anyway, she will probably outlive us all."

"A pity," he said softly. "Ah, well. You and I, my dear, shall not regard it, shall we?"

"Of course not." She smiled again, wondering at his meaning.

"I'd like to visit you tomorrow, if I may." Suddenly, the pressure of his hand brought them an inch or two closer. "I think you know why."

"T-tomorrow?" She nearly stepped on his foot.

His eyelids seemed to droop as he gazed down at her. "This is not the place for private conversation. As a mature woman, I'm sure you understand me."

Diana's heart leaped in her chest. He was going to make her an offer! Feeling as though the room was too warm, as if she were being suffocated by a situation in which she had no control, she somehow managed to stammer out, "Certainly, Sir Henry. I mean . . . why do you not come at two o'clock? I think I can arrange to see you . . . alone."

The last strains of the music drew to a close and Sir Henry gave her a formal bow. "Until tomorrow," he murmured.

Twelve hours later, Diana paced the floor of her bedchamber, fraught with indecision and self-doubt. Was she out of her mind? Was she really considering accepting Sir Henry's offer? Her hands clenched in nervous anticipation, she tried to review the facts as calmly as possibly. First of all, Sir Henry was, in essence, the physical embodiment of the man of her dreams, and though she was wise enough to realize this was not a reason to marry him, still, it could not help but weigh in his favor. Secondly, she had to admit that life as a widow might eventually become wearisome, even lonely. Not that she did not enjoy Tildy's company, but just lately

154

there was an odd discontent building within her, along with a new yearning, a *need* to take more from life, to feel complete in a way she had never experienced. It was most unsettling.

For some obscure reason, learning of Mrs. Clement had cast a damper over her spirits. Diana was finding it impossible not to dwell upon what her own life might have been like had she chosen to accept Lord Lucan's dishonorable proposal. Not that she would ever have seriously considered becoming the earl's mistress, but still, it did make one pause to consider the negative aspects of being without a husband. A woman alone had a great handicap, for the world she lived in was a man's world, built by and for the convenience of the male sex. At best, a respectable woman coped with rules and conventions designed to limit every aspect of her existence, at worst . . . at worst, she might be forced to compromise her own values—as Mrs. Clement must have done.

Who knew what trials the poor woman had been forced to suffer before she made her fatal decision? No longer horrified, Diana resolved not to pass judgment on Mrs. Clement, but she was also going to make very sure she did not emulate her. Determinedly forcing Mrs. Clement from her mind, she resolved to concentrate on her own problems.

As usual, she was interrupted. "Diana!" called Aimee through the door. "I . . . I'd like to talk to you, if I may."

Diana sighed. She could not very well put Aimee off, for her sister was obviously unhappy, and had been moping about the house all morning. Apparently, she had decided it was time to confide.

"I suppose you've noticed I've been a bit melancholy," floundered Aimee, upon entering. "I could not talk about it before, but I want to tell you that . . . that there is no question of my . . . my marrying Charles."

Her voice quivered as she spoke.

Wrapping an arm around Aimee's drooping shoulders, Diana drew her sister forward to sit upon the bed. "Tell me what happened."

In a forlorn little voice, Aimee related the details of the previous night's quarrel. "And then I told him I hated him, Diana. Of course I do not, but he was being so horrid that I had to say *something*. And now I feel so utterly wretched, I don't know how I shall go on living!"

Hiding her dismay, Diana searched for something positive to say. "Don't cry, dearest. Everything will work out." Since this did not seem to do the trick, she went on, "I'll tell you what I think. I have always thought Cousin Charles would make you an excellent husband, but I also believed the disparity in your ages might be too great. And then, observing him that first night, I had the distinct impression that he was, well, quite bowled over by you. And I began to wonder if I was wrong." At Aimee's involuntary squeak, she held up her hand. "But Charles is a man who believes in propriety, Aimee. He does not want a wife who flirts with every man she meets."

Aimee sniffed tearfully. "He called me a spoiled brat."

Diana sighed. "Well, you are a little spoiled, perhaps, but never a brat. You just need to grow up a bit more. That's why I hoped you would wait another year before coming to London." She patted her sister's hand consolingly. "Cheer up. You may very well have succeeded in making him jealous. From what you tell me, he must have been extremely upset to have reacted as he did."

"That's so, isn't it?" Rubbing her reddened nose, Aimee's piquant features took on a hopeful expression. "I didn't think of that before."

"You look tired. Why don't you rest for a while?"

Aimee rose obediently. "Yes, I think I will. I did not

get much sleep last night." She had almost reached the door when she turned around. "Oh, Diana?"

"Yes?"

"Remember I told you how I wanted to be adored? And how I might try to make some gentleman worship me so I could find out if I liked it?"

Diana nodded.

"Well," said Aimee tremulously, "I decided that wouldn't be very nice. I mean, it seems a rather silly reason to make someone else suffer, doesn't it?"

"Yes, I think it does," returned Diana gravely.

"So I shan't do it," said Aimee, and closed the door quietly behind her.

After some debate, Diana decided not to tell Miss Tilden about Sir Henry's impending visit. It was becoming Miss Tilden's daily habit to rest in her room after luncheon, and it seemed better not to give her news that might disturb her sleep. There was always the chance that her elderly companion might feel it her duty to stay and act as chaperon, which was really quite unnecessary. After all, she had promised Sir Henry that she would receive him alone, and alone she meant to be!

Two o'clock came, and as Sir Henry was ushered into the drawing room, Diana was struck anew by his elegance. The studied disorder of his golden locks became him, as did his coat of dark blue cloth, which fit his upper torso as if it had been sewn together as he stood in it.

In his leisurely fashion, he moved toward her, saying, with an engaging smile, "I am most punctual today, am I not? As we get to know each other better, you will find that I am frequently forgetting my engagements. But this is hardly one I could forget, is it?" He had taken possession of her hand as he spoke, and now raised and pressed it to his lips, rather lingeringly.

157

When he did not release her, Diana began to blush. "Sir Henry," she reproved, "you really must not—!"

He laughed softly, and reached for her other hand. "No, *really*, Diana! Do not tell me you are prudish, for that I refuse to believe. However, at this stage, I admit a show of reluctance is not unpleasant." His lazy eyes explored her face, then dropped to survey the rest of her. "What a beautiful creature you are, my dear," he added appreciatively.

"Sir Henry, you promised me last night you would stop saying these absurd things," she reminded him, very conscious of the warmth of his hands against hers.

In response, he pulled her closer. "My friends call me Harry. Do you think you could call me that?"

"I think," said Diana awkwardly, "that we had better sit down. Would you care for some refreshment?"

With a slight shrug, he set her free. "Very well. To please you, Diana, I am willing to play this hand however you wish. Some brandy would sit very well with me, if you have it."

Afterward, when the drink was in his hand and they were seated together, at his insistence, on the couch, he said, "Forgive me for proceeding with such haste, my dear. It did not occur to me that you would wish it otherwise."

Relieved that he understood, Diana said, "It is not in my nature, Sir—I mean, Henry, to rush into these things."

His eyes gleamed. "You are wiser, perhaps, than I, for I have been wanting this since I first saw you in Jermyn Street a month past."

"Oh?" she said, a little startled.

"But in the interim, I've grown quite fond of you," he explained. "And affection makes an alliance so much more enjoyable, does it not?"

The word *alliance* reassured her, for Diana had begun

158

to feel a trifle uneasy about his meaning. "Oh, yes," she agreed fervently. "Mutual affection is everything. Else I could not consider—" She stopped just short of saying "marriage," for he had not yet said that word, and she feared he might think her overeager. "I am fond of you, also," she said instead.

At this, he moved closer, so that there was scarcely an inch between them. "That pleases me more than you can know," he whispered, instinct warning him to honey his words. "In fact, it makes me quite the happiest man in London, Diana. I want to become the most important person in your life. When we're together, I want it to be the most wonderful event of our lives. Tell me you want that, too, Diana."

This was it, then—her first real offer of marriage. There was no magic, no fireworks, only a curious feeling of detachment, as if she were not a participant in the scene. Yet it was what she had been waiting for, what she had come to the conclusion was best for her in the long run.

"I want that, too," she heard herself say, and tried to force herself to believe it. Of course she *must* believe it. Hadn't she spent most of the morning convincing herself that marriage with Sir Henry Neyle was the best, the most logical course? That there were more reasons to say "yes" than "no"?

His expression turned triumphant. "Marvelous," he breathed, expelling air from his lungs as if he had been holding it inside. Then his right arm was about her shoulders, and he was pulling her against his chest. "Come closer, love, and give me a kiss to seal the bargain," he coaxed, his voice soft and urgent.

It was not an unreasonable request. Mutely, Diana closed her eyes, feeling his lips covering hers, growing more demanding, forcing her mouth open . . . Oh, God, oh God! It felt so much like Edmund kissing her, that,

159

repulsed, Diana's eyes popped open and she struggled to push him away.

"Is something wrong?" inquired Sir Henry, looking quite surprised.

Diana suppressed a shudder. "I . . . I'm sorry. I do not care at all for the taste of brandy," she stumbled, improvising rapidly. "It's nothing to do with you, Sir . . . I mean, Henry . . . *Harry!* Do not be insulted, please. It is merely the taste. I find it quite . . . repugnant."

He sighed slightly, and drew away. "Very few women care for brandy," he agreed. "I should have thought of that. Sorry, love. Next time will be better, I promise." His eyes narrowed thoughtfully, he rose to his feet. "I will give some thought to the arrangements."

As soon as he was gone, Diana flew upstairs and threw herself onto her bed, burying her face in her hands. What was the matter with her? Here was the most handsome, the most elegant man she had ever met in her life, and she was as repelled by his kisses as she had been by Edmund's horrid embraces! What was *wrong* with her? There had to be something wrong with her, something that made her different. Otherwise, how did other women *do* it?

It had been a mistake to consider marriage, she now realized. But, my God, what a scandal it would be if she cried off! He would tell people, it would get about before she could put a stop to it . . . what was she to do? Aunt Serena would kill her if she caused another scandal!

Slowly, Diana sat up and forced herself to think rationally. She could write him a note, explaining that she had changed her mind and could not marry him. Yes of course, Felix could deliver the note within the hour.

Her brow knit anxiously as she searched for flaws to her plan. She did not know where he lived. Had he ever mentioned it? But, no, that was a minor detail. Her footman could easily discover Sir Henry's direction. The important thing was to think of a plausible excuse, for she could not very well tell him the truth. She could not say she found his kisses revolting!

It was then that she heard it. A low, soft moan followed by a feeble thump, as of a foot scraping against wood. It was so out of place it pierced right through Diana's distress, forcing her head to jerk up, cocked at an angle to listen. Had she imagined it?

"Diana . . ." It was the merest whisper of a cry but it was enough to banish Sir Henry completely from her mind. Leaping up, Diana was across the narrow hall in three steps. Her heart in her throat, she flung open her companion's door, and for a bare instant, froze.

Miss Tilden lay crumpled upon the floor like a rag doll thrown by a child.

Chapter Nine

"Tildy!" she gasped. "Oh, my God, what happened?"

Her heart in her throat, Diana rushed forward, going down on her knees beside the elderly little woman. "How long have you been like this? Where are you hurt?"

Miss Tilden's complexion had a gray cast. "My ankle, Diana," she whispered, her face contorted in pain. "My foot . . . I think my foot must have been asleep and I . . . twisted my ankle . . . and fell. . . ."

Diana stared in shock as Miss Tilden went suddenly limp. Tildy had obviously fainted, and as for her ankle, it was probably sprained or broken. Either way, she thought grimly, they would need a physician at once.

Later, the events of that afternoon would blur in her memory and she would hardly recall ringing for Meg or the dreadful minutes that passed while her abigail rushed to find Felix, her footman. What would stay clearly in her mind were Miss Tilden's heartrending groans and the gratitude she felt toward Felix, who lifted Miss Tilden and set her back upon her bed as tenderly as if she were a baby.

Then came the long wait, while her footman set out to track down Dr. Hatfield, Great-aunt Serena's physician. It seemed like forever to Diana, but it actually took Felix little more than an hour to locate the doctor. This highly distinguished member of the medical profession was to be found, not at his home or at the bedside of some other ailing patient, but at a nearby coffeehouse where, his manservant woodenly informed Felix, he had taken his niece to enjoy that popular beverage. Familiar with the establishment to which he was directed, Felix quickly ran his quarry to earth. Why it was that the good doctor's plump arm was wrapped around his niece's waist, or why that young lady was giving her so-called uncle a flirtatious slap on the thigh, Felix neither knew nor cared. What mattered was that the doctor accompany him back to Jermyn Street with dispatch. Bearing this in mind, Diana's stalwart footman did not hesitate to make clear that the injured lady was a Dear Friend of the Dowager Lady Torrington's niece. Whether or not this nudge was necessary he would never know, for Dr. Hatfield surged instantly to his feet, prepared to depart despite the pouting objections of the young lady.

Dr. Hatfield's diagnosis was that Miss Tilden's ankle was only sprained, and that it was a minor miracle she had not broken her hip when she fell. Cook had managed to obtain ice while Felix was gone, but even so, the poor lady's ankle turned blue-black and continued to swell even after the ice was applied.

The doctor left, and such practical tasks as assisting Miss Tilden into her nightdress fell to Diana and Meg, as Aimee could only hover and talk, rather like an anxious butterfly. Shooing her sister away with impatience, Diana stayed by the elderly woman's side until her even breathing assured the young widow that she slept. Tildy had been in obvious pain, and had finally consented to take a spoonful of the laudanum which Dr. Hatfield had prescribed.

To pass the time while she was waiting for Miss Tilden to fall asleep, Diana had mentally composed her note to

Sir Henry, changing it over and over until she was satisfied. Worry and stress were beginning to take their toll on her energy, but as she had eaten little else that day, her appetite was as yet undiminished. Happily, she had also had time to recollect that Sir Henry was much too noble a gentleman to speak to anyone of their engagement before the news was inserted in the papers. Her equanimity thus restored, she descended to the dining room to eat her dinner.

Diana would have been aghast had she known that Sir Henry possessed few of the scruples for which she gave him credit, and was at that very moment preparing to brag of his victory to the one person his boasting would most enrage. He was a member of several men's clubs, but on this particular evening he had decided to drop in at White's, which he knew to be a favorite haunt of the Earl of Lucan's.

The earl was sitting in a large wing chair reading a newspaper when Sir Henry strolled languidly into the room.

"Why, hullo, Geoff, old boy," he said in his mocking way. "Mind if I join you? One's own company can get devilish boring after a while."

The earl lowered his paper, his gaze aloof. "Can it?" he said. Perceiving the other man's smug expression, he cast it aside altogether, adding with an air of resignation, "So what have you been at, Harry? You look as pleased with yourself as a cat in a pot of cream."

"Do I?" responded the baronet, pulling over the nearest chair. "Well, I've good reason to, old boy." He paused, searching the earl's impassive face. "I've beaten you, Geoff," he announced, a flash of exultation seeping into his voice. "I've vanquished the citadel." His long fingers toyed restlessly with his quizzing glass and the fobs which hung from his waist.

Lord Lucan betrayed no visible sign of alarm. "And which citadel is that?" he inquired, sardonically indifferent. "Your interests jump about so, Harry, I cannot keep them straight."

A smirk crawled over Sir Henry's face. "I speak of the beauteous Diana, of course. She whose face and figure we have both been coveting—for our disparate purposes. I thought you'd like to know who won."

His steel gray eyes pinned to the other man's face, the earl said, very levelly, "You had better explain what you mean by that, Harry. Exactly."

Enjoying himself, Sir Henry withdrew his snuffbox from his pocket. "Why, I intend to," he replied, "but first . . ." Prolonging his moment of triumph, he took a generous pinch of snuff and placed it on the back of his right hand. Lifting it close to one beautiful nostril, he said, "I paid a visit on our fair widow today," and inhaled deeply.

"And?" prompted the earl, his displeasure thinly veiled.

Sir Henry's mouth drew up in distaste. "Have you tried this mixture? It's the same sort Alvanley's been using, but I'm not sure I like it."

"Stop trifling with me, Harry, and get to the point."

With a careless shrug, Sir Henry snapped shut the hinged top of the snuffbox. "It's quite simple, old boy. You aspired to be the lady's husband, while I, on the other hand, cherished the desire to enjoy her favors outside the confining bonds of matrimony. And she has selected me."

If Sir Henry was expecting a violent reaction, he was doomed to disappointment. The earl's thick black brows drew sharply together, but he said only, "Gammon, Harry. You must be cast-away if you believe that—or if you think I'll believe it."

For an instant, irritation flickered in the baronet's eyes. "You think so?" His short laugh held a jeering note. "Well, you are free to believe what you will. However, not four hours ago, the incomparable Diana granted me an interview—alone—wherein I made my intentions plain. The fact is, old boy, that Diana has most charmingly consented to become my mistress. Sweet as nectar she was, when I kissed her," he taunted.

The earl was unprepared for the sharp, sickening pain which pierced his chest. "Harry," he said, after the briefest of pauses, "you are either foxed or lying." Somehow he spoke normally, controlling his urge to knock the other man senseless.

Sir Henry rose to his feet, all traces of good humor evaporating. "You may go and ask the lady if you like," he retorted angrily. "And then you may come back and offer your apology. I do not care to be called a liar."

The earl stood, too, and his voice was curt. "If you aren't lying, then you must have misunderstood her—or she you! Devil take the woman! Ten to one she thought you meant marriage! She is not the woman to accept a carte blanche from anyone, least of all you, my fine buck."

Sir Henry stared at him in consternation. "That's pitching it too strong," he objected, his lips twisted in a sneer. "I tell you I never once said the word *marriage!* No woman her age could be so naive!"

Lord Lucan's expression froze the other man's blood. "This woman could," he said icily. "And if you breathe so much as a syllable of this to anyone, Harry, and I mean *anyone*, I'll break every bone in your body, do you hear me?"

Sir Henry retreated by two steps, knowing the earl was well equipped to carry out his threat. "You go see her," he muttered. "You'll see I'm right."

"I intend to," returned the earl grimly. "Right now."

* * *

After a quiet dinner with Aimee, Diana excused herself and made her way down to the study. She had meant to write the note to Sir Henry immediately, but overwhelmed with fatigue, she simply sank into the desk chair and buried her face in her hands. This constant round of late nights was debilitating, for a lifetime habit of early rising made it difficult to make up her sleep in the morning. And then, of course, last night she had lain awake for hours thinking of Sir Henry.

Diana rubbed at her temples, reflecting upon the number of mistakes she had made in her life. Perhaps remaining so long in Wiltshire had been yet another mistake, for if her existence there had been pleasant, it had also been dull. Here in London, life was not always as pleasant or as insular, but at long last she was beginning to feel really *alive*, to feel like a living, breathing woman who was more than just a hollow shell, void of all emotion. It stimulated her, this new life. There were problems to be faced and dealt with, decisions to be made, the responsibility of managing a household and servants and Aimee; in short, a more normal life for a healthy young woman of four-and-twenty years. And yet, wasn't there even more than this? Was not the most normal life of all that of wife and mother?

A wave of depression slammed her with this thought, drenching her with its implications. As much as she disliked the more intimate aspects of marriage, she was well aware that without the act of love, she would never hold a child of her own in her arms. Could this be part of what she had been longing for of late? And if so, would crying off from her engagement with Sir Henry be still another terrible mistake?

In the frustration of indecision, Diana's fingers dragged through her hair, loosening its fastenings so that the thick golden mass fell about her shoulders. Absently, she reached to remove the remainder of the pins, shaking her head so that her tresses tumbled to their full length just short of her waist. What *was* it she truly longed for, she wondered, her fingers mechanically arranging the pins into a neat pile on the desk. Was it possible to know? Oh, why was it all so complicated?

Absorbed in introspection, Diana did not pay immediate heed to the commotion at the front door or hear the low voice of the earl demanding her whereabouts. It was not until his steady footsteps sounded in the hall outside the study that her head snapped up and her senses spiraled into alertness.

Framed in the doorway, the earl's expression was nearly as black as his hair. "Ah, here you are," he said, with a silky sort of brusqueness to his tone that she had never heard. "I want to have a word with you, if I may." Diana looked at him in astonishment. "Oh? And what right do you have to barge into my home without so much as a by-your-leave?"

Favoring her with another dark look, he stepped inside, shutting the door firmly behind him. "The right of someone who has your best interests at heart," he shot back. In three strides he was across the room and leaning over the narrow desk, his face thrust near hers. "I just spoke to Sir Henry Neyle a while ago," he informed her, his chilly gray eyes boring into hers.

"Oh, really!" Resenting his air of interrogation, Diana drew back indignantly, her chair bumping the wall. "And that should interest me, I suppose?"

"It should," the earl answered, keeping a tight rein on his temper. Straightening to his full height, he began to circle the desk. "I would have thought you'd want to take better care of your reputation," he said suavely, narrowing the gap between them with a purposeful step.

She leaped to her feet. "I have not the least notion what you mean," she retorted, backing away with a wary look. "Have you perchance been drinking?"

168

Shoving the chair aside, the earl took another step. "Believe me, I considered doing just that," he told her, a hard line to his mouth. "Instead, I came to tell you not to be a little fool. What in Satan's name goes on in that beautiful head of yours, Diana? Is your infatuation with Harry Neyle so strong you are willing to ruin yourself?"

Unable to fathom his meaning, Diana glowered up at him. "I don't know what you're talking about! How *dare* you speak to me like this? You are the most disagreeable, overbearing man I ever—"

His fist crashed down so hard upon the desk that the hairpins scattered. "Shut up, Diana, and listen to me," he thundered. "Are you aware that you accepted a carte blanche this afternoon?"

"*What?*" she gasped, her jaw dropping. "A c-carte blanche? I did no such thing! How dare you make such a . . . a *vile* accusation!" Something in his silence rocked her confidence, but she added, in dignified tones, "Not that it is any business of yours, but Sir Henry did me the honor to ask me to be his wife this afternoon, and I—"

"Damnation!" The harshly uttered word was enough to end her protest. "I thought it might be something like this. My foolish and very naive little widow, don't you recognize an improper proposal when you receive one?" Reaching out, he captured her hands in his, and drew her closer to trap them against his chest. "I just finished listening to Harry brag of his triumph and it was enough to turn my stomach. Good God, Diana, the man has been looking upon you as fair game ever since you arrived!"

Slowly, the color drained from Diana's face. "But . . . but he *asked* me . . ." she insisted, with desperate obstinacy. "You must be wrong."

"What exactly did he say?"

Her eyes fluttered shut in an effort to remember. "He spoke of an alliance between us. We talked of the importance of mutual affection . . ."

Sensing her bewilderments, the earl tried to be gentle. "Did he ever say the word *marriage?*"

Diana's eyes flew open, bewilderments in their brown-gold depths. "Not . . . not precisely."

He sighed. "Then I beg you will forgive my sharpness, Diana. There existed that slight chance that you actually understood. . . . It made me furious to think you might have knowingly accepted him. There are other kinds of alliances beside those bound by sacred vows, my poor innocent."

Despite the kindness of his tone, Diana's humiliation was crushing. "Naturally, I know that," she flared, snatching her hands away from his. "It simply never occurred to me that Sir Henry would . . . oh, I could *murder* him!" Her bosom heaved, and a familiar lump of misery burgeoned in her throat. How she hated being made to look the fool!

"Even so," she cried suddenly, "I don't know why you should be so vexed when you tried to offer me the same!"

If she had slapped him in the face, the earl could not have been more dumbfounded. *"I beg your pardon?"* he said incredulously.

Diana eyed him uneasily. "You meant to offer me a . . . a carte blanche, did you not? Before I stopped you, that is?"

In an odd tone, Lord Lucan repeated, "You thought I was asking you to be my *mistress?*"

"Are you . . . are you saying you were not?" she faltered, a curious weakness creeping into her knees.

"Hell's teeth, no!" he exploded, so loudly that she jumped. "I was *trying* to make an honorable offer, dammit! But you could not consider anything of a warmer nature—or at least that was the excuse you gave!" His eyes glinting with fury, he muttered, "Tried, sentenced and condemned, by God, for a crime I didn't commit! For the love of heaven, Diana, I could wring your pretty neck!"

Stunned to the core, Diana gazed up at him with stricken eyes. "I'm sorry, my lord . . . Geoffrey . . . what can I say? You gave me no reason to suppose . . . I mean, I simply assumed—"

"Well, you assumed wrong!" he snapped. "And I gave you *every* reason to suppose! I told you right from the start that I regarded you as a virtuous woman, but you just took it into that obstinate head that I was a womanizing scoundrel, despite anything I said or did!"

"Well, I had evidence!" she flashed, hurt by his derision. "Why, that very first day you threw me a kiss! If that is not a sure sign of a . . . a . . ."

"Profligate?" he suggested sarcastically.

"It is not," she returned with a glare, "the usual behavior of a gentleman."

Controlling his rage, the earl forced himself to alter his tone. "Perhaps not," he conceded. "I told you before, Diana, I don't live my life by other people's rules."

"You are fortunate! Being a peer—and a wealthy one, at that—you can afford to flout convention!"

"Yes, to a degree I can," he agreed. "And you could, too, if you married me. Rich countesses can set their own rules."

"Like Lady Uxbridge?" she said, without thinking.

"What the devil has she got to do with this?"

"Oh, nothing! I just thought perhaps . . ." Diana broke off, biting her lip.

"Thought *what?*"

"I wondered if you and she had been . . . close. And Mrs. Clement, too. It has not escaped my notice, my lord, that the ladies seem to find you vastly entertaining." Somehow, she could not keep the accusing note from her voice.

He stared, then disconcerted her by looking genuinely amused. "Well, I suppose it's a good sign that you noticed," he said, reaching once more for her hands. "No, Diana, I have never found Lady Uxbridge even

171

remotely appealing. And Cynthia Clement is no more than a friend."

Diana knew she was blushing. "I . . . I see. Then, I am sorry, my lord. I have misjudged you all along and you did not deserve it."

"No, by God, I didn't!" he said feelingly.

With lowered eyes, she added, "You must find me very stupid. I . . . my experience with men is not very great, I fear. It is my only excuse."

Before she realized what he intended, his arms had gone around her waist, encircling her loosely. His mouth was inches from her ear. "You're not stupid, Diana," he said softly. "Never think that about yourself, my darling. You're just woefully green." After another moment, he said, "Are you going to marry me?"

"I don't know," she whispered in confusion. "I'm just so tired, too tired to think sensibly." She did not add that his nearness was making it virtually impossible to think at all.

She was having the same effect on him. "Do you have any idea how beautiful you look?" There was a warm, seductive quality to his voice, a husky resonance which told of an unspoken need. "With your hair flowing down your back like a . . . like a river of golden honey?" His quickened breathing warned her what was coming next.

"Please." It was so faint a protest it deserved to be ignored.

"Please what? Don't try to tell me not to kiss you, Diana. You know it's too late for that."

Despite these words, for the space of several seconds he gave her a chance to deny him. Then his mouth slowly lowered to cover hers, exploring the sweet softness of her lips with his own. Wisely, he concentrated on making it a gentle kiss, curbing his ardor in the hope that restraint would find its own reward.

Too weary to fight him, too full of the knowledge of her

own blunders and stupid prejudices, Diana stood meekly in the earl's arms. Men needed this sort of thing, she told herself with a sort of muddled logic. And after misjudging him so dreadfully, perhaps she owed him this? At least this once? If she could only bear it, if she could only conceal her distaste, then perhaps she would stop feeling so horribly guilty and foolish and confused.

How many seconds did it take for her to realize that there was no distaste to conceal, no disgust to bear? Edmund's kiss had always made her flesh creep, Sir Henry's had made her ill, but Geoffrey Trevelyan's kiss was actually . . . why, it was actually pleasant! Marveling at the firm tenderness of his mouth, Diana parted her lips, daring to experiment with something she had feared she would always loathe.

Encouraged, the earl's arms tightened, crushing her against his body so she would know how much she aroused him. With less caution, his hands slid down the length of her back, caressing her warm body through the thin fabric of her gown. It was when he reached the curve of her hip that Diana experienced the first real stab of desire she had ever known.

Merciful heaven, what is happening? Diana's eyes had been closed, but now they burst open, full of unbound panic. She would never quite remember how she managed to tear her mouth from his, but suddenly they were apart, each of them panting and violently unhappy.

"No more . . . no more, please!" Surrendering to her own cowardly fear of the unknown, Diana choked the words out as if they were her last, her voice raw with pent-up emotion.

"What is it, Diana? What's wrong?" Though he said it very carefully, the earl's frustration was more than evident.

"I'm not . . . I'm just not ready for this." How lame and clumsy the words sounded, even in her own ears.

173

"Please forgive me," she whispered.

"Did you love Harry, then?" he asked flatly. "Is that what this is all about?"

Turning the question over in her mind, Diana was amazed by her own answer. "No, I didn't love him at all." Her eyes reached out to him imploringly. "But please try to understand. This afternoon I thought I was affianced to him and now you tell me I'm not. It's a bit of a shock, you know. And now, too, I must correct this odious situation before there is a scandal. Not to mention that poor Tildy sprained her ankle this afternoon, which really was dreadfully upsetting." Her hand swept across her brow. "And I am tired. My head is spinning with problems right now, and . . . and I can deal with no more."

"I see." The earl's face was inscrutable. "I am sorry to hear of Miss Tilden's accident." He hesitated. "And my offer of marriage? Will you consider it?"

It took Diana several seconds to form a reply. "My first marriage was terribly unhappy . . . I daresay you have guessed as much." Her voice was so low he had to bend his head to hear. "When I came to London, I believed I could never marry again. I'm still not sure I can. It seems like such a great risk to take—"

"Much of life is a risk," he interrupted.

She nodded wearily. "Oh, yes. But there are other considerations which . . . which I cannot explain. All I can say is that I would need time to think it over."

"You were willing enough to risk it for Harry," he pointed out in a dry tone.

"Yes, well, I have not told you the whole," she said awkwardly. "I know it sounds terribly capricious of me, but I was intending to cry off. After he left this afternoon, I realized I could not go through with it for . . . for various reasons."

The confession reheated the ashes of the earl's

174

patience. "Then it would obviously be unfeeling of me to press you for an answer this night," he responded. "If you will but agree to consider my offer, then I will be content."

She hesitated. "Yes, my lord, I can agree to consider your offer, but I cannot promise—"

"Of course you cannot," he said quickly. "I simply ask that you think it over. Later, when you are not so tired and overset."

Diana could do nothing but agree, for after wronging him so dreadfully, there could be no disputing that she owed him a fair, well-considered answer. Before taking his leave, Lord Lucan made Diana promise to take no action regarding Sir Henry, assuring her that he would deal with the baronet himself. Again, she was too tired to argue when he made it sound so logical. And from the hard look in his eye, there could be no question but that the Earl of Lucan was perfectly capable of dealing with any trouble Sir Henry Neyle might choose to cause.

Notwithstanding that it was the first night in nearly a week that Diana slept late, the moment she awoke, the flood of memories brought her to instant alertness. Recalling how she had nearly stepped headlong into the very kind of scandal she wished to avoid, Diana wondered how she was ever to trust her own instincts again. What could have fooled her into thinking Sir Henry so safe? Could it have been because he had never really touched her emotions at all?

Lord Lucan had called it an infatuation. That might have been true when she was eighteen, but this time around, she doubted it had been even that. To be strictly honest, had it ever been more than the simple wish to be the envy of those who had hurt her with their gossip? Or had she needed to prove to herself that, in her new maturity, she could succeed where before she had failed? Perhaps she had even had a subconscious desire to turn back time, to start from where she had left off before the night of Edmund's attack. With a regretful sigh, Diana came to the lowering conclusion that whatever the reason, she had behaved like a complete ninnyhammer.

But how could she have been so blind about Lord Lucan? Since the first day she had driven out with him, Diana had recognized his attractiveness, but that had only made him seem more dangerous. Until now. Now she no longer found him at all threatening. Odd, how easily she was able to summon his image when already Sir Henry's angelic countenance was faded and blurred. With new honesty, Diana acknowledged that the earl was a far more attractive, dynamic, *exciting* man than Sir Henry.

What was it that Aunt Serena said? *Sir Henry was as pretty as a girl,* that was it. Viewing them through new eyes, Diana was inclined to agree. The earl possessed an indefinable air of masculinity, a presence that outweighed and would probably outlast Sir Henry's fairness of face. Lord Lucan's features did not look like they had been chiseled from marble, but rather as though they were hewn from granite—as strong and firm as his touch. Such thoughts brought back memories of his kiss, and of the powerful sensations which had seemed to originate in the nether regions of her body.

Unfortunately, however, the sensations were now gone and therefore could not be subjected to reexamination. Had it actually been pleasure she felt? Or had it merely been part of her panic? Replaying the scene in her mind, Diana did not realize that the inner mirror in which she now saw the event was growing more and more distorted. Had she really felt anything at all? Perhaps she had only *wanted* to feel something so badly that her body had fooled her! Was that possible?

Engulfed in self-doubt, Diana forced the matter from her mind, and consequently remembered Miss Tilden and her injury. Honestly! Here she was lounging in bed, when Tildy should have been her first and primary concern. Meg had stayed with her during the night, of course, but still! Hastily snatching up her dressing gown, Diana was in the process of disentangling its sleeves when she crossed the threshold of her companion's room.

She found, however, that all had gone well in her absence. Assisted by Meg, Miss Tilden had already finished most of her breakfast and was halfway through her morning chocolate. Aimee was there, too, and had been entertaining Miss Tilden with an edited version of her London triumphs.

Tildy insisted that she was feeling better. "I daresay I shall be up and about in a trice!" she remarked. "The important thing is that I can still knit, for I have several more skeins of yarn to use up."

However, Diana's keen eyes took in the elderly woman's pallor. "Well, that may be, my dear Tildy, but today you must stay in bed. And I intend to remain home today to take care of you."

"Oh, but you will miss your outing!" objected Tildy in dismay.

With a start, Diana realized she had forgotten all about their plans for the day. "Ah, but you forget," she soothed, "I have seen Madame Tussaud's wax figures before. It is not so great a treat for me as you may imagine."

"Charles has been there several times," inserted Aimee with a nod. "He says that after you've seen them once, the whole thing becomes devilish flat . . . *sadly* flat, I mean," she corrected, with a quick glance at Miss Tilden. "But I still want to see for myself. I wrote him a note this morning to remind him, just in case he forgot our outing or . . . or changed his mind. It was a very polite, genteel sort of note, Diana, just to show that I have forgiven him."

"Forgiven him for what?" inquired Miss Tilden, stifling a yawn.

"Oh, he and I have been at loggerheads on one or two occasions," replied Aimee, rather airily. "But all that is going to change! Today, he is going to see me at my very best. I shall become the model of propriety and decorum he wishes. My eyes will stay modestly cast upon the ground, my remarks limited to the most circumspect observations. I shall shriek in horror at the gruesome displays of the victims from the French Revolution. I will clutch at his sleeve to show him that my sensibilities are simply too overset by it all. I have it all worked out perfectly!"

"That sounds a bit extreme," said Diana dryly.

Aimee shrugged. "Perhaps. But that is how a good many of these London girls behave, after all. And some of them are already betrothed! I have been watching them, you see, and although it seems nonsensical to me, it does seem to be what the gentlemen like."

"The best thing you could do is behave like the nice, normal girl you are," advised Diana tartly, "and forget all this play-acting! How is Charles to learn to care for you if you persist in changing personalities? Just be yourself, Aimee," she pleaded.

Aimee regarded her dubiously. "It may come to that in the end," she said with a sigh. "But I find it hard to believe that the real me could interest Cousin Charles."

"Fiddle!" Diana was about to turn to Miss Tilden for support when she saw Meg put a finger to her lips.

"She's gone off to sleep," explained the abigail softly. "I gave her another dose of laudanum with her food, for her ankle's painin' her some, though she won't admit it."

"Good," approved Diana, as they tiptoed from the

178

room. "Sleep is the best thing for her right now."

"I expect she'll sleep for most of the day, ma'am," offered Meg. "I don't mind sitting with her, if you'd rather go."

Diana glanced at Aimee. "I'd really prefer to stay here, if you think you will be all right. I've already told Tildy I'd be here, and besides, I need a chance to rest and . . . think."

"Don't worry about me," said Aimee with a sunny smile. "I shall be on my best behavior. Nothing can possibly go wrong."

Charles scanned Aimee's note three times before he made up his mind. Was she truly no longer angry? Or was this some childish trick?

He had been in a quandary about the outing, not knowing whether she would still be expecting to go. He had been furious the previous evening—even to the point of tossing off a few brandies before he went to sleep—but this morning, depression had replaced all the anger. Though she was not strictly beautiful, he considered his cousin Aimee the most engaging girl he had ever met. If only she were not so dashed unconformable! The woman of his dreams had always been lovely, circumspect, gentle . . . and, of course, devoted to no one but himself! She was not a wild, impulsive, flighty romp of a girl who flirted with other men. Oh, the deuce! Ruffling his hair, he wondered what he should do.

Should he court his cousin? He was reasonably sure it would please Aunt Serena, but for once, he did not give a damn whether it did or not. He tried to envision himself married to Aimee, and suddenly began to chuckle. It would not be the peaceful union for which he longed, that much was certain!

He glanced again at her note. She would be waiting, it informed him. Moreover, she had apologized very prettily for her indiscreet behavior, and assured him that he would have no further cause to be ashamed of her. Ashamed? Had he been ashamed of his cousin?

No, by Jove, he hadn't! The emotions which assailed him were nothing to do with shame. It had been jealousy, pure and simple . . . and hurt, too, when it came right down to it. Hurt that Captain Peterson's attractions had been able to lure her away from him so easily. He'd thought she'd been delighted at the opportunity to sit out the set with him. And then she had been gone!

Charles scratched at his head in uncertainty. Females, he reflected, did tend to do unaccountable things, so how could he expect little Aimee to be any different? Ah well. With any luck, today's outing would help him make this extremely difficult decision.

Chapter Ten

After flitting around the drawing room for a number of minutes, Aimee forced herself to sit, resisting the urge to fly to the window each time the rumble of carriage wheels reached her ears. She was wearing a new and very flattering gown of ice blue, but it was not doing as much to bolster her confidence as she'd hoped. Despite her brave words to Diana, she was feeling very nervous about seeing Charles, as evidenced by the restless fluttering of her hands and the strange churning in her stomach. She knew she had treated her cousin badly, and was firmly resolved to make it up to him. But would Charles forgive her? Had the apology in her note been enough? Would he come? If *only* he would come, Aimee prayed silently, she would be as meek and biddable as he wished.

For what seemed like the hundredth time, she glanced at the clock upon the mantelshelf. He was clearly going to be late, she thought. The only alternative brought back her nervousness; her stomach tightened into knots and her imagination leaped into action. He was not going to come. He had read her note, but instead of forgiving her, he had crumpled it, tossing it over his shoulder with a contemptuous curl to his lip.

Filled with foreboding, Aimee began to envision the

subsequent scene. She would go away forever, and only then would Charles realize that the only woman he could ever love had vanished from his life. She would waste away to an early death and when it was too late he would come (haunted with regret) to lay roses (preferably red ones) on her grave. Of course he would soon die of a broken heart and someone—perhaps Diana—would suggest that they be buried together. . . .

So affected was Aimee by this melancholy scene that huge tears welled in her blue eyes. She groped for her handkerchief, and sobbed into it with an abandon which would have been the envy of many an actress. The storm was of short duration, however, for an instant later, her cousin's familiar footsteps sounded on the stairs. With a muffled gasp, she dabbed frantically at one eye and then the other, blew her little nose and stuffed the sodden handkerchief under the cushion of the chair. By the time Charles entered the room, Aimee had managed to snatch up a book from a nearby table, reclaim her chair, and have the book open in her lap.

If her greeting held only a fraction of its usual vivacity, Charles gave no sign that he noticed. She gazed at him in trepidation, but to her astonishment, instead of hurling aspersions or indeed, displaying any sign of ill humor, he caught up her hands in a light squeeze, something he had never done before.

His first words surprised her even more. "You're looking as fine as fivepence this morning," he said, clearing his throat. As it happened, he had rehearsed this remark very carefully on the way over, but as Aimee's reddened nose and woebegone expression could hardly escape his attention, he abandoned the rest of his speech and said instead, a shade awkwardly, "I say, you haven't been crying, have you? Are you not feeling quite the thing?"

"No, no, I am perfectly well," she responded, then

blurted out, "Oh, I am so glad you came! I was afraid you might have . . . forgotten or even that you might still be . . . be angry about last night."

Charles's mouth curved in a lopsided smile. "Who me? No, no, I ain't one to stew for days, the way some do. Don't fret about it, kitten. I've forgotten it already." He hesitated, his expression turning doubtful. "But are you sure *you* ain't still miffed? I was dashed hard on you, I know. I can't think what made me say such brutish things."

His admission made her feel doubly ashamed. "No, you were quite justified, Charles," she protested. "It was my fault entirely. I ought to have known better than to allow Captain Peterson to . . . to . . ."

"Well, it won't happen again." he said gruffly. "You'll know better next time."

"I hope so." Deciding that this was as good a time as any to seem submissive, Aimee hung her head and said, "I *know* that as my only male relative here in town, I really must let you advise me. Being a mere female, I simply do not have the least notion how to go on. If only I were a man!" she sighed, raising ingenuous eyes to his.

This was doing it much too brown, and Charles gave her a suspicious look. Wondering if she could possibly be in earnest, he retorted, "Now, Aimee, there ain't nothing wrong with being a female. Why, it's a dashed fine thing to be! I mean, where would we all be without females? Nowhere, that's where!"

Aimee's nose wrinkled in perplexity. "Nowhere? Oh, you mean because we can make babies?"

"Well, I suppose that's what I meant," he answered, looking disconcerted. "Dash it, how did we get on to this? We'd better go!" he said, taking her by the arm.

Babies, however, had always been of great interest to Aimee. "But Charles," she argued, as he propelled her toward the door, "we cannot make babies on our own,

183

you know. Men are as—"

"Now, Aimee!" cut in her cousin hastily. "This really ain't the time to discuss this!"

She eyed him anxiously. "Oh, very well. I did not mean to make you angry."

"I'm not angry!" he insisted, sounding exasperated.

"Then why are you raising your voice? I'm not deaf!"

Charles strove to remain calm. "It's just that it ain't the kind of thing you ought to discuss with a man," he explained. "Delicate subject, and all that."

Aimee looked quite shocked. "Well, I know that! I wouldn't dream of talking of such things with anyone but you, Charles. But, you *are* my cousin, after all." She gave him a trusting smile, and tucked her hand under his arm. "You are different from all the other gentlemen . . . so much *nicer*—though you do lecture a shade too much! But I *do* feel safe with you, and I did *not* with Captain Peterson. In fact, I did not like him at all," she confided, "and I was *so* relieved when you rescued me! I could not help thinking you were just like Lochinvar!"

"Who?" said Charles blankly.

"Goodness, haven't you read *Marmion* yet? Lochinvar is a gallant knight who rescues fair Ellen from her dastardly bridegroom. You really must read it, Charles, it is so romantic! He rides all alone, and never stops, not even to eat! He just rides and rides—until he reaches a river that no one can ford, and then he swims across—"

"Sounds like a dashed noodlebrain to me," put in Charles with only mild interest. "Why didn't he just offer for her himself? Seems a lot more logical."

"Oh, but he did!" she explained. "But her father refused to consider his suit. So he stole her away, right in the middle of a ball!"

Charles's face was eloquent of skepticism. "Sounds like the poor fellow was touched in the upper works!" he declared. "Anyway, you're talking a pack of nonsense, Aimee! *I* didn't steal you from any bridegroom. Wouldn't

184

do that," he added, thinking it over. "Bad *ton!*"

"If you say so, Charles," said Aimee in disappointment.

"We'd better go," said her pragmatic cousin, whose definition of romance did not include having to swim rivers or do without his dinner. "My coachman don't like me to keep the horses waiting."

All the way to Madame Tussaud's, Aimee behaved with a flawless decorum which her cousin found unconvincing but restful. Madame Tussaud was soon to leave Blackheath to resume her tour of the country, and the newspapers had urged anyone who had not yet viewed her famous wax figures to do so before it was too late. Charles, no great admirer of wax figures, had nonetheless offered himself as escort when he'd discovered that Aimee wished to go.

"I can't say I'm wild about seeing 'em again," he remarked, giving her a hand out of the carriage. "But I don't mind it if it pleases you. As long as you don't take it into your head to drag me to the British museum!" he added, somewhat obscurely.

Within, there was a surprising crush of people, for the recent announcement—coming as it had at the onset of the Season—had brought out the curious in droves. Glancing around at some of the other visitors, Aimee grew stiff with annoyance. A little ahead, and not five feet to their right was that odious girl who had danced twice with Charles at *her* come-out ball!

Drusilla Low was clinging to the arm of a gentleman named Mr. Peacham. As it happened, Mr. Peacham was one of Aimee's most ardent admirers, and between this and the fact that Drusilla Low had obviously—as Aimee privately phrased it—*set her cap* for Charles, there would be little chance, she was sure, of avoiding them. Nevertheless, she attempted to point Charles in the opposite direction.

"Dash it, Aimee, don't push," objected Charles.

"You're going the wrong way."

"Oh," she replied, gritting her teeth as Charles steered the exact course she wished to avoid.

Naturally, since Mr. Peacham was extremely tall, his somewhat protuberant brown eyes noticed them at once. "Why, if it isn't Miss Farington!" he cried in delight. "Of all the wonderful coincidences!"

To Aimee's chagrin, they became a foursome within minutes. She was unsure just how this came to pass, but blamed it entirely on Miss Low, who was—as the seething Miss Farington later told her sister—nothing but a cunning little jade when it came down to it. (For what other reason could Miss Low have had for addressing the majority of her remarks to Cousin Charles, as if Mr. Peacham and herself were but two more of Madame Tussaud's wax figures?)

She would have enjoyed herself so much more had she been able to have Charles to herself, Aimee thought bitterly. Of course, it would have been the simplest thing to make them feel unwelcome, but Aimee's breeding forbade such a course. A proper young lady would allow no vestige of her resentment to show, she reflected with resignation. And was she not determined to show Charles that she was not a spoiled brat? Well, she would prove it! With this in mind, Aimee pinned a rather fixed smile to her lips and directed it at the other couple.

Actually, Miss Low was not as plain as Aimee previously thought. Her aura of plainness arose from her sallow complexion and the unfortunate fact that none of the pastel colors she favored suited her in the least. However, her features were regular and her eyes a fine shade of blue. She had a pretty laugh, but used it too frequently, as if everything either gentleman said was uncommonly amusing. She also had the unfortunate habit of appending any of Aimee's remarks with her own, which very soon began to take its toll upon Miss Farington's nerves.

When Aimee, regarding the figure of the great Horatio Nelson, remarked to Charles, "He is so lifelike!" Miss Low chimed in with, "Oh, yes, indeed! He looks as if he could step right off the pedestal, does he not, Mr. Perth?"

When they paused to examine the wise, benevolent features of Benjamin Franklin, Aimee said, "I wonder what it is like to live in America?" Miss Low immediately tacked on, "I have always felt it would be the most fascinating place to visit, don't you agree, Mr. Perth?"

At this, Aimee put up her chin and said, "I daresay it must be shockingly primitive there! What do you think, Charles?"

But Miss Low jumped in with, "Oh, yes! I should be far too frightened to go! A woman is better off remaining in the country in which she was born, don't you agree, Mr. Perth?"

"But I should very much like to meet an Indian!" said Aimee defiantly. "Wouldn't you, Charles?"

Miss Low shivered, and for the first time advanced her own opinion. "I am very sure Indians are quite horrible," she stated, but spoiled it all by adding, "Don't you agree, Mr. Perth?"

At this point, Mr. Peacham, who was obviously a proponent of accuracy, enthusiastically inserted, "Actually, in places like Philadelphia and Boston, I believe there is no danger at all. I am told that these towns are considerably less provincial than we English believe, and that no Indians reside anywhere near them."

No doubt Miss Low would have renewed her protestations in America's favor had not Charles suggested they move on, as there was a group of people pressing them from behind. Even as he spoke, he caught the eye of a large fat woman who was glaring at them.

"Oh, yes, *do* let us move on," urged Miss Low in agreement.

A short while later, as they paused before the figure of Voltaire, Charles put up his quizzing glass, ostensibly to better examine the great man's erudite features. Miss Low sighed, and expressed the wish that she were better acquainted with his work.

"Common sense is not so common," quoted Aimee in a sedate voice.

Miss Low's eyes narrowed suspiciously, Mr. Peacham looked impressed, and Charles said, "Eh?" in rather a startled voice.

Aimee tipped her head toward Voltaire. "He said it," she explained, looking pleased with herself. She was not about to tell them it was her father's favorite remark. Let them think she read Voltaire!

Miss Low made a quick recovery. "Why, how clever you are, Miss Farington!" she affirmed, with a warm smile for Charles. "Of all things, I do so admire an educated female do not you, Mr. Perth?"

Aimee's sharp eye saw Charles's lip quiver, but he said only, "Oh, aye!" in a tone of such cordiality that she stared at him. He was actually enjoying himself! she realized incredulously. How *could* he, when she was feeling so utterly miserable? Could he actually be flattered by Miss Low's fawning effusions?

It only grew worse. Charles began to make jocular observations about each of the figures, to which Miss Low would say, "Oh, Mr. Perth! You are so droll!" until Aimee longed to box both their ears. Mr. Peacham seemed oblivious, and continued favoring them all with more historical tidbits, to which, out of common civility, Aimee was forced to respond, "How interesting!" or "Indeed!" because Miss Low had ceased to pay him any heed at all.

Quite suddenly the room was too crowded, too warm. "Charles, does it not seem rather warm in here?" she murmured, staring fixedly at the waxy face of a young Queen Elizabeth. "There are too many people in here. It makes it difficult to breathe properly."

"It *is* warm," concurred Miss Low at once. "Perhaps you should sit down, Miss Farington. I would be happy to stay with you," she offered with sugary solicitude.

Charles frowned. "Are you all right?" he inquired, glancing down at her in concern.

"I—I think so. I do not want to sit down," replied Aimee irritably. "I want to see the rest of the exhibit!"

"Quite natural," agreed Mr. Peacham, bobbing his head. "It would be a severe disappointment to miss anything."

To Aimee's surprise, Charles gripped her arm a little more tightly from thence on. They soon entered the next room, which held the most grisly (and therefore the most popular) of the exhibits, the Chamber of Horrors.

It was this room which housed the ghastly replicas of the victims of France's guillotine, modeled by poor Madame Tussaud under gruesome circumstances. The French government, explained Mr. Peacham, had forced Madame to model the severed heads brought to her, no doubt many of whom had been known to her personally—including the ill-fated king and queen. Ironically, the murderers themselves eventually lost their heads, and these were also on display: Fouquier-Tinville, Hébert, Robespierre, and the murdered Marat lying in his bath.

What glimpse she got of them made Aimee feel nauseous. Recalling how she had bragged to Diana of how she would shriek with horror at the sight, she could only wonder at her own simplicity. It truly was a chamber of horrors, she reflected, feeling her head begin to throb. The problem was that her imagination was so very vivid.

"Charles," she whispered, tugging his sleeve. "I do not think I want to see any more. I'm afraid I don't feel very well after all. I am so cold all of a sudden . . ."

With what speed and efficiency Charles whisked her out of the museum she could only afterwards marvel. She did not, of course, realize how pale she had become, nor how distasteful Charles had begun to find their two companions. She was a little dizzy, and exceedingly grateful for the support of her cousin's arm as they exited the building. She never would remember just how Charles located his coach, but manage it he did, and with astonishing efficiency.

Once inside, out of all possible view, Aimee closed her eyes and leaned against Charles. Though her cheeks felt hot, she was shaking with chills that seemed to have taken over her small body. She did not even realize that his arm had gone around her or that her face was pressed against his waistcoat.

"Charles," she murmured, after a moment. "I think I should warn you that I might be sick."

She could feel his body shift. "Lord, Aimee, are you sure?"

"No." Her voice was very faint. "I shall try . . . very hard not to be . . . but if I am, you won't despise me . . . will you?"

Charles gazed rather wonderingly down at the soft black curls brushing his chin. "Where do you females get your crackbrained notions?" he said soothingly. "M'father says my mother is the same way. Always taking some odd notion into her head and clinging to it like a dashed limpet."

Aimee clutched suddenly at his waistcoat, and Charles braced himself. "No, I'm all right," she assured him, drawing an uneven breath. "You did not mind leaving

Miss Low, did you?"

"Of course not, kitten." His voice was queerly strangled.

"Charles?" she whispered, after a few more minutes. "This is the second time you have rescued me, you know."

Beneath her cheek, Charles's chest shook just a trifle. "Oh, is that what I'm doing?" he inquired, absently stroking her midnight curls.

"Oh, yes. For I should have disgraced myself utterly had you not been there."

"Just like that queer fellow with the odd name," he joked.

"Yes, just like Lochinvar," she whispered into his coat.

Shortly thereafter, they arrived back at Jermyn Street, and Charles, after explaining the situation to Diana, proved himself equal to the task of carrying his damsel in distress up two flights of stairs to her room. Even had she wanted to object—which she did not—Aimee was still feeling far too unwell to walk. Charles laid her gently down upon her bed, and after expressing his willingness to do anything in his power to help, promptly removed himself from the premises.

"Oh, Diana, I'm so sorry," moaned Aimee, as her sister helped her into her nightdress.

"Hush, now. I'm afraid you have a fever, my dear," Diana stated, touching her sister's brow. "You will have to stay in bed, at least for a day or two," she went on, tucking in the sheets. "But I have some news to cheer you up. A letter from Eliza arrived a short while ago."

"Oh, good," said Aimee, her voice whisper soft. "I'll wait and read it a bit later, I think."

As it transpired, Aimee was ill for more than a week,

191

and between nursing her and taking care of Miss Tilden, Diana was kept exhaustingly busy. Meg was a great help, of course, but theirs was a small household, and her abigail had many other chores to do. Moreover, Meg was equally fatigued, so that out of pure kindness, Diana insisted she take her afternoon off, as usual.

The house seemed filled with flowers, for a host of Aimee's admirers appeared to have discovered she was ill. The most prized of these arrangements were the ones from Charles, which took the place of honor at the side of Aimee's bed, but there were many others besides. Lord Lucan had sent flowers, also, but these were for Miss Tilden, which pleased Diana so much that she immediately sat down to write him a note of thanks.

Encouraged by the warmth of her letter, the earl presented himself at Jermyn Street the afternoon Meg was out. He had called twice before, but upon both occasions Diana had been tending to Aimee, and had come downstairs for only a few minutes to speak to him. This time, however, Chance favored him, for both patients were asleep and Diana had a few spare minutes on her hands. She was sitting alone, idly flipping through the first pages of a novel when he arrived.

She put it down at once, and had she not looked so exhausted and pale, the smile she bestowed upon the earl would have made him feel quite jubilant. However, since he was very worried that she, too, might succumb to influenza, he only frowned.

"You are not taking care of yourself, Diana," he said, in his blunt way. "You look positively hagged."

There was a time when such a remark would have kindled her temper, but Diana was so glad to see him she only laughed.

"Why, thank you, my lord," she said affably. "How pleasant it is to know that I may always count on you to deliver a pretty compliment!"

He smiled a little. "Yes, I've a way with words, don't I? Seriously, though, aren't you getting any rest at all? You don't look it."

"Not a great deal," she admitted. "But I assure you I don't regret it. Aimee is much better today, and is hoping to be up and about by the end of the week. And if only—" she broke off suddenly. "But let us sit down! What an uncivil hostess I am become!"

He waited for her to sit, then pulled a second chair close to her side. "If only what, Diana?" he inquired, reaching for her hand. "Is the little minx causing you more difficulty?"

His touch made her feel oddly revived. "You must not call her that," she reproached. "She has been feeling so miserable and has scarcely complained at all! No, the problem has nothing to do with Aimee. It is simply that her closest friend, Eliza Fingleshaw, is coming to town sometime next week and, well, I am not at all pleased. I'm afraid Eliza has the worst possible influence upon my sister."

The earl's brows shot up. "Oh? Then why do you not forbid the friendship?"

Diana laughed lightly. "Aimee is my sister, not my daughter, Lord Lucan. Moreover, the Fingleshaws are my parents' neighbors, and would undoubtedly take instant umbrage were I to suggest that their darling Eliza is of a sadly unsteady character—which she is!"

"Nonsense," he said impatiently. "If the girl encourages your sister to behave wildly, it is your duty—or that of your parents—to put a stop to it!"

"Yes, you are right, I know," she agreed. "But Aimee is so delighted, you see. And it is the only thing that has been able to cheer her up—save the knowledge that Charles has called a number of times to see how she goes on! I'm afraid *his* opinion is the only one that really counts with Aimee."

"Then ask him to use his influence," the earl advised. "Good God, Diana, you don't need to carry the whole burden yourself! What about your great-aunt? Why don't you speak to her about it?"

"I would, if I thought it would do any good. But it seems that Aimee and Aunt Serena have been getting along quite famously, and I should so hate to spoil that! You won't repeat this, I know, but according to Aunt Serena, she and Aimee are remarkably similar in character! I could scarcely credit it, when she told me!"

Lord Lucan looked unsurprised. "I can credit it," he said dryly. "They are both shockingly spoiled, molly-coddled by their relatives, their every whim catered to—"

"Surely I do not do that!" Diana exclaimed. "Oh, you are roasting me again—are you not? I am too tired to be sure."

"Let me take you for a drive," he urged. "The fresh air will do you good. How long has it been since you were out of the house? Days, I should guess."

"Thank you, I should very much like to," she replied casting a wistful glance toward the window, "but I have given Meg the afternoon off, and there is no other female in the house to attend to the patients. Tildy cannot put her full weight on her foot yet, so—oh, *pray* do not scowl so!" she said, impulsively squeezing his hand. "I promise I am not just inventing excuses."

His gray eyes probed her face. "Tomorrow then. Don't say no, Diana. I won't accept a refusal."

She could not help smiling at his domineering tone. "You are a shocking bully, my lord," she scolded. "I should refuse, if only to give you the set-down you deserve!"

"I only want to take care of you," he pointed out, in a tone that made her color up.

Diana's eyes dropped, then rose. "To own the truth,"

she confessed, "there is nothing in the world I would rather do than drive out with you."

"Good!" The earl had been clasping her hand all this time, and he chose this moment to raise it to his lips. "By the way, you may be interested to know that your 'betrothal' is now at an official end. I spoke to the gentleman in question, and he has promised not to trouble you again."

Involuntarily, Diana's fingers tightened in his. "How can I ever thank you?" she asked, her voice full of emotion. "I have worried and worried that perhaps I should have spoken to him myself, but—"

"Indeed, had it been an honorable offer, I daresay you would be right," he cut in. "But in such a case as this, I hardly think we need observe the niceties. Do not worry so much, Diana."

Her sigh was faint but discernable. "I do worry a great deal," she admitted. "It's in my nature, I think. But life is far from simple."

However, the earl was bent upon making life as simple as possible for Diana, and when he left her house a short while later, he paid a visit on Great-aunt Serena. The Dowager Viscountess of Torrington kept him kicking up his heels a mere twenty minutes before she deigned to put in an appearance, an interval which Diana could have told him was remarkably short for the old lady. He could not regard it so, however, and although he bore with good grace the intervening minutes while her servants fussed about arranging her cushions, footstool, and shawl, his patience had nearly run out by the time she dismissed them.

Comfortable at last, she turned her attention to her visitor. "Well, well!" she cackled, peering at him with interest. "Ain't this a surprise! Sit down—no, not there!

Over here where I can see you!" She watched as he obeyed, then went on, "Now, what brings you to see an old woman like me? Or need I ask?" she added archly.

The earl's bow had been courteous enough, but he was not about to beat around the bush. "Madam, I have just paid a call upon your niece," he told her brusquely. "Are you aware that she is on the verge of collapse?"

"How should I be aware of it?" returned the old lady curtly. "I ain't been there in over a week. And I don't plan to go, either, not while there's any risk of contracting an infectious ailment! My nieces are young. They can handle it—I can't!"

"I have no quarrel with that," he said impatiently, "but has it occurred to you, ma'am, to send an envoy to inquire how they are? Diana is looking burnt to the socket from the strain of playing nursemaid. In short, ma'am, she is in need of assistance."

"I see," said the dowager, after a pause. "And you came here to tell me of my negligence. Well, believe it or not, impudent young jackanapes, I received a note from Diana not two days ago assuring me she was perfectly well and in need of nothing! So what do you have to say to that, eh?"

"I say that if you know Diana as well as I, you must also know that would be her response. She is foolishly obstinate about some things, and likes her independence. But good God, ma'am! All you need do is send over one or two of your maidservants to give her some assistance! She has only the one to help her, and it is obviously not enough."

"And what business is it of yours?" inquired the dowager with sarcasm. "You seem to be mighty interested in things that don't concern you!"

Controlling his temper, he said, "Anything to do with Diana concerns me."

"Then why the devil don't you make her an offer?"

she said sharply.

"Dammit, I have!" he fired back.

The dowager's tongue clicked in dismay. "Oh, good God, do you mean to say the fool girl rejected you?"

The earl shrugged. "Not yet. To be honest, at the moment, I doubt that Diana is in a fit mental state to consider a proposal of marriage. Perhaps if she had some relief from her nursing duties, she could begin to consider it. But that is not my motive, Lady Torrington, so do not think it. I merely want to see Diana restored to her usual blooming health."

"Well, I ain't at all sure I have any maidservants to spare," snapped the dowager petulantly. "I don't waste good money on servants I don't need!"

The earl's lip curled. "In that case, ma'am," he said in a hard voice, "I will take up no more of your time."

"Oh, sit down, sit down," she barked. "Don't take everything I say so damned literally. Mayhap I could spare one of my girls. I'll have to give it some thought."

The earl bowed, but remained standing. "Thank you, ma'am. I am confident you will make a wise decision."

Aunt Serena took rather approving stock of the earl's solid six-foot frame. "In a hurry to leave, are you?" she complained. "Well, I can understand it. Why would you want to talk to an old bore like me? In my day I used to be what they call a diamond of the first water, but I daresay you won't believe it. Ha! Well, beauty don't last, does it? So make sure it's more than Diana's beauty that you want, my fine lad!"

"Have no fear of that," he said truthfully. "And whether you believe it or not, ma'am, I don't find you at all boring. You can be a most diverting woman—when you choose to be." To prove this, he sat back down, prepared to keep her company for a while.

"Toad-eater!" said the dowager viscountess, regarding him with sour pleasure. "You're as bad as Thurstan, then. Worse, actually, for there's some excuse for him! *He* remembers what I looked like when I was in my prime!" She paused. "I was acquainted with your grandfather, the fourth earl," she said abruptly. "Knew him well, in fact. You've something of a look of him. He was a devil of a rake, y'know."

"Indeed," said the earl, rather ruefully. "Well, it don't run in the family, ma'am, in case that's what you're wondering. My oats were sown long ago."

"Good," nodded Aunt Serena. "Diana don't need another one of those on her hands. Keep your chin up, boy. You've my blessing in this matter."

Chapter Eleven

When a fresh-faced young maidservant presented herself at Jermyn Street the following morning, Diana received her with some puzzlement. The girl, Mary by name, brought with her a note—as caustically worded as one might expect in a note from Aunt Serena—but as the dowager made no reference to the earl's visit, Diana was at a loss as to why she should have sent the girl at all. However, since she was ready to admit that they needed another woman in the house, it was with alacrity that she accepted the use of Mary's services. Mary's presence enabled Diana to get in a well-deserved rest, and by the time the earl arrived later that afternoon, she was looking and feeling better than she had in days.

She related the incident to the earl as they set out. "I cannot quite imagine Aunt Serena thinking of it on her own," she confided, as his well-sprung curricle carried them along the Mayfair streets. "It is most odd, don't you think?"

"Very odd," he said imperturbably. "She would have done better to have thought of it sooner, but it was good of her all the same."

Diana looked at him closely. "Actually, it crossed my mind that it is more the sort of thing you would do. But that is silly of me, isn't it?"

"Very silly," he agreed. "What a fine day it has turned out to be. That cloud formation ahead of us looks almost like some sort of running animal. A stag, perhaps? What do you think?"

"You are not trying to change the subject by any chance, are you, my lord?" she inquired in a suspicious voice.

"I?" Lord Lucan shot her a lazy look. "Since when have I ever been anything but direct with you?"

"To my knowledge, never!" she admitted. "But then, you have never seemed the sort of man to see fanciful creatures in the clouds, either!"

"No?" He sighed audibly. "Dear me, I suppose I have not. What a pity."

She eyed him for a few seconds, then decided to try a more straightforward approach. "I would rather that you do not play games with me, my lord. Why do you not simply admit it?"

"Admit what, my dear Mrs. Verney?" The earl's expression was as devoid of guilt as a small child's.

"Admit to sending the maidservant," she said with a touch of impatience. "Or should I say, of coercing my aunt into sending her!"

He appeared to debate his answer. "Coerced is a strong word, Diana," he replied at last. "I prefer 'suggested.' It has a nicer ring to it."

"Then it *is* you I have to thank." The words were not what he expected and he gave her a sharp look. "It was such a practical solution," she went on, unconscious of his scrutiny, "I was almost sure you must be behind it. I'm afraid it never occured to me to ask my aunt for assistance, though now I see that it would have been the sensible thing to have done."

They were nearing the entrance to the Park, which was congested with vehicles, and the earl sent his pair the signal to slow. As he maneuvered them unerringly into line, he remarked, a shade casually, "I had a notion that you would be up in arms at my presuming to interfere."

"Well," she said, thinking this over with a puckered brow, "I suppose a few weeks ago I would have been very much put out by it. But how ungrateful I would be to resent what was so sorely needed and was meant to be a kindness! It means a great deal to me that you took the trouble. We have become very close friends, I think."

"Yes, haven't we?" he concurred, rather tonelessly. Silence reigned as he navigated the curricle through the entrance gate to the Park. They were a little way along the carriage way when he said, "But I hope you do not forget that we might be a great deal closer."

Diana examined her fingertips as if she had never seen them before. "No," she answered, a note of constraint entering her voice. "I have not forgotten your offer, Lord Lucan. I know that is what you are hinting. But things have been so . . . so busy lately that I have been unable to come to any decision." As if her words were somehow hurtful, she added quickly, "I am greatly honored by your offer, Lord Lucan. I think I forgot to tell you that before."

"Yes, well, I was worried about that," he said flippantly, but could have kicked himself when he saw the way her hands jerked in her lap. "Forgive me, Diana. That was a shabby thing to say. I'm afraid I have no excuse."

She shook her head slowly. "Not so, my lord. You have every excuse in the world. I am treating you quite outrageously, I know, by not . . . not giving you an answer." She swallowed hard. "You cannot know how badly I feel about it. I must try your patience very much."

"On the contrary, I am pleased that you are willing to treat my offer as the serious matter it is. It was not lightly made, I assure you."

"I know." Her voice was unusually subdued. "And I shall give it very serious thought. I promise."

"I can ask no more than that," he replied evenly.

They were both unaware that several carriages behind, the eyes of a certain lady were upon them. Accompanied by her current lover, who also happened to be her distant cousin, Lady Uxbridge had also chosen that afternoon to take the air. Her motive, however, was somewhat different from Diana's, for she went to the Park because it was fashionable to be seen there, and because it usually provided her with some trifling new piece of gossip. During the fashionable hour, the congregation of carriages frequently came to a complete standstill, affording one the opportunity to converse with whomever happened to be at hand.

"It's a bit like the game of roulette, isn't it?" she murmured to her companion, a fair-haired youth at least fifteen years her junior. "Think of it! Why, one might meet anyone—even one's own spouse. That would be a novelty, wouldn't it? I do not think I've set eyes on poor Uxbridge in over a week." Her full lips slid into a satisfied smile. "Not that it matters when I have you, David, dear."

Knowing she did not require an answer, her companion smiled his beautiful smile and said nothing. He was simply an ornament on this occasion, a youthful foil for the countess's ripened perfection.

Lady Uxbridge was in a good humor this afternoon, and even as her brooding gaze rested upon the Earl of Lucan, her sunny mood did not completely recede. It had been so long since a man had rejected her so rudely that she could hardly believe it had happened. He really ought to be punished, she mused. Then her curious gaze shifted to the golden-haired woman beside him. So he persisted in playing escort to Edmund Verney's widow, did he? Her heavy lids drooped as she considered that interesting fact.

When the countess's coachman was forced to halt their progress a few minutes later, she was still deep in thought, and had she not looked up quite by chance, might have missed her opportunity to speak with Sir Henry Neyle. His knowing eyes were upon her, and since the baronet's peculiar brand of charisma had always appealed to her, she sent him her most tantalizing smile.

He doffed his beaver at once. "Good day, Lady Uxbridge. How very well you are looking, ma'am."

"And you, Sir Henry," she drawled in her languorous manner. "Always so gallant, so polished. I make no doubt you hold half the female hearts of London in your grasp."

He bowed. "You flatter me, ma'am." His eyes shifted to the face of her companion, and he cocked an inquiring eyebrow. "Dear me, let me guess," he said cordially. "*Not* the worthy Lord Uxbridge, and certainly not one of your own charming progeny."

She looked amused. "Certainly not. My children are far too young to live in London." She waved a white hand. "This is David. He is very shy."

Sir Henry reached for his quizzing glass. "Really?" he said, examing the youth in polite disbelief. "Are lapdogs shy?"

The countess's full lips curved. "You are very naughty, Sir Henry. You will hurt David's feelings. David and I enjoy a pleasant, cousinly friendship, don't we, darling?"

"Heavens, can it talk, too?" inquired Sir Henry with ruthless humor. "My dear Lady Uxbridge, with all due respect to your pretty companion, I implore you to do me the honor of joining me in my curricle. Send David home to play with his rattles."

She'd been hoping for the invitation, and did not care how it was couched. "Why, what a splendid notion," she replied. "I believe I shall do just that. David won't mind, will you, David?" She naturally did not add that she would pay him well not to mind in the least.

The transfer was soon made, and Lady Uxbridge settled herself contentedly beside Sir Henry. Each was anticipating a very pleasant interlude, and since both parties were well-seasoned in amatory matters, a great deal of ground was covered in a very short time.

"Now, why," pondered Sir Henry, not ten minutes later, "have we never done this before? I own I cannot think of a reason."

"Can you not? I can." The countess's side glance was replete with meaning. "I have seen how the suave Sir Henry amuses himself with the ladies. One might conjecture he has had his hands full enough."

Sir Henry's teeth flashed. "You flatter me, ma'am. But one does one's poor best."

"But how splendid," she murmured. "I so admire a man who tries to do his best. It makes me want to know that man better."

"For you, ma'am," he said gallantly, "I would strive to new heights of endeavor. Though I warn you I am no child, like your David. But experience yields other benefits."

"You interest me profoundly," she replied, rolling the words off her tongue in a way that made her meaning obvious.

His eyes dropped to the ripe swell of her breasts. "May I say, my dear lady, that your sentiments are entirely reciprocated?"

More by accident than design, Lady Uxbridge's gaze fell once more upon the Earl of Lucan, whose curricle was no longer so far in the distance. Almost without thinking, she said, "You used to be much more in his company."

"Who?" With difficulty, the baronet tore his eyes from her bosom, where the taut contours of her nipples were remarkably visible. "Oh," he said, following her gaze. "Now, that, dear lady, is quite another story. Hardly of interest to us, is it?"

In many ways, Lady Uxbridge was very intelligent. "Ah," she said, with a brittle smile. "There has been a rivalry between you. For the golden-haired lady in the earl's carriage, perhaps?"

Sir Henry looked vaguely disgruntled. "Aye. 'Tis still a sore point with me, I confess."

The countess looked thoughtful. "I know exactly what you mean, darling." She shrugged, somehow making the movement into a sensuous wriggle. "Never mind," she said softly. "A man like you needs a woman of passion and imagination . . . a woman like me."

Sir Henry's own imagination was well at work. "Where can we go?" he muttered. "Where, Sophia? And when?"

"Patience," she warned. "We go nowhere right now. Discretion, darling. Above all, remember discretion . . ."

Even after she returned home, a glow of cheerfulness enveloped Diana, and her feet were light as she mounted the stairs to her room. The outing in the Park had done her a great deal of good, and except for those few, uncomfortable seconds when the subject of matrimony had been raised, the earl had kept the conversation diverted from all but the lightest topics. How easily he could make her laugh, she thought with amazement. All things considered, she had seldom enjoyed herself as thoroughly as she had this day. She had even told him about her love of sewing and designing clothes, which was not something she told just anyone. And he had been genuinely interested!

Tossing her gloves and bonnet onto her bed, Diana hastened to take a dutiful peek at her patients. However, since they were both occupied—Aimee with the latest Gothic romance and Miss Tilden with a new pair of stockings—she left them in peace and withdrew once more to her bedchamber. She had a hazy notion that she might catch a quick nap before dinner, but unfortunately both mind and body refused to allow her this respite. It was impossible to relax, or indeed to do anything but stare out the window while her mind reviewed every minute of her drive with the earl with disturbing accuracy.

It was true that he had made her laugh, but in retrospect, she could see that his desire to possess her was as powerful as ever. It was in his gestures and his voice, in every syllable he uttered, in the warmth of his smile, in every expression that crossed his face—and it was in his eyes.

With absent steps, Diana went to the chair beside the window and sank into it, a long, ragged sigh escaping her lips. What *was* she going tell him? No matter what he said, it was wrong to keep putting him off like this. Of course, she had been very busy, and he had been excessively understanding about that, but common sense warned her that any man would grow tired of waiting.

He would make her a good husband.

The thought came winging out of nowhere, and with it came a wild longing to become his wife, a yearning to leap headlong into an alliance which offered, not only security, but a reasonable hope of happiness and tranquillity. It was a tempting proposal, but she suddenly realized that as tempting as it was, whether or not he would make her a good husband was no longer the primary issue.

Would she make him a good wife?

Oddly, this had become the crux of the matter, the concern which kept her from jumping at the chance to wed a man who was becoming more dear to her with every passing hour. It was difficult to pinpoint exactly when this shift in priorities had occured. How many days had it been since she'd acknowledged her own susceptibility to his charm? How long since she'd begun to let down—cautiously—some of her defensive barriers? Today, for instance, she'd realized that when his gray eyes smiled into hers she could smile back—spontaneously, naturally, and without a trace of a blush. When had that happened? And though she was still absurdly conscious of both his physical presence and his forceful personality, she no longer felt threatened by it. So why, oh, *why* did she suddenly feel so blue?

Tired of sitting, Diana abandoned her chair and began to pace, as if movement would help her make sense of the senseless, of the tangles and contradictions of her turbulent emotions.

First, despite all the progress she had made, the notion of marrying Lord Lucan still made her uneasy, even apprehensive. *Why?* His kiss had been pleasant, hadn't it? And even though she was convinced that those other, strange sensations had been a product of her imagination, at least she was certain his embrace had not been disagreeable. So why didn't her dread of intimacy simply abate?

She paused to scowl at her reflection in the cheval glass, as if it were somehow responsible for her quandary. Well, kisses were one thing, she mused, staring into her own troubled eyes. But the earl was going to want more than kisses. Intuition warned her that Geoffrey Trevelyan was not a man who would settle for anything less than a complete surrender. And he deserved nothing less.

Her mouth drooped at the thought. Yes, Geoffrey *deserved* a wife who was willing to surrender herself to him, body and soul. What he did not deserve was a wife who would try to foist him off as she had done with Edmund—though, to be honest, she doubted she could do it. Those gray eyes of his might smile at her, but they were also keen enough to see through any prevarication or excuse. What possible chance was there of fooling him? What possible chance was there of making him believe she desired his lovemaking?

On the other hand, assuming there was a chance of duping him, should she do it? Was it better to lie to him or to tell him the truth? Long, soul-searching seconds ticked away while Diana thrashed through the pros and cons of the question. Without doubt, the truth would hurt him, she reflected, but what good was a marriage based on lies? When it came down to it, neither choice was acceptable. She refused to hurt him and she couldn't lie to him. And, anyway, she reasoned despondently, even if she told him the truth, there was little likelihood that he would be able to accept it or understand it.

Which left her with a bleak third alternative. If she did not marry him, she would have to do neither. They could just go on as they were, and he would never need to know that there was anything wrong with her. Perhaps, if she were positive that he loved her, she would be brave enough to chance it. But he had never said a word about love.

By the morning of the following day, Aimee had finished the last of the romance novels she had borrowed from the circulating library just prior to her illness.

"Diana," she said, arriving at the breakfast table with a stack of volumes, "do you think you could return these and get me some more? Are you going anywhere near the lending library today?"

"Well, I wasn't planning on it, but there is no reason why I could not," replied Diana with a smile. "Mary can stay with you and Tildy, and Meg can come with me."

"Oh, good! Otherwise it is too tedious just sitting

around with nothing to do. If only I weren't so tired," she sighed, "I could go with you."

"Give yourself another day or two," Diana advised. "You are much stronger, I know, but not quite strong enough for that."

Aimee nodded glumly. "Oh, and Diana, if Charles happens to visit while you are out, may I receive him?"

"I see no reason why not. Did he say he would come?"

"No, but I am hoping he will. He has been quite attentive lately. Have you noticed?"

Diana reached for a slice of toast. "Indeed I have, and I am very glad. You had better make me a list of the books you have already read, by the way, so I do not borrow the same ones again."

"Yes, I'll do that right after breakfast. Thank you, Lawrence," she added, accepting her morning chocolate from the butler's hand. Her nose wrinkled as she surveyed the various dishes that Cook had prepared for them. "Oh dear. I still do not have much appetite. None of this looks at all appealing."

"But you must eat something, my dear. You have grown sadly frail these past few days."

Aimee gazed pensively down at her slim arms and tiny, delicate wrists. "I had a notion it was an improvement," she replied. "I thought it gave me a sort of ethereal look, like a heroine in a romance."

Diana shook her head. "Ethereal, no. Sickly, yes." Observing her sister's mulish look, she said hastily, "Do not forget, the sooner you recover your strength, the sooner you can begin attending parties again. And Charles does not want you to lose more weight. He told me he thought you were far too thin," she finished smoothly.

It was a masterful touch, and so near the truth it hardly signified. "Did he really say that?" Aimee asked, as eagerly as if it had been a compliment.

"Yes," Diana affirmed, "that was his meaning, though he did not state it quite like that. He is very concerned about you."

"Well!" chattered Aimee, excitedly reaching for the plate of eggs. "I had better eat, then! I think it is a good sign, don't you, Diana? After all, if he noticed I was thinner, that means he was *looking* at me! And if he is *concerned* about me that must mean he *cares* for me—at least a little. Don't you think so, Diana?"

Diana concealed a smile as her sister proceeded to heap her plate high with food. "Yes, Aimee. I think you may be right."

Colburn's circulating library offered its subscribers a widely diversified assortment of books. It had a congenial atmosphere, and for little more than four pounds per year, its patrons were afforded the considerable convenience of borrowing their books rather than purchasing them for a great deal more at Hatchard's.

Diana had always enjoyed coming here, and would have been quite content to spend the entire morning browsing among Mr. Colburn's well-stocked shelves. As it was, she spent some twenty minutes thumbing through one or other of the books until a pair of giggling young females disrupted her concentration. Reminded of Aimee, Diana replaced the book she had been skimming and returned to the section of the library where there was an abundance of lurid-sounding Gothic romances. Unfortunately, all the copies of the one book Aimee had particularly requested—*Glenarvon*—seemed to be absent, though she was able to find three other titles which looked to be just Aimee's cup of tea (including Mrs. Radcliffe's *Mysteries of Udolpho*).

She gathered these, along with the sole novel she had selected for herself—Jane Austen's *Emma*—and carried them up to the front counter. To her profound dismay, she arrived there at the very moment that Lady Edgerton entered the shop. She had seen the woman on one or two occasions, but this was the first time they were to be in such close quarters together.

Quickly averting her gaze, Diana took a deep breath and addressed the clerk behind the counter. "Do you have any more copies of *Glenarvon*?" she inquired.

The clerk, a sad-faced, little brown mouse of a man, peered at her over the rim of his glasses. "'Tis a popular book, ma'am," he responded in lugubrious accents. "Everyone wants to read it. I doubt there's a copy anywhere in here—unless someone returned one this morning, that is. Would you like me to look?"

"Please do." Diana inclined her head.

Lady Edgerton was standing directly behind her, and she could feel the woman's hard gray eyes boring into her back. With tautening nerves, Diana strained to recapture the insouciant attitude the earl had helped her achieve that first day in Hyde Park. To her surprise, the strategy worked better than she expected. The memory of Geoffrey Trevelyan's scandalous remarks regarding Lady Edgerton and her corset brought a resurgence of, not only her confidence, but the amusement she had felt about it afterward. Silent laughter welled inside her, sending an unbridled flash of pure daring coursing through her veins. Why should she be intimidated by this pitiable busybody? Why should she shrink from facing her, as though she had some reason to be ashamed? Abruptly, Diana made the decision to greet Lady Edgerton, if only to show that she cared not a straw for the woman's malicious gossip. Chin proudly aloft, she turned her head.

"Good day, Lady Edgerton." Diana's gaze was unwavering, her tone cool but meticulously polite.

At first, Lady Edgerton merely stared back. Then, in

211

the abrasive voice Diana remembered only too well, the woman who had once made life so difficult for her answered, "Good day," and allowed her lips to purse into a factitious smile.

Diana smiled pleasantly. "Such a long time it has been since we met. You do not seem to have changed at all," she went on, exulting inwardly as two bright spots of color entered Lady Edgerton's fleshy cheeks.

"Indeed," responded Lady Edgerton, looking as if she had just swallowed something extremely sour. Her eyes roved jealously over Diana's face and figure. "Neither do you," she added shortly.

"On the contrary, I have changed a great deal," said Diana seriously. "One cannot marry and lose a husband and remain unaffected. Some sort of adjustment is necessary. And as you have reason to know, my suffering was even greater than most." She watched with detachment as ugly crimson and purple streaks mottled Lady Edgerton's complexion. "But since then," she explained, "I have learned that there are ways to deal with unpleasantness—and those who derive pleasure from it."

Lady Edgerton's mouth fell open, then snapped shut tightly. "Indeed," she hissed, through shut teeth.

Knowing she had the upper hand, Diana was contemplating her next remark when the clerk returned.

"I'm very sorry, ma'am," he informed Diana, shaking his head gloomily. "No copies of *Glenarvon* have been returned. I feared as much."

For the first time, Diana noticed that Lady Edgerton held a book tucked under her arm. At the clerk's remark, she whipped it out and thrust it under the poor man's nose.

"Here is your *Glenarvon*," she spat, waving it wildly. "Here, take it, take it! It's disgraceful what they will publish these days. Caroline Lamb ought to be ashamed of herself!" She glared at Diana, the tip of her tongue snaking out to moisten her pale lips. "Ashamed!" she repeated with sudden relish. "No doubt Mrs. Verney will enjoy it." Then, like an indignant duck, she pointed her quivering nose at the ceiling and waddled out of the library.

The door slammed shut, and Diana and the clerk exchanged looks. "Is it truly that bad?" she asked him in amazement. "What can possibly be in it that is so objectionable?"

Looking doleful, the little man scratched his head. "Well, I don't rightly know, ma'am. I haven't read it myself. They say Lady Caroline put a lot of real people in it, which I reckon has got some 'em a bit riled." For the first time, the corners of his lips twitched. "Who knows? Maybe she saw herself in it," he said dryly.

Diana left the library with a proud spring in her step. She had actually done it! She had faced Lady Edgerton, spoken with her, and come out of it feeling reasonably victorious. And what was more, that spiteful insinuation at the end had not bothered her one jot. Not one jot! In fact, it had rolled off her as easily as if it had been no more than the commonest civility. She could not wait to tell Geoffrey!

Civility. Polite Society placed such importance upon civility, yet Diana had just discovered what a wealth of meaning might be conveyed within its boundries. It was quite possible to deal with people like Lady Edgerton in a firm, nonoffensive way. No doubt it was an art which required practice—but she had done it!

For perhaps the first time, Diana realized how much she had despised herself for being weak, for caring about the gossip, for allowing a woman like Lady Edgerton to make her feel uneasy. From now on, she mused, she would be strong and self-assertive. She would not run away from life, but would take it by the horns, give back measure for measure . . .

"If you please, ma'am," panted Meg, from five feet behind. "I can't keep up with you. I've got this bunion on my toe and it's started a-paining me again."

Diana slowed at once. "Why didn't you tell me, Meg?" she asked. "I could have brought Mary instead."

Meg shook her head. "I don't mind," she said bravely.

"Nonsense, of course you must mind. We shall hire a hack to take us home. And when Dr. Hatfield visits us later, I shall be sure he looks at your toe."

As she glanced up and down the street in search of a hired hack, a familiar voice floated through the air, raising goose pimples on her flesh.

"My dear Sophia, you look simply marvelous! No really, you *do*, my dear. It's the most flattering bonnet you could have purchased."

Not ten feet away, Sir Henry Neyle and the Countess of Uxbridge stepped out of a millinery shop. Diana's new-found confidence was about to undergo its first test.

Chapter Twelve

There was no time to walk away, no place to hide. And no *reason* to hide, she reminded herself fiercely. Braced with resolve, Diana's shoulders squared and her face took on an aspect of aloof determination. She would deal with this situation as effectively as the last.

By this time, Sir Henry had seen her. "Well, well," he drawled, his seemingly ever present smile curling his lips. "My dear Sophia, just see who is here. It is Mrs. Verney, my love. What a delicious situation! I simply *must* introduce you to each other."

Later, Diana would wonder if she'd made a mistake. But such was her animosity toward the smirking blond demigod before her that she acted on pure instinct.

She forgot civility. She forgot everything but the one lesson Aunt Serena had taught her the year of her come-out: the correct way to administer *the cut*.

If there was such a thing as a correct way to be rude, Aunt Serena had explained it in detail. The *cut direct* was for the most obnoxious. It meant crossing to the other side of the street, or going especially out of one's way to avoid the obnoxious person. The *cut indirect* was slightly less rude. Done correctly, one simply looked another way, as if one did not observe the obnoxious person in question. The *cut sublime* was a variation. One glanced up to admire the rooftops, or a handsome balcony or whatever else was about, so that the obnoxious person was outside the perimeter of one's vision. The *cut infernal* was the opposite. One stared at one's feet or the cobbles or pretended to search for a coin one had dropped.

Diana's cut was more than direct. She simply gazed right through Sir Henry as if he did not exist, allowing her eyes to sweep the surrounding area once, in a rather bored fashion. She then turned and strolled away in the opposite direction, while the astonished baronet stared after her in inarticulate fury.

He had good reason for that fury. Several amused onlookers had witnessed the scene, and some had tittered quite openly. Such episodes as this, he knew, had a way of becoming widely known. To his increased annoyance, even Lady Uxbridge was smiling.

"Poor darling," she purred, touching his arm. "She does not seem to wish for your acquaintance, does she?"

"Or yours," he muttered, his suaveness deserting him. "Bitch," he added, under his breath.

To which woman he referred was unclear, but Lady Uxbridge did not even blink. "Come, Henry," she murmured, with a shade less sympathy. "You make a fool of yourself by standing here like this, pouting like a lovesick school boy. The little slut is not worth it, believe me."

Reluctantly, Sir Henry pulled his gaze back to the lady he was escorting, his manner almost surly. "Come on, then," he growled. "I need to purchase some snuff."

She smiled complacently, knowing he needed more than snuff. They had had no chance to be together the previous day, for she had needed time to make arrangements, and to dispose of David. Though her young cousin was a fine stallion, in the final analysis he was too like a blank page for her taste. Sir Henry

216

possessed far more in the way of wit and sophistication—which one appreciated a trifle more when one had been without it for a while. Yet, in his own way, he too was a beautiful, sulky little boy.

Poor Henry had suffered a blow to his pride, but Lady Uxbridge did not for a moment doubt her ability to make him forget the whey-faced widow with the golden hair. When it came to men and their needs, Lady Uxbridge considered herself unsurpassed in knowledge. And she was going to make certain that Henry found this out very soon.

"How is your foot?" Diana asked Meg, once they were far away from Sir Henry. "I am so very sorry to have done that to you, but I'm afraid it could not be helped."

"It's . . . it's not too bad," gasped the abigail. "Goodness, ma'am, you certainly have a heap of hurry-scurry in you today."

"Er, yes, I suppose I do," Diana replied contritely. "But no more, I promise." Her eyes swept back to the street. "We shall find a hack—oh! Better yet . . ." She took two quick steps toward the busy thoroughfare and waved her hand.

Without doubt it was Aunt Serena's coach. Diana recognized it from the Torrington crest on the side panel as well as the brawny coachman on top. But surely, Aunt Serena would not be out so early? The dowager viscountess almost never ventured out of her house before three in the afternoon.

The coachman also recognized Diana, and brought the coach to a halt. "Morning, ma'am." He touched his top hat respectfully.

Diana smiled up at the man. "Good morning, John. Is my aunt within?"

"Nay, 'tis 'is lordship," replied the coachman with a

wink. "Do ye be needin' a ride, ma'am?"

Before Diana could reply, Lord Hervey stuck his head out the window. "Oh, it is you, my dear," he said brightly. "I thought I heard your voice. 'Pon my word, what luck! Tell John where you wish to go, and we shall take you there at once. And in the meantime, p'haps you can give me some advice."

Once inside, Diana sank into the squabs with a grateful sigh, while Lord Hervey beamed at her from the other seat.

"And how is that pretty little sister of yours feeling? Did she receive my flowers? Serena told me she had the influenza, and that you, Mrs. Verney, were on the brink of collapse."

Diana raised her brows. "The brink of collapse? Where can she have—oh, Lord Lucan must have told her that. It is a slight exaggeration, my lord." She smiled. "And, yes, Aimee received the flowers, thank you. Her health is much improved, and we are hoping she will be able to resume some of her activities quite soon."

"Good, good." Lord Hervey's double chin wagged with enthusiasm. "Serena said she sent one of her girls to help out. Now isn't that just like Serena? Your aunt's a generous woman, y'know. And regal! I always tell her she should have been a queen. Could have run the country better than . . . ahem. Well! It don't do to criticize our sovereign, of course. God save the king, and all that."

Diana repressed a smile. "Yes, Aunt Serena is very much the *grande dame*."

"Aye, she is that," he agreed. He stared pensively out the window for a few seconds then looked back at Diana. "Her birthday's coming soon, y'know. That's what I wanted to talk to you about."

"Oh?"

His head bobbed. "Wanted to do something special for

her, y'see. Throw a surprise party—something of the sort."

"That is very kind of you, Lord Hervey, but I am not completely sure that is a good idea. Surprises make her feel enfeebled, and are bad for her heart—or is it her digestion? I cannot quite recall."

"That won't do, then." Lord Hervey's chin sunk to his chest. "Well, let's see what you think of my other notion. I'd like to have the Torrington diamond reset for her. Thought it would look well in a necklace instead of a tiara. Serena pretends she don't like that diamond but that's just a lot of twaddle!" His voice dropped to a confiding whisper. "Ever notice your aunt has a little vain streak?" He nodded indulgently. "The truth is, she hasn't worn that tiara since her hair turned gray! So I thought, why not put the Torrington diamond in a necklace? A thing like that ought to be worn once in a while," he added simply. "No sense in owning it otherwise."

Diana sighed. "Lord Hervey, I really wish I could advise you, but I just do not know what to say. You will simply have to put it to Aunt Serena. If she likes the notion, I think it would be splendid. No one has seen the Torrington diamond in years."

Childlike pleasure spread over Lord Hervey's pudgy countenance. "Aye, I'll do that, I think. A woman like your aunt ought to wear a necklace fit for a queen."

With much the same amount of delight, Aimee's blue eyes lit when Diana presented her with the library books. "Oh, good!" she exclaimed, examining the titles intently. "And you were able to obtain *Glenarvon*! I'll read that one first."

Diana's gazed musingly down at her sister. "I'm not at all sure I should let you," she said half-seriously. "Whatever it's about, it seems to have set a great number of people in a bustle. I have it from no less a personage than Lady Edgerton that it is quite shocking."

Aimee looked up quickly. "Lady Edgerton! Oh, Diana, was she there?"

"Yes, indeed." said Diana calmly. "And I even spoke with her."

"Goodness, Diana, why? Whatever did you say to her? Was she polite? And were you?"

"Well, I was, but she was barely so. And the reason my dear, was mostly to prove to myself that I could do it. Never mind her. Did Charles visit while I was gone?"

"Alas, no," said Aimee, sighing wistfully. "It has been very boring while you were gone. I sat with Tildy while she finished another pair of stockings, but then she wanted to take a nap, so I've just been lying here thinking."

Diana surveyed her with interest. "Oh? About anything in particular?"

Aimee eased herself into a more upright position. "As a matter of fact—yes. I've been thinking about you."

"Oh? What about me?" For some reason, Diana was disconcerted.

"I've been wondering," said Aimee, rather timidly, "about you and Lord Lucan. I've been wondering if perhaps you ought to marry him, Diana. I know it is none of my business," she went on, rushing her words as if she feared interruption, "but I have seen such a difference in you lately. You seem so much more animated. And it is all because of him, is it not?"

Diana walked to the window, her back to her sister. "What makes you say that?" she said in an odd tone.

"I say it because it is the only possible answer. Just because I am young, Diana, does not mean I am blind. I told Mama before I left home that I would find you a husband. I haven't done much of a job of it, I'm afraid, but I think perhaps you found him by yourself."

There was a long, heavy silence before Diana swung

around. "Well, you are wrong," she stated dully. "I do not need a husband. I am happy the way I am." Sensing her sister's disbelief, she added, almost angrily, "For God's sake, Aimee, I have been through all that once! I've *earned* my independence. I'd be a fool to relinquish it!"

"But, Diana," faltered the younger girl, "doesn't every woman need a man? Isn't that the natural order of things? And anyway, if husbands are so . . . so horrid, why are you anxious for me to have one?"

Diana came close, and took firm hold of her sister's hand. "You are mistaken. I was never anxious for you to have a husband at your age, Aimee. But, sooner or later, the world we live in dictates that young girls marry. What other choice do we have? Men deem us inferior creatures whose mental powers cannot possibly be as great as theirs. We are considered unworthy of a good education, and those few of us who manage to live by what wits we possess are scorned, or considered outré. Why, even those of our own sex take this stand. Look at Hannah More, who says that young women should keep silent, so as not to *usurp the authority of men!*" Realizing that the faint furrow on Aimee's brow had deepened considerably, Diana paused. "Well, just listen to me," she said, more lightly. "I daresay I am as much a hypocrite as any. However, few men are monsters, and if I seem anxious it is only because I want you to marry a kind man, a man like Cousin Charles, who will treat you gently and with consideration."

"But, Diana," said Aimee, her eyes troubled, "don't you think Lord Lucan a kind man? Don't you believe he would treat you well?"

Diana sat back, and her eyes grew distant and faintly moist. "Yes," she whispered. "He is an extraordinarily kind man."

"Then, why not marry him, Diana? Hasn't he asked you?"

'Yes, he has asked."

221

"Then, *why?*"

Diana struggled to answer. "Because . . . because . . . oh, it's so complicated, I scarcely know myself! No, that's not true. You see, part of it is that I love him." Her head was bowed so that she missed her sister's incredulous look. "Yes, I think that's it. I've loved him for a long time now, but I'm afraid it is not enough."

"I don't understand."

Diana rubbed her temples wearily. "No, I don't expect you to understand. I don't want you to understand."

"Well, that's all right. After all, it's not for me to understand," replied Aimee, with unaccustomed logic. "But don't you think Lord Lucan will want to understand? It doesn't seem fair not to have a reason you can explain, Diana."

"No." Diana chewed her lower lip reflectively. "No, it doesn't, does it?"

Tossing aside his shirt, Sir Henry eyed the elaborate Chinese screen with impatience. "Aren't you ready yet?" he called out.

"Patience, darling . . ." Lady Uxbridge's throaty voice drifted low and sultry from behind the screen.

They were in someone else's house, someone he did not even know, but who, according to Sophia, owed her this favor. It scarcely mattered. He did not give a damn where they went, as long as he could put an end to the ache in his loins. He had reached the point where he neither knew nor cared whether it was Sophia or Diana his body craved. He only knew that Lady Uxbridge would serve the purpose adequately enough.

"Henry."

He glanced up, and in an instant all thoughts of Diana trundled from his head. What she wore was so transparent it could scarcely be called a gown, and what was under it was altogether spectacular. As experienced as he was, as many women that he had seen in their most natural state, he did not think he had ever seen her match.

"Sophia," he whispered, taking a jerky step forward. She held out her arms. "Come to me, darling."

Her emerald eyes were assessing his physique with a frankness which equaled his, and when he seized her, her hands were just as eager.

"What a beautiful man you are," she remarked, her head cocked to the side. With a teasing laugh, she tried to plant a kiss on his nose, but he forestalled her attempt with his mouth.

"On second thought," she murmured, after his long, hard kiss, "I think I should call you a boy." An irresistible, spoiled little boy," she added, her voice languorous. "And I know just what little boys like."

"Then show me," he mumbled, his lips roving her throat. "Show me, Sophia."

She drew back a bit, toying with him still. "Polite little boys say 'please'," she said playfully.

His nibbling kisses dropping ever lower, he responded, with more of his characteristic mockery. "But I . . . was never . . . a polite . . . little boy."

After partaking of a small nuncheon, Diana went upstairs to keep Miss Tilden company, and was just in time to witness the completion of the two hundredth pair of woolen stockings.

"I am becoming a trifle tired of making stockings," Tildy confessed, putting her needles down with relief. "I think I will make scarves for a few weeks instead. But I must find a way to get these stockings to the Foundling Hospital right away. Not that it is cold, of course, but the

223

children do need them eventually. We may as well send them along while we are right here in London."

Once Miss Tilden switched projects, Diana knew she would fret until all of the first had reached its intended beneficiaries. She therefore said, without hesitation, "I will take them there myself, Tildy. Perhaps even this afternoon, for I have nothing else to do today."

"It is too good of you, my dear," quavered the elderly woman, pressing her hand gratefully. "I do so hate to ask you, but you see, I always think of the children when I am making them, and how pleased they will be to receive something new." She sighed wistfully. "I wish I could go myself, but my ankle is still much too weak."

"But healing very nicely, according to Dr. Hatfield," said Diana bracingly. She leaned forward to kiss Tildy's soft, wrinkled cheek. "I shall have Mary pack up the stockings directly. But before I go anywhere, why do we not sit here and have a nice coze, and perhaps play a hand or two of piquet?"

*

At much the same time, the earl was scanning through some documents relating to his estate in Cornwall. At least he was *trying* to scan them, but unfortunately he had done so three times already and absorbed next to nothing in the process. How could he read when, instead of words, he saw Diana's lovely, vivid face? How could he focus upon anything but her radiant smile and sparkling eyes?

No woman had ever had such an effect upon his ability to concentrate. On the whole, he had no particular objection to being thus distracted (indeed, it was extremely pleasant) but he wanted to understand the rationale behind it. Was it possible that he had actually fallen in *love?* The earl's lips twisted in sudden self-mockery. Was a logical man like himself going to admit that such an emotion existed?

Casting aside his papers, the earl leaned back, linking his fingers behind his head. Love was such a difficult concept, he reflected. It was impossible to define, which was why he had always been so skeptical about it. In his salad days, he had fancied himself in love a hundred times, but in the end each of his loves had drifted away and he had never cared. Would he care if Diana went away? If he was never to see her again? Astonishingly, the very notion flooded him with such an ache that his eyes screwed shut with the pain. Well, that gave him his answer, said a taunting voice in his mind.

But would it last?

He spent a number of minutes pondering the question, but concluded that it was something that only time could decide. And it was really quite irrelevant, he thought, with unconscious arrogance. He had made up his mind that she was the woman he wanted for his wife, and that was final.

If only *she* would make up *her* mind! He had told himself over and over that she would accept him, that she *must* accept him, that there was no reason why she should not accept him. And when she did, he thought suddenly, he knew exactly what he was going to do—down to the last, intimate detail . . .

Damn! He shifted uncomfortably, aware that he ought to cut off this particular daydream before he had cause to regret it. Night and day he'd been dreaming of Diana, and unfortunately, his heated imagination was getting too good. But, sweet Jesus, he wanted her badly. He wanted to hold her in his arms and make love to her, kiss those sweek pink lips and chase away all her fears. He longed to assure her that whatever she wanted for the rest of her life would be hers, for he would make sure that she got it. Instinct told him that if he could only put his arms around her, he could convince her to accept him. But for some inexplicable reason he wanted her to say 'yes' without his using the force of their physical attraction as persuasion.

Just lately he'd begun to feel confident that she would soon come to the only reasonable conclusion. She must realize that a strong rapport existed between them, and it was obvious she was attracted to him. Since he was a man, the earl reasoned with masculine logic. Thus he could not think of a single reason why Diana should not accept him. So why the devil was she taking so long to decide?

Puzzled, he stared reflectively off into space. Confound it, he wished he understood. Was it her freedom she feared losing? Or was it something else? Was it something about him? Without realizing it, his fingers began to crumple the thin sheet of paper beneath his hand. He glanced down, then smoothed it mechanically and heaved a long, exasperated sigh. Well, there was obviously no use in trying to read any more documents today. His secretary would not be happy with him, but his secretary could go to the devil.

He would go and see Diana, and hope to God that this would be the day she would accept him and put him out of his misery. For after all was said and done, nothing could possibly be worse than this wretched, damnable waiting.

"Do you wish to play again?" Diana glanced at Miss Tilden as she gathered up the cards, deftly reducing them to a neat pile within seconds. Her long, graceful fingers automatically began to reshuffle the stack.

Regarding her former charge fondly, Miss Tilden leaned back against the pile of feather pillows which served as necessary prop to her frail body. "You are so clever with cards, my dear," she remarked. "I am no match for you, am I?"

"Certainly you are," replied Diana, still shuffling, "when you concentrate. But perhaps you are too tired to play again?"

"I am a little tired," the elderly woman admitted. "I'm getting old, I suppose." She semed to hesitate, and Diana shot her an inquiring look. "I hope I'm not too much of a burden to you," she said suddenly. "I worry about that, you know."

"A burden?" Diana was genuinely amazed. "Wherever did you get such a foolish notion? Tildy, I *love* you. You could never be a burden to me."

"You are such an angel," said Miss Tilden, much moved. "All your family is dear to me, but you, Diana, have always held a special place in my heart. You are like the daughter I never had. But I do wish I could see you looking happier."

Diana gave a little laugh. "But Tildy, I *am* happy. I have never been happier in my life than I am right now."

Miss Tilden shook her head. "Not so," she said wisely. "You are not satisfied with your life, Diana. And that is understandable. You need more than the company of an old woman like me, or even your sister, bless her heart. You need a husband and children of your own."

Diana sighed. "Perhaps I should tell you that Aimee and I had this same discussion a short while ago." She paused, choosing her words with care. "Well, I will tell you what I told her. I do not think that marriage agrees with me. I have not told you this, but Lord Lucan has asked me to marry him, and I have given his offer a great deal of very serious consideration. To be honest, if I were to marry he would be the only man I could consider." Her mouth turned down sadly. "But I have come to the conclusion that . . . that it would be best if I do not accept."

Miss Tilden's eyes were not as sharp as they had once been, but they saw more than one might suspect. "I see.

Have you told him yet?"

"No."

"And when do you plan to do it?" she prodded gently.

"I don't know." Diana shrugged.

Miss Tilden frowned. "Do you plan to reconsider your answer, or is it absolutely final?"

"I don't know," Diana repeated. Her fingers were suddenly clumsy, and the deck of cards flew from her hand to spread over the counterpane. She quickly gathered them up, and smiled the bright, false smile which Tildy found so disturbing. "Let's not discuss it anymore, shall we? If you are tired, I will send Mary to fetch your drink, and then, my dear Tildy, I plan to take those stockings straight to the Foundling Hospital where they belong."

"Very well, my dear," replied Tildy submissively. There was nothing she could do, after all. And when Diana bent to kiss her brow and tuck in the sheets, Miss Tilden did her very best to smile. Even though her heart was very heavy.

Diana descended the stairs intending to send Felix to fetch one of Aunt Serena's carriages, but the earl's arrival made this unnecessary. Her pulse leaped the instant she saw him, but rather than dwell upon the possible reasons for this, she put it down as simple cowardice. She absolutely dreaded having to tell him she was not going to be his wife.

"You are going out?" he asked, observing her carriage dress, and the large valise near the door.

She cleared her throat. "Yes, but I am in no hurry. I can visit with you for a short while before I leave."

Perhaps she should tell him now . . .

As usual, he had taken her hand, and was standing far closer than a gentleman ought. "Where are you going?" he asked sharply. "You are not leaving town, are you?"

She smiled slightly. "Goodness, no. The valise is full of

228

Tildy's stockings. I am off to the Foundling Hospital to deliver them."

He looked incredibly relieved. "Then, you must allow me to take you there," was his prompt response. "My curricle is just outside."

Diana wavered. "Thank you, my lord. It is very kind of you," she said finally, knowing she was being a coward. She would put the dreaded interview off until later, when the stockings were delivered. In the meantime, she would try to gather the requisite courage.

As soon as they were underway, she told him about her encounter with Lady Edgerton, which seemed a safe enough topic. She'd been certain he would find the story humorous, but he surprised her by saying, quite seriously, "Be careful how you deal with her sort, Diana. That woman can be quite vindictive when aroused to it." She was silent for so long he glanced down at her curiously. "Come, tell me what's wrong."

He didn't miss much, she thought. She'd been staring straight ahead at nothing in particular, but her thoughts had traveled far back in time . . .

"I was only remembering what happened six years ago. Foolish of me, I suppose. To look back on a painful part of one's life can do no good."

"If looking back serves a useful purpose, there's nothing wrong with it," he countered, guiding the horses around an apple cart. "Sometimes one gains enough in wisdom and understanding to justify it."

Diana sighed. "I suppose you are right." Seeking to change the subject, she said casually, "I saw Sir Henry today."

The earl's head swiveled. "And?"

"And I cut him. Quite publicly." She waited for his reaction, her eyes in her lap.

He said nothing for so long she glanced up, and saw that his lips were tightly compressed. "Was I wrong to do so?" she said anxiously. "He was about to address me, and he was with that odious Lady Uxbridge." When his face darkened with anger, her voice filled with the need for reassurance. "Are you angry with me, Geoffrey? It all happened so fast I did not have time to consider." Her use of his name was an unconscious slip.

"No, of course I'm not angry with you, Diana," he said curtly. "Nor am I sorry you did it. What infuriates me is that the blackguard spoke to you at all. He swore upon his honor he would not."

"Well, I doubt he will do so again," she said hopefully. "I did not dare to look back, but I would think he'd be quite angry with me now. I daresay he will no longer wish for my acquaintance."

The earl's eyes glinted a little. "Yes, I'm sure he was quite put out. But to be certain he does not forget himself again, I will pay him another visit."

Something in his tone made her eyes fly to his face. "You will not do anything absurd, will you?"

"Absurd? Such as what?" he inquired, amused despite the anger burning inside him.

"Oh, I mean hit him, or . . . or call him out," she explained.

He shrugged. "I'll do whatever is necessary. Are you concerned for his safety?"

She stared at him. "*His* safety! Good God, I don't care a jot about his safety. It is *your* safety which concerns me, my lord. Sir Henry is obviously a man without honor. I shudder to think what he is capable of doing. I—I simply do not want you to be hurt on my account."

"My dear Mrs. Verney," said the earl, his spirits considerably lightened. "I am touched. Fear not for my safety, ma'am. I am fully capable of taking care of myself. Has no one ever told you that boxing is one of my pastimes?"

"No, of course not!" she retorted. "Why would

anyone tell me such a thing?"

"Well, it is," he replied. "It's something I do rather well, in fact."

"Then that explains why you're so—" Realizing what she had nearly said, Diana blushed to the roots of her hair.

His black brows shot up. "So what, Diana?"

"Oh, I . . . never mind."

How appallingly inelegant it would have been to comment upon his muscular physique! It would make him think she had studied him in a most unladylike fashion—which to her shock she realized was the truth. . . .

Of course, he guessed what she had meant to say. "Dear Diana, you are so very sweet," he said, quite tenderly. "So very respectable."

She made no answer, for his words were like a hot knife twisting inside her. She was not sweet at all, she thought in despair. He would not think so highly of her later, nor would he speak so gently. Not after she had turned down his offer of marriage.

Chapter Thirteen

"Would you care to stay for tea, my lord?"

For the first time in over two hours, Diana's voice was hesitant, even a little shy. While delivering stockings to the Foundling Hospital, she had been perfectly in control, and the ride back to Jermyn Street had been companionable and peaceful. Somehow she had managed to steer clear of any topic even remotely connected with marriage, and had even managed to keep her private thoughts on other paths. Yet now, as she stood beside the earl upon the front steps of her house, she suddenly longed to be done with it. It was time to tell him.

Something told her he knew it, too. Whether it was the flicker of his eyes or that instant of stillness about his stance she did not know, but whatever the case she was certain he knew it. She also had no doubt that he was anticipating her acceptance.

"I'd like that very much," he answered, gazing down at her with a pensive air. With a jerk of his chin, he instructed his groom to continue on to the mews. "Providing, of course, that you offer me something to eat," he added, in a joking tone.

"Naturally," she replied with dignity. "I need no reminder, Lord Lucan. I am as hungry as you are."

Her reproachful look made him laugh, and as they stepped into the house, he placed a proprietary hand at her waist. He did not ordinarily touch her thus, but he was obviously in high and very confident spirits and Diana found she could say nothing. Indeed, the knowledge that she was about to dash those spirits weighed heavily upon her, although it did not quite account for the bewildering tingle which went racing through every nerve in her body at very much the same instant.

Once inside, Diana composed her features and forced what she hoped was a note of cheerfulness into her voice. "Goodness, delivering those stockings took much longer than I expected! Aimee and Tildy are sure to have eaten already so I shall not ask them to join us. Aimee, in any case, is probably engrossed in *Glenarvon* and would not wish to be disturbed." She untied the ribands of her bonnet and laid it carefully upon the pier table at her elbow. "Lawrence, pray send up the tea tray immediately. And some of those delicious cakes which Cook made just this morning. It is well past tea time and his lordship is famished."

"Yes, as it happens, I am," remarked the earl, his hard mouth slanting ruefully as he handed the butler his hat. He followed her toward the stairs, saying, "You allow your sister to read books like that?" He sounded mildly surprised.

"Books like what?" she inquired over her shoulder.

"Books that are written out of spite, meant to stir up trouble rather than to instruct or entertain. It's not even well written," he added, as they reached the first floor.

"Have you read it?"

He shook his head. "Not word for word. I wouldn't waste my time on it." He saw her inquiring expression. "My dear Diana, it's the sort of story that will only encourage your sister to engage in foolish histrionics. Its

233

characters are so clearly cast from life they are completely recognizable. Lord Byron is the hero—if one can call such a dastard a hero—and Caro Lamb is the heroine. And Lady Caroline's representation of her mother-in-law, Lady Melbourne, is purely malicious. She has set the seal on her own social disgrace by airing her grievances so openly."

"Oh." Diana mulled this over, then said in a placating tone, "Well, I cannot actually forbid Aimee to read it, but I will drop a hint in her ear. Better yet, I will ask Charles to do so." She took a seat and patted the chair next to her invitingly.

Lord Lucan strode forward, a glint in his eye. "An excellent notion but for the fact that she will very likely be done with it by then," he agreed. He sat as if he were in his own home, stretching his long legs out in front of him.

Despite her apprehension, Diana could not prevent her lips from twitching. "Well!" she said, her manner more relaxed. "I believe that is what you sporting gentlemen call a *flush hit*? Or am I mistaken?"

He grinned. "Are we sparring again? I meant only to offer a little friendly advice."

"And I should hardly be so uncivil as to ignore it," she said, more seriously. "But I still contend that your opinion of my sister is too severe. Reading is merely a diversion for her, my lord. She does not pattern her life around such melodramas."

He shrugged. "If you say so. It is none of my affair, after all."

Normally, she would have made a point to agree with him, which would have set off another whole round of such banter. However, there were more important matters on Diana's mind, and until Lawrence arrived with the tea tray and the necessary accouterments for their repast, she scarcely knew what conversation passed

234

between them. As soon as the butler left, she noticed that the earl sat straighter, and there was an air of expectancy about him which brought a tightness crawling into the pit of her stomach. How on earth was she going to do this?

As calmly as possible, Diana poured the steaming tea into two dainty china cups. "Is this one of your sugar days, my lord? Or will you drink your tea black?"

"Sugar, by all means," he replied lightly. "I'm in a festive mood."

The tension felt like tiny needles pricking at her skin. With a curious kind of detachment, Diana noticed that her hands were quite steady as she passed over the teacup. How very strange that was. And how ludicrously fragile the cup looked in the earl's hand.

Although there was no longer any reason to put off the inevitable, she heard herself say, "Do try a cake, my lord. They are very good."

Inwardly, she castigated herself, scorning her own cowardice, despising her weakness. It was stupid and cruel to keep procrastinating merely because the interview was bound to be painful. Had she not decided to be strong? Yet a part of her knew this was not quite fair, for it was not fear which made her hesitate, but a reluctance to hurt the man she loved.

She sat stiffly, unable to do more than study the earl over the rim of her teacup. How, she wondered, could she ever have thought him unattractive? Loving him as she now did, she believed him superior in every way, and this included physical appearance. Indeed, she mused, how could she ever have thought to resist a man so compellingly masculine? Especially when the entire force of that masculinity was centered so flatteringly upon herself?

His dynamic presence filled the room, dwarfing everything in it. It had always been so, she reflected even that first day he had visited her, and even six years before

235

that. At age eighteen, she had been in awe of him, mistaking his blunt, forthright manner as something threatening or formidable. However, at four-and-twenty, she had been unable to preserve this attitude, despite all efforts to the contrary. Looking back, she could now admit that not once since her arrival in London had she ever been truly angry with him. In fact, every one of their encounters had been impossibly exciting, and her so-called anger had been but a willful self-delusion, an excuse to engage in verbal sparring matches that acted like a tonic upon her frozen emotions.

She must tell him. But could she possibly hope to make him accept her decision when it was not what he wanted? She doubted he would give up easily. He was a man who met life boldly and confronted every challenge head-on. Could she convince him that—this time—the conservative approach was best? She had to try. She had to do what she believed was right, though it made her feel as treacherous as Judas. Taking a deep breath, Diana set down her teacup and cleared her throat.

"Geoffrey—"

Her use of his name was inadvertent and probably unwise, for it brought an intensity to his eyes that made her nerves jump. She stumbled over her next words.

"I—I know you will not mind if I call you Geoffrey . . ." *Dear God, why did she have to sound so foolish, so gauche, so young?* Diana flushed, and made her voice firm. "I've been thinking about your offer."

"And?" The earl set down his cup and leaned forward, his eyes locked on her face.

She moistened her lips. "This is very difficult for me to say, but I'm afraid I . . . I cannot marry you. I thank you for your offer but my answer must be . . . no."

What poise she possessed caved in with a crash. Lord Lucan's expression barely altered, yet the room was all at once a void, full of nothing but stark, rigid silence. The

236

afternoon grew colder, the shadows longer, and a chill wrapped itself around Diana's heart.

A handful of seconds slipped by before he spoke. "Well, that was short and sweet," he remarked, with unnatural flippancy. "Is that it? Shall I go now?" His disappointment was so tangible she could feel it.

Stricken with guilt and remorse, Diana stretched out a hand, but he pointedly ignored the gesture, and her hand dropped limply back into her lap. Her face was very pale.

"Please listen, Geoffrey," she begged. "It's important to me that you understand." His mouth was tight and uncompromising, but she went on, imploringly, "Whatever you may think, this has not been an easy decision for me to make. If you think I do not care for you, you are wrong. Quite the contrary, I care for you very deeply— too deeply to marry you."

He frowned, but his mouth lost some of its pinched, icy look. "I think that you had better explain that," he said carefully.

"I am trying to!" Unable to stay still, Diana stood and walked to the window, her arms wrapped under her breasts in an unconsciously shielding gesture. Now that she faced him, she realized that she would have to tell him the whole truth, that there could be no half-measures or cowardly evasions. Feeling his gaze on her back, she swung around, endeavoring to put into words what she had been unable to tell Aimee.

"You see, my first marriage was a disaster in every sense of the word. I've told you that, I think. Edmund cared less than nothing for me, and to be frank, I felt the same for him." Her voice wavered a little, but she controlled it and looked him straight in the eye. "I am no innocent girl, Geoffrey. I was Edmund's wife in the fullest sense, and I know what is involved."

The earl stared at her, baffled. "Naturally, I assumed as much," he replied, a note of harshness in his voice.

"But what the devil does that have to do with us?"

Sensing his frustration, Diana's eyes clouded with anguish. "Geoffrey, what I am trying to tell you is that I found that particular part of marriage excessively distasteful. Edmund knew it and went to other women for his pleasure—with my blessing, I am ashamed to say."

Those piercing gray eyes were riveted to her face, unrelenting and keen, demanding an explanation that she hardly knew how to supply. He was making this horribly difficult for her.

She swallowed hard. "You see, it is because I . . . I love you that I cannot marry you. I owe you a great deal, I know. These weeks with you . . . have brought me out of my cocoon. Because of you, I have felt so *alive* and . . . and *whole* . . . and for a while I really thought it might work. But it's not enough. I love you with all my heart, Geoffrey, but marriage is not for me. I . . . I could not suffer through . . . all *that* again. Not even for you. And eventually you would despise me for it. And if you went to someone else, I could not bear to live."

Lithe as a panther, the earl was out of his chair. "Diana," he said stubbornly, "at the risk of sounding like an utter coxcomb, I think you might find the experience different with me. Edmund Verney was the lowest kind of vermin, my dear. I doubt he tried overmuch to please you." He had planted himself directly in front of her and was scowling fiercely.

A fleeting smile touched her lips. "Edmund never did anything to please me," she agreed, reaching up to trace the line of his jaw with her finger. "But, Geoffrey, I have decided I cannot take that chance. I cannot, in all conscience, accept your offer because I know I would make you miserable. It is for your own good."

He closed the remaining gap between them, his hands clamping around her wrists with unconscious force. "Dammit, Diana, I am miserable now!" he retorted, his fingers tightening as if he longed to shake her. "Forget your damned scruples and marry me! Give me a chance to prove I can make you happy! I think what you are saying is complete rubbish, but if in truth you find that you cannot stomach me, why then I'll—I'll leave you alone. I swear it."

His grip on her wrists was too tight, but she ignored the pain, for it was nothing in comparison to the wrenching agony in her heart. Perilously near tears, her voice quivered.

"A little while ago you told me I was sweet, but it is you, Geoffrey, who are sweet. Sweet and hopelessly unrealistic. It would never work, my dear, don't you see? Were I to deny you, sooner or later you would go to another, and though I would try to understand, I fear my love for you would suffer as a result. I know many men have mistresses, but I could not just look the other way. I would want to kill her, whoever she was. Don't you think that would be an odious marriage? Do you see that I am right?" Now that she was finally telling him, the words came tumbling from her mouth. "Why risk it, Geoffrey? If we do not marry, we can remain friends which is far better, for we will not lose each other. It is a good compromise. Please, please, try to see that I am right."

Hearing the obstinancy behind the plea, he stared at her in despair, racking his brain for some magical words to make her see things his way. Out of nowhere, his own advice came back to haunt him. *There are no magic formulas . . .*

"This is not logical, Diana," he said inadequately.

"But it *is* logical," she objected. "Think about it, my dear. If we can remain friends—"

"Dammit, Diana, I don't want you as my friend!" he exploded. "I want you for my wife. I want you in my bed so I can make love to you as often as possible, preferably every day for the rest of my natural life. I want you to bear my children, Diana. I want sons who look like me and daughters who look like you with topaz eyes and glorious golden hair. I want to be able to—"

"You seem to want a great deal!" she interrupted, with new coolness. "And I do not think you are even *trying* to understand! I have spent *hours* agonizing over what is best for both of us. But it seems that you only consider what is best for you!"

"Not true!" he retorted, stung. "I know what you need better than you do, my girl. What you need is to be kissed and bedded by someone who knows what he's doing! And you need someone to paddle some sense into you so that you'll stop torturing yourself—and me, I might add— with these harebrained, foolish flights of fancy—"

"Flights of fancy!" she echoed, in sudden, vibrant fury. Something inside her snapped at the phrase. "If you think for one moment," she blazed, "that Edmund Verney's crude, animalistic embraces were merely some flight of fancy, or some . . . some figment of my imagination, then pray allow me to correct you. My husband hurt me, Geoffrey Trevelyan! On my wedding night he left me with nothing. Not my virginity, not my pride, not my self-respect, and certainly not with any expectation of future happiness." She laughed, and the laugh was laced with bitterness. "No, let me correct myself. He did leave me one thing. Pain. A great deal of it, in fact. I vowed long ago never to repeat that experience—at least not voluntarily. So, my lord, unless you are prepared to force me against my will—"

The injustice of the suggestion cut him to the quick. "Don't be ridiculous," he rasped, finally giving her that shake. "Dammit, Diana, you're not listening to me! If you think I would treat you anything like that cur treated you, then you're out of your senses!"

"Oh, really! You're a man, aren't you?" she cried, too near hysteria to consider the wisdom of her words.

The earl's face whitened with rage. "Why, how clever of you to notice!" he said sarcastically. "Since the game is up, I shan't scruple to give in to my bestial instincts. We men are all the same, you know. When all is said and done, there is little to choose between us."

As he spoke he jerked Diana against him, his expression more savage than she had ever seen it. Before she could do more than stare up at him, his mouth was seizing hers, his lips cleaving hungrily while his thrusting tongue forced its way forward. It was an aggressive kiss, yet it did not inflict pain, and it evolved so quickly into one of passion and sensuality that Diana's senses skittered and spun. It was a kiss that might have won the day if he had not gone a step farther and slid his hand between them to caress her soft, quivering breasts.

But Diana was not yet ready for this. Dazed to the point of numbness, she recoiled from his touch, pushing against his chest with the whole of her strength. Then the earl, failing to comprehend his mistake, compounded his error by trying to renew the embrace, but this only made Diana struggle more. Ugly memories of Edmund erupted in her mind, and for a moment she forgot who it was that held her, forgot that she loved him, and acted on pure instinct. Recalling something she had once done to Edmund, she raised her knee, aiming for the earl's groin.

The earl's quick reflexes came to his aid, enabling him to turn just enough so that she barely grazed his thigh. However, though he tried to catch her, the force of her attempted kick put Diana off balance, and she tumbled to the floor.

For an instant, he stood over her like a conqueror, his legs spread wide, his fists planted firmly on his lean hips. But as she stared dully back, it was as though a curtain had been ripped away, and for the first time he really saw the dark torment behind the brown-gold eyes. He had sensed that there were things she preferred not to

241

discuss, things which had to do with her unhappy marriage, but now he was truly beginning to understand. Wishing it were possible to murder Edmund Verney all over again, he dropped to his knees beside her.

"Forgive me, Diana!" He said it twice more, gathering her into his arms with a tenderness so at odds with his previous behavior that Diana simply accepted it and clung to him, sobbing into the white material of his shirt.

"God, I'm sorry, love," he murmured, over and over in her ear. "I'll never do that again to you, darling, I swear upon everything I hold sacred. I'll never hurt you again, Diana. Please stop crying, darling."

"But you didn't hurt me," she gasped, fighting for composure. "And I know you're not like Edmund. I don't know what made me say that."

"No, I promise you I'm not," he said, kissing the top of her head. "So it hardly makes sense to assume that going to bed with me will be unpleasant, does it?" he inquired. He pushed her hair back out of her face, stroking the soft golden curls which had escaped confinement. "I did not think I was that unappealing to you."

"You don't understand. It's not you," she insisted, her voice husky with emotion. "It's—it's me, Geoffrey. I didn't want you to know, actually. I'm horribly embarrassed to tell you, but there's . . . there's something wrong with me."

"Nonsense," he replied. "What could be wrong?"

"I don't know," she almost wailed. "But there is something different about me. I'm just not like other women."

He gazed at her in tender bewilderment. "I'll vouch for that," he said, his lips twisting. "You're far more beautiful, muddled, and maddening than any other woman I've ever known!"

"Don't tease me," she begged, and amazed him by pressing her lips to his hand. "Let's forgive each other

242

and forget this ever happened. I don't want to brangle with you."

"Nor I with you," he agreed, helping her to her feet. "You've said you care for me—well, I care for you, too. A very great deal, in fact." His hands cupped her face, and for a long moment he stared into her tear-soaked eyes. "You *must* marry me, Diana," he urged. "There's nothing wrong with you. Let me prove it to you."

It would be so easy to give in, but having come this far, Diana was determined to stand firm. After all the soul-searching, after all the procrastination and vacillation, she had done what she had to do. As difficult as it had been, she had finally told him, and now it was evident that she would have to be strong for them both.

"No, Geoffrey," she said bravely, ignoring the leaden ache in her chest. "I refuse to do something that will only cause us both more pain."

His clenched jaw was set in an obstinate line. "You know I'm not going to give up, Diana. You think about it some more, won't you, darling? Promise me you'll think about it some more."

Uncertain whether such a promise would be more cruel than kind, Diana hesitated, but before she could answer, there were footsteps on the stairs.

"Forgive me for interrupting, madam," said Lawrence a moment later. "But you have visitors."

"Visitors?" Diana repeated blankly. "Who can be calling at this hour?"

His fastidious fingers held a small calling card by its corner. "A Mrs. and Miss Fingleshaw, madam. I took the liberty of putting them in the morning room. They appeared to know you."

Slowly, Diana sank into the chair behind her, her gaze fixed on the butler. "First Lady Edgerton, then Sir Henry, and now, *now* Eliza Fingleshaw," she said faintly. "What could possibly happen next?"

Chapter Fourteen

In the end, Diana was obliged to invite Eliza and her mama to stay for dinner, for they showed no disposition to keep their visit short. They had arrived in London only that afternoon, having bounced around for the better part of the day in Mr. Fingleshaw's rumbling old traveling coach.

"It is dreadfully antiquated," complained Eliza, a tall, angular girl with sandy hair and pale bluish-gray eyes. "But as many times as we have mentioned it to Papa, he refuses to spend the money on a new one."

"My husband has the most tiresome notions," stated her mother with a trill. "Only fancy! He did not want me to bring my darling Eliza up to London to visit her bosom friend, the *confidante* of her entire childhood!" Her chair creaked as she made impatient gestures. "Can you conceive of anything more nonsensical? As if we should be infringing somehow upon dear little Aimee's Season— which I know we could not possibly do."

Eliza giggled, and looked at Aimee. "I have *so* much to tell you, but I shall wait until I have you all to myself. Mama says I can invite you over just as soon as we are settled. Of course, I am not officially *out*, but Mama says there are still a number of things I can do. It will be such capital fun!''

"Perhaps I should warn you that Aimee has been ill," interposed Diana firmly, "and may not be quite ready for all the activities you are planning."

Mrs. Fingleshaw's alarmed gaze shifted between the two sisters. "Ill? I do trust it was nothing serious? I noticed she looked thinner, but I put it down to the unaccustomed strain of town life."

Diana folded her hands. "Well, she is much better now, ma'am. But, yes, it was fairly serious for a spell."

Eliza turned to Aimee. "Have you had a great many offers?" she asked, bouncing a little. "I cannot wait to hear about all those suitors you mentioned in your letters! Who was that scowling gentlemen who left just after we arrived? I saw him through the morning room window, you know. He is not one of your suitors, is he, Aimee? I thought he looked quite frightening, and not at all handsome."

"Goodness, no, Eliza," scoffed Aimee, with a swift, sidelong glance at her sister. "Lord Lucan is too old for me. He is Diana's friend."

"Lord Lucan?" repeated Mrs. Fingleshaw in an impressed voice. "My dear Diana, do not tell me that a peer of the realm has chosen to honor you with his attentions?" Her eyes goggled as she strained forward in her seat.

"Not at all," lied Diana. "Lord Lucan *is* a friend, but nothing more than that."

Despite this assertion, an arch smile sprang to Mrs. Fingleshaw's lips. "Silly goose! You need not keep secrets from me, my dear. Think how long your mama and I have been acquainted! I am perfectly aware that she and your papa yearn to see you happily established and that you are a dutiful, sensible girl. It would be the most natural thing in the world for you to look about for a husband while you are here. There is not the least occasion for you to pretend otherwise."

Concealing her annoyance, Diana kept her reply courteous. "Indeed, ma'am, I think you do not understand. I have no wish to remarry. And my parents want only what is best for me."

But Mrs. Fingleshaw was obviously unconvinced, for she waved a waggish finger, and said, "Now, now, my dear. I shall say no more. No one will ever be able to say that I, Eudora J. Fingleshaw, do not know how to keep a secret!"

They soon went in to dinner, where the conversation quickly turned to the subject of Aimee's success and the host of delights in store for Eliza.

"Freddy has told me all about Vauxhall Gardens," Eliza announced, rather breezily. "Perhaps he will be able to take us there himself, for he is right here in London. In fact, though Mama did not tell you, that is the main reason for our being here. He has been sent down from Oxford for the rest of the term."

"What, again?" said Diana involuntarily.

For the first time, Mrs. Fingleshaw appeared a trifle discomposed. "Yes, is it not the most tiresome thing? My son seems to have gotten in with the wildest set of young men. They are constantly getting him into one scrape or another. I don't scruple to tell you that Mr. Fingleshaw is enraged, but I think it preposterous to believe that our Freddy has anything to do with these shocking schemes they hatch. He was always such a good boy." She sighed, abandoned her obstinate defense of her son, and dabbed her mouth with her napkin. "Mr. Fingleshaw has bidden me to bring him home," she added glumly.

Diana remembered Freddy Fingleshaw as having been a very nasty little boy, but tactfully refrained from making reference to the multitudinous troubles he had caused during his more youthful years. Instead, she suggested that they repair to the drawing room for coffee.

"I fear I cannot ask you to stay much longer," she said pointedly, "as Aimee needs her rest. I am hoping she will be herself again in a very short time."

"May she visit me tomorrow?" asked Eliza hopefully. "We can just sit in my room and talk. She can even lie on my bed if she wishes."

Diana hesitated, but was unable to think of a reason to refuse. "I don't see why not," she said finally. "It sounds like a perfect arrangement. I think Aimee is ready to begin making some short outings."

Aimee and Eliza exchanged eager glances. "Oh, good!" they said, so nearly in unison that they both went into a fit of the giggles.

"Oh, Eliza! I am so glad you have come!" cried Aimee, reaching impulsively for her friend's hand. Then they both laughed again in a giddy, girlish way that set Diana's teeth on edge.

Thanks to Eliza Fingleshaw, she reflected gloomily, Aimee's behavior was already backsliding.

That night, Diana was too tired to do more than fall instantly asleep, but a loud crack of thunder awoke her sometime near morning. Still drowsy, she lay for a while listening to the hard, steady beat of rain, but instead of drifting off again her mind grew gradually alert. She thought of her childhood, and of the carefree existence she had led until Edmund entered her life. She thought of her wedding night, and of the many long, lonely nights she had lived through since then. She recalled how she had locked her door against Edmund, and why it had been necessary to do so. And she thought about Geoffrey Trevelyan.

Every fiber in her body ached to be with him. How wonderful it would be, she thought, to have him sleeping next to her, to hear the reassuring sound of his breathing in the dark. She could imagine how blissfully safe she would feel knowing that he was right there within the reach of her hand. It had been a long time since she had felt that kind of security, security derived from the knowledge that there was someone strong to lean on—someone who cared. She was honest enough to acknowledge, however, that the strange, restless ache inside her was a great deal more complicated than a simple need for protection.

She had to admit that what he said made sense. How could intimacy with him be anything like intimacy with Edmund? Geoffrey would be caring and considerate; he would never try to hurt her—at least not intentionally. Many years before, her mother had told her that it was a woman's duty just to lie still and let her husband do what men were intended to do. That it was all that was required of her, that it was what a good and dutiful wife did. It had sounded depressing at the time, and it sounded just as depressing now. Why, oh *why* could women not enjoy it? At least just a little?

But perhaps they did. She wished she knew another woman with whom she could discuss the matter. Aunt Serena was out of the question, and as for Mama, the subject had obviously made her extremely uncomfortable. Rolling to her side, Diana pulled the blanket up to her chin and gazed rather sadly into the blackness. If only she had a close friend, someone with whom she could discuss things of a private nature, perhaps she might understand a little more about it. But there was only one person in her life who came anywhere near to fitting this description. And that was Geoffrey himself.

The following morning, Cousin Charles came by to inquire whether Aimee was fit enough for a drive in the Park. Though the ground was still wet, the rain had cleared the air and the sun was peeping over the tops of the houses in a most determined fashion. Diana's gray mood began to lift as she observed Charles's attentiveness to her sister. Under her approving eye, he handed Aimee into his carriage as tenderly as if she were a china doll, and tucked a blanket over her knees with the most painstaking regard for her comfort.

At least things were going well in that quarter, she reflected. Cousin Charles would surely be making her sister a declaration quite soon—at least, as long as Eliza Fingleshaw did not put a spoke in the wheel.

Diana reentered her house with a sigh, and decided that it was time to pay a visit on Aunt Serena. She had not done so since before Aimee had taken ill, and though this could hardly be said to be her fault, she could not banish the feeling that she had been derelict in her duty toward her aunt.

Apparently, Aunt Serena shared that opinion. "Well, well!" she remarked, as disagreeably as ever. "Fancy you taking the trouble to come all the way to Arlington Street only to see me. What cataclysmic event can have prompted this, I wonder?"

Preserving her calm, Diana dropped a quick kiss on her aunt's cheek and sat down. "No, I'm afraid we have had no cataclysms today, Aunt Serena. Is your stomach troubling you again? Is that why you're so peevish?"

The dowager eyed her with disfavor. "Impertinent girl," she grumbled. "I don't know why I can't get any respect out of you. Your sister's just as bad."

"Now that is unfair and you know it. Would you prefer that we bow and scrape? I thought you disliked that sort of thing."

The dowager's cane thumped the floor. "Hang it, girl. I do! For land's sake, now, don't go looking smug just because I agreed with you. How's little Aimee? Why didn't she come with you?"

Diana sat back and adjusted her skirts. "Cousin Charles has taken her for a drive. She is much better, but still a trifle weak. I am planning to bring her to see you as soon as I can."

Aunt Serena's chin drooped thoughtfully. "See that you do. I like the chit. She knows what she wants and has the spunk to try to get it. Behaves a bit silly, of course, but she'll grow wiser with time."

"I certainly hope so," agreed Diana, a shade dryly.

The dowager shot her a look. "You've got spunk, too, Diana. But you've got to learn to take what you want from life, and stop namby-pambying around. It puts me completely out of patience with you."

Diana's mouth hardened. "Oh, does it?" she said coolly. "Well, I am sorry to hear it, for I plan to continue namby-pambying my own way through my own life, Aunt Serena. Perhaps I should inform you that my chief concern at this time is Aimee. I want to see her married to someone who will be kind to her. And I am hoping very much that someone will be your grandson."

"Hang it, of course she's going to wed Charles," replied the dowager, glaring impatiently. "If she wants him, she'll have him. The boy hasn't a prayer's chance of escaping. What you should be concerned about is yourself, birdwitted girl! Are you going to marry Lord Lucan or not?"

Diana returned the glare. "And just what makes you think he's asked me?"

"Hang it, I *know* he's asked you. He told me so himself!"

"Well, he should not have!" snapped her niece, keeping her temper with difficulty. "And, no, I am not going to marry him!"

Once more, the dowager's cane thumped. "Confound it, girl, why the devil not? Haven't you the wit to see the man's in love with you?"

For a time Diana did not reply. Then she said, more quietly, "I know he cares for me, Aunt Serena. Whether he loves me or not is another thing entirely." She shifted restlessly, her hands massaging her knees through the thin muslin. "But after much thought, I have decided that I do not wish to marry him."

The dowager looked disgusted. "Pah! Of course you do, addlepated girl. Where on earth have your wits gone? Why, any sensible woman would want to marry a man like that. I'd marry him myself if I was forty years younger!"

"Oh, would you?" said Diana stiffly. "Simply because he is wealthy and bears a title, I suppose."

"There is that, of course," nodded Aunt Serena. Then she leered, and began jabbing the air with her finger. "That and the fact that he's put together damned nicely! Most of these high-born young whippersnappers mincing around London wouldn't strip to half such advantage. Manly, that's the word for him. A discriminating woman learns to appreciate such things."

Though she knew she ought to be shocked, Diana amazed herself by laughing. "For pity's sake, Aunt Serena," she begged, "*do* keep your voice down. The servants are likely to hear!"

Paying no heed to the suggestion. the dowager scratched her nose reflectively. "What's more, it's my guess he'll know what he's doing between the sheets. Well, at his age, he should, but that ain't always the case," she added inconsequently. "At any rate, he ain't a philanderer, which is a strong point in his favor. He told me he's sown his share of oats, but that he's done with all that. He's ready to settle down now."

Diana sat back and stared at her aunt. "Well! You and he are certainly on intimate terms," she remarked, rather crossly.

Aunt Serena preened. "Yes, I always had the knack for

251

getting a man to talk. Some women are born with it, others just ain't!"

Abruptly, Diana decided it was time to change the subject. "Has Lord Hervey spoken with you about your birthday?" she asked.

"My birthday? Oh, you mean that business about resetting the Torrington diamond?" Aunt Serena cackled. "Imagine Thurstan thinking of such a thing. The man's completely besotted with me. He even took a house on Bennet Street just to be near me!"

Diana sighed inwardly. "Yes, he seems very devoted. So you think it's a good notion?"

"Lord, no!" scoffed the dowager, smiling fondly. "What do I want with another necklace? I told him the diamond belongs in the tiara. It was a gift from Charles II, for land's sake. One doesn't chop up an heirloom like that!"

"I thought you might feel like that. But he seemed so delighted with the notion I was reluctant to say so."

Aunt Serena stared off into space for a few seconds. "He keeps asking me to marry him," she said suddenly. "But I keep turning him down."

Diana was surprised. "Oh? Why?"

She received a sharp look for her pains. "I don't need a reason, missy. When you reach my age, you can be as peculiar as you choose. It'll be your prerogative, but right now its's mine."

With a sigh, Diana studied the old woman's face, her gaze softening as she took in the fine, aristocratic bones beneath the wrinkled flesh. "You are a little, ah, unconventional," she admitted. "But as often as you annoy, confuse, and bewilder me, there are times when I really don't think I would have you any other way. It seems very strange," she added musingly.

Great-aunt Serena grinned. "Ha! Thank God there's

some sense in you, Diana. There's hope for you yet!"

For the next few days, Aimee divided her time fairly evenly between Eliza Fingleshaw and Cousin Charles. She and Eliza spent the bulk of their time gossiping and giggling—concerning what, not even Diana cared to guess. One might arguably claim that the healthy glow in Aimee's cheeks owed its restoration to Eliza's visit, but in her elder sister's opinion, it was merely the natural consequence of fresh air, increased activity, and improved appetite. These, in turn, were all linked to Charles and his efforts on her young sister's behalf, for Aimee's mornings were almost exclusively taken up by her handsome cousin.

Unfortunately, Aimee's recent and rather engaging display of good judgement had all but vanished. She no longer seemed to think before she spoke, and to Diana, what came out of her sister's mouth seemed more foolish than ever. The day that Cousin Charles escorted Aimee and Eliza for a walk in Green Park was not, as it later proved, the culmination, yet at the time, it crowned what was clearly becoming a threat to Aimee's future hopes. Diana was never to know exactly what occurred, but the look of stoicism on Charles's face when they returned might have been laughable had it not seemed so ominous. Ominous, too, was the speed with which he made his departure, so that when, an instant later, Eliza went into one of her fits of insane giggling, Diana rounded on her guest with a most uncharacteristic snap.

She soon left the room, for she could not quite care for the bold way Eliza returned her gaze, or the manner in which her pale eyes glinted back. And knowing that Miss Fingleshaw was fundamentally just as much a mischief-maker as her brother, Diana could not help feeling

253

uneasy. She reassured herself, however, with the reminder that Eliza's mother intended to leave London by the end of the week, and so was able to push the matter from her mind. She might not have done so had she been privileged to hear the ensuing conversation.

"Aimee," whispered Eliza, when Diana's footsteps had faded away, "it's all set with Freddy. All we must do is smuggle your evening clothes out of the house. You had better give them to me today, so your sister does not become suspicious."

Aimee nodded slowly, "Yes, but, Eliza, I'm not at all sure I shouldn't simply tell Diana what we are planning. To own the truth, I would feel a great deal better if I had her consent."

"Absolutely not!" hissed Eliza. "You must do nothing of the sort. She would only spoil everything! Anyway, you do not need her permission. She is only your sister, not your guardian."

When Aimee frowned, Miss Fingleshaw's voice turned coaxing. "Oh, do not be so provoking. It will be such fun! Freddy is bringing some of his Oxford friends, so we will have a surfeit of male protection. Nothing can possibly go wrong, and your sister need never know anything about it."

Aimee's blue eyes held a troubled look. "Yes, but I keep thinking that . . . that Charles would not like it," she said.

"Oh, pooh," said Eliza, scorning this sentiment. "Who cares what he thinks? That cousin of yours is not nearly as remarkable as you led me to believe. He is positively stodgy, Aimee. I cannot see you married to someone like that. You need to meet a more exciting man, a man who knows how to flirt!"

"Charles is not stodgy!" objected Aimee indignantly. "At least, he is a little, but in a rather endearing way. You

254

will like him more when you are better acquainted."

"Perhaps," conceded the other, "but does he ever flirt with you? Ever?"

"Well," said Aimee weakly, "not exactly. But he did take me home when I thought I was going to be sick . . ."

Eliza began to laugh. "Oh, Aimee," she gasped, clutching her side, "you cannot know how ridiculous that sounds."

Aimee eyed her bosom companion ruefully. "I suppose it does. You know, Eliza," she said sadly, "I think I have changed."

Within Castle Tavern, at Holborn, Charles Perth and Lord Lucan were drowning their disparate sorrows in a glass of daffy. Charles was feeling very much put out, and in consequence, had imbibed more than his usual amount of the sporting gentleman's favorite drink, known in certain circles as Blue Ruin, and in the Daffy Club simply as daffy.

"Y'know," he said moodily, "I ain't at all certain I ought to get married. Females are a deuced lot of trouble when it comes down to it."

"True, but they also offer certain undeniable compensations," replied the earl, as sympathetically as possible. His mood was not much better than Charles's, but the other man obviously needed to talk.

Raising a shoulder, Charles rapped the table with his knuckles and stared into his glass. "She's been thick as thieves with that Fingleshaw hussy ever since the cursed girl arrived. All I hear these days is 'Eliza says this' and 'Eliza says that'!" he groaned. "Frankly I'm fed to the teeth with Eliza, and I don't give a brass farthing what she says or thinks! You'd think she was a damned oracle or something! If it were up to me, by God, I'd send her to

255

Jericho and never bring her back!"

The earl raised a dark brow. "Well, then, why don't you?"

Charles glanced up. "What d'you mean?"

"I mean," said his companion patiently, "that according to her sister, your opinion carries great weight with Miss Farington. I think she would listen to you if you tried to, er, suggest such a course."

Charles shook his head. "Diana told me something of the sort, too. Thought she must be thinking of somebody else. Aimee never listens to a word I say. At least, I don't see a sign of it." He sat up straighter and cocked an inquiring and slightly befuddled eye at the earl. "What about you? Going to pop the question soon?"

The earl's lips twisted bitterly. "If memory serves, I've offered for Diana three times already. And I feel like I've done nothing but knock my head against the stable door."

Charles shot him a commiserating look. "In love with her, eh?"

For a few seconds, the earl said nothing. "She suits me," was all he finally got out. He was not sure he could talk about his problems, at least not without a little more daffy in his system.

Under normal circumstances, Charles might have held his counsel, but he had already had enough gin to make him feel expansive. "She more than suits you, I'd say," he said shrewdly. "I thought you was looking devilish out of sorts lately. Knew another fellow who had just that look. Sick with love, he was. Married the girl in the end. She made a new man of him."

"Sick with love?" repeated the earl derisively. "He sounds like a damned milquetoast."

Charles hooted. "Jack Brinvilliers? Not on your life, my friend. Ever hear of the Marquis of Vale? Course you have. He had the devil of a reputation until last year. Then he fell in love and, well, that was that. He didn't come up to town this Season because Amanda's increasing," he went on, gesturing vaguely. "Won't leave her side. Expecting an heir in June."

The earl drained his glass, eying the other man in rather somber silence. "Do you really believe in love?" he said suddenly.

Charles's glass stopped en route to his mouth. "Hang it, man, of course I do!" he said in surprise. "Don't you?"

"I mean a love that never dies," the earl explained. "A love that . . . that *nourishes* without destroying. A love that doesn't burn itself out with the spending of passion." His gray eyes seemed lit from within, as if illumed by the intensity of his emotions.

Charles fortified himself with another swig of daffy before replying. "I do," he said, wiping his lips. "Can't say I ever thought about it quite like that, though. I ain't got much of a way with words. But I know I love Aimee Farington, and I know that love ain't going to disappear tomorrow, or next year, or ten years after that."

"Then you are fortunate," the earl told him with a frown.

Charles refilled both their glasses. "Why?" he asked. "You think your love for my cousin Diana ain't going to last?"

His companion stared at the floor. "No. No, actually I'm beginning to believe it will."

Charles's brows shot up. "Well, then? What's the problem?"

"Well, for one thing, it leaves me feeling too damned open!" The earl sounded unsettled. "I may be a blunt, logical man, but I'm considerate, too, I think. But Charles, I've never in my life worried about a woman's feelings like this! I've never worried about what other people might do to hurt her, or what kind of pain she's suffered in the past. I don't mean to say I'm usually callous about such things, but—"

"—but you never cared about anybody as much as you care about Diana," Charles finished with a grin. "Aye, you're showing all the signs of it, my friend." He took a few swallows of daffy, and added, reflectively, "I s'pose it's because you've more than just yourself to worry about now. You feel protective, but you also feel a bit . . . a bit opened up. That's the word you used, ain't it? *Open.*" He shrugged. "Not much you can do about it. It comes with the territory."

Having lost complete track of how much gin he'd consumed, the earl prepared to toss off some more. "Well, here's to love," he said, raising his glass. "The most disconcerting emotion around! Though since she won't have me I don't know what the devil good it's going to do me!" he added in frustration. "And that's the second part of the problem!"

Charles sucked on his lower lip, trying to think of some sensible advice. "Stop askin' her," he said suddenly. "Give her a chance to get worried."

The earl grimaced. "You don't know Diana. She'd be delighted. She'd think I'd finally come to my senses. She'd think I wanted to be her *friend!* Her *platonic* friend," he added, with a meaningful belch.

Charles shook his head sympathetically. "You've got a problem," he admitted. "I've got a problem, too. Eliza Fingleshaw's my problem. It's ain't as bad as your problem, but it's a problem." He scratched his head. "Y'know, I always thought I would marry a docile girl . . . someone quiet and submissive . . ." He stopped and puffed out his cheeks, looking thoughtful.

The earl decided to be helpful. "Docility can be deceptive," he pointed out. "Boring, too."

"Boring," repeated Charles, refilling their glasses. "No, Aimee ain't boring." He took another swig of gin and rolled it around his mouth. "By George, I'll do it!" he said with an air of decision. "I'll offer for her! Just as soon as the Fingleshaw girl leaves town, that is," he added with a wink.

"Coward!" mocked the earl. "Does Eliza the Oracle frighten you as much as that?"

"Aye!" Charles grinned drunkenly. "She's worse than my grandmother!"

Chapter Fifteen

"Damn him."

Sir Henry grimaced as he fingered his jaw, and forgot, for once, to admire himself in the mirror. There were lines of discontent about his mouth and eyes, but these were cast into the shade by a large and singularly resplendent greenish gray bruise. Still, it could have been worse, he supposed—considering the solidity of Lord Lucan's fist. The old boy could have broken his jaw if he chose.

"Why didn't you hit him back?"

The baronet's reverie broke, and he swung around. "Really, Sophia," he answered wryly, "physical violence has never been my forte. It's such a shocking waste of effort, my dear. I don't hold with it at all." He dusted his fingers on the front of his dressing gown, a fastidious gesture which was becoming a habit.

"Nevertheless, it is monstrous that he should treat you so," she exclaimed, crossing to his side. "And all because you spoke to the whey-faced widow!"

"Whey-faced? Diana Verney?" Sir Henry's brows rose quizzically.

Sophia Uxbridge tossed her thick red mane from her face. "I think her so. Do you disagree?"

He sensed a challenge in her voice, and responded accordingly. "I could never disagree with you, love. You hold me in the palm of your hand." He saw her quick smile and recollected her appreciation for a double entendre. "And I always rise to the occasion," he whispered, with his most engaging grin.

The lady's smile widened, but then she noticed the wince that accompanied his grin. "But, darling, *something* must be done," she insisted, studying the bruise. "You cannot simply accept his insult."

He shrugged. "What can I do?"

"Has it never occurred to you that words can be more vicious than any weapon?"

His expression became a little meditative. "Now that you mention it, love, yes, it occurred to me when I was a sniveling brat of five or so—but I won't relate the reasons for my enlightenment. It's *so* boring to talk about the past." There was a puckering about his mouth, but it faded quickly. "Suffice it to say that I have kept my tongue sharply honed since then."

"Then let us use our tongues, Henry darling. You say he wants to wed this woman, well? Then let us cast a little doubt upon the lady's reputation. A little gossip can do a great deal of harm—if one desires to be thought respectable."

Sir Henry hesitated, then his voice turned faintly malicious. "Why not?" he said, reaching out to pull her against him. "The little bitch deserves it. But I think I'll leave the details in your very capable hands."

The countess's capable hands slipped through the opening in his dressing gown. "You please me so much more than David," she whispered. "Touch me."

Sir Henry's angelic blue eyes darkened. "As always, Sophia, you find me perfectly willing to oblige . . ."

*   *   *

261

"Do you have everything?" Diana regarded her sister anxiously. "And are you *quite* certain you feel well enough to do this?"

Not quite daring to meet her sister's eyes, Aimee glanced idly around her bedchamber. "I feel fine, and yes, I think I have everything. My night dress, toothbrush and tooth powder, hair brushes, clean clothes for the morning . . . what else is there?"

"And you won't stay up too late or do anything foolish?"

Aimee gave a light laugh. "Goodness, Diana, you really must stop worrying. Spending one night under Eliza's roof will not send me into a decline, you know!"

Diana sighed. "I know. It's just that you are still so thin, and between the two of us, Eliza's mother is *not* as reliable as I would like."

"You forget that I am seventeen, not seven," said Aimee firmly. "Even Mama does not worry as much as you."

Holding fast to the knowledge that Eliza would soon be gone, Diana forced a smile. "Very well. I shan't say another word."

"Oh, I just remembered." Aimee pulled open the drawer next to her bed and pulled out a book. "I promised Eliza I would lend her my copy of *Glenarvon*."

"What did you think of it? Did you like it?" asked Diana curiously.

Aimee's nose wrinkled. "Not really. I don't know why exactly, but in a way it seemed rather silly." Her expression turned prosaic. "But I daresay Eliza will love it. It is just her sort of thing."

"I see. Well, you are probably right about that."

"Aunt Serena says Lady Caroline Lamb is nothing but a nasty little hussy," stated Aimee. "She says people who purposely cause horrid scandals should be banished to the Antipodes—though I daresay she did not mean it."

262

She sighed. "Personally, I think Charles is far nicer than Lord Byron. Not as romantic, perhaps, but, well, *nicer!*"

"Then you do still wish to marry Charles?" asked Diana bluntly.

"Well, of course, I do!" Aimee sounded startled. "How can you even ask?"

Diana hesitated. "Be careful, then. I do not think he likes Eliza. You wouldn't want to . . . to drive him away."

"Drive him away? What do you mean?"

"Well . . . if and when a gentlemen contemplates marriage, I am sure he likes to receive, oh, a great deal of notice . . . or attention, if you prefer, from the object of his affections." At Aimee's bewildered stare, Diana went on hastily, "Naturally, I am no authority on the male sex—God knows my experience is limited—but one cannot help making certain observations about gentlemen in general. They are a bit like children, I think—at least many of them," she amended. "I am concerned that if you devote too much time to Eliza, Cousin Charles might feel, well, slighted. Just lately, I thought he looked a trifle put out, so to speak."

To Diana's surprise, her sister nodded. "Yes, I thought so, too," she said. "I said something about it to Eliza, but she only laughed. Almost, Diana, I felt a little angry with her at that moment." She frowned at the memory, then said, with brooding hesitancy, "Diana, do you think there is any chance that Eliza could be jealous of me?"

Grateful that the possibility had finally occurred to Aimee, Diana replied, "As a matter of fact, I think it quite likely. I hope you know that I have no wish to spoil your friendship, but neither would I like to see Eliza spoil your future expectations."

"Oh," said Aimee, thinking this over. "No, neither would I." She sighed suddenly. "I told Eliza I had changed, and I really think I have, for there are some things about her that I no longer like. I really think I'll be glad when she leaves." Then she smiled cheerfully. "In any case, one more day and she will be packing to go home, and then, Diana, I will be sure to devote myself *entirely* to Charles. I intend to make it indisputably clear that I am the perfect wife for him."

Though Diana still felt a twinge of foreboding, she made the firm decision to dismiss it. Obviously, Aimee was not so taken in by Eliza as she had thought, while her own tendency to worry was working overtime. Beneath her silliness, Aimee appeared to possess an intrinsic streak of plain common sense that would, in all likelihood, see her safely through these early stages of adulthood. Perhaps, she reflected, Aimee *was* a little like Aunt Serena, after all.

"My God, Eliza! What have you done to my dress?"

Garbed only in her stockings and chemise, Aimee stared in dismay at the neckline of the evening gown which they had smuggled out of the house the previous day.

Eliza smirked. "I knew you'd be surprised. I worked on it 'till midnight last night. What an improvement, eh?"

"An improvement?" Rushing to the mirror, Aimee held the rich blue fabric up to her thin frame. "Diana would kill me if I wore this in public!" she wailed. "Oh, Eliza, why did you do it?"

Eliza pulled a gruesome face. "Pooh! Who cares about Diana? I did you a favor, ninny. I thought you wanted to have some fun."

"I did." Aimee eyed the other girl doubtfully, then her eyes dropped to the dress. "I wonder how it will look," she said, fascinated by the notion.

"Well, there's only one way to find out, isn't there?"

Aimee pulled the dress over her head and twitched it

into place. The neckline was nearly two inches lower than it had been before, highlighting the shadowy cleft between her young breasts. Several seconds elapsed while she stared at herself in bemusement. "If Charles saw me in this," she said candidly, "he would be quite, quite shocked. I cannot even think what he would say."

Eliza rolled her pale eyes. "Then he must be the stodgiest man alive! Haven't I told you time and again that gentlemen adore seeing a little glimpse of bosom? I heard Freddy and his friends talking about it one time, and you should have heard the things they were saying." She giggled. "It makes them feel queer all over, and the most peculiar thing happens to a certain part of their anatomy. Of course, they must have been foxed, for I heard them say—"

"Eliza!" cut in Aimee, rather apprehensively. "They will not be foxed tonight, will they? Because I really cannot even consider going if—"

"Rubbish!" Eliza was contemptuous. "You want to see Vauxhall, don't you? Freddy says it is the most vastly exciting place in London! And the fireworks, Aimee—you know you've always wanted to see them! Think how much more fun it will be without stuffy Diana and stodgy Charles along to spoil the fun." Her words must have amused her for she began another round of giggles.

Aimee eyed the other girl as if she were some rare zoological specimen. "But what on earth will your Mama say? She will think me shockingly fast!"

Eliza's sharp shoulders rose and fell. "Oh, Mama is not nearly so nice about these things as you imagine. And it is not as though I were wearing it, you know. She will probably think it all the crack, especially if you tell her your stuffy sister bought it for you. Everyone knows she has been a model of propriety since her marriage."

Aimee's sapphire eyes glinted with wrath. "It would be better for our friendship," she said stiffly, "if you refrain from making any more personal remarks about my sister and cousin. Otherwise, Eliza, I am going to become very angry."

Eliza's startled look quickly faded to amusement. "Oh, very well," she said grudgingly. "But do let's finish getting ready. Freddy and his friends will be here soon!"

While Aimee's conscience continued to prick her, Diana was sitting at home, plowing determinedly through the final pages of *Emma*. For a while, she had played piquet with Tildy, but the elderly woman tired easily, and had soon gone off to sleep. Once or twice, the sound of a rumbling carriage reached her ears, but otherwise the house was quiet. The servants were in the kitchen, and though their voices occasionally drifted up to the first floor, they did not penetrate inside the drawing room.

The clock struck ten just as she finished the last chapter, and she put the book aside, stretching the cramped muscles of her arms and legs. Odd, how greatly her evenings contrasted with those first, hectic days in London. Aimee's illness had caused her to miss nearly three weeks of the Season, and one by one, her many beaux had drifted away to hover around other, more available girls. Two or three of the most devoted still came to call, and occasionally sent flowers, but of these none seemed at all suited to be Aimee's husband. Perhaps Cousin Charles's frequent presence had been noted and deemed significant, for the stir her sister had created had quietly dwindled to nearly nothing. So it was that Charles remained the only possible candidate for Aimee's husband. Not, Diana reminded herself, that it was at all necessary for Aimee to be married at so young an age. But that would mean more London Seasons, and who would play the chaperon if not herself? Certainly not Mama, for she would never leave Papa for so long, and Papa hated to travel because of his back. Aunt Serena continued to harbor the fantasy that she could do it, although Diana had rarely seen her leave her chair at any ball or reception that they attended. And since Lord Hervey was always monopolizing her ear, the dowager viscountess scarcely noticed what Aimee was doing at all!

Shoving aside her sister's concerns for the moment, Diana absently traced one of the stripes in the sofa's fabric. She had blocked the earl from her mind all evening, but now she allowed herself the luxury of wondering where he was and what he was doing. She was feeling very lonely. She was often lonely these days, but just now it was worse than usual, a dull, heavy weight in the center of her chest. And it was useless to pretend ignorance of the reason. Earlier in the evening, she had paced the floor in a caged fashion, trying unsuccessfully to erase the suspicion that she was the biggest fool who ever lived.

Well, now that she had played cards with Tildy, finished her library book and had a glass of wine, there seemed to be nothing else to do—nothing to prevent her from going over it again. Of course, she *could* go and write to Mama, but her frame of mind was so dreary that she feared it would show in her letter. No, she had better finish hashing it out now, so that—hopefully—when she retired for the night, she might be granted a peaceful, dreamless sleep.

Diana's lip curled a little. That was the worst time, wasn't it? Those occasional nights when she could not fall asleep, and was forced by some inner demon to relive every mistake she had ever made. The truth was, for the past six years she had cherished a very poor opinion of herself, and her behavior of late had done nothing to improve it. It had not always been so, of course. The carefree days of childhood had been unfettered by guilt, and if her father had been more interested in his books than in any of his offspring, she could not recall it greatly troubling her. Her mother, too, had always been sweet and loving, and Miss Tilden had been yet another blessing.

No, it was in the later years when it began, for she had never stopped blaming herself for Edmund. She had never quite banished the belief that she deserved what she got, that it was her rightful punishment for that foolhardy, hopelessly indiscreet venture up those stairs. That belief lay buried, but alive and ever-present, a skeleton in her own personal closet of memories.

Oh, her emotions were so muddled! Lord Lucan had thrown her life into a havoc, just when she had begun to sort it into some semblance of order. Yet she was glad, yes *glad*, he had done so, she thought fiercely. To know him was an honor, to love him, a privilege. That he wished to marry her was beyond wonderful, beyond anything she could ever hope to express in mere words. She could delude herself no longer. With every shred of her being, she wanted, yearned, and *ached* to be his wife.

Her lower lip tucked between her teeth, Diana tried to sort it out a little more logically. He had asked that she reconsider her refusal. Well, what if she did just that? With sinking spirits, Diana realized that her conscience would demand she confess her secret. And if she did, would he still want her? He believed her modest and respectable, even virginal. But what would he think if she told him that six years ago she had crept up those stairs like a thief, intending to eavesdrop shamelessly on Sir Henry and his partner? He had disparaged Aimee's inconstant behavior, but even Aimee had done nothing as bold and brazen as that! How highly would he think of her then?

Diana shifted restlessly. If only she could be sure that he loved her. He had said he cared for her, but she could not believe it was the same thing. True love was more than caring—it was all-encompassing, inviolable, uplifting. It was both elemental and spiritual, disordered pulses and unquestioning trust. It was a connecting of eyes, a yearning to drink in every feature of the loved one's face, a contentment in his presence. Love was forgiving anything, even what one could not understand. It was *not* the same as caring, she thought broodingly. One could care for a pet, for God's sake.

Since their last meeting, she had come to believe that if he truly loved her, she would be able to tolerate his caresses. She might never truly enjoy them, but would that matter? The children she would doubtless bear would more than compensate for the discomfort. He had spoken of sons and daughters as if he wanted them as desperately as she. How easily she could envision them— gray-eyed sons with black hair, perhaps daughters who resembled herself. She longed for them almost as much as she longed for him.

Jumping to her feet, Diana went and poured herself another glass of sherry. She almost never drank spirituous beverages when alone, but tonight it seemed to calm her nerves. All she had to do, she told herself staunchly, was tell him she had had a change of heart. Phrased like that, it sounded as easy as adding a column of numbers. And after that, she could confess her disgraceful conduct, and await his response.

As she sipped her drink and contemplated this course she heard the faint ringing of a bell. Curious, she listened intently. Who could be calling at this hour? Had Aimee changed her mind and decided to return home?

A minute later, her butler's measured footsteps sounded on the stairs. "A dispatch for you, madam," he revealed, placing a small, white envelope in her hand. His normally wooden countenance looked mildly disapproving.

It was from Aimee, and judging from the nearillegibility of the hand, it had obviously been written in considerable haste.

Dear Diana, it read, *I am writing to tell you that I have gone with Eliza to Vauxhall Gardens. I am sorry now that I deceived you, but I truly did believe that Eliza's Mama meant to go, and that everything would be Perfectly Respectable. Eliza did not want me to write to you, but my conscience dictates that I make a clean breast of it. Freddy and three of his friends are to escort us, so I daresay everything will be just fine. I did not lie to you about feeling well, so do not worry about me! As long as you know where I am, then I think I will be able to enjoy myself.*

Scrawled across the bottom was, *Your loving sister, Aimee.*

"Oh, no!" moaned Diana, scanning the note twice through. "Oh, Aimee, Aimee, how *could* you?" Then the set of her mouth began to harden. "Drat those odious Fingleshaws," she muttered, wadding the note into a tight ball. "This is positively the last straw!"

She threw it into the fire and reached angrily for the bell cord.

Meanwhile, Aimee was finding herself in a far less enviable position than she had anticipated. Freddy Fingleshaw had been ogling her for most of the evening, while his three friends, wild young bloods wholly unsuited to be their escorts, proved themselves so lost to propriety that they, in turn, ogled almost every female who passed, one even going so far as to chase one straw-haired damsel across the lawn.

They had located a vacant supper box easily enough, but the four gentlemen (if such they could be called) had ordered a great quantity of rack punch, and seemed bent on consuming it all in the first hour. To Aimee's further

270

distress, Eliza appeared to be on far too friendly terms with one of Freddy's friends, a young man called Boxy, who flirted with them both and sat with his arm around Eliza's waist. For the hundredth time that hour, Aimee wondered how Eliza had inveigled her into coming. She had known it was wrong, and indeed had been much inclined to refuse simply because she had not yet recovered all of her strength. Though she had felt well enough when they departed the house, fatigue was beginning to creep into her muscles, and she began to wish she could lie down.

As she watched Eliza whisper into Boxy's ear, she realized what little affection she retained for her friend. She would never have believed Eliza could behave so vulgarly. Recalling how Diana had always disapproved of Eliza, she decided her sister's opinion had been warranted. Somehow or other Eliza had changed, transformed from the fun-loving, rather mischievous compatriot of childhood into an ill-bred creature she scarcely knew. Moreover, it seemed strange to Aimee that Mrs. Fingleshaw had permitted the excursion when she was not able to come along. If Eliza's mother had the headache, Aimee reasoned, then they ought to have stayed home. It was unfortunate, however, that these revelations had not occurred to her an hour sooner.

"I say," said Freddy Fingleshaw, quite suddenly, "let's go for a bit of a stroll, Aimee. I'll show you some more of the Gardens."

Dismayed, Aimee glanced at Eliza's brother, taking in the sharp-featured face with its wispy blond eyebrows and reddish eyelids. "No, thank you, Freddy," she answered, as politely as she was able. "I'd really rather not."

Freddy puffed out his cheeks, his shortsighted gaze flicking over her insolently. "Why not? Not afraid of me, are you? Known me all your life, haven't you?" He took a another swig of punch and wiped his lips, staring at her in a challenging manner.

Eliza tittered. "Oh, why don't you go with him?" she urged playfully. "He only wants to kiss you, you know."

A certain hauteur crept into Aimee's voice. "Nonsense, Eliza. Freddy and I are like brother and sister to one another."

"Now *that's* moonshine," protested Freddy, leering a little. "You're far too pretty to be a Fingleshaw! Fact is, you look hellish fine in that gown." His head turned. "Don't she, Boxy? Bang up to the nines, eh? Eliza never looked half so good in her life, I'll swear. All the Fingleshaw females are deuced chicken-breasted," he added, eyeing the soft swell of Aimee's bared bosom with lewd appreciation.

Eliza stuck out her tongue, but Aimee favored him with a reproving look. "Well, this is really too bad of you, Freddy!" she said with dignity. "I think you must be foxed, for I have never heard you speak so discourteously before."

"Not foxed yet," he replied, laughing unpleasantly. A nasty gleam entered his eye. "What's the matter with you, anyway? You're hellish high in the instep tonight. P'haps we ain't good enough for you now that some fancy honourable is waving his handkerchief in your face?"

Goaded by this disparaging reference to Charles, Aimee snapped, "Well, at least my cousin treats me with respect, which is a great deal more than I can say for you! I would not go walking with you if you were the last man in London, Freddy Fingleshaw, for I do not trust you at all! Nor you, Eliza, for it is obvious that you betrayed what you knew was to be kept in strict confidence!" She rose to her feet and glared at them mulishly. "I am excessively sorry I came, and I would very much like to go home!"

This announcement was greeted with general mirth.

"Oh, come *on*, Aimee," said Eliza, rather mockingly. "Don't put yourself into such a taking! Freddy didn't mean anything did you, Freddy?"

"I want to go home," repeated Aimee stubbornly.

"Well, who is going to take you home? You won't go with Freddy, will you? Do be reasonable, Aimee!"

Freddy, who was far closer to being foxed than he was willing to admit, looked sullen. "I say, Aimee, I don't think I like your manner very much." He came round the table and seized her by the arm. "If I want to take you for a walk, then by God, you are going for a walk!"

"Oh, no, I'm not!" Aimee drew back her foot and kicked him hard in the shin—twice.

Freddy let go with an undignified howl. "Why you little she-devil!" he exclaimed, rubbing his leg. "Now where the devil are you going?"

Aimee had darted away, and was bolting over the grass with gazellelike speed. She had an excellent sense of direction, and was already calculating the exact location of the Garden's entrance when by pure chance she caught sight of a familiar face. Filled with relief, she changed course at once, for Freddy was now hot in pursuit, and she was already starting to get a stitch in her side.

"Oh, Sir Henry!" she gasped, hurling herself at the baronet. "Thank God you are here! Can you help me, please? I am being followed!" She clutched at his arm, hardly noticing that his companion—a very beautiful lady—was inspecting her with cold green eyes.

Sir Henry Neyle could not conceal his astonishment. "Why, it's . . . Miss Farington, isn't it?" His hooded blue eyes had just taken in her disheveled appearance when Freddy arrived.

"Who the devil are you?" demanded Eliza's brother, before being lanced to the quick by Sir Henry's cool stare. Freddy goggled wordlessly as the baronet lifted his quizzing glass and surveyed him with clear contempt.

"I *do* beg your pardon," replied Sir Henry, sounding bored, "but is it possible I know you? Miss Farington, I hope you will not tell me you are acquainted with this gentleman?"

"I am, indeed!" shot back Aimee wrathfully. "And he is no gentleman!"

Sir Henry's shoulders shook slightly. "But, my dear girl, I thought you craved excitement?" he murmured.

She glanced at him in surprise, then remembering, blushed. "Not that sort of excitement," she said tartly. "Now, *do* go away, Freddy! You look quite nonsensical standing there with your mouth open." She tucked her small hand under Sir Henry's arm. "*This* gentleman will take care of me," she added innocently.

A trifle startled, Sir Henry exchanged a meaningful look with Lady Uxbridge. "This, my dear, is Mrs. Verney's little sister. Pretty, isn't she? But, of course you have met. You were at Miss Farington's come-out ball . . . *and* dinner."

As Freddy stalked away, Aimee eyed Lady Uxbridge with interest. "Oh, yes. I remember. You sat next to Lord Lucan and flirted with him quite shockingly. I was watching you, you know, to observe how it was done."

Lady Uxbridge looked taken aback. "How what was done?"

"Flirting," explained Aimee. "I wanted to see how you went about it. You looked to be just the sort of lady who would know."

As the countess's eyes narrowed, Sir Henry quickly intervened. "Come, Sophia, let us enlighten the young lady on a few of the finer points. Her education has been sadly neglected."

Aimee frowned. "Oh, but I want to go home. You see, I am still a little weak from being ill. I should not have come here tonight at all. If Diana knew what was intended, she would never have—"

"Your sister does not know you are here?"

Aimee looked embarrassed. "Well, actually she does, but—oh, it is too complicated to explain! Please, could you just escort me to the entrance and summon a hackney to take me home?"

His blue eyes gazed down into hers rather pensively. Then he bowed. "I shall be happy to oblige you, Aimee, love—after a bit." He covered her hand with his own. "But first, let us talk a little while. If you are weary, little one, I will gladly find you a place to sit."

Suddenly, Lady Uxbridge gave a shrug. "Go with him, my dear," she urged. "I promise you will find him good company. *I* always do!"

Aimee hesitated. "But . . . will you not come with us?"

The countess looked amused. "Goodness, why would you want me along? I shall find some diversion or other to keep me entertained. Henry, shall we meet, say, in an hour?"

He bowed. "I will meet you right here, Sophia." Then he turned his attention to Aimee, projecting the full force of his charm. "And now, little Aimee, I intend to provide you with some of that excitement you crave . . ."

Chapter Sixteen

With supreme effort, Diana thrust her fury aside and reviewed the situation from a sensible standpoint. It was very likely, she decided, that Aimee really was as safe as she claimed; nevertheless, inaction was completely out of the question. Aimee's note had intimated that Mrs. Fingleshaw was not to accompany them, a circumstance which in itself was enough to rekindle the angry glitter in Diana's eyes. She had always thought the woman's sense of responsibility was lacking, but such laxity as this surpassed everything! No, there was no help for it. She would have to go to Vauxhall herself, retrieve her sister, and while she was at it, give the Fingleshaw offspring a raking-down they would long remember! However, Vauxhall Gardens was a huge place, and at night it was unwise to venture there alone. She therefore made up her mind to take her burly footman along for protection.

She would have preferred Lord Lucan as escort, but there were several excellent reasons for not seeking him out. For one thing, locating him would be sure to entail a delay, and for another, there existed a distinct possibility that wherever he was, Cousin Charles would be with him. And if their cousin got just one whiff of this, there was no saying but what it might destroy whatever desire he might still have to offer her sister marriage. No, it was best to deal with this herself, and hope to God that the whole situation could be kept as secret as possible. At any rate, fetching her sister home should be simple enough with Felix along.

However, as they approached Vauxhall Gardens, Diana began to feel less sanguine about the matter. Illogical as it was, she had the oddest presentiment that Aimee was in trouble, which sharpened her ·sense· of urgency.

"Stay close to me," she instructed Felix, as she paid their entrance fee, "and if you see anyone who looks even remotely like my sister, for goodness sake, tell me! Thank God it is not a gala night, for the crowds would have been horrendous."

"Yes, ma'am!" replied her footman, his enthusiasm ill concealed. Game for a fight, he flexed his large hands hopefully. Any rascal who had the bloody nerve to bother his mistress would be in for a regular set-to!

As they traversed the gravel-lined walkways, Diana paid scant heed to the twinkling Chinese lanterns hanging in the stately elms, or the fragrant flowers, or the songs of the nightingales in the distance. She ignored the openly admiring glances cast her way by pleasure-seeking bloods on the strut for an available female, but such looks increased her unease. Her nerves on the stretch, she strained her eyes every time she saw a young girl with dark hair or heard a high-pitched giggle or shriek. But it was never Aimee.

Eventually, she and Felix headed for the supper boxes with the hope that the Fingleshaws might still be dining. There were more than a hundred of them, and she found it distinctly embarrassing to have to peer into each box— particularly because of the ribald remarks this elicited from some of the occupants. Nevertheless she did so, for her determination to locate her sister was increasing steadily. She was thankful she had taken the precaution to bring Felix, for without doubt she would have been accosted many times over but for his presence. Because she felt so safe, however, all Diana's attention was focused to the fore—and so she never noticed that at one point a silent figure slipped quietly from one of the supper boxes to trail behind them like a shadow.

In the end, Diana heard Eliza Fingleshaw before she saw her, for Eliza's voice was loud and her abrasive laughter carried on the breeze.

"There they are," she told her footman with a grim gesture.

"Don't you worry, ma'am" he replied. "We'll whisk Miss Aimee 'ome in a pair o' winks!"

Diana was within ten feet of the Fingleshaw's box when she realized that Aimee was not in it. Indeed, the scene which met her eyes was so much worse than she had bargained that she stopped dead and stared in disbelief. A young man with a slurred expression had his arm curled around Eliza's waist, while Freddy and two others had acquired a pair of garish-looking females of dubious reputation. None of them took any notice of Diana.

Her first, ruling emotion was utter fury. Fixing her eyes on the sandy-haired blond, Diana's voice rang out clear and cold with contempt. "All right, Eliza, where is my sister?"

Eliza Fingleshaw looked up, and her pale eyes widened. "Oh, my God," was her sole response, "I told Aimee not to write that wretched note!"

Diana's features were icily stern. "I asked you where Aimee is, Eliza, and I expect an answer—now!"

To her consternation, Eliza only shrugged. "I've no notion at all." She pointed an accusing finger at Freddy. "My clodpole of a brother chased her away, then was poor-spirited enough to surrender her to someone else. It

278

was only a little while ago, so . . ." She shrugged again, drifting into awkward silence.

Diana transferred her gaze to Freddy Fingleshaw. "Do you mean to tell me," she exclaimed, "that you *left* my seventeen-year-old sister in the clutches of a perfect stranger? And that none of the rest of you had the common decency to be concerned? Who the *devil* is she with?"

Freddy looked uncomfortable. "Hang it, *I* don't know. She wouldn't come back with me. Doesn't like me. Anyway, he wasn't a stranger. Said she knew him, or some such thing."

Diana's temper flared. "Both of you ought to be thoroughly ashamed!" she said scathingly. "Have you *no* sense of propriety? You conduct yourselves as though you were raised in a brothel! Eliza, you may consider yourself no longer welcome in my house. I am completely disgusted with you. You may be sure I intend to tell your mama about this—and do not think I will omit to mention it to your papa, either!" She turned, addressing her footman in a decisive tone. "Felix, you must locate Lord Lucan and beg him to come at once. I do not know where you may find him, but try his house first, then my cousin's and then White's. After that, I leave it up to you. Why do you hesitate? Go! And hurry!"

She whirled to face the others. "And now, Freddy, you and I are going to search for Aimee. You will give me the protection of your escort, for it is the very least you can do after your disgraceful behavior. Perhaps I may then tell your papa that you did something useful."

Her threat apparently struck home, for Freddy Fingleshaw scrambled to his feet. "Oh, very well," he muttered, casting her a look of dislike. "Where do you want to look?"

"I believe you can best answer that. Where would *you*

279

take a young lady in this place?"

Freddy cocked his head, and exchanged significant looks with his companions. "Depends," he said rudely, "on my intentions."

"Assume they were dishonorable!" she said with a snap.

"Well, I suppose it would have to be the Dark Walk, then. One likes one's privacy, y'know." Freddy affected a knowing sneer.

Someone guffawed, but Diana merely held out her hand. "Come on, then," she said curtly. "And do not forget for one instant that I am depending on you for my safety. If you *dare* to abandon me, you will never cease to regret it!"

Unfortunately, it soon became evident that Freddy was more inebriated than he had first appeared. He was able to walk and talk, but his gait was rather lurching, and his interest in rescuing Aimee appeared meager, at best.

"Honestly, Freddy," cried Diana, when he stumbled and nearly fell, "you are worse than useless! How much have you had to drink?"

"Not foxed yet," he mumbled. "Only slightly disguised. Feel a bit queasy, though. Like to sit down."

"Well, you cannot sit down," she told him severely. "We must keep looking for Aimee."

"Aimee?" His tone was vague and rather pettish. "Pretty little filly, ain't she? Only wanted to kiss her, y'know. Don't know why she ran away."

"Oh, just be quiet, Freddy!" she snapped.

On this path there were no Chinese lamps to guide them, and what light there was filtered down to them from the moon, which was nearly full. Diana kept her ears attuned for any sound that might reveal Aimee's whereabouts, and continued to hush Freddy whenever he tried to speak. There were a profusion of leafy alcoves along the Dark Walk, and from the muffled giggles, scuffling sounds, and occasional shrieks, it was obvious that many of them were occupied. Again and again, she called out her sister's name, but each time she was disappointed.

They had nearly reached the end of the walk when first a small figure and then a larger one materialized some twenty feet ahead of them. Could it be Aimee? Some sixth sense told her it was, but then the man spoke, and for an astonished instant, Diana checked her steps.

"Now, now, love," drawled a familiar voice, "I really must protest. We both know there were no snakes in there. First, spiders, then bats, and now, snakes. Egad, what other excuse can you invent, I wonder?" A soft laugh sent chills down Diana's spine. "You promised me a kiss if I listened to your story, and having done so, my dove, it is time for you to pay the forfeit. You babble *quite* charmingly, but Scheherazade you're not. Don't struggle so. I don't want to hurt you."

"But you have not heard the most diverting part of the story yet! And there *was* a snake! It went right over my foot!"

It *was* Aimee!

The hysterical edge to her sister's voice brought Diana surging forward. "Let go of my sister, Henry!" she cried out.

"What the devil—!" Sir Henry's head jerked around, and Aimee wrenched herself from his grasp.

"Oh, Diana, thank God you have come!" A tiny sob escaped her lips as she stumbled into Diana's arms. "I am so very tired, and Sir Henry had been most disobliging and ungallant! Please, please, take me home, Diana, and make him go away."

The light was far too dim to discern Sir Henry's expression, but the sardonic silkiness in his voice warned

Diana that he was very angry.

"So," he purred, "the fair widow has come to rescue her little sister. Almost, Diana, my admiration is roused. And you appear to be unescorted, my pet. Do you think that is wise?"

Diana lifted her chin and peered at him through the evening shadows. "Of course I am escorted," she replied. "Freddy, come here this instant and show yourself!"

There was no response, and she turned around. To her acute dismay, Freddy lay slumped upon the ground and from the faint, whiffling sound emitting from his mouth, he was obviously fast asleep.

"Oh, Freddy!" she said despairingly. "I should have known better than to trust you!"

Sir Henry had taken the opportunity to move, and his hands closed on her wrists with unexpected strength. "I cannot quite decide which one of you is more delectable," he mocked. "Your sister is a mouth-watering little morsel, but you, Diana, are indisputably an entree. Would that I could sample you both at once," he added crudely. "'A titillating notion, don't you think?"

"Let me go!" She struggled, but he twisted her arm behind her, at the same time reaching for Aimee. "Go into the arbor," he directed the younger girl, giving her a push. "Go, or I'll break your sister's arm. Move!"

"Let her go, Harry."

This time, everyone jumped. Diana did not recognize the woman's voice, but it was plain that Sir Henry did.

"Why, good evening, Cynthia," he remarked, after a stunned moment. "Did you think this was a party? I hate to be rude, but it is not, you know. Do go away, love. I am otherwise engaged."

Cynthia Clement did not move. "Perhaps it is too dark for you to see I have a pistol in my hand. Release Mrs.

Verney at once or I will be forced to shoot you."

Sir Henry snorted a laugh. "Or Mrs. Verney," he countered, gripping Diana tightly. "Or yourself, or some other passing fool. What the devil are you about, Cynthia? What is Diana Verney to you?"

"That is none of your affair," she answered. "And there is nothing to prevent me from walking so close to you that I see precisely where to aim. Give up, Harry. This is not the sort of game you like to play. The odds are too much in my favor."

Diana heard her cock the pistol, and realized in horror that the woman was not bluffing. So, apparently, did Sir Henry for he let loose of her arm and thrust her at Mrs. Clement.

"Oh, very well," he said, making a clucking noise with his tongue. "I wouldn't *really* have broken her arm, you know. Egad, no. *How* distasteful." With disconcerting aplomb, he strolled past them and melted into the darkness.

Diana turned to Mrs. Clement. "Thank you," she said, a shade hesitantly. "But . . . why? We do not even know each other."

"Perhaps we should leave talking for later," advised their rescuer. "Right now, I believe your sister requires assistance. Take her left arm and I shall take the right. It leaves my pistol hand free," she added dryly.

The three women made their way to the end of the Dark Walk and out into the wider lane at the end. Once more, Chinese lanterns twinkled, and Mrs. Clement tucked the tiny, silver-chased pistol back into her reticule.

"I always carry a pistol when I go out at night," she said calmly. "On occasion, it has saved me considerable distress and inconvenience."

Wondering which term she would apply to their

encounter with Sir Henry, Diana gave her a curious look. "I see. Well, we are both extremely grateful for your assistance, but I do not understand how it comes about that you were there to help us. Almost as if you appeared on cue."

Cynthia Clement smiled at the phrase. "Almost," she agreed. "Let us just say that I am acquainted with Lord Lucan. I knew he would want you to come to no harm, so I took what I felt were the appropriate steps."

Diana could not help stiffening a little. "Oh?" she said, her tone very casual. "You are closely acquainted with his lordship, then?"

"Not in the way that you are thinking, my dear. He is no more than a friend." She glanced around. "Oh, good, there is a place for your sister to sit down."

Recalling that this woman was noted for her discretion, Diana felt it wisest not to pursue the matter. Instead, she assisted Aimee to the bench, saying, "As it happens, I have sent my footman to convey a message to Lord Lucan. I am hoping he will come and . . . and take us home."

Though Diana did not know it, she sounded a little uncertain. What if Felix was unable to locate him? They might be forced to wait a long time, and Aimee's face was white with exhaustion. Ought she to wait?

"A wise move," approved Mrs. Clement with a nod. "He should be here soon then."

Diana eyed her with half-jealous fascination. That another woman should be so certain about what Geoffrey would or would not do aroused a mixture of emotions in her breast. Had Mrs. Clement been his mistress? She was not pretty, but she had an interesting face, with a pair of expressive, dark eyes which looked as though they had seen a great deal.

"How can you be so sure?" Diana asked at last. "That

is, if you are only a little acquainted with him . . ."

Mrs. Clement touched her arm. "My dear, one cannot spend ten minutes in his lordship's company without knowing him for a gentleman one could rely upon in a crisis. What a pity you did not bring him with you tonight. That other young man was quite worthless."

"Freddy Fingleshaw," sighed Diana. "Yes, perhaps I should have gone straight to Geoffrey, but . . ." As if he were there already, Diana glanced around hopefully.

With characteristic tact, Mrs. Clement switched her attention to Aimee. "Do you feel well enough to begin walking toward the entrance? It would make it simpler for Lord Lucan to intercept us."

Aimee nodded, and rose to her feet. "Thank you," she said. "My knees are not nearly so shaky as before. Keeping Sir Henry at bay was the most wearying thing I have ever done, you see. I have never talked so much in my life."

Mrs. Clement's brows rose. "If you succeeded in holding him off, you must be very clever indeed. Harry can be a most persistent gentleman . . . when he is not feeling indolent, that is."

"Oh!" Aimee digested this for a moment. "Do you know him then?"

"Oh, yes. Everyone knows Sir Henry." Mrs. Clement's voice was light, but Diana read volumes into her reply.

They were halfway along the Grand Walk when Diana spied the earl. She knew a wild longing to run into his arms, but could hardly succumb to the impulse in such a public place. Still, a wellspring of happiness flooded her heart, so that her chest felt ready to burst with the mere joy of seeing him. In a matter of seconds, however, it became obvious her delight was not shared.

"What the deuce is going on?" rasped the earl. "Your

footman said you were in trouble." His eyes shifted. "What's the trouble, Cynthia?"

Diana was taken aback by the roughness in his voice, but when he turned and addressed Mrs. Clement before she could even speak, her mouth dropped open with sheer outrage. The fact that he made free use of the widow's Christian name only exacerbated the situation.

"Thanks to Mrs. Clement," Diana put in acidly, "there is no trouble now. I do not wish to go into detail at the moment, but Aimee has had a bad experience and I require some assistance in getting her home. I had meant to ask you to help us, Lord Lucan, but perhaps it is too great a thing to ask!"

Ignoring her sarcasm, the earl's eyes flicked over Aimee, taking in the lowered neckline of her gown. "What the devil has she done now?"

His arrogant assumption that whatever occurred had been Aimee's fault infuriated Diana. "She has done nothing!" she countered, with an angry look. "What an insufferable thing to say!"

The muscles of his jaw tautened. "So I'm an insufferable man," he flung back. "Cynthia, perhaps you would care to enlighten me?"

However, once again Mrs. Clement proved herself the soul of tact. "Forgive me, my lord, but it is not my story to tell. I know you will see to the ladies, so if you will excuse me, I will go. A friend of mine is waiting for me."

As she started to walk away, Diana said quickly, "Oh, but I have yet to thank you properly! Do call on me tomorrow, so we may become better acquainted."

Mrs. Clement looked back, but her eyes went past Diana to the earl. Then slowly, as if she had received some signal, her head shook with regret. "I'm sorry, my dear. I do not think that I can do that."

Perplexed, Diana watched the widow hurry away, then her attention returned to Aimee. "Please, Geoffrey," she urged, concern for her sister cleansing the anger from her voice, "Aimee is exhausted. Please help me to get her home."

Though the set of his mouth was still rather grim, the earl's reply was far more civil. "Of course. My coach is at the entrance. Do you wish me to carry you?" he asked Aimee in a neutral tone.

Aimee's laugh had a listless quality. "Gracious, no. If we do not go too fast, I . . . I can manage. Charles did not come with you, did he?" she asked fearfully.

"No." Lord Lucan gave her a curious look. "No, I'm sorry, he did not."

"Oh, thank goodness! Please do not tell him about any of this!" she begged. "Promise me you will not tell him!"

"Very well. I promise," he said, soothing her agitation as best he could. "Now, come along, Miss Farington."

They reached the carriage in a short time, and Diana let out a sigh of relief as they settled back against the cushions. She held her sister against her, and within a few minutes, Aimee's eyelids had drooped shut. She was fast asleep.

"What happened?" said the earl. He spoke in the quiet authoritative voice of a man who expected the complete truth.

Diana shrugged. "Except that the whole episode is due to Eliza Fingleshaw—and her odious brother, Freddy— I'm not actually sure." Oddly reluctant to mention Sir Henry's involvement in the scene, she said, "She ran away from Freddy only to be waylaid by . . . by another gentlemen who compelled her to accompany him to the Dark Walk. Fortunately, I arrived before things were . . . out of hand."

She knew the earl's penetrating eyes rested on her

face, for the gas-lit street lamps cast a margin of illumination through the coach's windows. Weird, elongated shadows slid along the inner panels, then repeated as each lamp along the avenue was succeeded by the next. He still had not spoken, and, unnerved by his silence, Diana went on in haste. "What I cannot understand is why Mrs. Clement felt obliged to rescue us. I hope you mean to explain that to me."

"What do you mean 'rescue *us*'? What happened, Diana?"

Inwardly, she cursed the unconscious slip. "Oh, it was merely this, ah, man threatened me also—just for a moment. Naturally, there was no real danger. Then your friend Mrs. Clement arrived, so conveniently, and frightened him away with her pistol."

She could almost see the curl of his lip. "A man threatens you in such a place, and you say there was no real danger? I can't believe you're really that naive, Diana. Why don't you tell me the truth?"

"And why don't you?" she countered.

"What the devil is that supposed to mean?"

"It means that I would like to know just how close you really are to Cynthia Clement. You told me before you were only friends, but something she said made me wonder. Was she your . . . your *mistress?* And did you set her to spy on me?" Diana's heart thumped painfully as she waited for him to answer.

She heard him sigh. "To bed a woman once or twice doesn't make her your mistress. For God's sake, Diana, why does it matter so much? It's in the past."

"I don't know," she whispered. "Perhaps it doesn't matter at all. But I wanted to know." She noticed he had not answered the second part of her question.

Another few minutes passed in silence and the coach slowed to a halt in front of Diana's house. "Shall I stay a little while?" he asked, when they stood outside the coach. A unmistakable flame of longing burned in his eyes. "We could . . . talk."

She did want him to stay. Tonight, more than ever, Diana yearned for his company, a yearning so powerful she came near to being vanquished. But she had yet to cope with Aimee, and was herself too tired to parry the questions she knew he would ask. And when Geoffrey learned the truth, he was bound to be furious. She knew he would condemn her decision to rely upon Freddy for protector—which admittedly had been an error in judgement—and although she was grateful to Mrs. Clement for her timely rescue, the woman had unfortunately made Diana more conscious than ever of her own deficiencies. Cynthia Clement had succeeded where Diana had failed, and quite frankly, it rankled just a little.

Yet, Diana's eyes were hungry as she gazed up at the earl. "You'd better go," she said finally. "After all, it must be nearly midnight. But . . . thank you for coming when I needed you, Geoffrey. You are so good to me."

He gave her a rather ironical bow. "Yes, well, that's what friends are for, isn't it?" he replied flippantly.

Aimee slept until noon the following day, but other than that, she appeared to have suffered no ill effects from her ordeal. She confessed the entire tale to Diana, and promised with wholehearted fervency to renounce her friendship with Eliza Fingleshaw. It was necessary to give Miss Tilden a slightly edited version of Aimee's adventures, since she was naturally surprised to find her home, but other than that, the two sisters both agreed to put the entire adventure behind them.

Diana had every intention of paying a visit on Mrs. Findleshaw that afternoon, so that when Aimee suggested that she and Mary take a quiet stroll in Green Park—which was, after all, within yards of Aunt Serena's—she gave her immediate approval to the scheme. When Aimee grew tired, she could return to the dowager's house until Diana came to fetch her in the carriage.

The interview with Mrs. Fingleshaw went far better than Diana expected. Mrs. Fingleshaw professed herself quite horrified about the entire episode, and even went so far as to declare that when her son had sufficiently recovered from the consequences of his excesses, he would make his apology in person. Diana coolly assured her that this was unnecessary, and though both Eliza and Freddy were obviously in store for a rare dressing-down from their parent, it was clear that in the future, the Fingleshaws and the Faringtons would be seeing considerably less of each other.

As she had half-known she would do, Diana decided to pay a call on Mrs. Clement next. She had discovered her direction some weeks before, during the first stages of her fascination with the woman, and now that she had an excuse, the temptation to visit the woman was irresistible. When she was ushered into Mrs. Clement's drawing room—which was as tiny as her own—she could not help being amazed by the lavish touches amid the general shabbiness. Mrs. Clement evidently had a taste for luxury which did not match her income.

"Ah, yes, I thought you might come," said the widow from the doorway. Gliding into the room with a fluid grace, she shook Diana's hand and invited her rather gravely to sit. They did not immediately speak, but studied each other overtly, a weighing-up process made necessary by their interest in the same man.

"I have seen you from a distance," stated Mrs. Clement musingly, "but up close, in the light of day, I can more fully appreciate your beauty. I understand

290

what it is he finds so attractive."

There was no need to ask who "he" was.

Diana cleared her throat. "I came to thank you once more—and to discover your true motives for assisting us."

Mrs. Clement smiled. "You are suspicious of me. That's understandable, of course. But, in truth, it is much as I told you last night. Lord Lucan had expressed to me his concern for your welfare, and I merely sought to do what I thought he would wish. He is a good friend, and a good man."

"That is all he is to you? You do not love him?" Diana's fingers were tightly laced together in her lap.

The widow gave her a considering look. "I have always had a soft spot in my heart for Geoffrey. I shan't lie to you about that. And yes, we spent some time together— briefly—a few months after his wife died."

"You were lovers, you mean," said Diana curtly.

Mrs. Clement looked amused. "You desire frankness, then? Yes, Mrs. Verney, on less than a handful of occasions we were lovers. But love had very little to do with it, my dear. And I tell you that only because you are in love with him yourself. You have a need to know."

Diana nodded. "It's true," she replied pensively. "You do understand."

"I wonder if you realize how much I envy you. You're fortunate I have not a vindictive temperament."

"Why should you envy me? You appear to have everything you need, and your freedom besides."

"On the contrary, I have almost nothing," countered the widow. "I am constantly in debt, and the various gentlemen with whom I share my time are only generous when the mood moves them. There is no security in such an existence, Mrs. Verney, which is why I have decided to remarry. I am glad you came today. I wanted to tell you about this myself."

Slow dread crept over Diana. "Remarry?" she echoed sharply. "Who?"

"Lord Bathurst, your late husband's uncle, has made me an honorable offer," replied the other, with dignity.

Diana's mouth gaped open. "*Lord Bathurst?*" she repeated incredulously. "But . . . but he is the most top-lofty, pompous man alive! . . . although very worthy, of course," she added, guiltily recalling the man's kindness to herself. "But he is much, much older than you, surely!"

The widow's shoulders lifted. "Yes, he is dreadfully pompous and tedious, but even the dullest man needs a woman," she said prosaically. "I appeal to him, you see, because I remind him of some long lost love of his youth. It's an amusing situation, actually. You see, I believed he was offering me a carte blanche . . . and it was only after I accepted him that I discovered it was a proposal of marriage!" She said it almost merrily. "You cannot imagine my surprise! But I grew accustomed to the notion almost at once, for I'm sure you are aware that he is a wealthy man. I thought it best to explain all this to you, for it will put us more or less in the same family. I shall be sort of an aunt to you, I suppose—at least until you remarry, of course."

Diana looked a little bemused. "And do you . . . I mean, is it possible that you *love* him?"

Mrs. Clement laughed, a pleasant, musical sound that nevertheless held a dash of bitterness. "Forgive my amusement, Mrs. Verney. It has been a long time since I was asked such a question." Slowly, her smile faded to seriousness. "No, I do not love him. Nor does he love me, though at the moment he believes he does. I intend to provide him with an heir, however, which should go a long way toward binding us together."

A tiny frown furrowed Diana's brow, and she moistened her lips, daring to ask the question foremost in her mind. "But . . . without love . . . do you not find the whole notion . . . rather distasteful?"

Mrs. Clement regarded her shrewdly. "Distasteful? You are speaking of the marriage bed, I collect. What an odd conversation we are having!" Observing the flame of color in Diana's cheeks, she said, "No, don't apologize— I am not offended, I promise! We have something very basic in common, don't we? You feel it, too—I know you do."

In the brief period of assessment which followed, her gaze grew unexpectedly sympathetic. "I am not known for my candor, Mrs. Verney, but you may trust that I speak from experience when I say that all men are not alike. Their needs are similar, yet the way each man translates that need into being can be as individual as the man himself. Many men have not the least understanding or interest in what we females need or want, but there are some who do—and others who are willing to learn."

Embarrassed, Diana's eyes lowered, yet her desire to *know* overcame her reticence on the subject. "And is it possible to feel nothing at all with one man, and . . . and something with another?"

Mrs. Clement nodded slowly. "It is not only possible, it is inevitable. *If* you are lucky enough to find a man who will give of himself, then my advice is to cherish him . . . *love* him, if you can. With such a man as that, you will not find the marriage bed distasteful, I assure you."

The ensuing conversation was no less frank, and when Diana rose to leave, it was with the knowledge that she would always recall this interview with mixed feelings. Mrs. Clement was both candid and encouraging—but she also laid bare her scarred past to the possibly censorious eyes of a woman she scarcely knew. In times to come, there would be moments when something would jog Diana's memory, and she would remember Mrs. Clement's courage and compassion, and from whence was born the sage advice she offered.

But it was not this which made Diana's spirits soar as she headed back to Aunt Serena's house. Her thoughts were only of Geoffrey and the future, a future suddenly gleaming with the promise of happiness. However, a rude shock awaited her back in Arlington Street. It seemed that Aimee and Mary had never returned from their walk in Green Park. In fact, they had vanished without a trace.

Chapter Seventeen

"What do you mean Aimee is missing?" Midway into Aunt Serena's Yellow Saloon, Diana came to a frozen standstill, her heart lurching as the first and worst possible explanation leapt into her brain.

"I mean exactly what I said!" bellowed the dowager from where she sat, swaddled in shawls. "She told me she'd return in an hour, and it's been nearly three! She ain't here, and she ain't in the Park either! So where the devil is she?"

Diana pulled off her bonnet. "Well," she said, after a stunned moment in which she denied her initial fear, "she must have decided to return home, or—"

"Do you take me for a fool?" There was a heavy, ominous quality to her aunt's voice. "Hang it, girl, Jermyn Street was the first place I sent 'em to look! I didn't cut my milk teeth yesterday, y'know! And where have you been all this time? I was beginning to think you'd disappeared too!"

"I had a call to pay," Diana answered shortly. She moved to the nearest chair and perched on its edge, frowning.

Aunt Serena thumped her cane. "You've got more things to worry about than paying calls," she said in a grim tone. "Not only is your sister missing, but something else is afoot. I suppose you've been too damned preoccupied to notice that the gossipmongers are on the attack again?"

"No!" Diana's eyes widened in dismay.

"Oh, yes! You've done it to me again!" the dowager informed her. "It's beyond me why other women can manage to be discreet, but *you* have to start a scandal every time you come to town. They're saying he sleeps under your roof every night. Is it true?"

Diana gasped. "Good God, of course not! Who on earth would say such a spiteful thing?"

Aunt Serena did not mince words. "Lady Edgerton, for one," she retorted, "along with a handful of other hens with nothing better to do than flap their beaks together." She made a sweeping, rather irritable gesture. "It's time to end this namby-pambying around with Lucan. I'm going to send the announcement of your engagement in to the newspapers, and drop word of it in one or two appropriate ears. Better yet, we'll say you've married him already—that'll clip their wings!" She cackled gleefully. "We'll steer the gossip the way *we* want it to go! We did it once, and we'll do it again—"

"No, you will not!" interrupted her niece, springing to her feet. "Don't you dare meddle, Aunt Serena! I must speak to Geoffrey about this at once, and *we* will decide what must be done!" Though she did not notice, the decisiveness in her voice brought a hint of approval to the dowager's expression. "Never mind that," she went on with an air of decision. "Right now we must discover where Aimee is! Could she have gone shopping, perhaps?"

Aunt Serena glanced at her clock. "Hrumph . . . not likely at this time of day. It's near five, now. And she'd have come here first so that one of the carriages could be sent for, wouldn't she?"

296

"I suppose so." Diana's forehead creased with thought. "I don't like this at all, Aunt Serena." She began to retie the strings of her bonnet.

"Where the devil are you going?"

"I'm going to consult with Lord Lucan," she said unevenly. "I've a dreadful suspicion Sir Henry is behind this. Do not ask me to explain, but . . . Geoffrey will know what to do!"

In the event that Aimee had returned home in the interim, Diana went first to her own home in Jermyn Street. She had been making use of Aunt Serena's landaulet, and it was this which conveyed her, less than ten minutes later, to her own front steps. Leaping from the carriage, she hurried forward, and was about to throw open the door when a folded slip of paper tucked into the crack attracted her attention. She snatched it up, and seeing it addressed to herself, unfolded it with trembling fingers.

As she read, the color drained from her face. "My God," she whispered. "Oh, Aimee, Aimee!"

Whirling, Diana lifted her skirts and dashed back to the landaulet, instructing the coachman in a harried voice to drive immediately to Bruton Street. As they rolled through the cobbled streets, she reread the note several times more, then shoved it into her reticule with a small moan. Please, she prayed silently, please, *please* let Geoffrey be at home!

It seemed to take forever to reach the earl's residence, for it was the fashionable hour, and a plethora of vehicles were beginning to clog the streets. Strictly speaking, it was improper for her to visit an unmarried man in his own home, but Diana could hardly allow such considerations to weigh with her at such a moment. As before, she ordered the coachman to wait, and sped up the steps of the earl's house to bang the knocker repeatedly.

Like any worthy member of his profession, Lord

Lucan's butler allowed no vestige of his surprise to show when he opened the door to discover a beautiful but highly agitated Lady of Quality demanding to see the earl on a matter of Great Urgency. He ushered her ceremoniously into the drawing room, but when she very prettily begged him to hurry, he did allow himself to wonder what could occasion such turmoil in so lovely a female breast. None of this, he hoped, was visible in his demeanor as he bustled up the stairs to the floor above.

Lord Lucan, as it happened, was expecting a guest, and had just donned his coat when the astounding intelligence that Diana was below reached his ears. It caused him to utter a stifled oath, and to head for the drawing room with such swift strides that both his valet and butler were to form some rather interesting conclusions about his visitor.

Diana was pacing up and down the carpet when he entered. "Oh, thank God you are here!" she cried, moving toward him with something very like a sob. When his arms opened automatically, she threw herself into them without reserve. "Oh, Geoffrey, Geoffrey," she wept, "It is all my fault! I should have told you the complete story last night, and now he has taken his revenge. He wants the Torrington diamond!"

With her soft body pressed so distractingly against his, the earl found it difficult to think, or indeed, to make any sense at all out of what she said.

"Diana," he replied shakily, pressing his lips to her hair, "I don't know what you're talking about. What are you doing here? You should not be here at all." Somehow, he forced himself to push her away. "You're pale," he added with concern. "You'd better sit down before you explain."

He led her to a chair, but he himself remained standing, his alert gray eyes fixed on her face.

Blinking back her tears, Diana fumbled to draw out the

ransom letter. "It's Aimee," she blurted. "She and Mary left Aunt Serena's for a walk in Green Park and never came back! And then—"

"Not again!" he cut in roughly. "After that Cheltenham tragedy last night I'd have thought your sister would have had enough of pranks—"

"This is not a prank!" Diana thrust out the note with its carefully printed, chilling message. "Read this!" she said wildly. "I found it on my own doorstep not a quarter of an hour ago."

The note was brief, and Lord Lucan took in its contents in seconds. "Your sister's life for the Torrington diamond," he commented, glancing up. "And you think you know who sent this?" His voice was cool and steady, full of common sense.

Diana struggled to mirror his calm. "It's got to be Sir Henry!" she said. "You see, it was he who . . . who waylaid Aimee in Vauxhall Gardens. I was afraid to tell you last night because I knew you'd be angry . . . perhaps say something cutting to her when she was already feeling so wretched."

The earl's dark brows snapped together. "Oh, really? Dammit, I wish you'd learn to trust me a little more, Diana. And I wish to God you'd come to me last night, instead of dashing off on your own—"

"But I do trust you," she protested in a watery voice. "I came to you now, didn't I?"

"True," he conceded, after a pause. "So Harry has still not learned his lesson, eh? It seems I underestimated him." Abruptly, he glanced toward the door. "A damned good thing your cousin is due at any moment—this is as much Charles's concern as mine! I rather think that choking the truth out of Sir Henry Neyle should be his privilege, though I daresay I would enjoy it even more."

He did not elaborate, and in the moment of silence which followed he was obviously thinking hard. Con-

299

scious that half her panic had subsided the moment she was in his company, Diana fell to studying the hard planes of the earl's face. His sensual lips were set in a forbidding line, yet she was sure he was not unsympathetic of her sister's plight.

Then suddenly, she remembered. "Aunt Serena says the gossips are talking about us," she said without preamble.

"*What?*" The roar in his voice took her by surprise.

"I said . . . people are saying you and I are . . . lovers." Her voice was low, but somehow she managed to keep it unwavering, her tone matter-of-fact. The earl's reaction was far less controlled.

"That tears it, then," he growled, cursing beneath his breath. He began to pace the room, his athletic frame moving with the taut grace of a jungle animal—or so Diana thought. The comparison rang true, yet seemed odd when one considered that he was elegantly garbed in the civilized clothing of a London gentleman.

Before Diana could summon the courage to say anything more, footsteps on the stairs heralded the arrival of her cousin.

Charles Perth did his best to hide his surprise at finding her in the earl's drawing room. "Why, hullo, Diana," he said, bowing politely. "Uh, what brings you here?"

Charles's face darkened as the earl, in cool, precise terms, furnished him with a summary of recent events, To her approval, he did not forget his promise to her sister, and looked to her to contribute what specifics she wished about the Vauxhall incident.

Before the story was finished, Charles Perth's green eyes were blazing. "God blast it!" he exploded. "That pretty-faced scoundrel ain't going to be so dashed pretty when I'm through with him! Rascally, lousy, little cur! I'll kill him so help me God if—" He ranted on for a bit

300

longer, and finished with, "Hang it, what are we waiting for? Let's go find the worthless bugger!" The words were flung over his shoulder as he plunged from the room.

"I'll be with you in a moment," called the earl after him. Taking Diana's arm, he guided her firmly toward the door. "Go home," he ordered, "and wait for me there. You have a carriage?"

Diana nodded, her fingers clutching his sleeve. "Aunt Serena's landaulet. But I want to come with you and Charles!"

"Don't be ridiculous. We can't take you to Harry Neyle's house. And if he is not there, lord only knows where we may track him down."

"Aimee may be there," she said stubbornly. "She will need me."

"And she may *not* be there," he returned. "Don't argue, Diana. If, as you say, your reputation is once again under fire, then for God's sake let's not feed the tabbies any more food! Go home! I promise I'll come there the instant I learn anything."

She heard the steel in his voice, and though she did not like it, she knew there was sense in what he said.

"Oh, very well," she said crossly. "But do not forget that Mary is missing, also. You have two females to rescue you know."

For the first time, he smiled, a reassuring smile that warmed his eyes and held a teasing glint. "Don't look so put out," he murmured. "I won't forget you while I'm gone." He raised her chin with a finger and planted a firm kiss on her lips. "You just stay home like a good girl," he added, "and leave the rescuing to us."

It was positively infuriating. No woman of spirit could fail to appreciate the maddening aspects of the situation, thought Diana pugnaciously. Flouncing to the window, she peered out for what must surely be the dozenth time since she arrived home half an hour before, but there was as yet no sign of the earl. Of course she loved him immeasurably, but still, she reflected, it was extremely arrogant and superior and thoughtless of him to expect her to wait while *he* got to go and watch her cousin plant Henry Neyle a facer. At least, she believed that was the phrase the sporting gentlemen used. It certainly had a satisfactory ring to it.

Just stay home like a good girl . . . In retrospect, it sounded positively condescending, and she wished she'd had the wit to tell him so at the time. Something warned her that being married to Geoffrey Trevelyan was going to have its challenges, that she would have to be sure not to let him have his way too often. Not, of course, that he would do so intentionally, but he obviously had a dictatorial streak. Diana had a sneaking suspicion he'd been trying to conceal it from her, but she was not fooled in the least. Did she love him anyway? *Dear God, yes.*

Nevertheless, he needed to be taught a lesson. Surely if she put her mind to it, there was *some* way she could contribute to Aimee's rescue. Tapping her fingers on the windowsill, Diana cudgeled her brain in an effort to think logically. Well, if they were unable to find Sir Henry . . . or if they *did* find him and he refused to talk— an unlikely contingency, of course—then Aimee would still be missing. Of course, Geoffrey would find her, but in the meanwhile, no whiff of scandal must be allowed to drift to the gossipmongers. How many of Aunt Serena's servants knew what had occurred, she wondered uneasily?

Well, Aunt Serena would naturally tell them to—good heavens! She had forgotten the dowager completely! Aunt Serena would be practically foaming at the mouth by this time, she reflected, rushing up the stairs to fetch

302

her cloak and bonnet.

"Diana? Is that you?" called Miss Tilden from her bedchamber.

Diana suppressed a flash of impatience. "Yes, Tildy? Is anything wrong?"

"No, my dear. It's just that it's so quiet here, I've been wondering where everyone was. I could do with a spot of tea, if you would care to join me."

Diana groaned. "I'm sorry, Tildy, but I cannot. I have to go to Aunt Serena's immediately. I'll send Meg up with tea and cakes, if you like."

She gave her abigail the instructions, adding, "When Lord Lucan arrives, tell him I went to Aunt Serena's house, if you please. Keep a sharp ear out for him, now. Where is Lawrence?" she asked, glancing around for the butler.

"'Tis his afternoon off, ma'am. He should be back any minute now, though."

Diana nodded. "Very well. See that he knows where I am, too."

Her abigail curtsied, and Diana hurried from the house, indifferent to the promise of rain hanging heavily in the air. As she walked, intermittent gusts of wind whipped her gown against her legs, reminding her of that first encounter with Geoffrey. How greatly she had changed since that day, she mused. Her whole outlook was no longer focused inward, no longer distorted by a brooding lack of faith in the entire male sex. Thanks to Geoffrey, her ability to trust a man had been completely revitalized; she knew now that Edmund had been but a bad apple, while Geoffrey—and for that matter, Cousin Charles—where men upon whom a woman could rely, men who would protect and value a woman instead of wounding and scorning her. Surely they would be able to find Aimee soon, she thought, as she reached the end of the street.

Jermyn Street ran perpendicular to St. James's Street; while directly across, Bennet Street led from St. James's to Arlington. Diana did not normally care to cross St. James's at this hour of the day—particularly without a maid—but she had long since sent the landaulet back to the mews, and it was simpler and faster to walk. She had not forgotten that Ladies of Quality did not visit St. James's in the afternoon, but in her view, *crossing* it was hardly a fracture of that rule. Thus it was not propriety which made her hesitate upon the curb but the vast number of swiftly moving vehicles bowling along without any apparent regard for the safety or existence of pedestrains. Twice she stepped out, and twice she was forced to leap back or risk being run down, which made her wonder whether she would be able to cross at all.

She almost did not notice the hackney coach until it slowed to a stop beside her, and then she was startled and a little apprehensive until she recognized its sole passenger, his round, good-humored face peering out at her with doddering geniality.

"Oh, Lord Hervey!" she cried, moving eagerly forward. "Thank goodness it is you! Would you mind terribly if I joined you? I must get to Aunt Serena's at once!"

His lordship pushed open the door, and reached out a pudgy hand. "Climb right in, m'dear. Here, let me help you. There! Always pleased to oblige a lady." He took in her slightly disheveled appearance. "In a hurry, you say?"

Diana nodded. "Yes, the most dreadful thing has happened. I must speak to Aunt Serena at once."

Lord Hervey looked at her intently. "Nothing serious, I hope?"

Diana hesitated. "Well, yes, it is serious. I suppose

Aunt Serèna will not mind my telling you. You see, my sister has disappeared."

"I said, *where is she?*"

Of his two uninvited guests, Sir Henry Neyle considered Lord Lucan to be the most dangerous; however, it was Charles Perth who had led the charge into his bedchamber, and it was Charles who appeared the most irate. The earl merely blocked his escape by propping his broad shoulders against the closed door, leaving it to Mr. Perth to shout wild, incomprehensible accusations and wave his doubled fists at the startled baronet. Keeping his wary gaze on them both, Sir Henry beat a strategic retreat behind his washstand, his celestial blue eyes regarding the intruders with considerable alarm.

"I really have not the least idea what you mean, old boy," he quavered, trying to sneer. "I haven't seen Miss Farington in ages. Sweet little gal, isn't she? Not my style, of course . . ."

Lord Lucan snorted, and Charles stepped forward in a menacing fashion, which had an oddly stimulative effect upon Sir Henry's memory.

"Wait now, ahem, er, yes. Now that you mention it, I *do* seem to recall seeing her at Vauxhall Gardens last night." When Charles made a savage gesture, Sir Henry's voice grew a trifle shrill. "I swear the chit did nothing but talk my ear off!" he insisted. "I never heard such a little prattlebox in my life! For hell's sake, I never even got a kiss for my pains!"

"I'd break his nose if I were you," offered the earl in contemptuous accents.

Sir Henry gave a horrified gulp. "Egad, Geoff, such violent inclinations you have! Every feeling is offended, I assure you! Think of what *ma mère* would say—she would never forgive you if you spoiled my face, y'know." Licking his lips, his eyes darted nervously between the two men. "Anyway, now that the little chit is so thin, she isn't nearly as appealing as before," he added unwisely.

The washstand did nothing to save Sir Henry; it tipped over with a crash as Charles dove forward to grab him by the neck. Cursing furiously, Aimee's raging suitor rammed the baronet's head against the wall.

"Just one more word," he grated, "just one more word about Miss Farington and I will personally change the shape of your nose! Better yet, I'll wring your scrawny neck, you complacent little turkey cock. Now, for the last time, what the devil have you done with her?"

"Nothing!" screeched Sir Henry. "You're both mad! Let me go! Ouch! You're choking me!"

"I don't think he knows anything," said the earl suddenly.

"The devil he doesn't! Look at the lily-livered coward. The fellow's positively shaking in his boots! He's hiding something, sure as check."

"I think he's only worried about his face. It's his only hope of winning a rich wife." The earl's tone was sardonic. "Buck up, Harry. We won't damage that spectacular countenance if you cooperate. Have you seen Aimee Farington since last night?"

"No!"

"You did not write a ransom note, by any chance, and address it to Mrs. Diana Verney?"

Sir Henry goggled. "Ransom note?" he echoed, a shade squeakily. "Why the devil should I do that? Diana Verney hasn't any money. At least not the kind I want."

The earl exchanged looks with Mr. Perth. "I suppose we could take him with us," he suggested. "Knowing what he does, I wouldn't trust him out of my sight, and he might be useful."

Charles released his captive with a derisive snort. "Useful? This fellow's never done a useful thing in his life."

Sir Henry was edging toward the mirror. "So sorry to disoblige," he protested, "but I really do have other plans." His head craned forward in an attempt to get a clear view of his mangled neckcloth.

"What plans?" said the earl, his lip curling. "Don't worry, Harry. You look fine."

"Personal plans," retorted the baronet, his voice resuming its normal tenor. "With a lady who is none of your concern, old boy."

"Dammit, *who?*"

Sensing that further dissembling would only result in damage to his person, Sir Henry lifted a petulant shoulder. "If you must know, Lady Uxbridge. She and I have struck up a bit of a friendship just lately."

The earl's voice altered abruptly. "Ah," he said, an unpleasantly soft edge to his voice. "And does this 'friendship' include the friendly practice of spreading malicious gossip?"

Sir Henry started guiltily. "How the dev—?" Knowing he had betrayed himself, he cried out, "Devil take it, Geoff, it was Sophia's idea. I swear I had nothing to do with it!"

"I see." Lord Lucan's face was cold with contempt. "For this, Harry, you are going to pay, unless you can tip the scales in your favor very quickly. As you must have already guessed, Aimee Farington has been abducted and is being held for ransom. She must be found as quickly as possible, and if you can think of some way to expedite the process, I strongly suggest that you do so."

*   *   *

307

"Disappeared!" repeated Lord Hervey in a thunderstruck voice. "Why, how can that be?"

"I fear the whole story is a long one, my lord. She appears to have been abducted, for the nefarious object of extorting money from my aunt. Or to be more precise, it is the Torrington diamond that this . . . this person wants"—Diana's lips trembled—"in exchange for my sister's life."

"The diamond," he echoed. "Yes, I s'pose it is worth a fortune, ain't it? But not as much as a human life, eh? Never fear, Serena will give it up," he told her, patting her hand comfortingly. "She don't have a selfish bone in her body, y'know."

Diana cast him a quick glance. "Yes," she agreed, a shade uncertainly. "But I think it wrong to yield to an extortionist, don't you? My hope is that we can catch whoever did this vile thing before any real harm befalls my sister."

"We?" inquired her portly companion in an odd tone.

"My cousin, myself, and . . . Lord Lucan," she explained, coloring slightly. "You see, we think we know who is responsible."

Under her startled gaze, Lord Hervey's complexion grew queerly mottled, and his hamlike hands began to open and shut until one, as of its own accord, shot across to close around her wrist. "Who?" he uttered, almost hoarsely. "Whom do you suspect?"

"I think it better if I do not say," she replied, with new wariness. "It is quite possible that we are mistaken. Pray, release me, my lord. You are hurting me."

He did so at once. "Beg your pardon, m'dear. I'm just sick about this whole terrible thing, y'know. Can't bear to think of your aunt being upset about this. And that pretty little sister of yours, too! She must be sick with fright! Well, at least she has her maid with her. I daresay you'll get them both back right and tight once the ransom is paid."

"How did you know Mary was with her?" asked Diana bluntly.

"Eh?"

"I asked you how you knew the maid was with my sister," she repeated.

Lord Hervey's mouth gaped open. "Why, you said so, m'dear. I heard you . . ."

Diana's head shook. "On the contrary, I said nothing whatever about Mary. What have you done with them, my lord? What have you done with my sister?"

Chapter Eighteen

During the heavy silence which followed, Lord Hervey seemed to wilt before Diana's eyes. A faint, staccato tapping on the roof marked the beginning of the rain, and this, combined with the oppressiveness of the air inside the coach, somehow added to her sudden fancy that the scene was unreal, a vivid nightmare conceived from her own wild imaginings. Yet the perspiration beading on Lord Hervey's brow was only too real, as was the ugly transformation of his complexion, which had turned quite muddy. He looked, she thought, as if he were going to be ill.

"What have you done with my sister?" she asked once more, her eyes pinned to his. The insistent question hovered between them, its silent echo begging for an answer.

When he finally spoke, there was a choking edge to his voice. "If only Serena had let me have it reset. I was going to have a copy made, a good one, so that no one would ever notice it was not the original. If only she had let me do it . . ." His fumbling fingers dragged a handkerchief from his pocket.

To Diana's dismay, his lordship's eyes were brimming with tears. "I am so sorry," he sobbed. He swabbed his

310

upper lip and brow with the small square of white linen, then blew his nose on what remained. "So very, very sorry," he added, his mouth quivering like a child's.

He sounded so despairing that Diana was seized with terror. "My God, do not tell me you have *killed* her—!" she cried, going quite white.

"Oh, no." His head shook. "No, course not. I wouldn't hurt a pretty little gal like that," he insisted with pathetic dignity. "Even for the Torrington diamond." Another large tear rolled down his cheek.

Unburdened of this dreadful fear, Diana collapsed against the squabs, one hand pressed to her breast in an effort to still her own shaking. Within seconds, however, this relief gave way to an anger so powerful her hand itched to slap him across the face.

Resisting the impulse, she said sternly. "Well, being sorry is all well and good, my lord, but you must stop crying and tell me where Aimee is. Now look, we have reached Aunt Serena's. Do you wish to talk inside, or—?"

"No, no!" he whispered, shuddering visibly. "Serena mustn't see me like this. Tell the coachman to keep driving—please! Tell him to take us to Covent Garden."

"Covent Garden! What on earth for?"

"That's where she is," he said simply. "Her maid, too. Tell him Maiden Lane, near Covent Garden."

Hearing the hackney driver's impatient shout, Diana pushed open the window and gave the order; she then sat back and fixed the plump little man in front of her with an unwavering stare.

"I hope you mean to explain what my sister is doing in such a place," she said. "If she has suffered any ill, I can asssure you that Aunt Serena will—"

"Promise you won't tell her!" he interjected in a panicky voice. "I don't want her to know. We'll get little Aimee back, but for God's sake promise you won't tell Serena!"

"I can make no such promise, Lord Hervey. What you have done is wicked and dishonest and—"

"Aye, aye, but you don't understand. I was desperate," he explained, looking shamefaced. "Y'see, I'm rolled-up . . . ruined. I've got a pile of debts as high as St. Paul's—gaming debts, most of 'em. Serena despises gamesters, but I ain't a gamester, really. I just had a run or two of bad luck. Still, she'll despise me if she finds out!" He regarded her earnestly. "Y'know, I was pretty well up in the stirrups five or six years ago, but now—! Now, I'm a fair hop into Dun territory. My own fault, of course. I admit it. If I could do it all over, I'd do different."

"But you can't," she pointed out.

He sighed deeply, his hands resting atop his big stomach. "No," he agreed in a sad tone. "The Torrington diamond would've solved all my problems, though. It was either that or go to a shark, but I figured that wouldn't fadge. I'd have to be insane to get myself caught in the toils of a moneylender." He paused for an instant, and when he spoke again, his voice shook with emotion. "Y'know, it hurts a man's pride to depend on a woman for his blunt, and it's worse when other people start to suspect. They gossip about you, call you a parasite behind your back. And, by God, it's true!" He lifted his hand, ticking off a list on his fingers. "I sold my curricle. I sold my traveling coach. I sold my carriage horses. Did it quietly so Serena wouldn't know. Private sales, all of 'em." His hands spread. "And what's left? Not much! Now I hire a hackney or take one of Serena's carriages when I need to get about. And people notice," he nodded. "People notice."

"But, my lord, *stealing* is no better—in fact it is much, much worse!"

"No, it ain't," he retorted. "That big old rock ain't

312

doing nobody any good lying around in a locked box. S'pose you think I'm selfish and evil. *I* don't think so. But like as not I'll have to flee the country like that poor devil George Brummell. Ten to one I'll die in some cold, dirty French garret, instead of spending my old age with the woman I love. Serena won't marry me, but I know she loves me. Wants me to visit her every day, and how can I do that if I'm wasting away in some filthy garret or debtor's prison?"

Diana's brow furrowed in thought. "Well," she said slowly, "there must be some solution, and I daresay we shall think of it if we set our minds to it for a bit. But before that, my lord, it is of the first importance that we bring Aimee and Mary back as quickly as possible. Where are they exactly?"

Once again, Lord Hervey looked uneasy. "It was my manservant's idea," he said defensively. "*I* didn't like the notion, but Jacob said they'd be safe. He said that sort of place knew how to keep its females away from its customers—when it chose. He's the sort who should know."

"What kind of place do you mean?" Diana looked at him blankly.

"Well, I guess you could call it a fancy house," he said, rubbing his head, "but it ain't one of the better ones. I didn't like it, but it was the only one where Jacob knew the abbess well enough to ask a favor."

Diana stared in appalled comprehension. "Do I understand you to mean my sister is in a . . . a *brothel?*" she exclaimed, both face and voice awash with indignation. "An innocent young girl of gentle birth?"

Lord Hervey looked ashamed. "Aye. When you put it like that, it does sound wicked. I admit it, and I'm sorry for it."

Again, she almost slapped his face. "Yes, I do think it wicked!" she flashed. "And you had better hope that neither girl has suffered any harm, for if they have, I, for one, will not rest until I see you brought to book for this outrage. And as for Aunt Serena, I will not even venture to guess what she will say, but you can be very sure it will be unpleasant."

She might as well have struck the man, for he flinched just as much. "Your sister is safe and well," he insisted, but his voice was laden with such doubt that she could not be reassured.

Trembling with fury, Diana merely turned her head away, for she could think of nothing civil to say, and railing at the ineffectual little man certainly did no good. Instead, she directed her gaze toward the rain-splattered streets, and wondered suddenly what Geoffrey and Charles would say when they discovered she was not at Aunt Serena's. She rather thought Geoffrey was going to be annoyed, for not only had she gone off without him again, she had left not a trace of a clue to tell him where she might be found. Suppressing her qualms on this count, Diana forced herself to stop worrying and relax. At best, it would teach him to leave her behind, wouldn't it? And at worst—well, she would not think of the worst.

Geoffrey, as she would eventually learn, *was* a little annoyed to find Diana gone from her home, however as she had most thoughtfully left a message providing him with her destination, he was not unduly perturbed. He therefore betook himself, along with Charles and the ever-reluctant Sir Henry, off to Arlington Street, it being his intention to reexamine the ransom note, in case he had missed some subtle clue as to the writer's identity.

The three men arrived at the dowager's residence just short of half-past five, a time when the dowager was normally enjoying a light repast with Lord Hervey. Today, however, she was eating alone, a circumstance

314

which did nothing to improve the surliness of her disposition. It grew worse at their entrance, for it was at that moment that she inhaled a crumb, and spent the next minute coughing while her well-meaning grandson pounded her on the back.

"Let be, Charles, let be! Are you trying to kill me, for God's sake?" she shouted, launching into a tirade about people who jumped into rooms and startled defenseless old women. At length, she said, "And what the devil do you want, anyway? And what did you bring *him* for?" she added, pointing at Sir Henry Neyle. "I don't like the fellow, and I don't want him in my house."

"Now, Grandmama—" began Charles. He rolled an expressive eye at the earl, who quickly came to his aid.

"I would think you'd know why we are here," he said, ignoring the majority of her speech. "May I speak to Di— Mrs. Verney, please?" He glanced around in obvious puzzlement. "She *is* here, isn't she?"

"Diana?" repeated the dowager viscountess, scowling at him. "Of course she ain't here! The silly girl ran off to find *you* over an hour ago. Took a notion that you would know how to—" She broke off, and favored Sir Henry with an imperious stare. "Does he *really* have to be here?"

"I'd be more than happy to leave," offered Sir Henry with a well-bred bow.

"You can speak in front of him, ma'am," said the earl ironically. "Unfortunately, he already knows about Miss Farington's disappearance. Well, where is Di—Mrs. Verney, then? Her message said she was returning here." He glanced down at the dowager, his forehead creased with disquiet. "You see, ma'am, we had some reason to believe Sir Henry might have been responsible for the entire business. So far, it seems we were wrong," he added. "Diana assured me she would remain at home while we went to Sir Henry's lodgings, but she apparently changed her mind." He paused. "I suppose you know nothing about the ransom note?"

"Ransom note?" Aunt Serena sat up straighter and reached for her cane. "Confound it, man, what ransom note? No one bothers to tell me anything!"

"Someone wants the Torrington diamond," put in Charles angrily, "and when I find the miserable swine I'll kill him. If he's hurt one hair on Aimee's head, I'll kill him, so help me God."

Aunt Serena looked stunned. "The Torrington diamond . . ." she repeated in such an odd tone that all three males looked at her curiously.

"Yes, ma'am?" prompted the earl in an urgent voice. "You have an idea that might help us?"

Slowly, the dowager shook her head in disbelief. "I wouldn't have believed he'd go that far . . ."

"Who?"

It was the first time the earl had seen her falter. "Thurstan," she finally answered. "So that's why he ain't here."

"You mean Lord Hervey?" he said. "Are you serious?"

"Well, personally, *I'm* not surprised." The remark came from Sir Henry, who had taken up a negligent attitude against the wall. "The fellow's up to his ears in debt—debt he can't possibly pay."

The earl looked skeptical. "How do you know that?" he asked. "The man must have assets—property he can sell, investments he can tap into. I've heard nothing about him being that far under a cloud."

Sir Henry gave him a superior smile. "That's because you don't move in my circles, Geoff, old boy. You've all the blunt you need, but some of us don't. Some of us," he emphasized, flashing his teeth, "can hardly be blamed for taking advantage of the circumstances. By George, I rather admire the fat little fellow. The Torrington diamond, eh? Well, well. I wish I'd thought of it myself."

"That man," said the dowager emphatically, "is starting to give me palpitations. I wish you'd get rid of him."

"Why the devil did we bring him anyway?" inquired Charles, who was pacing the floor in frustration. "I can't see any use for the fellow at all."

The earl shrugged. "It was just a hunch."

Sir Henry sidled toward the door. "Does this mean I am free to, uh, make my departure?"

"*No.*"

A clap on his shoulder could not have been more effective than the one clipped word. Sir Henry stood in a frozen posture, regarding Lord Lucan with fresh alarm. "Why not?" he whined. "What do you want with me?"

"You seem to know a great deal about Lord Hervey's financial circumstances," continued the earl, in a hard voice, "and I don't find your reason all that convincing. I'm beginning to think you're hiding something, Harry."

"*I?* Hide something from *you*, Geoff, old boy? You cannot honestly think that—" The sentence ended in a squeak as the earl bore down on him. "Beg your pardon, old boy. It's merely that I've an agile mind. Don't know anything for certain, of course, but I *can* add two and two."

"What the devil are you trying to say?"

Sir Henry affected a languid smile while backing cautiously away. "Life is full of the oddest coincidences, don't you know? Let me tell you an amusing little story, old boy. One day I was strolling along Bond Street and I spied my own manservant walking ahead of me. Well! As far as I knew, Isaac was at my lodgings, and I was curious as to why he should have abandoned his duties. I called out to him, naturally. He turned, and after speaking with the fellow, I discovered that he was not my Isaac at all, but his brother, Jacob. His *twin* brother, I should say.

Isaac and Jacob . . . *so* biblical, don't you think?"

"Get to the point, Harry."

Sir Henry licked his lips. "The point is, old boy, that Jacob is Lord Hervey's servant. And the two brothers sometimes go out carousing together when they have the chance. Apparently they share a common interest in, er, debauchery. Rather charming, what? So the full sum of my story is that upon occasion Isaac has some rather interesting stories to tell. And that's all I know!"

"But what has this to do with Aimee's disappearance?" exclaimed Charles in disgust. "It's a sheer waste of time listening to this silly fellow's babblings."

"On the contrary," said the earl grimly, "he has provided us with a lead. I think we had better have an interview with this Jacob immediately."

Not to be outdone, Aunt Serena began spewing directives. "You find my nieces, Lucan!" she bellowed, brandishing her cane. "You bring 'em back safe—both of 'em, and you tell Thurstan I want a word with him! And then you marry Diana, do you hear me? No more namby-pambying around with my niece, do you hear me?"

Lord Lucan bowed. "There's nothing wrong with my hearing, ma'am," he responded. "I beg you will not shout."

"Impertinent!" sputtered the dowager with a gleam of appreciation. "Insolent, impudent young devil! My God, if I was forty years younger—!"

Maiden Lane proved to be a dark, constricted street, its narrow houses crammed uncomfortably together, its inhabitants shabby and ragged in appearance. Ill at ease, Diana made sure Lord Hervey bade the hackney coachman to wait, since it seemed the height of folly to be trapped in such a place without a means of transportation. She stepped daintily over a pile of refuse and

318

glanced around, suddenly conscious of silence, of foul smells, and of numerous pairs of eyes watching from the shadows. Four or five urchins had been splashing in the gutter puddles, but their activity had ceased when the hackney rolled into the lane. They all gaped, and one ginger-haired lad crept cautiously forward, his bright, black eyes fixed on Diana, his grubby hand raised as if to seize her skirt.

"Back with you, now," growled Lord Hervey, shaking his fist at the boy. "Get back! Haven't you ever seen a lady before? Get back!" He added, in an undervoice, "Hope you ain't too shocked, m'dear. Once you get into these smaller streets, it's all pretty much the same."

"Oh?" It was all Diana could think to say, but her heart was torn with pity for the wretched youngsters. "And this is where my sister is?" she asked, and found herself wishing that the man beside her was tall and powerfully built, rather than short, elderly, and portly.

"Aye," he mumbled, taking her by the arm. He led her to the largest house in the street, and pounded on the door.

The girl who admitted them was not at all what Diana expected. True, she was young and uncommonly pretty, but she was also clean, and the simple gown she wore was modest in its cut. Furthermore, she displayed no vulgar curiosity at their purpose, but invited them in with a respectful curtsey, her soft brown eyes downcast. If all was as it seemed, and this sweet, unaffected girl with her cultured accent was representative of the inhabitants in this house, then perhaps, thought Diana, just perhaps there was nothing to fear.

Lord Hervey gave the girl his hat. "I need to speak with Mrs. Creech as soon as possible. Is she available?"

The girl curtsied again. "I will go and see, sir. If you and the lady will follow me?"

She left them in a small salon, which, though not elegant in the true sense of the word, had a distinguished appearance, as if it had been furnished with the desire to make a visitor feel secure. Lulled by these surroundings, Diana's apprehension receded; then her pleasant illusion shattered as somewhere above them a door slammed, and a shrill, cockney-accented voice screeched a long stream of obscenities.

Diana's eyes flew to Lord Hervey. "Why didn't you ask her about Aimee?" she said nervously.

"She ain't the one to ask, m'dear. Mrs. Creech's the abbess of the place. It's her domain."

Ten agonizing minutes passed before the door opened, and a woman of approximately fifty years of age came into the room. Mrs. Creech was small and round, with shrewd gray eyes and a complexion so pale it gave her a bloodless look. Coarse yellow curls clung to her head, her neck was incongruously long, like a goose's, and her lips were tight and hard and smiling.

"Ah, Lord Hervey," she said smoothly, "I was not expecting you. How can I help you now?" Her eyes flicked briefly over Diana, then attached to his lordship's face.

Lord Hervey coughed. "I've come for the girls—both of 'em. Apologize for the inconvenience and so forth, but I've, uh, changed my mind and want 'em back."

For a few seconds Mrs. Creech did not speak, then all at once her smile broadened. "Unfortunately, my lord, this is not the way I conduct business. Our arrangement was somewhat different, if you recall. If you now desire the return of your merchandise, you must pay for it."

An involuntary protest ripped from Diana, but Lord Hervey only swallowed resignedly, and said, "How much?"

Head tilted, Mrs. Creech folded her arms. "I think the quality must be taken into account. Two such attractive

320

young girls, both probably virgins. I think two hundred pounds might cover the cost of my trouble so far today."

"Two hundred pounds!" Lord Hervey's face went pasty white.

Diana could no longer keep silent. "But this is preposterous!" she cried, stepping forward. "You have no right to refuse us! You are holding those girls here against their will, and I demand that they be—"

"You demand?" interrupted Mrs. Creech in amusement. "You come into my house and dare to make demands?"

In an unconscious imitation of Aunt Serena, Diana's expression turned haughty. "Certainly," she replied, with Olympian coolness. "I not only demand, but I promise that I have no intention of leaving here without my sister or the maid, Mary. Be advised that I am not without connections, Mrs. Creech. If you prefer to be brought before a magistrate—"

"And now you dare threaten me!" Mrs. Creech was still smiling, but her eyes had narrowed to icy slits. "I can think of uses for you, my fine lady, where such threats will earn you nothing but the beating you deserve." She was moving sideways as she spoke, and too late Diana saw her hand snake out to drag open a small drawer. "Don't bother to scream," she continued, raising a pistol. "In this neighborhood, no one will bother to take notice."

Lord Hervey moaned and dropped shudderingly into the nearest chair. "Oh, God, God! Serena'll never forgive me for this! Never!"

Mrs. Creech's lips curved in a contemptuous line. "Men! They're all fools. Weak, helpless fools, useless save for one thing only. I've changed my mind," she went on, her eyes running over Diana in an assessing, insulting manner. "There's a market for young women like you, and as for him"—she waved the pistol at Lord Hervey—"if he's found floating in the Thames come

321

tomorrow morning, who's to connect it with me? Neither Jacob nor Isaac will say anything." Her smile spread. "My sons will not betray me."

Mrs. Creech would doubtless have been enraged to know that one of her sons was not as encumbered with filial allegiance as she believed. In fact, several well-placed blows to various portions of his anatomy had persuaded Jacob Creech to become quite voluble. Bruised and sullen, he now lay against the wall of Lord Hervey's drawing room, glaring balefully at his persecutors.

Even with his back to the scene, Sir Henry Neyle had winced at every sound. "*Are* you quite finished, old boy?" he inquired, finally daring to peer over his shoulder. At the earl's curt nod, he reached for his quizzing glass. "Good heavens," he drawled, surveying his manservant's twin with a shudder of distaste. "You know, I never would have thought to associate *my* Isaac with *that* Mrs. Creech. So your mama runs a bawdy house, eh, Jacob? How bloody convenient."

"Only you would think so," was the Earl of Lucan's dry comment. "Do you accompany us there? Or would it be too much for your sensibilities to handle?"

"Let's leave the tiresome fellow," spluttered Charles. "What the deuce do we want him for?"

"I tend to agree," said Sir Henry languidly. "Surely I have been adequately, er, helpful?"

"Helpful?" Lord Lucan's face hardened. "You've barely begun to scratch the surface, Harry." He took a threatening step forward. "Very well, you may go—on one condition. You and your friend Lady Uxbridge will oblige me by spreading another rumor as fast as possible. The rumor is this: that Diana Verney is a lady of unimpeachable virtue and that I have been courting her with marriage in mind. You may add that there is likely to be a formal announcement at any moment. Do you have it?"

Sir Henry smiled. "Oh, to be sure. Anything you say, Geoff, old boy."

The earl pointed to Jacob Creech. "If you fail to do as I bid, or if that other rumor you started does not die a swift and permanent death, then you, Harry, are going to look far worse than he does. Do you understand?"

"Perfectly," responded Sir Henry, the smile wiped from his face. "Sophia will know just how to go about it."

"See that she does," said the earl coldly. "You have twenty-four hours to do it, and after that, Harry old boy, it is you who will pay the forfeit."

Sir Henry fled.

Diana shifted her body, and struggled once more against the cruel ropes that held her prisoner. Where on earth was she? Vaguely, she remembered that Mrs. Creech had struck her with the pistol, which accounted for the strange floating sensation in her head. She remembered, too, that Lord Hervey had cried out, but beyond that it was all a sickening blur.

She decided she must be directly under the roof, for the beat of the rain came through distinctly, and the room was cold and dank. Vaguely, she knew she was shivering, either with shock or cold or fear, or some ghastly combination of the three. The straw upon which she lay was damp, and she wriggled sideways, hoping to locate a dryer spot. Instead, she managed to roll directly under an area where the roof leaked and the floor was drenched with water.

Sobbing with frustration, Diana inched her way back to her original position. The whole left side of her gown was soaked, and her wrists and ankles throbbed from where the bonds cut into her flesh. Exhausted and

323

disoriented, she lay gasping, her mind spinning with pain. Whoever had tied the knots had not been gentle, nor had they intended her to escape.

Oh, Geoffrey, help me ... please, please, come quickly ... where are you? ... oh, my beloved, please come ... hurry ... I love you so ...

For the next little while, Diana slipped in and out of consciousness, a tangle of dreams and half-formed ideas drifting through her head. Despair had driven everything from her heart but the earl; he was her obsession and her hunger, and she focused on him as her only sane thought.

He would find her. Somehow he would find her and bring her out of this awful place. He would find Aimee, too, she thought hazily. She had been foolish to come here without him, and no doubt he would rant and rave and scold, but he *would* find her, and if he would only hurry, she would gladly bear his tongue-lashing. And when he was done, she would make very sure he knew how pleased she was to see him ...

For a while, Diana's dreams were only shifting patterns of bizarre colors, then they faded to something far more agreeable, a marvelous dream wherein a door opened and the earl came into the room. He was calling her name, over and over, with such a queer, passionate intensity that it banished the colors and patterns for good.

"I knew you would come," she croaked, suddenly certain it was no dream, and that the Earl of Lucan really *was* there. And from the unspeakable things he was muttering under his breath, Diana knew also that her Geoffrey was in a black rage, which somehow seemed so completely right that she merely gazed at him and reveled in his curses.

"Thick-skulled female!" he growled, sawing through her bonds with something she could not see. "Empty-headed, *obstinate* woman! Do you know what a fright you gave me? I don't know whether to kiss you or strangle you! Brainless, *stubborn* girl!"

Diana eyed him lovingly. "You forgot maddening," she quavered, her voice small and cracked.

"There's several words I forgot," he responded, with tender asperity. "I'm saving them for a more appropriate moment."

Then he was rubbing her wrists and ankles, massaging the sensation back into them until she cried out from the pain.

"There, darling, I . . . I think you'll be all right," he said, his voice shaking oddly. "Don't cry now, there's a brave girl."

With a final sob, Diana flung her arms around the earl's body and pressed her dirty, tear-stained face to his chest. She hugged him with all her strength, and in turn, received the most crushing embrace of her life, a hug so forceful she thought her bones would crack.

Later, she would try to understand what there was about the moment that made it the right time to tell him. Somehow the entirety of her inhibitions had vanished, peeled away by shock, by the earl's tenderness, and by her own raw emotions. When he would have taken her away she begged him to wait, and to listen, while in a little voice, she spilled out her long-kept secret. It was time he knew the truth about the Edgerton ball and what it was that Edmund had caught her doing. It was time to unload the burden for good.

"—so you see, Geoffrey, I really am not as . . . as good as you think. I crept up those stairs intending to . . . to spy . . . to eavesdrop upon Sir Henry . . . and I was guilty of vanity because I believed that I was . . . the one he should have been walking with . . . and . . . why are you smiling?"

"Because you are such a goosecap," he said, kissing the tip of her nose. "Oh, Diana, my sweet, sweet love, you can't really believe you did something terrible? Do

you mean to tell me that all these years you've been—"
He saw her expression and stopped, and when he spoke
again, it was a trifle unsteadily. "So because you, an
innocent young girl, formed a *tendre* for a handsome man
and behaved in a human manner, did you really believe
you deserved to be . . . to be mauled and humiliated and
socially ostracized? Did you really believe you deserved
to be forced to marry a man you loathed, and be
mistreated by him?"

When she gazed up at him mutely, he swore under his
breath. "If it takes me the next thirty years, I will make it
up to you," he promised, his arms tightening about her
slim body. Then he kissed her once, hard on the mouth,
and scooped her into his arms.

"No more talk," he said. "I'm getting you out of this
hellhole."

Chapter Nineteen

"And Charles says that if Papa gives his consent—
which I know he will!—we can be betrothed at once, but
that we must wait a year before we marry. He does not
want it said that he married a girl just out of the
schoolroom, you see. He thinks I should be given the
chance to grow up a little more." Aimee's voice was half-
rapturous and half-wistful. "Also, he says he wants to be
sure my affections are genuinely engaged, but I think I
have succeeded in convincing him that they are!" She
giggled. "Kissing Charles is such fun, Diana. You can
have no notion!"

"Is it, my dear?" Diana smiled absently. "I am very
happy for you."

Diana was still in her nightdress, and at everyone's
insistence, had been in bed ever since the earl had
brought her home from Maiden Lane the previous
evening. Dr. Hatfield had examined her then, and again
this morning, and in the end pronounced her injuries to
be very minor. Indeed, except for a few bruises and a
lump on the side of her head, she felt quite her usual self,
and had been chafing to get up for some time.

"What time did Lord Lucan say he would be here?"
she inquired for at least the third time that hour.

Aimee hid a smile. "About one o'clock or thereabouts. Charles is coming back too. They had to deal with certain things pertaining to our misadventure, as well as Aunt Serena, of course. Charles says she is taking the whole thing amazingly well. She refused to press charges against Lord Hervey, which one might have predicted, but what surprises me, Diana, is that she seems willing to forgive him." Aimee's expression was solemn. "I think she really does love him, don't you?"

Diana sighed. "I suppose so. I myself find it very hard to forgive him, but perhaps in time I will feel differently." Her mind very much occupied by private matters, she gazed pensively at her ringless fingers, then pushed back the bedcovers with decision. "And speaking of time, I think it is past time I got up. What a sluggard I am! I must decide what to wear to see Geoffrey and—oh, my goodness!" she exclaimed, catching sight of herself in the mirror. "Something must be done with my hair!"

By the time Lord Lucan was due to arrive, Diana was looking her very best. She was wearing one of her most alluring gowns—its color a shade of blue she had reason to know he particularly admired—while her hair, newly washed and golden as a new-minted guinea, cascaded over her shoulders and down her back in soft, shimmering waves.

When he first entered, Geoffrey Trevelyan's eyes were both unsmiling and possessive, concern for her welfare as yet the reigning emotion in their gray depths. Indifferent to the presence of Charles and Aimee (who were deeply involved in their own greeting), he strode forward and caught up her hands, as ever giving the gesture an intimate flavor by raising them to his lips.

"You are well?" He said it tersely and his look was more critical than complimentary.

Diana nodded. "Beyond a few bruises, quite well," she said, reassuring him with a smile. "But I hope you do not

328

plan to be as cross as you look, my lord, or you will send me into a fit of the dismals."

She basked in the way his eyes flashed and changed to something warm and deeply amused, something that made her feel a little breathless, and sent strange shivers racing over her flesh.

"I had no notion my moods affected you so," he replied, a teasing glint in his eye. His gaze ran over her anew, this time with an air of masculine appreciation. "You look beautiful," he murmured.

They were simple words, spoken without embellishment, yet laden with such a wealth of meaning that Diana blushed with pure pleasure.

"Thank you," she said quietly. "Thank you for everything."

He sat beside her on the couch, while Aimee and Charles pushed a pair of chairs together for themselves. Lawrence brought in hot tea and freshly baked scones, and while the butler was in the room the conversation remained desultory. The moment he was gone, however, the talk immediately shifted to the subject occupying all their minds.

"On the face of it," explained the earl quite seriously, "a daylight abduction such as Lord Hervey planned seems an utterly mad scheme, almost impossible to carry out successfully—at least in this section of London. It worked for two reasons. First, because he had access to the Dowager Lady Torrington's coach, and second, because he had managed to obtain two sets of livery almost identical to that used by the servants in her household. One was for Jacob Creech and the other, of course, was for his brother, Isaac. It was Isaac who was driving the coach."

"*Was* it?" Thinking back, Aimee's head shook in perplexity. "I was completely taken in. When the footman came up to me with a message from Aunt

Serena, it never even occurred to me to question him. I had never seen his face, but the livery was familiar, so . . ." She gave a little shrug. "When Aunt Serena sends a summons, one tends to listen. Mary told me afterward that she did not know him, but of course, she assumed he'd been hired since she came to work at our house. Until the carriage took off down Piccadilly, of course. Then we both knew something was wrong."

Diana gazed at her sister. "And you thought Aunt Serena sent the carriage out of consideration for your health, I expect. But you did not notice the coachman?"

"No." Aimee still looked a little uncertain. "I don't recall even glancing at him. And his back would have been toward us, wouldn't it?"

"But, good lord!" exclaimed Diana, with a startled glance at the earl. "Where *was* Aunt Serena's coachman, then? Surely he would not just hand over the coach to a pair of strangers?"

"Stunned by a blow, just as you were," he answered tightly. He reached for her hand, holding it firmly so that it rested between both of his. "Apparently, the two brothers simply walked into the mews and took the coach. Thanks to an order sent down from Lord Hervey, the horses were already harnessed and ready. I suspect the Creech brothers must have bribed one or two of the stableboys to absent themselves at the crucial moment, but more investigation will have to be done before we know for sure."

"We're dashed well going to find out," said Charles grimly. "I'll have no disloyal servants in my grandmother's employ."

The coach was found abandoned near Leicester Square," added the earl. "They were too shrewd to steal the horses, of course. It would have been much too dangerous."

Diana sipped pensively at her tea. "So Lord Hervey

330

knew that Aimee would be in the Park—Aunt Serena told him, I suppose—and sent the order. Then the two brothers must have been ready to act at any moment."

Lord Lucan nodded. "Yes, he admitted as much to your aunt. They had been ready for some weeks, it seems. His lodgings are very close to hers, so it did not take him long to return there, apprise Jacob that it was time, and send Jacob to fetch Isaac."

Aimee sighed. "I keep thinking what a pea goose I was to be so easily duped. And even after I was in the coach, I could not conceive of what was happening. And then Mary went into a fit of the vapors, and by the time I had calmed her down, I no longer recognized what street we were on." She frowned suddenly. "Oh, yes, and the handle to the door was jammed. I tried it, because I was wondering whether we ought to try and jump out."

"Well, it's a dashed good thing you didn't!" retorted Charles, looking startled. "You might have broken your neck!"

Aimee gazed coyly up at him from under her lashes. "It's quite plain I need someone to look after me," she complained. "Someone tall and forceful and very, very ardent—"

"Now, Aimee," chided her future husband, very hastily. To Diana's amusement, he turned a trifle pink. "S'pose she told you I made her an offer," he said in a gruff voice. "Ought to have waited to speak to her father first, but—"

"—but I made it *dashed* difficult," finished Aimee with an irrepressible smile. She reached for the teapot and refilled each of their cups, saying, with dancing eyes, "Oh, Diana, you should have seen Charles come dashing to my rescue! I swear he cast Lochinvar completely into the shade! We must ask Sir Walter Scott to compose something in his honor."

The tips of Charles's ears went even pinker. "Well, I'm

glad you can joke about it," he said with extreme feeling. "I know *I'm* going to have nightmares for a twelve-month! The whole business was deuced unnerving."

"Gracious, yes!" agreed Diana with a shiver. "I was utterly terrified, especially when I knew what—" Her voice fluctuated with emotion and the earl's tanned fingers tightened while for a few seconds she fought back the fearful memories. Drawing strength from him, she looked up, her gaze connecting with his in a contact more comforting than any words.

"Should we tell her?" she asked him in a low voice. "She does not yet know the whole of it."

"You mean what Mrs. Creech really intended?" the earl shrugged, and leaned forward to select another scone with his free hand. "Perhaps it would be best," he said, addressing Charles. "It might induce her to cultivate a little more caution."

Aimee was beginning to look indignant. "What are you two talking about? What should I know?"

Charles cleared his throat. "I ain't at all sure she ought to know—"

"Of course I ought to know!" she cried. "Tell me at once, Charles!"

"Well," he said uneasily, "it seems that Mrs. Creech had connections with the criminal underworld of which Lord Hervey was unaware. I ain't exactly sure why he thought he could trust her, but it's devilish clear he couldn't. *His* plan was simply to get as much as he could for the Torrington diamond and the rest of the jewels in the tiara, pay Mrs. Creech a small fee for holding the girls, and have them released. He ain't exactly what you call awake on every suit," he added disparagingly. "Only a Johnny Raw wouldn't have known the woman would try to stab him in the back."

Aimee's eyes grew round. "You . . . you mean she did not intend to release us? That is what she told me. That is why I was only a . . . a little afraid."

"Unlikely," put in the earl harshly. "From what she said to Diana, and from what she told Lord Hervey before she had him trussed up and tossed into her cellar, it seems clear that her plans were more ambitious. She does not admit it now, of course."

Charles patted Aimee's hand. "Hate to tell you this, kitten, but you had a dashed narrow escape. The Creech woman was going to take Hervey's blunt, and then, er, toss him into the river, so to speak. You and Mary were destined for something . . . worse."

The earl nodded. "When Diana arrived, Mrs. Creech was forced to alter her plans. I imagine she still hoped to get her hands on the Torrington diamond, but she now had Diana, too. Three healthy English girls, all well-looking in appearance, two of gentle birth . . . and apparently someone who was willing to pay dearly for them. Much as I hate to say it, there are still illicit markets for such women—particularly in some of the eastern countries."

"Edmund mentioned something about that once," put in Diana slowly. "I thought he meant it as a sick jest or . . . or said it only to disgust me. I could not believe such things were true. But when Mrs. Creech said . . . what she did . . . then I remembered." Once more the earl squeezed her fingers, and just as before, it helped.

"But could they really hope to get away with such a wicked scheme?" asked Aimee in a constricted voice.

"Probably not," said the earl, observing her white face. "In any case, Mrs. Creech has broken enough laws to be transported. In particular, any form of slave-trading has been a criminal offense in this country since 1811, and if it can be proved—" He broke off at the sight of Aimee's expression. "But we need not go into that any further just now. The important thing is that Mrs. Creech has been caught. Unfortunately, both her sons have eluded the authorities thus far."

"We should have tied the fellow up," exclaimed Charles, clapping a hand to his brow. "Why the devil didn't we think of it before?"

Lord Lucan looked equally rueful. "It was incredibly stupid of us, I agree. All I can say is that I, at least"—he cast an inscrutable look at Diana—"had something far more important on my mind."

"And what might that have been?" Diana made a strict effort to keep the question casual, and if there was a slight huskiness in her voice, she blamed it entirely on the earl, whose thumb had begun to caress her wrist in a most disturbing manner.

He gave her an amused look. "Why, I fear I cannot call it to mind at the moment," he replied, with a smile that made her heart thud.

"So Sir Henry was not involved in this after all?" said Aimee suddenly. Her eyes flew inquiringly to Charles.

"No, dash it! And I was sure the fellow was guilty!" His vexation evident, Aimee's betrothed popped the remainder of his fourth scone into his mouth and chomped on it savagely.

"In fact, he was actually instrumental in achieving your release," added the earl, reluctantly dragging his eyes from Diana's. "I would have questioned Lord Hervey's servant, of course, but without Sir Henry's information, I'm not sure I would have thought to, er, offer him physical violence—at least not to quite such a degree." His gaze returned to Diana, who was looking dismayed. "I'm afraid it was the only way we were able to get anything out of the man," he explained, with a faint air of apology.

Charles snorted. "His nose'll never be quite the same, and who cares? I'm devilish sure I don't!"

"Speaking of noses," remarked the earl in an altered tone, "do you agree that Sir Henry has earned his reward?"

Charles stared at him. "Reward? What sort of reward?"

"I thought we had both expressed an interest in rearranging certain of his features?"

"Oh!" Charles sat back with a grin. "Aye. I s'pose we ought to let him keep his nose," he stated, with careless magnanimity. "As long as he continues to mind his manners!"

After this, the conversation wended its way into more general channels, and when it turned eventually to horses, Aimee began to beg Charles to take her riding. Mr. Perth was not entirely sure that his beloved was ready for such strenuous exercise, but he found himself completely unable to resist her coaxing, and since she very meekly agreed to tell him the moment she began to feel fatigued, he finally yielded to her entreaties. He was, after all, only human, and there were a number of rather private sentiments he wished to impart (again) into her ear. A ride in the Park would offer them a chance to continue one particularly interesting discussion that had begun just after he had slashed the ropes which bound her prisoner in Mrs. Creech's house. And perhaps, he reflected, if he was very lucky, and they found themselves in an unoccupied area of the Park, they might be able to exchange another kiss. He therefore took himself off to his lodgings to change into riding clothes, while Aimee scurried upstairs to do the same.

Grateful to be alone at last with the earl, Diana turned to him eagerly, but was shocked to realize that he, too, was rising to his feet.

"But . . . but you are not leaving *now*, are you?" she faltered.

Observing her forlorn expression, he immediately sat down again and pulled her into his arms. "Don't look so wounded, love," he said, raising her chin with his finger. "I don't *want* to leave you, "—there was a queer flicker in his eyes—"but I have several important matters to attend to this afternoon and if I stay another minute I won't be able to drag myself away at all." Diana's unconscioulsy provocative pout nearly changed his mind. "You want me to kiss you, don't you darling?" he murmured. "Well, and why not?" His lips came down to brush hers lightly, hovered for an instant, then withdrew before it ever became a real kiss.

"On second thought, I think you are crediting me with more willpower than I possess," he said, expelling a jagged breath. Her topaz eyes were wide and doubtful, and he pulled back enough to look down into them for a long moment.

She stared back, seeing something that was at once hard and soft, candid and enigmatic. "You don't want to kiss me?" she whispered in confusion.

"Dammit, of course I do, Diana. But the next time I kiss you,"—he said it roughly, deliberately—"I don't intend to stop before we're finished."

The words were suggestive enough to make Diana's mouth go dry. "I'm sure I don't know what you mean," she lied, her heart knocking against her ribs. Fearing he might explain, she added quickly, "And I don't know what could possibly be so important that you could not stay a short while longer." She did not care if she sounded pettish, and neither did the earl, apparently, for he merely grinned and ruffled her hair.

"Oh, can you not?" he retorted rather lazily. "Well, you soon will, my love. I'll take you for a drive tomorrow morning, how about that? Do you think you can be ready by eleven o'clock?"

"As to that, my lord, I shall have to consult my social schedule," she replied with spirit. "It is quite possible that I am engaged to drive out with some other gentleman. Someone with enough courtesy to request—"

"I *did* request!"

"—the pleasure of my company. Someone who inquires

336

whether I am feeling well enough for such exertion—"

"My dear Diana, if I thought for one moment that you were not—"

"Someone," she continued in deeply piteous tones, "who does not run off and abandon me only hours after I have sustained a severe shock—a shock, I might add, which would have sent *most* females into repeated fits of hysterics! Which reminds me, my lord, I should like to know just why my companion is not here. Aimee informs me that you descended upon us this morning while I was still asleep and *abducted* poor Tildy!"

"Miss Tilden," he responded, without remorse, "was not abducted. In fact, she offered to go and help sustain your aunt in her Hour of Need. Your Great-aunt Serena evidently took a liking to Miss Tilden, for she specifically requested her attendance."

"Oh. I—I see," said Diana, abandoning her theatrics. "Very well, then. If it is as you say—"

The earl's patience was dwindling rapidly. "My dear Diana, I am still awaiting your answer with bated breath. Dare I hope that you will accord me the honor and pleasure of your charming company for a leisurely ride in my carriage tomorrow morning? At approximately eleven o'clock?"

"My dear Lord Lucan," she said, her eyes cast demurely downward, "since you phrase it so gallantly, how can I possibly refuse?"

Though she would not have liked him to know it, Diana was wearing a track in the drawing room carpet more than thirty minutes before the earl was due to arrive. Over and over, her fretful gaze swerved to the clock upon the mantelshelf, then moved to the mirror above, where she anxiously inspected her appearance. Why hadn't he come early? Wasn't he as eager to see her as she was to

337

see him? Was he actually going to be *late?*

It was ten minutes past eleven before she heard the bell ring, and by then, Diana had worked herself into a fume. It was outside of enough for him to have deserted her yesterday, just when she'd been about to blurt out all her feelings for him, but now, *now* when she was positively languishing over him, he had to go and be late! How could he be so infuriating?

When Lawrence announced the earl, however, Diana was seated in a chair with her back to the clock. "What, is it eleven already?" she remarked, feigning an airy little start of surprise as she twisted around, "Gracious, I had no notion of the time! Where *has* the morning gone?"

Moving toward her with long strides, the earl grinned his appreciation. "Miffed again, Diana? Lord, what a scolding little fishwife you are going to make me!"

Diana's brows arched. "Why, what can you possibly mean? Simply because you are ten minutes late, does not mean—" The sentence ended in a small squeak as he reached down and pulled her manfully into his arms.

"In reality, my dear delight, I am as punctual as always. I told you that blasted clock was wrong, didn't I?"

The heat of his nearness made a clever response impossible. "Well, I was hoping you'd be early," was all she could manage, on a shred of reproach.

"I would have been but for your aunt," he said wryly. "She sent me an early morning summons, and what could I do but obey? Come, are you ready?"

"What?" With difficulty, Diana focused on the latter question. "Oh, yes, of course. No, wait—I must put on my bonnet." This delectable confection of feathers and flowers lay beside her gloves atop a nearby table, and as she tied it under her chin, she said in some bewilderment, "But what on earth can have possessed Aunt Serena to send for *you?* Especially at such an hour?"

"She likes me," replied the earl, shepherding her toward the door with determination.

"Yes, but that hardly explains—"

"Can you wait until we're outside?" he demanded. "I'll explain it all to you then."

It seemed judicious to do as he desired, but the moment they stepped out of the house, Diana's curiosity received a startling new stimulus.

"But . . . but this is a traveling chariot!" she protested, staring at the light, yellow-bodied chaise-and-four standing in the street.

"So it is, he agreed, urging her forward with his hand. "I purchased it only yesterday so there are no crests on the door panels as yet. I did not think you would care about that."

"But, Geoffrey, there are *trunks* strapped to the boot. Are you—we—going out of town?"

"Clever girl," he approved, as the postilion hurried to let down the steps. "I usually hire a post-chaise, but I thought it high time I bought my own conveyance. Do get in, love."

For some unfathomable reason, Diana found she lacked the will to refuse. In fact, an unexpected, heart-jarring excitement was rushing through her, so that all she could do was say, in as blithe a tone as she could manage, "I presume you mean to tell me where we're going!" and climb into the coach.

The earl did the same, settling himself beside her with an air of intense satisfaction. "That was certainly easier than I expected," he remarked. "I envisioned having to sling you over my shoulder and—"

"What was easier?" she interrupted, her voice rising a little. "Geoffrey, I really must insist you explain what this is about."

"I have every intention of explaining," he retorted. "You see, my dear delight, I'm abducting you."

"What?"

"I said I'm abducting you." Both his tone and expression strongly suggested that he was uncommonly pleased with himself.

"Geoffrey," she said, after a brief struggle with her emotions, "this is quite unnecessary. I am perfectly willing to marry you."

"Ah, but you see, I'm no longer asking you to marry me," he replied, to her utter astonishment. "The offer is withdrawn."

Diana was almost certain she saw his lips twitch, but to her, it was hardly a laughing matter. "I'm afraid I don't understand," she said, rather shakily. "If you don't want to marry me, then why . . . go to all this trouble?"

"I do wish you would pay attention, Diana," he complained. "Did I say I do *not* want to marry you? No! I said I have withdrawn my offer of marriage." He reached for her hand and carried it to his chest, holding it where she could feel the steady thud of his heart. "I'm still determined to have you, Diana, but the fact is, I have proposed—or tried to propose—marriage to you three times, and each time have had the infelicitous experience of being turned down! First," he said in an aggrieved tone, "you made false assumptions about me, then you hemmed and hawed over the whole business until I was ready to tear out my hair with frustration—"

Diana's conscious-stricken expression vanished. "I was not hemming and hawing!" she said indignantly. "I was simply considering—"

"—and considering and considering," he went on, growing wrathful. "I never met a woman so given to thinking things over! Then you said you loved me—"

"And it's true!" she protested.

"Yes, thank God, I'm aware of that. But then you gave me some cock-and-bull story about how you were not a normal woman with normal responses—"

"Well, how do you know it's not true?" she inquired

340

in a small, breathless voice.

The earl's expression was laughing and tender—but it was also mixed with a hint of steel. "I know," he said firmly, "because I've held you in my arms. I know because I've kissed you, Diana, and I can tell a quiver of desire from a shiver of revulsion. There is nothing wrong with you, and I intend to prove it before the day is out."

His meaning was more than plain. "You would really take me without marriage?" she whispered.

"If that's the only way," he told her bluntly. "One way or another I intend to show you that your fears are misplaced! However, I just happen to have a special license in my pocket, only inches from your fingers, my sweet." Her hand jerked, but he recaptured it and carried it to his lips. "You know, as much as I enjoy kissing these pretty fingers," he teased, "there are a number of other parts of you that I'm even more anxious to kiss."

Diana was too upset to be diverted. "But, Geoffrey," she objected, "you are making no sense. Either you do wish to marry me or you don't—"

"Oh, didn't I explain?" He made a pretense of looking surprised. "*You* must ask *me* to marry *you*."

Diana's mouth fell open. "But—that's absurd!" she said, finding her voice at last.

"Why?" He grinned. "I should like it above all things, you know."

She thought this over. "Then you *do* love me?" she asked hesitantly. "I mean, *love* me . . . not just *care* for me?"

He stared at her in astonishment. "For the love of heaven, Diana, haven't I made that clear? Of course I love you! I'm mad with love for you, darling!"

His arms reached out to crush her against him, an embrace which ended with her snuggled cozily upon his lap, and what remained of her bonnet shoved into the opposite corner.

"Lord, what a clunk I am not to have said it!" he

341

murmured, stroking her hair. "Love was just a meaningless word until I met you." He kissed her ear, then the tip of her nose. "Oh, granted I loved my parents, but . . . the love I feel for you transcends anything I have ever felt. You have taught me to love, Diana. I adore you, every blessed inch of you, and I plan to spend the rest of my life proving it. And I'll love you just as much when we're old and fat and all our teeth have fallen out!"

Diana saw no purpose in hiding her delight. "That is absolutely the most romantic thing anyone has ever said to me," she remarked, sighing dreamily. "In that case, Geoffrey, will you please, please marry me? For I *do* love you so very much!"

Her words were simple and sincere, and as far as he was concerned, the sweetest words she could have spoken.

"In a very short while," he promised, his voice unnaturally husky, "we will find a clergyman and attend to the matter."

His broad shoulder offered an enticing spot for her head, but too many unanswered questions still crowded Diana's mind. "But, Geoffrey," she said, after a few moments, "I still do not quite understand why we are leaving London. And you've not told me where we are going, either!"

"We're on the Bath Road," he said, "which I'm sure you know takes us eventually into Wiltshire. I seem to recall you telling me about a certain set of parents and siblings in that area, who have, by the way, been apprised of our imminent arrival. And the reason we're leaving, dear delight, is because there are too many blasted rumors flying about London for my comfort!"

In reply to her look, he grumbled, "The first, of course, you already know. Then there's a second rumor which suggests the we are *not* currently engaged in a liaison of a passionate nature, but that a formal announcement of our approaching nuptials is expected at any moment. That one, by the way, is being circulated by our dear friend Sir Henry at, er, my suggestion. And now a *third* version has sprung up!"

Diana blinked. "A third?" she echoed. "What is it?"

"An unnamed personage," he said sardonically, "has started a rumor that we are already married, and in fact have been so for a great many weeks! And as of this morning, it seems to be the most prevalent of the three!"

"Aunt Serena!" A variety of emotions swept over Diana, but the strongest—mirth—won out within seconds. "Oh, Lord, I might have known!" she said, between giggles. "I wonder what reason she invented to account for it? Why are you scowling? Her story scarcely does any harm, does it?"

He smiled reluctantly. "Oh, I agree it's the best of the three, for it cancels out the stench of the first. However, when every gossipmonger in town feels free to bandy my future wife's name about, I find it puts me in a devil of a temper."

Back in March, Diana would have been horrified by the notion, but now she merely leaned up to kiss his chin, her eyes dancing with laughter. "Never mind, I daresay it will all soon die down. In fact, I can think of a few other details I am more concerned about."

"Oh? And what are they?" he inquired, one dark brow rising quizzically.

She traced the line of his jaw with her finger. "You, my dear Geoffrey, may have had the foresight to bring every stitch of clothing you own, but I have brought nothing. And if you mean to tell me I can purchase more, it seems to me a shameful waste when I've so many things, and *furthermore*, we have brought neither maid nor valet with us, which is going to look rather peculiar, don't you think?"

The earl's chest shook with laughter. "Have you no faith in me, my little pea goose? Thanks to your abigail,

343

one of those trunks up in the back is filled with your clothing—although I confess I added a few items of my own choosing. The weakest part of my plan, you see, was that you might notice half your gowns were gone."

"Well, I didn't!" she said, with new asperity. "Indeed, how could I? Everyone made sure I lay about like some sort of vaporish invalid and did nothing for myself! And how shockingly *high-handed* of you to persuade my abigail to go behind my back! How did you manage it?"

He smiled wickedly. "You could say it was a combination of your aunt's influence and my own personal charm."

"Oh, really?" she retorted. "So Aunt Serena knows about this, does she?"

"And totally approves—except about the business of a church wedding, for I don't expect to find a clergyman before the noon deadline. But I *won't* wait another day Diana, so don't ask! Your aunt and I had that out already, both yesterday and again this morning. I only got away by promising we'd be married a second time *in* a church, *in* her august presence!"

"This seems to be getting rather complicated," Diana complained.

He looked amused. "No, it's actually quite simple," he said, gently pinching her chin. "We will be married once today, most likely in Reading since we are due to change horses there shortly. That will enable us to live as man and wife in *your* house, Diana, rather than in your parent's. Yes, I thought you might see the advantage of that. By sometime next week, your aunt will have arrived, along with Aimee, Charles, Miss Tilden, my valet, your abigail and her, er, husband—"

"Meg is married?" interrupted Diana in surprise.

"Yes. To your footman, it seems. Their romance appears to have taken place under your very nose, my dear, but that is another story. Now, to continue: I dispatched a letter to my own mother this morning, whom I hope will also be able to attend our, ah, second wedding. She ought to be able to arrive by next week also, but if not, we will wait until she does."

Diana regarded him with near astonishment. "Oh, this is all very simple, indeed! And then what?"

His eyes glinted. "And then, my darling, we shall go anywhere you like and do anything you like. As long as you do it with me."

They were married in Reading by a stout, elderly clergyman with three chins and a fatherly manner. The earl had not forgotten to purchase a ring, and when he slipped this—a large sapphire surrounded by diamonds and pearls—onto Diana's finger, the fit was as close to perfection as anyone could wish. When the ceremony was over, the Earl and Countess of Lucan shook hands with the clergyman, signed the register, and proceeded to *The George* for what they jestingly called their "wedding breakfast"; they then returned to the chaise and recommenced their journey through the Berkshires. An hour and a half later they had crossed into Wiltshire and were skirting the Savernake Forest, the edge of which, Diana informed him a trifle absently, was but three miles from her home.

At this point in the journey Diana fell abnormally silent, and when she frowned suddenly, her concerned husband was quick to demand the explanation.

"Geoffrey," she answered in a serious tone, "I have been thinking."

"Have you, my darling? What about?"

"Now that we are married, it has just occurred to me that I no longer have any need of Edmund's money." She turned anxious eyes to his face. "Do you have any need of it? For if you do not, I should very much like to give it

345

to my parents, for they *do* need it, you see. They would not accept my help before, but I think perhaps that under the present circumstances they might."

He was conscious of a profound feeling of relief that her frown had not arisen from second thoughts about their union. "A capital notion, my love," he approved heartily. "They are welcome to every penny of it, for I have more than enough for our needs." He did not add that he wanted nothing of Edmund Verney to remain in their lives, for she very likely knew that.

Diana's frown vanished. "You are so very good," she said, emotion creeping back into her voice. "Oh, but now I have recalled another favor I must ask you."

"Here it comes!" he groaned, in mock despair. "The never-ending list of wifely demands."

Diana poked her husband in the ribs. "No such thing! I merely wanted to ask if you have any objection to Tildy living with us. She is getting old, and has no family of her own, and while she *could* live with my parents, of course, I think she would be happier with me. We are very close, you know."

"Miss Tilden is welcome to live with us for as long as she pleases," he stated. "From what I have observed, she is very much like my own mother in disposition. In fact, my mother is also a knitter, so I daresay they will form a lasting friendship. You will like my mother, by the way. She is not at all high in the instep."

"And do you think she will like me?"

He smiled. "She will be in transports about you. She still blames herself for allowing me to make a loveless marriage the first time around. Not that she could have prevented me, of course. At that time I did not believe in love, so I did not seek it."

He sounded so rueful Diana reached up to touch his cheek. "Your first wife ran away from you. Did she hurt you, my dear?"

346

His head shook. "My pride, perhaps," he said honestly. "But to be hurt, I think, one must love—and I loved Laurette no more than she loved me." His arm tightened around her. "One must come to terms with one's past, Diana," he added meaningfully. "The future is what concerns me. *Our* future."

She nodded. "It is the same for me," she told him quietly. "Edmund is truly gone for me, now. The future is what counts."

Diana did not argue when her husband insisted they go first to her house rather than her parents', for she had sensed his growing impatience to make love to her ever since they left Reading. The woman she had left in charge of the house greeted them warmly, as did her burly husband, who hurried to unload the trunks and take charge of the chaise and horses. Seeing the way Mrs. Piper's eyes kept darting to the earl, Diana hastily informed her they were married, and with a blush which deepened as she spoke, went on to say that they intended to take a short rest and must upon no account be disturbed. The journey was quite exhausting, she explained in an increasingly flustered voice.

The earl's face was very bland during his wife's speech, but when they were mounting the stairs to the second floor, he chuckled and whispered. "You did not deceive her in the least, you know!"

Any reply she might have made was trapped in her throat, for his hand was caressing her hip in a manner which drove away her voice.

Within her bedchamber, Diana turned to her new husband with confidence. She knew no apprehension, nor dread, nor even nervousness, for no shadows from the past lingered to sully the moment with doubts. This was *excitement* she was feeling, a pure, restless sort of excitement, an unguarded yearning to give all of herself to the man she loved. And deep down inside, she knew she was going to make him a very good wife.

To Geoffrey, Diana still looked as vulnerable as ever, but though he studied her carefully, he saw no hesitation or fear in her face. Complete trust was shining in her brown-gold eyes—trust in him, along with the first stirrings of knowledge, a half-awakened awareness of her own feminine needs. Reassured, he held out his arms to her, and she went into them with a choked little laugh that meant more to him than a thousand words of affection.

As his lips sought hers, Diana went up on her toes, pressing herself against him with an abandon she had never known. She wanted him as much as she loved him, and the two mingled within her to form something more powerful and potent than she had ever dared imagine. How strong, how splendidly, solidly *male* he felt beneath her hands! Her eager fingers stroked the nape of his neck, dragged through his raven black hair, then almost of their own accord went down to grip the top edge of his waistcoat, where the pounding of his heart reminded her that this was only the beginning.

"My beautiful wife," he whispered against her upward tilted lips. "My beautiful, wonderful wife."

Then he was claiming an even more demanding kiss, a blending of mouths that took Diana into an entirely new, compellingly fundamental arena of sensation. Before her reeling mind could comprehend her own delight, his tongue was sliding down her neck, then up again to her mouth with a hungry, thrusting movement that sent a stab of pleasure to her very core.

His hands were fumbling at the ties of her gown, then she felt him pulling it up and off so that she stood before him in nothing but her undergarments. Trembling a little, Diana bent to remove her shoes and stockings, aware that her husband's eyes were devouring her, scorching her with the intensity of their gaze. Then she straightened, and, pushing away the last remnants of self-consciousness, took off her chemise.

"Diana—!" Geoffrey's voice caught in a throat grown thick with desire. She was just as he'd imagined, only better because she was really here and she was finally his. Her rosy-tipped breasts were perfect, just the size to fit into his large hands, while the rest of her was even more heavenly. But he would go slowly, he promised himself. He would court her senses so that she would feel everything, so that she would never again doubt that she was anything but the most flawless, the most exquisite, the most vital of women. In turn, he wanted to witness her pleasure, to know that every sigh and tremor was for him. With iron control, Lord Lucan lifted his new wife and placed her tenderly upon the bed.

"I adore you," he said, raking her with possessive eyes. "And if I can get this damned thing off"—he yanked impatiently at his neckcloth—"I mean to prove it! Unfortunately, gentlemen's garments are not so simple to remove," he added, with a lopsided grin.

Diana forgot her nakedness in the joy of watching him undress. His body was hard and lean and utterly masculine, so unlike Edmund's that it was ridiculous to compare. Moreover, Geoffrey's love for her seemed as solid and tangible as his body, and it was partly this which made it impossible to look away or be afraid.

To her surprise, his lovemaking was almost too leisurely at first, his caresses featherlight and teasing when some unreasoning part of her longed for haste. Then, once or twice, he did something which startled her, but each time this happened, he whispered something so outrageous that instead of tensing, she giggled and yielded to his mastery. He wooed her with consummate skill, slowly building their hunger until it reached a new summit where nothing existed but the fierce interdependence of the masculine and the feminine. And when he

349

finally entered her, she opened to him like a flower to the sun, welcoming his thrusts into her body with soft, gasping cries that spoke of a pleasure as great as his.

Afterward, they did not talk at once, but lay with limbs entwined as lovers do. At length, however, the earl rose up on his elbow, and regarded her with a mischievous grin. "I told you it was a cock-and-bull story."

He sounded so smug Diana hit him with a pillow. "*Oooh*, you! Impossible man! I suppose you will tease me about that for the rest of our lives!"

He gave a mock yelp as she swung again. "No, no, I promise I won't! On one condition, that is."

Since he was still grinning, Diana eyed him with suspicion. "And what is that?"

"That you never wear a corset!" he replied, grabbing the pillow away from her. "I cannot abide the things, and I want to be able to do this—"

"Geoffrey!"

"—and this—"

"*Geoffrey!*"

"—without unlacing you for half an hour!"

"I don't even own a corset," she informed him with dignity. "In the meantime, if you can possibly attend to something serious, I wanted to tell you where I would like to go for our wedding trip."

He pulled her closer, so that the full length of their bodies touched. "Where?" he whispered in her ear.

Trying not to be distracted by his nibbling kisses, she replied, "Cornwall. I want to see your home, Geoffrey. It is a part of England that has long intrigued me, and—will you stop doing that?"

His lips rose from her neck long enough to say, quite fervently, "I am glad you desire to go there, for it is the one place above all others on earth I wish to show you. There is more beauty in Cornwall than one could absorb in a lifetime! Just thinking of it, I can taste the salt air and

350

hear the pound of the sea." He dropped a kiss on her chin, his harsh face growing animated. "I will take you to visit the fishing, farming, and mining communities so you can hear their superstitions and legends for yourself. You'll be highly entertained by their stories, my love. And we'll ride the moors together, Diana, the miles and miles of moorland stretching far as the eye can see. There is nothing like it, I promise. And we can still come up to London whenever you like." He said it eagerly, as a small boy offering to share his candy with a friend.

She smiled at his enthusiasm. "I'm sure I will, my dear. I would love any place in the world if I could live there with you."

"And when we're done with riding, we will find a private place and work on producing the next generation of Trevelyans," he added roguishly.

Diana's arm slid around his waist. "Shall we, indeed? I think I would like that very much."

"On second thought," he murmured, nuzzling into her neck, "why wait?"

This was obviously not the time, reflected the new Countess of Lucan, to reprimand her husband for his high-handed tactics. It would have to be done, of course, but on this particular occasion, she could not help but feel that it was wiser to let him have his way. Husbands had to be humored, didn't they?

It was the easiest decision of all.

Julie Caille welcomes letters from readers and invites you to write to her c/o Zebra Books, 475 Park Avenue South, New York, NY 10016